1973

ROGUE'S LEGACY

ROGUE'S LEGACY

A Novel about François Villon

BY BABETTE DEUTSCH

DRAWINGS BY ALLEN POPE

COWARD-McCANN INC NEW YORK

Typography by Robert Josephy

ROGUE'S LEGACY

Chapter One

The place was Paris. The scene was what night and June could make of it. The time was the end of the Middle Ages.

The dark-visaged young man lounging under the clock tower of St. Benoit was fully aware of all his senses reported. It was odd he should not have recognized that an end was looming. He felt the suppressed tumult of the town, the echoes of the festival just over, the promise of an empty hour. He knew the quarter, the cloister, the brothel, and the University, the wealth of the Church, the depths of poverty. He would have told you that he knew everything but himself. Yet he knew his own power, and its frustration.

He sat relaxed on the stone bench, one arm round the girl,

Ysabeau, a malicious eye cocked at the priest on the other side of her.

"God, I feel thin! We might pose for a fresco: Death and the Priest, or Death and the Lady. Pity Ysabeau is no lady."

"Reely!" Ysabeau wriggled in his embrace.

"Nowadays, sweetheart, we know the difference. It's not as when the queen gave the kiss of peace to one of your sort in church."

"Because she wore a gold belt, I suppose. And what harm? It's bad for trade"—Ysabeau shook her bangles—"when they don't let you dress decently."

A fat man's chortle from the priest.

"Quiet, Gilles. What do you wear under here?" The young man plucked up the priest's robe. "You could play tennis in that sooner than grant me absolution."

"I doubt I could grant you absolution in any dress, Master François." The priest pushed his hand away.

"But forgiveness of sins is your trade, my Father, while sin is Ysabeau's," grinned Villon.

"St. Mary of Egypt!" murmured the girl.

"And she was a whore."

"Philippe never spoke to me like that." Ysabeau was between howling and cursing this devil of a student.

"Philippe Sermoise?" Villon's dark face twitched scornfully. "I hear he is looking for me."

Ysabeau stared at him with gooseberry eyes. "Ooh, I don't half like that."

"What are you afraid of, my poppet? Perhaps he wants to confess me: he's a priest, too. God's bread, I thought he was a friend of yours."

"He was," said Ysabeau, "until"—she smiled up at Villon with professional sweetness—"you came along." And turned her head aside to spit. "Ugh! Let's not talk of him. Give us a song, Master François."

Villon thrust his fingers under his cape obligingly, drew out a short dagger, held it in his arm as though it were a lute, and plucked amorously at imaginary strings.

"Sing the one about Jeanne de Bois," pleaded the girl. *"You know:*

> *"Jeanne de Bois came back again*
> *Tuesday late, and never mind*
> *Where they had to go to find*
> *Jeanne . . ."*

"Where do I go to find you, wench?" grinned Villon. "At the Holy Innocents most likely."

"What's the one about mustard?" asked the priest. "Trumpetty tumpty tumpty tum . . ."

"I have it!" Villon thrumbed on his bare blade:

> *"Open your door to me, Guillemette,*
> *She's gone for the mustard, hot hot hot!"*

"You're hot stuff without that, Ysabeau, eh?" Gilles laughed. "Go on, Master François."

Villon ignored him. He thrust his dagger back into its sheath and pulled his cloak closer about his bony shoulders.

A few hours ago there had been music of another sort in the quarter, as the Church dignitaries, flowers falling before them, banners floating above them, had marched solemnly in procession, to the swinging of silver censers, the flicker of torches and tall candles. The Feast of Corpus Christi had been over at twilight, the dubious hour between the dog and the wolf. But the summer night seemed still to tremble and glow with the tramp and glitter of the ecclesiastics and the slow wonder of that mo-

5

ment, suddenly eclipsed by the pushing crowd, as the Host, under its canopy of cloth-of-gold, hung with white violets and roses, was borne past on its way back to the tabernacle.

The fragrance of incense and of flowers, for the churchmen too had gone garlanded in marjoram and violets, lingered on the air, mixing with the usual smells of the street, and half-hiding the stench from the small common opposite with its eternal hillocks of filth.

From behind, deep-toned Mary, the clangorous bell of the Sorbonne, tolled curfew for the University. Nine o'clock. But for a little Villon was content to sit on the stone bench with the priest and the prostitute, swinging his heels and thinking of nothing. Not, certainly, of Katherine de Vauselles. The better not to think of Katherine, he began playing with Ysabeau's pliant hand.

He looked down the street. It was as familiar as the forgiving smile of old Guillaume Villon, nay, as familiar as the slippery eyes and the jerking shoulders of René de Montigny. With a gate opening into the cloister, and the tavern opposite, the rue St. Jacques held associations both with the good canon of St. Benoit and the prodigal son of the Montignys.

At this hour the street was so quiet it was a wonder it did not bore him. There was no light save what came from the early June sky, the lamp swinging under the image of the Virgin, and the candle in the notary's window. Villon noted the crosses looming faintly in the cemetery across the way. Ah, the poor dead! He heard the house signs swaying in the wind, as a gibbet creaks, but less noisily. The Sign of the Fleur de Lys, the Sign of the Wild Man, the Sign of the Image of St. Anne, farther down, where the grocer lived, the Sign of the Golden Mortar, and, just beyond, the Sign of the Mule, with its sprig

6

of cypress and its barrel hoop like a whiff from the cask promising good drink and low company.

From the alley came a belated cry of "Mustard, hot mustard!" The signboards creaked. There was no other sound. Across the street a near-sighted man stumbled against a barrow in the dark, spat out an oath, and vanished into the night. The cloister, with its huddle of gables above neat gardens, its market stalls, empty now, and the old church over all, was dark and silent as its own charnel.

"Sing us a proper song, do," begged Ysabeau, disturbed by the quiet.

"Yes," urged Gilles, an ancient hatred stirring in his fat bosom: "one about the Goddams—they're the best!" He began reciting with gusto: " 'Don't be afraid to thrash 'em, they've stuffed their paunch with peas; one of us is worth four of 'em, or at the least worth three.' "

Villon took up the verse to the right tune:

> *"Then bring 'em on, we'll have our fun,*
> *As many as you've got:*
> *The Goddams to the gallows,*
> *And there we'll hoick the lot!"*

Ysabeau put an arm around the lean throat and breathed a shuddering "ah-h." But Villon only pulled her ear and laughed.

"Don't fret: the University will take care of her own. You forget that I am a master of arts and a man of letters."

"Who might have been a bishop," sniggered Gilles.

"Reely?" cried Ysabeau.

"I never could get fat enough for that office," explained the young man. "You know a bishop by his robes, but do you know that the lining of his stomach is also prescribed: partridges,

7

goslings, carp, and only the very best Beaune are rich enough. For myself, I have eaten too many herring. I have even"— Villon made a wry mouth—"been known to swallow beer."

He pinched Ysabeau so that she squealed. He would swallow vinegar, and think it hot and sweet, if the demoiselle Katherine were here beside him instead of this girl of the streets.

" 'Reely'!" he added, mocking her, and stopped, with an upward glance.

Out of the shadows, as secretly as the shadows, had come two men. One, by his dress, was a student, the other wore a priest's gown. They stood confronting Villon for as long as it takes a chime to die on the air, a curse to echo in the ear. He recognized Philippe Sermoise, scented trouble, grinned.

Sermoise nudged his companion.

"I was right, le Mardi! The dog is here and the little bitch too."

He turned on Villon, snarling.

"By God, I have found you, Master François! I'll make it hot for you!"

"Messire Philippe! Are you overheated?"asked Villon ironically. "What can I do for you?"

The scornful "Messire" was pepper in a raw wound. But Villon's malice did not stop there. He had vaguely anticipated entertainment this evening. Was he to find it in a quarrel with this priest over his whore? He recalled a line from the Mystery he had seen performed earlier in the day, and, imitating the lisping choirboy who had played the child Joseph, he addressed Sermoise: " 'Dear Brother, nowithe have I done you wrong.' "

He rose, as though to offer the offended priest the place he had warmed for him. Sermoise thrust him back.

Ysabeau melted into the darkness. Gilles ran. Le Mardi was on the point of following.

8

Villon accepted the stone slab, onto which Sermoise had pushed him, as though it were a chair at my lord bishop's and kicked lightly at a small boulder that might have served as a footstool. He looked up at the priest with a wicked grimace.

"Damn you, you laugh!" Sermoise snarled.

"Bless you, would you have me weep? But of course"—Villon's tone turned melancholy as a jilted lover's—"it is sad to see a priest with horns: he might be mistaken for a devil in the dark."

"Devil's offal!" growled Sermoise, and reached under his skirts for his hidden sword. With a quick stroke he slashed Villon's upper lip so it could never curve quite that way again.

Howling, Villon leaped up and flung himself on Sermoise. He felt his knife go into the flesh. He pressed hard, harder. The dagger pierced the priest's groin and stuck there. With a shriek of agony Sermoise rolled into the street.

His scream drew le Mardi out of hiding. The student bent over the wounded man. Villon, weaponless, his mouth full of salt blood, stooped for a stone.

It bashed the priest full in the face. His groan followed Villon as he ran.

He dodged up one black alley and down another, fear bitter as copper to his palate. It might be murder. And the man he had killed belonged to the Church. That was a hanging job. He began to sweat. The pain in his lip was frightful.

There was a barber-surgeon in the cloister, Jean Flastrier. He might just have finished his nightly game of chess at the Red Door with the old canon, Guillaume de Villon. But young Villon had no wish to see the nephew of his foster father. Flastrier would dress his wound, but he would also ask questions. He was a man who respected the law, even more than his uncle, who taught it. One question he would not need to put: the name of the young man who came to him this night with a slashed lip.

The canon had given his own name to François de Montcorbier when he took the lad in a dozen years ago. And what had the son of the poor farmer of Montcorbier, God rest his soul, done with the gift of his foster father? Nothing to cast glory on the name of Villon but some marvelous wicked verses. A good deal to make it known in the wrong quarters. He winced and pressed his cloak against his bleeding mouth.

Hurrah! That was the house of a barber, the basin swinging before the door. He hangs a basin up, you note, although he cannot milk a goat, thought Villon. But, even if the song spoke truly, he must get help here.

At last the bolt was shot back, the door opened, and the barber, a man of middle age and past surprises, let him in. He was not too slow in lighting candles and preparing the hot oil and the plasters. Villon, watching him, groaned inwardly.

"Now," said the barber.

Ah-agh, but that hurt! A burning dazing pain.

How did they bear it, those who were bound to the stake to die in the fire, like the good girl, Jeanne, whom the Goddams burned the year he was born? The flames creeping up and up, wrapping the tender flesh in agony. How did they bear it, those others, thrust into the monstrous vats, to writhe there like nothing human, for no worse work than coining false money?

Oh, the pain! This lip that had touched Paradise, brushing the fingers of Katherine de Vauselles, was tasting hell-fire tonight. Funny, to think that, if she let him, he could not kiss her now.

"Well, I have patched you up as best I could. My name, sir, is Fouquet."

And yours? he would ask next. It was hard for Villon to

mumble his thanks. It was devilish hard to have to spend his few coins paying for such misery. Fouquet might have grumbled at the smallness of the fee, but it was plain there was no more to be got out of this customer. A poor rowdy from the University, by his dress, but a notable face. Those feverish eyes! Even with the patch across his mouth, a notable face.

Now it was coming. The barber had his inkhorn ready, his quill poised.

"And how did you get this nasty cut?"

"I was attacked, without provocation, by a brigand of a priest. His name is Philippe Sermoise." Speech was difficult. Villon had to lisp, which reminded him of that fat fool, Tabary, and made him want to grin, but he could not. "Philippe Sermoise," he repeated. "He'll be put under arrest tomorrow if the sergeants know their job as you do yours."

"Thank you, sir," said the barber drily. "I will do what is necessary."

Villon bowed. He would gladly have bidden Fouquet good night, but the barber, who wrote deliberately, had another question to ask.

"As you know, I must set down who was the victim of this . . . eh, Philippe Sermoise." Fouquet looked up curiously at the thin dark face with the quick malicious eyes. "Your name?"

"My name," replied Villon promptly, "is Michel Mouton."

The barber nodded, pursed his lips, and wrote: Michel Mouton. Villon watched him with an inward movement of relief.

Sermoise might already have been picked up dead or dying. The only witness had been his companion, le Mardi. Gilles and Ysabeau would lie low. You can be dragged into prison for murder, Master François. A life for a life. That is the law.

To be strung up for ridding the earth of that fighting cock

of a priest! To choke to death, to do a jig on the air, to give your eyes for crow's meat. There were those who denied the right of confession to the condemned. Villon felt his bowels churning. Christ Jesus, he could not go that road.

The scraping of a stool recalled him to the candlelit room, the smells of the surgery, the serious commonplaceness of the barber Fouquet, in his nightcap, anxious to get back to bed, bowing him out.

Out, into the black street again. Out, and down the rue St. Jacques, slipping along swifter than the Seine runs, past the quiet convent, past the muffled lights and noises of the Mule, past the silent shuttered houses, to where the rue du Petit-Pont turned off toward the public baths (oh, for a steaming tub now!) and the stench of the slaughter house killed your pleasure in the roof garden on the ramparts. Damn the fortress, its flowers and its prisons. Six of the Watch were on duty. You must walk boldly not to be challenged. Villon waved a hand as a lantern flashed in his face. "A fine night, Messire!" Very fine, since he was not stopped.

Skilfully he picked his way among the covered barrows of the Petit-Pont. The smell of chicken feathers and fish thickened the air, but the usual screaming traffic was dead at this hour. There were no sounds but the rusty voices of vagrants huddled there for the night and the slapping of the water under the stone arches of the bridge. He was across and moving through the Cité like a shadow.

At the sound of hooves he drew back into a doorway, snickering to see another shadow slipping around a corner: as wary a night bird as himself, that one. The horseman clattered past, singing. Some man who had had his pleasure and need not repent it. Villon breathed deeper and ran on, leaving the swampy street that stank of drains, on toward the Church of the Madeleine, past the countless darkened shops, to the Sign of the Pine Cone swinging before Robin Turgis's tavern.

He might halt here for the cup of wine he needed so badly if he could open his poor lips for it. He might find Montigny. Montigny would have money or know where to lay hold of it. He could work his brother-in-law through Jeanne Chartrain if only there were time.

The door opened. The tavern fumes were sour and keen in Villon's nostrils. He had a glimpse of sprawled bodies, a nose like a boiled shrimp that might be Jean Cotart's, and a girl on a table swinging her legs. There was a crash and a roar of laughter. The door closed.

He shrugged. No sign of Montigny there. The hulking fellow in the corner looked like a sergeant.

He must go on. He must go quickly. He crossed the planks of the Pont Notre Dame at a run, turning up toward the oat market, with its comfortable smell of the stable, and so into the wide emptiness of the Place de Grève. There were a few strolling couples, a sergeant having a noisy set-to with a drunken old woman, a lantern moving along under the eaves—the usual traffic of the night. But Villon had a waking nightmare of the crowd that surged by day into the square, the thousand-headed monster, shouting with savage joy to see a man hanged. He to make such a show for the people of Paris? Ah, God, no.

His side ached with running. This was the neighborhood of the hottest of the college riots. Beyond was the great house where the Provost and his bride had entertained. A brilliant evening, Master François, if you recall. And you not the least dazzling, with your rapier wit.

Yes, and Sermoise?

This night's work meant good-by to all that. His hot head pulsed to the lilt of Deschamps' ballad, bitterly true: good-by, my love, good-by, dear generous girls; good-by Grand Pont, markets, steam rooms, and baths; good-by to handsome clothes, doublet and hose, good-by to studded harness and to plain; good-by soft bed, rich covers, tender breasts; good-by to dances and those haunting them; good-by to Paris and her little tarts!

He had no elegant gear to lament. The cloak whipping about him as he moved was stained and stiff where he had clapped it to his lip. His dagger, a cheap one he had picked up second-hand, was sticking in Sermoise's groin, if the student hadn't pulled it out, and the priest's life with it perhaps. A man with nothing to lose, thought Villon. Fleeing, he would leave nothing of value behind. Except some precious scribblings. But to part with Paris, with Paris and her little tarts. With the clangor and color of the greatest city in the world, with the fierce coarse life of the streets by day and the secret excitements of the night. With everything that made his verses. With the demoiselle Katherine. Good-by, my love.

He was dizzy and sick as he skirted the great church of the Celestines, the monstrous stone casket of jewels, that told him he was in home territory. He stumbled down the darkest street of the quarter and swayed on his feet as he waited for the meanest door in it to open to his knock. The first door he had known.

"It is I, François," he whispered hoarsely, hearing the old woman's fingers fumble at the bolt. He was inside before she could speak.

"François! At this hour!"

She was surprised. But why? Nothing he did should surprise his mother. Not if he were to commit murder.

"Who else should come at this hour?" he asked. "The King of England?" He dropped onto a stool. Black and white spots were dancing like juggler's balls before his eyes.

Her voice recalled him, harsh, angry, anxious. Isaiah spoke of grinding the faces of the poor. But it was their voices that were ground to an edge by the endless quarrels over a rotten carrot, over a leaky pot, over a dirty man. He saw her face above the stub of candle and became conscious of the sweat on his own, the patch across his lip, the dried blood on the edge of his cape.

"It's nothing," he told her. "You don't have a drink in the cupboard?"

"Here."

She brought him a jug, the heel of a stale loaf, a piece of cheese. She wondered he could swallow.

He lifted the jug and sniffed at it. "Not beer," he answered unhappily and tried to grin.

"It is what I drink."

He took the jug then and, with difficulty, wetted his dry throat. His lip stung. His head ached. His legs felt as though they had been drawn on the rack. He shook himself, unfastened his cape, and flung it to her. She must clean it for him, not tomorrow morning on the river front, tonight, with the water in the fire bucket if necessary. He could not wait. He added—it was an inspiration—that there was a pilgrimage to be undertaken at dawn.

She gripped his cape as though it were part of him. Was he doing a penance? Had the devil put that seal on his mouth? Holy Virgin, she cried at him, she was his mother, she would wash his cape, she would wash his filthy soul if she could, but how could she pray for him if he hid his sin?

He shrugged and shivered. No use telling her the stupid story. She was no lawyer. She could not sign her name.

Now it was the canon: she thought he had come from the canon.

"You can go to the Red Door tomorrow and tell him I'm sorry I couldn't see him." This, Villon reflected, was no lie. The canon knew the law, and he had powerful friends. He and Montigny. One of Montigny's uncles was a crony of Master Guillaume de Villon. He added, with a letter of remission in view: "Tell him I will write."

His mother paused in the act of wringing out the edge of his cape. "Yes, you can write." She began cursing the womb that bore him, cursing him, dragged out of the muck, with what pains the Holy Virgin knew, to grow learned, to grow great, and dropping back into his native muck again like the spawn of hell.

You do not make pilgrimages like this, she thought, hanging his cape over the bench so the damp end would dry. You do not leave Paris like this. What had he done, then? He was silent as a carcass. She did not know where he was going. If he stayed, what would happen to him? If he went off, Mother of God, she might never see him again, alive or dead. She poured out her rage as a woman empties a pail of dirty water.

"Nothing like a mother's blessing," he murmured. Her heart was ripped, like his lip, and she must howl, as he had, with the pain of it.

"I may get to Angers," he said to turn her thoughts from himself. "Have you a message for my uncle?" wishing he were one of Montigny's kin.

"You think your uncle can do for you what the canon cannot do? Or," she asked impatiently, "the good God?"

He did not answer. The good God had done no major favors for him so far. Nor for his mother. Looking down, he saw a beetle crawling across the worn trestle table toward the crust he had left. He was reminded of the evenings in his childhood when he had waited in the cold dark room for his mother to come home. He dared not go out to meet her. On every street there were men as naked as the dead on the gallows, men with sore stumps instead of feet and terrible eyes and long hands like claws that snatched at you: "I am dying of hunger. For Christ's sake, give! I am dying of hunger." No one noticed except to walk faster. But François would stare, fascinated. He kept wondering if the beggars would turn out to be Flayers, those wild men who kidnapped boys and cut their throats for a brass penny. It was a good thing he looked as though he never had a penny.

The worst place to pass was a dump heap with dogs and men fighting over the refuse. The men looked like dogs, and the dogs like wolves.

His mother told him the howling he heard when he woke late at night was only the wind, but he knew it was the wolves. They had come in to Paris from the country, following the starved farmers. If they caught you, they took you by the throat, like that woman who was found near the Holy Innocents with her throat ripped open—they tore you to pieces with their teeth. The most secret, the most horrible was the Wolf With No Tail. Was it really a wolf, or worse?

He was a naked hungry boy, waiting for his mother to come home. O Holy Virgin, let my mother come home, let her come now, even if she doesn't bring anything, let her come home before it gets darker.

Perhaps she wouldn't come. Perhaps on the way back the Flayers had followed her. No, she had stopped off at the Celestines to light a candle: the aunts would have given her money. The great bell at the Celestines began tolling. It was already vespers. O God. Where is my mother? François crouched on the floor, shrugging together in a little bony shuddering heap. Was this how you felt when you had the fever? The funeral

17

bell did not stop ringing in the streets. In rich houses they kept priests to chase the devils away with holy water. But they were too poor to think of such a thing. Suppose his mother never came home. He would be all alone. He would be sick alone. He would die alone. What was that rattling?

There was a blast of icy air.

"François, where are you?"

He jumped up, with a cracked whoop. He was well again. He was warm again. He was ravenously hungry.

And she had brought turnip tops again.

Even when he had eaten, he was too cold to sleep. They lay huddled close to each other, her body covering his, her cold feet chafing his.

He had been afraid? He should have told the Holy Virgin. She watched over little boys: She had had a boy of her own— that was how you got round Her, said his mother shrewdly. She would tell him a story to prove it.

"Once upon a time there was a poor widow." "Like you, my mother?" "Like me, François, why not? And she had an only child, a son." "Like me, my mother?" "A little like you—but older, big enough to be a soldier." "Yes, go on." "Well, so of course there was a war, and the young man went away to fight, and the enemy took him prisoner. His mother found out what had happened to him. She could not ransom him, she had no money for such doings." "But if he had been a knight, she could have." "That's different: they were poor people. So she prayed to the Holy Virgin to give him back to her. She waited and waited. But he did not come. So what did she do? She went to church, to the statue of the Holy Virgin holding the infant Jesus, and she knelt down before Her and said: 'Heavenly Lady, I have asked Your patronage for my son, but You re-fused. Very well, then. My son has been taken away from me:

now I shall take Your son, and I shall keep Him hostage until mine is given back to me.' Then the widow took the statue of the Child from the breast of the Virgin, and she carried it home with her and wrapped it in spotless linen and locked it away in a box. The very next night the Holy Virgin appeared to the young man. She opened the doors of his prison. 'Go, my child,' she said, 'tell your mother to return My Son to Me as I have returned hers.' He was amazed, eh? He went home at once and told his mother the miracle. You can think how quickly she unlocked the box and lifted out the little Jesus and took Him back to the church. There she placed Him safely in the arms of His Mother. Then she knelt down before the Virgin and said: 'I thank You, Heavenly Lady, for giving me back my child. In return I give You back Your own!' "

François sighed deeply. His mother must tell him another. Oh, but just one more. Then he would go straight to sleep. He would sleep so soundly that he would not kick her, not even once. She could not see him grin in the dark. He had his arm round her neck.

"Well, then . . .

"Once upon a time there was a priest . . ."

Oh, not about a priest. What then? About a robber? she joked. Yes, yes, about a robber. Lying close to your mother, you could listen comfortably to stories about assassins. Now she thought of it, there was a story. . . . Listen.

"Once upon a time there was a robber. He was not such a thief as you find on every street in Paris nowadays, a poor man who stole from hunger. He was a great rogue, who made a business of robbery. He would lie in wait for merchants' caravans on the road, and stop them and take away bales of goods. Or he would find his way to a lord's manor and snatch up a page, some rich man's son, and hold him for ransom. Or he would break into the house of a powerful banker, like Jacques Coeur, when he was off on his travels and the servants were busy with their own affairs, and carry off gold and silver plate. It is not known that he ever broke into a church. That sin he did not commit. But, short of sacrilege, this robber did every wicked thing a man can do. He was not afraid, either, to seize by force what he could not get quietly. But see, François, when the robber saw that he must use force, he would first make a prayer to Our Lady. Every time this sinful man first asked forgiveness of Her. So the years went by, and in the end the robber was caught. He was flung into prison, and he only came out of it to mount the steps of the gibbet. They put the rope around his neck, and they hanged him properly. But listen now. The Holy Virgin looked down from Heaven and saw what was happening. And Her heart was sorry for the man who had always asked Her pardon when he was about to sin. So She came down to earth and went straight to the gibbet, and with Her own hands She held him up, while he hung there, so that he did not die. And this went on for three days. And on the third day all saw that it was a miracle, and they took him down and pardoned him by the grace of Our Lady, and She was able to go back again quietly to Her throne in Paradise."

There was not much robbing in the story, after all. But it was well to know that you could depend on the Holy Virgin to rescue you from a tight place. François decided to be better about saying his prayers, and maybe, since his mother was determined to send him to Master Guillaume de Villon and make a clerk of him, he might study hard and earn real merit in the eyes of God's Mother. He murmured a Hail Mary sleepily into the warm neck of his own mother, and soon, soon, all was quiet, and he was about to bite into a marvelous cheesecake, and then he was being chased up the steps of the gibbet by the Wolf With No Tail, and now he was being strangled by the rope, and he kicking madly to be free of it, and the Holy Virgin was scolding him for a thief. "You have taken all the covers, François! Turn over! And keep your legs still for as long as it takes to say a paternoster at least."

He woke up to find a torn strip of blanket twisted round his neck and his feet pushing his mother out of bed. The Virgin Mary had vanished, along with the gibbet and the Wolf With No Tail. And alas, the cheesecake also was only a dream.

It was all a dream. It was all part of the ghostly past. Only the death-faced men crying, "I am dying of hunger," were hard to forget.

Through the darkness the bell from the Celestines began sounding matins. Villon thought of Sermoise, lying stabbed, with a broken head, and glanced at the hand that had flung the stone. And saw again, with a grimace, the beetle that had turned back for him the hands of the clock. With sharpened senses he smelled the stale air of the little room, saw the yellow flutter of the candle in its pool of tallow, the worn soiled boards, heard the resonant pealing of the midnight bell.

He covered his eyes with his hand and mechanically muttered the familiar syllables. He felt his mother at his side like a dragging weight, saying her prayers as she used to say them with him when he had been a sleepy shivering child. The prayer ended in a sardonic grin that pulled at his lip and made him groan.

He must go.

She had hardly done crossing herself when he had taken her hand and was asking in that gentle way of his that would coax a smile from Henry the Hangman, "Now you have prayed for me, my mother, now you must show me your Christian charity. You would not have me go like this." He flicked out his purse and exposed its nakedness.

She shrugged. It was his own gesture.

Here. She fetched from behind the broken boards where it was hidden the stocking that held such money as she managed to keep. On the road he would need it. And the protection of all the saints. The worst company in Paris was kinder than what you met beyond the walls. Gangs of thieves: they would steal the jewels from the Queen of Heaven; soldiers out of a job: they would cut your throat for a clipped coin—wolves, not men; vile women: runaway nuns, girls from the stews, pretty pieces of filth. François could deal with that lot.

She counted out the pieces, small ones they were, and some queer bits, of no value any more, while he stood watching with greedy eyes.

"Yes, yes, take it. You will need it." She closed his fingers over a fistful of odd coins and a round bright one that it was an ache to let go of.

He hugged her, rubbing his cheek against hers and "God bless you for this, mother!" pocketing the money before she could repent. "You don't grudge me that, either?" His eye had lighted on the knife lying beside the loaf. He thrust it hastily into his belt. "I left my dagger with a fellow—a priest, he was. Fine doings, eh?" he mumbled.

"François!" She made the sign of the cross over him. "You will take care of yourself?" The Holy Virgin had often shown kindness to men of evil life. And Her Son, though He was Judge of all and could send you to worse than the gibbet, would listen to Her when She spoke: not look everywhere else at once like François.

He was going.

22

"You'll see me yet," he lisped gaily, "with a chain round my neck." It could be made of hemp, too.

With a mocking finger at the patch across his mouth, he tossed her a kiss. She stood there, choking with tears. A moment since she had cursed him. The words would have soiled the ears of the demoiselle Katherine. But Katherine, parting from him, would not have had the kindness to cry.

"My love to the canon. Tell him I will write."

And to Katherine de Vauselles nothing, since that is what she wants. He might be making his testament, he thought, and grinned, and winced.

He shook himself. He had no time to make a will when he might be wanted for murder.

Chapter Two

He was beyond the walls, putting Paris farther behind him
with every step. The devil of it was that the Mounted might
catch him at night on the road. You could always make a deal
with the foot sergeants if they weren't fighting drunk. But the
Mounted were another matter.

Villon appraised his companions. The likeliest of the lot was
the peddler, a sharp-nosed, sharp-chinned old codger. He must
have seen a bit of life in his day and undoubtedly talked the
jargon. What were his ribbons and rosaries for, his belts and
combs and gloves and buckles, if not to hide the stolen goods
at the bottom of his pack? But this strong sun that stripped
you naked was no help to confidential talk. The four friars

were silent as oysters—dull-looking beggars who smelled of garlic. Even the stout pardoner had stopped his Roman stories. The juggler looked like a jolly child. He was drawing out the lame fellow in armour—it was dark with rust and badly dented.

"So when you were camped across the river you lay low for a bit. But what of the captain's hose?"

"Nothing left of 'em," answered the soldier. "And his shirt—it looked like a cheese the rats had been at. The baron's men were on the other bank. They knew what bad shape we were in. We could see 'em doing their laundry. That was our chance."

"You made a raid?"

"We did that. While their shirts were drying."

"How many prisoners did you take?"

"It wasn't prisoners we were after. We took their wash. By nightfall we'd patched the captain's clothes so that they could be the envy of the whole tailor's guild."

The juggler capered, and the soldier uttered a hoarse laugh.

If you were a man of learning, Villon addressed the fellow silently, you could quote Virgil now on the fine savor of hardships remembered. But if you were a man of learning you'd not have known those hardships. You'd have known others, and worse maybe. Here, trudging the roads with knaves and fools, is a university man, François Villon, M.A., who remembers iron cold and a pinched belly, fever and thirst, bloody fighting and shrieks in the street, night and the terror of dying—this dish of misery set before a child.

Memories foul as the fruit on the gibbets at Montfaucon: memories glittering like the golden-fisted Emperor of Byzantium. Villon escaped to them from the fears that nudged him, from the dusty road that wearied him, from the fellow-travel-

25

ers who bored him. His lip itched, healing. His throat was dry with thirst. His feet burned to rest on a tavern table.

He wished himself back home, sitting at the Sign of the Pine Cone, with René and Colin cracking jokes over their winnings, all warm with drink and song—another warmth than that of this cruel sun; or wandering through the booksellers' quarters, fingering his slack purse and thinking books should be stolen as readily as tripe from the butchers' stalls; strolling by the Holy Innocents under the gaunt frescoes, with the shopgirls in the arcade throwing him the latest slang and the gilded youth a spectacle, their fashionable shoes flopping over their ankles; hearing the familiar boom of the thousand and one church bells or the strumming of a lute in the dark or the salty clamor of the fishwives on the bridge; standing under the clock tower of St. Benoit in the unquenchable hope that Katherine de Vauselles might come by on her way to mass. He was almost willing to be perched on a high stool in Guillaume Perdrier's anteroom, drudging over the ledgers to the harsh tune of Perdrier's voice fretting over some bad accounts and quarreling with his sons.

It was growing late. There was a gilt rosiness in the sky that sharpened Villon's homesickness.

He had played the fool once too often. But, if his luck held, they would not lay hands on him before he had sent word to the canon and with his good help got the royal letter of remission. Even if Sermoise were dead, the blow had been struck in self-defense, and, though Sermoise was a priest, Villon was a clerk: the University would care for her own.

Cheer came with his first glimpse of the gables of a little inn. All he needed was a drink. But he held his hat before his face as he entered, and sent quick stabbing glances into the corners as though he would pierce the sergeant with his black eyes if one were there.

Some stout citizens making a pilgrimage occupied the center tables. In the corner a group of students had pushed their cups away and were throwing dice. Near the cold hearth sat a smooth fellow, silken, curled, and scented, with the brassy voice and the curious self-importance that marked the heralds of the realm, who treated the news they announced as if they had invented it. The bearded man beside him looked like an inquest judge, and there was a young churchman whose horsey profile reminded Villon unpleasantly of the pontifical notary, Master Ferrebouc.

The peddler, he noted, sat down in the far corner, next to a patched vendor of simples whose box of herbs and ointments lay on the floor beside him. Villon looked twice at this one. Attached to his cap was the badge of brigandage: a neatly scalloped cockleshell. It might mean nothing. Pilgrims to the shrine of St. James at Compostella wore cockleshells as a matter of course. But that short fellow in the shabby jerkin, his face trenched and weatherbeaten, his eyes set too close together, was no pilgrim. Villon was ready to swear that he was a sly subject of the Great Khan, who took tribute from all the thieves and ruffians in France and paid none to the King himself. René and Colin had urged him to join that guild more than once. A dangerous trade, but more profitable than all his odd tutoring and copying and bookkeeping jobs lumped together. Villon had always sheered off. It meant rich pickings. But a man of imagination flinches from the prospect of the gallows.

As Villon watched, out of the corner of his eye, he saw the old peddler cock his head in the direction of the churchman and spit deliberately. The sign could not be mistaken. When

27

the Companions of the Cockleshell would hint at danger they spat.

Villon shrugged. His danger was his own secret.

He slipped across the room to the table where the young men were shouting over their game. These boys could serve him. If one of them should be on his way to Paris, he might be the bearer of a letter to the Red Door that would set the canon working for a pardon.

Shabby, travel-stained, with the face of a gypsy and the swagger of a player, he must look for snubs. But he could shake his own dice and win something to pay for his drinks.

A couple of new card tricks were Villon's introduction. He found that the youngsters were ready enough to be entertained by this odd stranger, who was a University man himself. They hailed from the law school at Orléans.

Villon had lived under the same roof with a professor of canon law for upwards of fifteen years. He made the most of it now. His gambit was the name of Master Ferrebouc of St. Benoit, who was handling the case of the redemption of the girl Jeanne. Forthwith the hopeful lawyers were at it, hammer and tongs. Alone, one staunch Burgundian dared to maintain that the Church had known what it was about when it handed her over to the English to be burned.

"You might as well make a saint out of that witch as impugn the Inquisition!"

The Orléanists hooted him down. He was mad-drunk. He was a damned foreigner. The seeds of heresy were in him. Maybe he believed that the King of France had been crowned by a she-devil?

Villon grinned wryly. He had heard it all before. He remembered when the Goddams held Paris. The terror. The cold. The wolves. Famine and pestilence. A jolly childhood. Those

28

miseries would never be out of his bones, no matter how softly he might lie. What did these infants know of all that? Shake the dice and forget it.

He had been brought up in the house of the canon. Who was a Burgundian. But with the rest of St. Benoit the canon was on Jeanne's side. What the Church had done, the Church could undo: the machinery was at work to turn black white, and nothing could stop it. Now the Seine had been leaching the poor girl's ashes these twenty years and more. Shake the dice.

"D'you know what they say in Paris?" asked the "heretic."

"You come from Paris?" Villon was on the alert. It was not impossible the lad should have been in the neighborhood of St. Benoit, heard something of the affair Sermoise. He might yet learn if the rowdy priest were alive or dead.

"But just. They say . . ."

The others shouted him down again.

"What's it like—Paris?" interrupted Villon, as a man bites on a sore tooth.

"The signboards are all new," said the young man.

They laughed at that. But Villon wagged an admonishing finger.

"The lad has a noticing eye. And whom has Paris to thank for her new signboards? The students!"

"You mean the college riots?"

"The University shut up shop, didn't it?"

"When they raped the stone in front of that rich widow's house?"

"Not one stone," said Villon, "two of 'em: she set up another after they stole the one called the Pet-au-Diable, and the students carted that one off too. And took the Pet-au-Diable from the Palais Royal, where the sergeants thought they had it safe—marched on the Palais in a body, mind you: the Arts students and the medicos, and the theologians and even the lawyers, the masters in all the glory of scarlet and miniver." He saw it again with a sharp delighted eye. He rejoiced in an audience that would find the story fresh and jolly.

"We fought the sergeants like men," Villon proceeded with relish, though he had only cheered the fray from the edge of the crowd, "and set up the Pet-au-Diable and its mate in front of the University. On our way through the City one of the Arts students climbed a ladder to fetch a tavern sign that took his fancy and fell and broke his back. But that was all in the day's work. We had our stones. And we lit bonfires round 'em and didn't stop dancing till cockcrow. We crowned the Pet-au-Diable with rosemary. The stones got new hats every Sunday and every feast day set by Mother Church."

"It must have been sport," sighed the Orléanists.

Villon snorted.

"That was only the beginning. We made a tour of Paris, and ripped all the house signs and all the tavern signs from their brackets. And then we had a wedding: the Sow married the Bear."

"You mean the signboards?"

"I mean the signboards. With the Sign of the Preacher to officiate and the Sign of the Two-headed Man to see to the arrangements. There was wine from the Sign of the Barrel and the Sign of the Bottle and the Sign of the Gold and Silver Cup. The meats were furnished by the Sign of the Bull and the Sign of the Two Sheep, with the Sign of the Caldron to cook 'em. The remnants of the feast were dumped into the Sign of the Basket to be distributed among the poor.

"There were games after dinner, too. We had the Sign of the Dice from the street near the steam rooms and the Sign of the Tennis Ball. The knights and ladies came to the ceremony in the Sign of the Chariot (that's a good tavern, by the way), or they traveled by water in the Sign of the Silver Ship. We didn't forget the bridal bed either. There were rich drapes for it from the Sign of the Blue Squirrel, and we put the bride and groom to bed when the Sign of the Bell before St. Catherine's rang vespers. Sport?" Villon would have whistled but for his sore lip. "Yes, they've new signboards on every street now."

"I'll bet the burghers didn't take it lying down."

"Not exactly." Villon grimaced. "They went to the Provost. He's a good fellow, Robert d'Estouteville, but he had to satisfy 'em. There was a set-to between his men and ours. That was where the butchers' hooks came in. We armed ourselves with those. I took one myself from under the nose of the Master Butcher," he lied happily. The Master of the Butchers' Guild had indeed nearly had him by the collar when he ducked and fled. "The sergeants got the better of us that time. They had sharper weapons than butchers' hooks. They made their arrests."

"But the University won?"

"Only after another fight. In May, that was, and a bloody fracas too. The Rector himself headed a deputation to the Provost to demand the release of his innocent lambs. It was granted, of course, and we cheered the Provost in the streets. Then we marched back, a thousand strong, to the University. But there was a little company of sergeants in the way, with a hot-head of a captain. He ordered them to draw. We hadn't any butchers' hooks that day. One student was killed outright, defending the Rector. The University closed down after that for a year. No lectures. No sermons in any church throughout all Paris. The Provost made honorable amends. He apologized to the Bishop. He made restitution to the University. There was a hanging, and one sergeant belonging to the Chatelet had his hand struck off at the wrist. The University, my young friends, is the most beloved daughter of the kings of France and the nurturing mother of her churchmen. She will always come off victorious, and God damn the butchers."

They drank to the damnation of the butchers, but Villon heaved a great sigh. He had written a whole epic on the affair of the Pet-au-Diable, in which he had not played too brave a part. Heaven alone knew where the scrawled sheets were lying now.

His audience had failed to take his bait. The visitor to Paris had looked blank at his mention of St. Benoit. The name conjured up no story of a recent row in that neighborhood, and the tale of the college riots had merely made them guffaw and forget poor Jeanne. None of these children would carry a letter to the Red Door for him. They had listened joyously to Master François, and lost a little money to him. But now it was finished. He must look for help elsewhere.

Villon shrugged one shoulder and pocketed his winnings. He waved an ambiguous farewell to the Orléans crew and sauntered across the room. As he passed the corner table the short shabby man bent down hastily over his box of medicines.

"How can I serve you, sir? I have remedies for the itch and the scurvy, and a strong salve against wounds that refuse to heal. And here is a tried cure for loss of vigor. . . ." He spoke in a high droning voice, glancing up at Villon from under his eyelids, his fingers hovering coyly above his wares.

Villon gave him a sour grimace. He felt vigorous enough for a hotter night's work than he could afford. He leaned over and with a side glance at the old peddler muttered two words of the jargon in the quack's dirty ear. The peddler laughed noiselessly, showing black stumps of teeth. But the quack merely repeated stupidly:

"An ointment for your lip, sir?"

"By the Great Khan," muttered Villon, "I think you have something better than ointment there. Are you on your way to Dijon?"

The fellow shrank together.

"What do you want?" he whined. "I have a salve . . ."

The man was afraid of him, of him, poor François! Here was a joke. Villon began talking the jargon, but he was out of practice. The quack looked sulky and refused to respond.

The old peddler scratched his sharp chin with a swollen finger and got awkwardly to his feet.

"Come out into the yard with me, young man," he said. "You don't want apothecaries' stuff. I need a mouthful of air."

Villon followed him outside. The quack remained sitting at the table, staring after them with his little close-set eyes.

The peddler took Villon by the arm and led him to a corner of the yard near the stable. A wagon stood there, with one wheel missing. He settled his old bones on that.

The medicaster, he explained, had reason to be cagey with strangers. Himself, he was not afraid of Villon. A man who talked the jargon that way could be trusted.

Slowly, with the first stars coming out overhead, and the sound of church bells drifting to them from the four quarters of the little town, the old man confided to Villon the bitter story of Dijon as he had just heard it from the fellow within.

The city was the hunting preserve of the Burgundy gang. Their headquarters were Jacquot's brothel. He would receive anything, from a stolen horse to a scabbard studded with Indian rubies. He gave a fair price for what you turned over, but he made his profit and more, what with the drinks he sold and gambling games and of course his girls. They said he worked under the Great Khan himself. But it was all up with Jacquot now. Some damned traitor had passed the word to the Dijon authorities. The peddler had it from the quacksalver that the guard had come down on Jacquot's house at one o'clock in the morning. The procurator himself had headed the raid. There was no buttering him. The place was crammed with stuff: silks, plate, jewels, enough to hang every man jack of them.

Villon craned his lean neck and made a stifled clucking sound in his throat, so that the toothless old rogue lisped sharply: "Don't do that!"

Those who weren't hanged, he went on, after an angry pause, were thrown alive into vats of hot oil, and the small fellows were put on the rack until they squealed on those higher up. It was a miracle any escaped. And the crew there was at Jacquot's that night: Companions from Gascony and Italy, from Spain, and all the way from Scotland, not to speak of Parisians like René de Montigny.

"René?" Villon lamented again his inability to whistle. So that was why he had lost sight of his chum. A slight shiver ran through him, and he smiled strangely, as the old smile at the death of a contemporary. It would be a joke if René, the foxy René, were the first of them to be caught. "Is he . . ." and Villon made the same throttled noise, with his fingers knotted at his throat.

"God saved him," said the peddler.

Villon nodded. God was always saving him. Or his fine relatives. It would go otherwise with Colin de Cayeux, the locksmith's son. Or with himself. He swallowed. His gullet was dry.

"Well, old bag-o'-bones, thanks for your news. René taught me how to suck eggs, so to speak. I should be sorry to see him in a hempen necklace."

34

The peddler shook his head, as though commiserating René in advance, and sighed.

But Villon jogged him out of his mumpish ways with a quick query:

"Where do we go from here?"

" 'We,' is it?" the peddler asked, chuckling in his young friend's face till Villon wrinkled his nose at the old man's foul breath. But Villon added firmly and jovially in the jargon:

"We're not for Dijon, at any rate."

The peddler had been for Dijon—hidden under the glass beads, lute strings, combs, and gloves was merchandise that would have interested Jacquot. But, after the medicaster's news, he must take another road. He might try Angers.

But, he groaned, he was getting feeble. His eyes were bad. And his hearing not much better. He didn't sleep well of nights: his bones ached so bad. He'd thought he had a hard life of it, sweating in the galleys for Jacques Coeur when the banker owned the Pope and was money lender to the King. But there was no hard life while you were young and tough. The burden of his lay was that Villon should bear him company, lend him eyes and ears while the roads were being thrashed for the rest of Jacquot's gang, and share the profits on the disposal of the goods he carried. There were bound to be good pickings when they came to Angers; it was a city of churches, a rich city. What did his young friend think of it?

Villon scratched his elbow. They could not lay hands on him in Angers. The Companions would help him to keep in hiding. He might even win the protection of another René, the King of Anjou. If only he could get a letter to the canon first.

"I am for you," he said at last, clapping the old man on the shoulder so that he giggled, and groaned again. His bones ached bad, he said mournfully.

35

It was a weary life, trudging in the hot sun, snitching their victuals from fields and orchards, drinking well water, and the women so busy in the fields they would not throw you a smile, much less haggle over a packet of needles or a picture of St. Eloy to pray to against quinsy.

Villon had been over that road once before in better company. No less a man than André Courant, solicitor to King René, had obliged the canon by taking his ward to Anjou to see the tournament with his own eyes.

Villon grinned, remembering how for days before he left he had plagued his fine friend de Montigny to tell him what went forward when such a company assembled as he would find at Saumur, and sat eagerly at the feet of Big Jehanne for tales of the old Provost, who gave her the protection he so kindly afforded the prostitutes of Paris. He was to be at the tourney with his wife, the wealthy Baroness d'Ivry, and his daughter, Ambroise de Loré, who bore her father's name, though they said she was no more like that jovial old soldier than a rose is like a wine barrel.

As he footed it wearily beside the limping peddler, Villon entertained the old man with incredible stories of that first journey, and the wonders of his visit.

He had believed such scenes lived only in the imagination of painters and of hungry children like François Villon. But this was real. The castle, with its black towers, lording it over the slate-blue roofs of the village far below, and the painted pavilions with pennants flying, near at hand, was reality as solid as the vineyards and woolen mills and glass factories that maintained it. The spacious lawns, the rose gardens, the trees clipped into leafy grotesques, the fish ponds with the jeweled life moving dreamily in their clear depths, were actual: you could walk on the grass, pinch the hedges, smell the flowers, plunge your fingers into the water to scare the fish. For contrast, there was the enormous clamor on the tilting-ground: armourers hammering, horses stamping and snorting, stableboys cursing the trumpeters who got in their way, squires straining to fasten the thongs of shields, noisily buckling on helmets, little knots of people everywhere, arguing the strength and weight of the contestants. After the silence, the sweetness and emptiness of the gardens, you soaked in joyously the noise, the bustle, the strong language, the sharp smells of the stables.

You could spend hours in the great halls, studying the tapestries, the paintings, the Persian rugs, the elaborate Venetian glass, the fine red leatherwork, the King's library: François had handled the Virgil, the Plato, the Boccaccio with greedy fingers. Later, he would be wild for the manuscripts he had not opened, the treasures he had had no eyes for. Then, all this luxury had been a frame, a background for the men and women who accepted it with such enviable ease. The courteous talk, the ready laughter, the intervals of music, the ceremonious accompaniments of the war games had seemed splendidly symbolical of power, of race and wealth.

The peddler listened doubtfully to Villon's recital of these glories. They might pay a visit to the castle and do a bit of business there. But he had no hope of coming closer to the riches of Anjou than the postern gate. It was a queer thing for a man who had seen the Provost of Paris jousting for his bride to be trudging the roads with a packman. Villon had to swallow his boasts as often as not. His companion kept interrupting him to complain of pains in his legs and his heart.

Back at home, Villon had sometimes thought he might fancy a packman's life, traveling from door to door, bandying words with the women and showing them what a blade you were, given half a chance. In fact, it was as tedious as any other job.

37

Your feet burned with walking. You had to keep sorting your goods again and again, because no woman could resist turning the ribbons and trinkets upside down for nothing but the pleasure of handling them. A pot would boil over, her brats would start quarreling, and you lost a sale. Or she shut the door in your face. There was neither money nor poetry in it.

Villon planned to shake the peddler as soon as they got to Angers. There he could join up with one of the companies of players that made the city more famous than its countless costly churches. They might travel to the court of King René, or he could work his way with them back toward Paris and stay in hiding on the outskirts until a letter of remission made it safe to return. If he got it. The road had not shown him a soul by whom he could send the necessary word to the canon.

But first he must spend another night under a hedge.

Villon had almost become reconciled to the night air, the stars, the maddening country silence. The solitude he could never get used to. Hell itself could not be so bad: it would not be so lonely.

He waked at cockcrow with the sky lightening in the east till it turned from the grey of a dishclout to that of a wine-soaked napkin. His mouth was dry. His skin prickled. He had a crick in his neck. He sat up, shrugging, as though he could shrug off his discomfort and his drowsiness. He yawned. He staggered up.

The old man was lying as he always did, with his pack for a pillow. Villon picked up his staff, and prodded him with it. He would have kicked him awake, but something about the peaked grey face, the unshaven scrawny throat, made him think of the canon. Another old man, with a different face, a different fortune, and the same end when all was said and done.

38

"Come on," cried Villon, hoarse with rheum. "Do you want to make dog's meat?"

The peddler did not answer. He lay stiffly hunched, his mouth gaping black between his sharp nose and his sharp grizzled chin. His knobby purple hands were open, clutching at nothing.

Villon bent over him. The man was dead.

Villon glanced over his shoulder. There was not a creature in sight. The birds were beginning to twitter. He heard a cock crowing far away. Villon made the sign of the cross. Then he bent down swiftly and, with a gentleness he had not shown the old rascal in life, drew the box away from under his head. His fingers worked hard at the buckles, but his face was quiet as the dead man's. At last he had the straps undone. It took another moment to sling the pack over his own shoulders and fasten the buckles again. Now he knelt beside the peddler and lifted his wallet.

He rose from his knees and turned his back on the dead.

He misliked leaving the old man to the crows and the wild dogs, who might find him before the farmer did. But he must move on. He shrugged, glanced keenly up and down the road, and hurried away. He had always turned it off with a jape when he saw a man roll over in a tavern brawl or met a funeral procession coming from church or, as long ago, picnicked at Montfaucon with the smell of rotting carcasses on the wind to flavor the taste of the wine. But the joke was on him. All his wit was dazzling swordplay to hide his horror.

The old rogue was dead. What of it? So was Aristotle. So was Alexander. So were uncounted soldiers, serfs, and clerks, and priests. Villon lashed the heads off the roadside daisies with his staff, thinking abruptly of Sermoise. Was he dead?

François Villon must die one day. But not before he had

39

made verses that would live long past his time. Not before he had conquered that proud heart, Katherine de Vauselles. And Katherine must die. What would conquest itself mean then?

He heard a dog bark and took a firmer grip on his stick. Suppose she were to see him now, his clothes torn and stained, his face darker than ever with a tramp's beard, and he panicked by a farmer's bitch.

He swore to himself that when he got back he would be so fine that she would never guess what he had suffered. She was bored by poverty, ignorant of pain. She admired him for having been noticed by the young Provost and the Provost's gracious lady, Ambroise de Loré. She was amused by his escapades, the college riots, the "free feeds" that had kept rowdy students alive at the expense of outraged butchers and bakers and taverners when the University closed down. She scarcely knew his songs. What she did not know would fill more books than enriched the library of the Sorbonne. He mocked her. He worshiped her. If he had been born to another station he might even have married her. The thought of Katherine was more terrible to him than the memory of what he had left behind under the hedge. It drove out hunger, darkened the morning.

He pushed on.

That night too Villon slept in the open, a wretched sleep, full of bad dreams in which the dead peddler and Katherine, the Provost and the bloody-browed Sermoise came and went. He woke early and walked fast in the direction of the city.

To give himself heart, he began thumping out the good old song about the Abbot Adam of Angers, who had so mighty a thirst, and satisfied it with draughts from such huge pots that his skin was tanned with liquor as hides with myrrh and his wine-soaked body was incorruptible. The metre was superb for a marching song, and Villon found himself going at a good pace. He had learned the verses from a student of Verona who swore that they were five hundred years old.

If the Abbot of Angers were preserved as well as the song about him, his mummy would make good medicine. Villon grimaced. Death and death and death. He could not be rid of it, no matter how fast he walked or to what tune. He peered eagerly toward a distant spire that caught the rays of the noon sun. With wine in his veins and a girl on his knees, he could forget that he must die. He could forget that his love must die.

It was late when he reached the little town. There was no business there to put money in his pocket. The taverns offered little to choose among them. Villon entered the most promising, one eye cocked to discover a Companion who would be his mentor in this foreign place and lead him to a fence with whom he could leave the peddler's stolen goods. But he was disappointed. The food and drink were poor. The girls—there were only two of them—were homely.

Villon was restless. He was haunted. He wanted the spice of an adventure to make him stop chewing on his ugly thoughts. He longed to be bathed and shaven, dressed in smooth silks, with a chain about his neck, a proper figure to present himself before King René, if he should travel that far. He was sick of a packman's shabby habit, a packman's dreary life.

He wandered out into the streets, asking himself how a man like his friend Colin de Cayeux amused himself in such a hole as this. But, of course, an accomplished picklock plied his trade. There was risk in that, which cooled your blood with a pleasant chill on a hot midsummer night. And profit too.

Villon halted in front of a draper's shop. There were goods

there that would make a gentleman of him. He glanced down with disgust at hi/ stained tunic. And up again at the rolls of cloth. With a shr ag of the shoulder, he turned away.

But when ni ht came and he ached with boredom over the dismal entert inment afforded by the tavern, he turned out again into t' e streets. The stable provided him with a dark lantern. H escaped the curiosity of the inn keeper. He was careless of the Watch.

As though by a magnet he was drawn back to the draper's shop. The shutters were closed. The doors were bolted fast. One of Colin's crowbars would turn the trick. Villon had never taken seriously what Colin had to teach a man of house-breaking. He cursed himself for a lazy dolt. He had never troubled to learn anything thoroughly but a new tune or an old rhyme-scheme. He flashed his lantern downward to explore the entrance to the cellar. God's bread, but it would be a pity if he could not get in somehow.

Chapter Three

There was a narrow cellar window that looked hopeful. He would try it. Why not? What else could he do in this damned town? He needed stuff for a suit more than the draper did. He set to work.

He sweated so that he almost forgot the risk before he pushed the cellar window open and slipped through like an eel.

He scrambled up the steps, hearing like something outside of himself the hammering of his heart. This job was more exciting than the "free feeds" had been. Then you had had half the University men with you to help you gull the baker out of his rolls or the taverner out of his wine. This was solo work. In a strange town. And if he were caught—he was damned if he would be caught. After the Dijon affair, the authorities thought the Companions were lying low.

As he grasped the handle of the door leading into the shop proper, Villon remembered Colin's advice to turn it slowly, and lift the door so as to take the weight off the hinges. He grinned secretly. There was no one but himself to notice if the door should creak. And remember, Colin had said, frowning, how you breathe: you hear better when you are inhaling. It had amused Villon that a thief must breathe as carefully as a singer. At the moment, it was of no importance. There was no sleeping householder here to disturb. There were only the bales of cloth. And the huge shadows.

He stood still a moment, listening. He was alone as he had never been alone before, the trembling center of an enveloping darkness into which he would have sunk, away from the small miseries of his exile and the recurrent dread of capture, content to be part of the night, the silence, the shadows, only the quickened throbbing of his heart making him fearful of himself, the one living thing in this hushed breathless dark.

The scratch of a mouse in the wainscot nipped him out of his trance. He must work quickly. Soon the church bells would be ringing. These little towns woke earlier than Paris.

He lifted down a bale of stuff that felt like silk. He could not hope that it would be the Venice sort. But it was deliciously smooth to the touch. He stooped for his lantern to see the color.

A noise below made him stiffen sharply. The Watch on his rounds? Villon listened, his mouth gone dry, the back of his neck suddenly cold. No, it was only the cellar shutter banging in the wind. He had not fastened it behind him properly. Fool! Should he go down now and make it tight? Or chance it, and look over the possible loot first?

44

He believed in his luck. He would examine the goods and let the shutter go.

He raised his lantern, searching for shears with which to cut the cloth. He could not carry away too bulky a roll.

Ah, there!

Villon placed the roll on a counter, and started measuring out a length of stuff. He was beginning to feel at home in the dark shop. It would be like planning a costume for one of his players in a Paris farce, but more satisfying because this would be for François Villon himself. Who deserved a decent suit. There were those who thought they could make up for the poverty of their wit by a show of magnificence. He was not one of that lot.

He began to hum below his breath. The click of the great shears ticked off a pleasant accompaniment.

Suddenly he stopped cutting. He held his breath.

It all happened so quickly that he could not tell how it happened. There was a noise that he mistook for the wind at the shutter again. There was a light that did not come from his own lantern. There was a heavy hand on his thin shoulder and the point of a knife pressing disagreeably between his ribs.

He was in the hands of the Watch. Villon had barely time to invent a plausible story and an alias—Jehan de Loges—to throw them off poor François' track when the draper, shivering, and absurd in his bedgown, came tumbling into the shop. He must have been sleeping in a room beyond that Villon had failed to take account of and been roused by the clamor of the Watch.

"Carry me, I pray you," Villon pleaded, "to the Bishop's prison."

Hearing his own broken voice, Villon asked himself dis-

45

consolately why so clever an actor should have stooped to thievery. And here, close to Angers, whose perpetual Passions and Mysteries and roaring farces made it the players' paradise.

He clutched his breast with the gesture of the young man whom Jesus bade give all to the poor. The rich chain he had removed for safekeeping from the bottom of the peddler's pack was safe unless they searched him. He could feel the stones of the cross that hung at the end of it rough against his skin.

The Watch shook him by the shoulder.

"The Bishop's prison?" he repeated, between doubt and scorn.

"No, no!" panted the draper, who was fat and frightened, with pearls of sweat on his pale face. "It was from there a thief escaped only last Easter."

"I swear by St. Nicholas I'll not escape," vowed Villon, twisting his neck like a chicken about to be slaughtered.

"St. Nicholas, patron of thieves!"

"Patron of clerks," Villon corrected the fat draper politely.

The Watch pulled down a corner of his mouth.

"You're a clerk, are you? You don't look it."

"A man of letters," Villon mourned, "who would give all his learning for a loaf of bread. Oh, sir"—he turned his gypsy face toward the draper—"it was hunger drove me to it. I wish you no ill. Believe me, I feel for you. You are no common draper, I see that," he smiled flatteringly. "You have beautiful stuffs, beautiful! That Florentine cloth there. You buy your silks in Venice and hang the cost—isn't it so? You pay duties every step of the road, you are taxed to the teeth: the way of the merchant is hard." He wagged his head. "But then"—his voice brightened—"you have something to sell. You are a man of substance. You can take care of your wife and children.

46

Mine, if I had them, would starve with me. Poor things!" He paused over the sad reflection, adding: "And I know Aristotle."

The fat merchant was mollified by Villon's sympathy with the draper's lot and puzzled by the reference to Villon's imaginary wife and children. Perhaps the thief was light-headed with hunger. He boasted that he knew Aristotle: was that a friend of the Bishop's?

But the Watch looked sullen.

"Come along now," he growled and jerked Villon's arm. "If it's not the Bishop's prison, our Seigneur can stow you away." The Watch had bethought him of the great house where his wife's niece was in service. He would quench his thirst there.

So he did. But Villon did not.

The hell of it was that, in the little hole off the scullery where they stuck him, all the noises that he heard reminded him of food and drink. The closetlike room gave him nothing else to think of. It was bare except for the stool he sat on and a heap of old straw in a corner.

He struggled to put away the thought of his sins, of the precious chain next his shirt, of the revenge the fat draper would take on a thief caught red-handed, of the possibility that this peccadillo would lead to the discovery of what had happened in Paris on the night of Corpus Christi.

These honest folk! "Do you who uphold the rights of the law, when the hard hap befalls you that it is your work to condemn a man for his crime and to destroy the handiwork of God, do you have care for your justification that pity move your heart! It behooves you to love him and to hang him: to love him for that he is your brother and to hang him because he is a thief." The draper could not know that Jehan de Loges, once Michel Mouton and before that François Villon, might be wanted in Paris for murder. Had Villon too destroyed the handiwork of God? What it was to be without news! What it was to be without breakfast! He groaned. As the morning wore on, he could have made a poem to a pasty.

He leaped up as the door was unbolted and a servant came in carrying a dish of broken meats and a cup of sour wine. Villon was nearly as hungry for company as for food. As his teeth met over a greasy morsel his sharp eyes devoured the man who had brought it. The servant returned his stare impassively. He was a stocky fellow with a broad face that was ageless and misshapen feet. Villon lifted the wooden cup to him in a health.

"This is a great house that your Seigneur enjoys," he said between hasty mouthfuls. "Do they treat you well here?"

The servant shrugged slightly.

"I can't complain."

"You know where your dinner is coming from and with whom you will sleep at night," said Villon.

"So do you, now."

"It is weeks since I was so certain," Villon admitted.

"Well, fall to, fall to," urged the man, as though Villon had not done so greedily, and turned toward the door, limping.

Villon waved a crust at him to stop him.

"You have corns, eh?"

"What's that to you?"

"I used to know an old woman who had them," said Villon, with a reminiscential grin. "Every time she got a twinge in her big toe she'd say a soul was descending into Hell."

"The devil couldn't find room for 'em all by my big toe." The man sighed.

"A pity I haven't my pack here," said Villon, wiping his fingers on his breeches. "I have a corn cure there works miracles."

48

The servant looked down at his lumpy feet.

"You'd have made a sale, young man. I'd try anything."

"You could have had it for nothing."

"So?"

Villon jumped up and put a nervous hand on the servant's arm.

"I'll give you something better than a corn cure if you get me out of here tonight."

"So?" repeated the servant, and a slow smile broke his moon-shaped face into a dozen wrinkles. He shook his head. "Not possible."

Villon dug out a worn leather purse.

"Aristotle says that the impossible is more possible than the improbable." He would make fun of Aristotle in any company.

"Hush now!" whispered the man, "someone's coming." Before Villon could turn, the door was opened and shut again and bolted. He was locked in alone.

He shrugged and flung himself down on the straw. It was old and nasty but softer than the stool. The serving man was smooth, and never smoother than when he had pocketed that coin. Villon yawned thoughtfully and, less despairing than afraid of despair, addressed himself to sleep.

He dreamed that he was back in Paris, in Robin Turgis's tavern, playing cards with Colin and René. René was urging him to come to a meeting of the Companions at the Sign of the Mule: why waste the best years of his life teaching dolts when a bit of quiet work would make him rich enough to live like a lord? And then the scene changed to the dark corner back of the locksmith's shop, where Colin used to take him as a child and François, fascinated, would watch his friend handling the tools of his father's trade with the fingers of a magician at a street show. Colin bent his sullen face over the slivers of metal with complete concentration. He was apprenticing himself to a more rewarding trade than that of his absent parent. To François it was a mystery, dangerous, wonderful, and, when Colin labored too long and too earnestly, a trifle boring. The dingy airless back part of the shop was the familiar place of their common childhood, but in the dream Villon was not a child. He was the young man who had just been laughing at René's stories of the tricks the Companions used, and half-consenting to join the party at the Mule. The lock over which Colin was frowning would open the door of the library of the Sorbonne, but Villon knew that, once he got in, he would find, not the serious fellows, robed and hatted as the rule required, dragging the great tomes on their clanking chains to the lecterns under the windows, but a garden, sunny and fragrant as the rose garden at Anjou, and hidden there, awaiting him, who but Katherine de Vauselles? In his impatience Villon seized the tools from Colin to try his own inexpert fingers at the task, but Colin snarled at him savagely, and when Villon, with a crow of triumph, made the pick turn in the lock and the door swung open, he saw, neither the library nor the garden, but the charnel house of St. Benoit, cold and grim in the dusk, and the bashed skull of Sermoise threatening him from the top of the heaped bones.

It was a disagreeable dream, and he was relieved when he woke. But he had no sooner satisfied himself that it had all been a dream when he began puzzling wretchedly for its significance. Did it mean that Sermoise was dead and that the man who had killed him must die for it and lie with those moldy fragments of mortality? Did it mean that he had no hope of Katherine forever? Did it only mean that the fat draper intended to press charges against him? They had not taken him to the Bishop's prison: they did not believe he was a clerk. God knows he looked more like a common thief, not even one of René's gilded Companions. Mechanically he put his hand to his breast and felt the chain concealed there. He blinked at the bare room, dull with twilight, his nostrils twitching with the smell of the old straw where he had lain. Even that moon-faced servant would be better company for him than François Villon now. He had always hated solitude, except when he was making verses. And it was weeks since he had been pricked by the excitement that made him sing. His heart must be brimming with delight or squeezed by a crowding pain before it could beat in the rhythm of a poem. Now he was bare of joy and too anxious to peer into the bottomless pit.

He would bribe whoever came with as much as he had on him, with everything but the precious necklace, only to get out. Once he was on the road again, he would beat his way back to the outskirts of Paris. God, if he could run into René! René knew the ropes, and how to get free of the rope, Villon punned to himself wryly.

He looked up eagerly as the key turned in the lock. It was the moon-faced man again with his evening victuals. Villon was ready for him this time. He did not so much as look at the food before he began to hint that he had about him a fine present for whoever would be Christian enough to help him out of this place. The servant stared at him impassively. He was waiting to be shown.

Villon turned his back on the man and fumbled in his breast. He detached the cross from the chain and held it out in the palm of his bony hand. It was too dark for the garnets set in their silver-gilt frame to make any showing. But Villon's glib tongue might have been that of the jeweler who had wrought it.

"And—you cannot see it, that's true, but there is a sliver of the great toenail of St. Paul worked into the setting. This is a relic worth more than you will earn in ten years' service. And the cross has been blessed by the Pope."

The man's face did not change, but he peered over Villon's shoulder as though the papal blessing would take visible shape and aureole the precious object lying in his hand.

"The nail," pursued Villon unctuously, "was lost on the road to Damascus."

"How did you come by it?"

"It was given me by a holy man for whom I did a kindness," said Villon, recalling the stories told by the pardoner who had been his fellow-traveler on the Orléans road. "He charged me never to sell it, even in my sorest need, for some of its virtue passes from it unless it be used as a gift. I would not part with it now, but that I am on my way to my poor mother. She is lying at death's door, and I would see her once more before the end. Take it, good friend, for pity's sake, and enjoy its magical powers. God will reward you doubly if you get me out of this place tonight."

The man hesitated, rubbing his chin with a broad hand.

"Do you think any harm can befall you for forgetting to lock me up safely if you have this to protect you?"

Villon had fallen into misfortune in spite of his carrying the cross with its sacred relic. But he judged rightly that this would not at once occur to his moon-faced friend.

The servant shook his head, blinking at the cross with a mixture of greed, reverence, and suspicion in his pale eyes. Then he held out his hand, and Villon dropped the bribe into it with a sigh of relief that did duty for regret at parting with so rare a treasure.

"God bless you, my man. You will never repent this," he cried softly.

52

The servant departed without further word, and Villon ate his cold supper behind bolts. But he did not expect treachery from Moon-Face, and indeed, late at night, as he listened warily to such small sounds as could only sharpen the silence of the sleeping household, he noted that the door swung slowly open and remained ajar in the conspiring dark.

He slipped out with never a challenge, thanking Heaven for a starless sky, and made his way quietly down the road.

He had lost his pack. He had nothing to dispose of but the necklace, which he purposed keeping for Katherine. He liked feeling it against his skin and imagining that it would yet be hers. For a while he revolved in his mind the notion of going on to Angers. He had not much to hope for from his old uncle, the monk, whom he had never seen and who would scarcely rejoice to lay eyes on a relative as disreputable in appearance as poor François at this juncture. He could take up with the players. Even if he managed to avoid going to a fence with the necklace, he might run into some of the Companions.

He was haled back by his dream about Sermoise. The knowledge that after all his wanderings he had not yet set the canon moving the powers of the realm to grant him a necessary pardon dogged him wherever he went. He turned his back on Angers and began working his weary way north.

The days ran into weeks, the weeks into months. There were the summer suns that burned his back and turned the stones of the road to hot coals under his feet. There were the thunder showers that drove him, drenched and cursing, into impossible shelters. There were the star-spangled nights when he lay awake, tortured by the terror of the midsummer sky and the memory of Katherine, and sometimes there were games by candle light in dismal taverns, when he kept a roomful of travelers roaring at jokes that Paris had forgotten long ago.

If only he could get back, he would give up his vagabond ways. He would slave in Perdrier's bank, he would teach dolts to speak the Latin of a papal nuncio, he would be an obedient son to the canon, and earn a job as secretary or librarian in some great house. He would be prudent, would grow rich and plump, and hold all tramps and thieves and roisterers in scorn, knowing their life for the torn spotted ugly thing it was. He would write verse that would be talked of in high places, not sung by rowdy students only. He would make Katherine proud of him. And be invited to the parties at the Provost's. And stop in at the Mule on the way home . . . So his fantasies ran, from noble intentions to happy dreams, and all alike remote, tormenting him.

Here he sat, then, in a tavern in the little town of Bourg la Reine, fiddling with an empty cup and wondering how he would get news of home. He rubbed his chin gloomily. It bristled with a week's growth of beard. He was grateful that it hid the white scar on his upper lip where Sermoise had slashed it. But he felt dirty, and tired of feeling dirty. At the same time he was conscious of being stared at.

Before the cold hearth, with his gown pulled up and a neat pair of legs stretched out as though it were deep winter and the fire roaring, sat an abbot with a shrewd blue eye fixed on Villon. He had the smooth cheeks of a girl. Villon envied him that and his plump complacency. There was something disturbing about his blue-eyed stare. If he had been a woman, Villon would have started a flirtation. But no woman would look at him now, he reflected sourly.

He put his hand to his breast to feel the necklace, which he had luckily saved through all his misadventures. It gave him a morsel of comfort and fortitude, and a twinge of fear too, when he touched it. Then he got to his feet and strolled across to the abbot, trying to make up for the dullness of his appearance by the brilliance of his smile.

"You appear to be at home here, good Father," he said. "Is your abbey in this neighborhood?"

"Some eight miles east as the crow flies," answered the churchman in a low husky voice. It reminded Villon oddly of that stout wench, Marion l'Ydolle.

"But then you should hail from Port Royal," he said. "There is nothing in that place but a nunnery. One has heard of the abbess"—he grinned—"Huguette du Hamel."

The scandals at Port Royal were a by-word. Never too strict a nunnery, it had changed for the worse since Huguette headed it. It was common knowledge that Master Baudes le Maistre, her lawyer, had been given not only the seals of the abbey but the keys to the abbess's bedchamber. There were more circumstantial stories. One night, when Huguette and Baudes were about to bathe together, the abbess invited a pretty nun named Alison to follow suit with a cousin of Baudes', a clerk who was enjoying the hospitality of the convent. Alison protested. Huguette insisted. The abbess ended the argument by seizing the prudish virgin and throwing her, in her nun's habit, into the bath. They said that the refractory sister had ended as a concubine of the abbot of Saint-Riquier: a gift to him from his daughter Huguette. Villon wondered if this rosy-cheeked abbot would entertain him with other lively tales of Port Royal.

He made no answer to Villon's remark, merely continued to survey him with an appraising stare.

Villon looked harder at his companion.

"A bath would be a good thing now," he pursued, rubbing his chin again.

The strange prelate laughed huskily.

"I see you know the story," said Villon. "Do you know the abbess too?"

"Possibly. Would you like to meet her?"

Villon grinned knowingly.

"It would be an honor I do not merit. Although"—he glanced down at his shabby habit—"I deserve better than you would think to look at me. I was caught in a thunder shower and have had no chance to change. We should not judge by appearances, should we?" he grinned.

"No," said the abbot.

"Huguette would not look twice at me now. And yet, if she were here, I believe I could make her merry."

"Yes?" said the abbot.

"As you see, good Father, what I need most at the moment is a barber."

"Yes," repeated the abbot.

"When I was a bec-jaune at the University," murmured Villon in the wistful voice of reminiscence, "they shaved me before I was shriven. If I had a barber to shave me now and your reverence to shrive me, I should be clean without and within: I would not know myself."

"Do you only know yourself when you are dirty and sinful?"

Villon closed one eye in what might have been a wink as he answered:

"God made us out of dust, and we are all miserable sinners."

"Yes," admitted the abbot and, pulling his gown about him, stood up.

"Let us go to my friend, Perrot Girart, with whom I have certain business. He is a master barber and will treat you like a king."

"But I can only pay like a poet," Villon confessed.

"It is the same thing," answered the abbot reasonably. "Come."

As they stepped down the road together Villon thought to himself that Huguette du Hamel must indeed have an eye, if she could see beyond his travel-stained clothes and bearded face to the man who had indeed every hope of making her merry. She could know nothing of the necklace close against his skin. But as they moved on he made his eyes shine for her like black diamonds.

"This Perrot Girart, what manner of man is he?"

Huguette replied that Perrot was a simple soul, a widower, who had a daughter . . . Pretty? Truly! Complaisant? But yes. Aha!

"Not so fast, young man," protested Huguette. "She is not in Bourg la Reine. She is at Port Royal." And to keep her there, for of course every nun brings a dowry to the convent, the barber must pay what was necessary. But the good man was slow. The abbess had come to collect.

She might have sent Baudes, but perhaps she loved him more than she trusted him. Rather than send an envoy, in any case, she would attend to the matter herself. Villon guessed her reasons. Every company of pilgrims could hold an interesting stranger, like himself. Every thicket on the road bristled with adventure. She had not worn the gown of an abbot all the way: she had put it on to impress Perrot. He would be reminded that traveling was risky for a woman unescorted: her disguise was her protection. Yes, Perrot was simple. And here, thank God, was the barber's basin swinging before his door.

They were not disappointed in their welcome. Perrot was a short plump man with a fringe of hair round his bald spot that made him look like a tonsured clerk. But there the resemblance ceased. He showed the humility of the mere crafts-man before the Church, with the debtor's eagerness to please, and a native generosity. Rubbing his palms together, he ex-plained joyfully that they had come in the nick of time, for the old sow had littered and, if they would but stay for the roast-ing, they could dine on a sucking pig as tender as a baby; and, if the abbess would consent to stop the night, his bed was at her service; and had they ever seen such fine weather for November; and it was such a journey from Port Royal: he prayed that his daughter was a good child and knew her duty to the abbess; and did the abbess prefer white wine or red? Huguette nudged Villon and lifted her chin, amused, while the barber chattered on like an old woman. But Villon wanted only to be shaved, for he would cut a figure with the abbess and you must have a clean lip to relish roast pork even when it is tender as a baby.

Perrot fussed and fumbled over the job, chattering all the while, till Villon could have bitten the barber's hand. The abbess looked on, mightily entertained. But there was comfort preparing: the buttery fragrance of the little pig roasting began to fill the air. The abbess had spoken for red wine to begin with and white wine to follow. She had graciously consented to stop the night, accepting Perrot's bed. And she had made it plain to Perrot that she would excuse him after dinner and that she had no wish to be disturbed by him or his maid or his man, for then she would have work with her secretary. Villon had been elevated to this post by casting up his *beaux yeux*.

So there they sat, at last, alone together in the smoky kitchen, the rich fragments of the feast spread out on the table where Villon now leaned his elbows, having eaten and drunk a little more than he was able. He smiled lazily into the abbess's face. It wore the look of serenity that is sometimes seen in a saint who has foregone the world, sometimes in a woman who is holding it carefully in two smooth hands. The abbess, Villon guessed, measuring her through half-closed eyes, might have turned thirty. An old woman. But with the privileges of age. She had the look of Dame Richesse, in *The Romance of the Rose,* powerful and prideful, secure in satisfied lust: she would not care to play the coquette. Hastily he poured himself another cup of wine and launched into tales of the wild days at college, which would amuse the abbess as they had amused the young Orléanists, as, longer ago, they had amused Katherine.

When he had done the abbess laid a hand on his arm and asked in her husky voice if he thought the University could instruct the Church in such matters as these.

Did he know about the lady Clotilda, who envied the abbess Leubover of Poitiers her appointment to the headship of that convent? Villon confessed that he was usually bored with the minor details of church history. But, he added with a sly look, he was sure that Huguette could make even a nunnery interesting.

"Listen, my lad," replied the abbess. "Clotilda was no ordinary woman. She was kin to kings and more powerful than most queens. She had a band of outlaws under her thumb, ready to commit murder at a nod. And when she heard that this Leubover was appointed to head the convent she coveted, she ordered her followers to put her rival out. Leubover was no better than she should have been, in any case. She had made a gown for her niece out of a precious altar cloth. At least so Clotilda claim:d. And Leubover was a coward. And, besides, she suffered from gout."

"That is a sin," said Villon gravely.

59

"You cannot drink good wine when you have gout," retorted Huguette. "So what is life worth, though you are an abbess?

"Well, when Leubover heard Clotilda's people breaking in, she begged to be carried for safety before the altar of the Holy Ghost. It was dark when the band entered, they knew nothing of the abbess's gout, and they seized the prioress by mistake and carried her off, like one of your Paris house signs, but in tatters and shrieking. So Clotilda held Poitiers, and the bishops were in such terror of her that they would do nothing. It took the king's soldiers, charging them with lance and spear, to put down those brave sisters. Is not Clotilda as worthy of admiration as any scholar in your company? She had no University of Paris behind her, remember. She had nothing but her own strong will and the wild men—"

"And the wild women," interrupted Villon.

"And the nuns under her," concluded the abbess smiling.

Villon nodded, but his laugh rang false to Huguette.

"What are you thinking about?"

"I was wondering of whom you remind me," he said, thinking gloomily of Katherine and of how she never repaid his stories with one of her own, for she had none, and how he preferred her silence to the abbess's maddest laughter.

"Of whom, then, do I remind you?" asked Huguette throatily.

"Why, of the lady Clotilda, of course," he answered with mocking sweetness.

Huguette looked him in the eye.

She would not fear to do the cut-throat's job herself, he reflected. Though she could always hire the proper sort for dirty work.

"I have never known a woman like you." It was God's truth.

"You have not known me," retorted the abbess in the husky voice that again recalled curiously the harlot, Marion l'Ydolle.

"Have we drunk all we wanted?"

"For this night, yes," said Villon, playing his glances against her own. Suddenly he grasped the nearest candle and held it up to her face. "You are older than I." She did not flinch at this: she might have guessed what was coming. "And more learned than I in certain matters. You can undoubtedly instruct me . . ." He leaned closer, setting the candle down. She pushed back her chair. He seized her hand, raising her to her feet. Before she could speak she was in his arms, and he had pushed aside her gown, and his face was buried in her neck.

"It is a good thing," she panted, with a short low laugh, "that Perrot's bed is wide."

"And you are not narrow," punned Villon, releasing her and quickly snuffing the candles, one after another. She had not seen his grimace at his own wit. Even so bold a woman as the abbess of Port Royal, he felt, would be more at ease in the dark.

But as he unbuttoned his jerkin and flung it into a corner, he suddenly touched the necklace. For the first time since he had taken it from the dead peddler's pack he had forgotten it.

Chapter Four

"How slow you are!" Huguette's husky voice pricked him.

He would have run to her, but the disposal of the necklace troubled him. All these months he had been dreaming of the hour when he should be back in Paris, his own man again, Katherine beside him, and he placing the necklace about her throat.

"Are you saying your prayers?" the abbess mocked him.

Hastily he removed the chain and stuffed it into his wallet.

She was not too curious. He thanked God for that. Perhaps she believed it was a rosary of no value. Her laughter drew him into the room where Perrot's bed waited.

The abbess was clever. She was gay. She was kind. For a little Villon forgot that the woman he held was Huguette du Hamel. But when, at last, the amorous play was done and he lay satisfied, a sudden anguish wrenched him, his fingers closed on her breast, and he half-whispered, "Katherine!"

Huguette stirred and lifted her head.

"What did you say?"

"Cara—it is what the Venetians call their lovers."

"I thought you said 'Katherine'."

Villon suppressed a groan.

"Tell me about her," said the abbess.

He was silent. Then he said, teasing his own pain:

"I love her. I cannot have her."

"And you have had me. But you do not love me." Huguette laughed now. "Where is she?"

"In Paris."

"You were on your way there?"

"I was not," said Villon, adding recklessly, "though I am wanted in Paris."

The abbess moved so as to look at him. The room was in darkness, but the eyes of both had grown accustomed to it. She put out a finger and touched the scar on his lip.

He nodded.

"Because of that scratch," she said. "How did you come by it?" And when he did not answer, "You need not be afraid to tell me. I have seen worse."

"I don't doubt it," he said, thinking that she might have given worse, too, this Huguette du Hamel who was so wild a lover. And then he told her. It kept him from speaking of Katherine.

She found the story almost as entertaining as the tale of the Pet-au-Diable. But when she had listened and tried to laugh him out of his fears, she began to yawn. The abbess of Port Royal was not one to fret over the killing of a priest. Through hours of crushing loneliness Villon lay awake, thinking of punishment, while she slept sweetly beside him.

When morning came he was thoroughly tired. But the abbess was no sluggard. She was up and ready for business before Villon had wiped the sleep from his eyelids.

She did not trouble herself with him that day. The better

part of it she spent explaining to the barber how ill things went at the abbey for want of funds, how she was cheated at every turn by villainous millers and vintners and chandlers, how she had had to dispose of a most valuable piece of land in order to settle an old debt to Rome, and how, if the remainder of his daughter's dowry were not speedily forthcoming, she would have to pack the girl home again to Bourg la Reine, a consummation whereat neither father nor daughter would rejoice.

Perrot was full of excuses and explanations, and ended by begging that the good mother of the convent be patient for a day or two, or three at the most: he was coming into a bit of money from a delayed inheritance which he had counted on receiving years ago, and, besides, he would send her back to Port Royal with a keg of the very wine she had been kind enough to praise the night before, not to mention some bags of fine wheat flour and a sack of the richest raisins. It made Villon's mouth water to hear him, though the conversation was tedious enough, the two of them at it hammer and tongs and the abbess getting a bit more than she bargained for with every wag of her naughty head, every shaft from her masterful blue eyes.

It was getting on toward vespers when she turned her attention from the barber to Villon's more attractive but less profitable company. He looked so grim that she asked him if his old scar refused to let him smile.

"Come," she said, "let us walk down to the orchard. Dinner will be some time preparing, and I am tired with all this blather."

They walked slowly through the kitchen garden to where the fruit hung reddening on the twisted boughs. She chatted easily as they strolled along, reminding him, as much by her tone as by her words, that she was the abbess of Port Royal and knew the world as an abbess must.

She had been thinking over his little affair, she told him, making herself at home, as she would anywhere, on a boulder beside the brook.

"Have you no friends in Paris who will take care of it for you? What does your father do now?" she asked.

"Whatever they do in Purgatory, I suppose," answered Villon with a shrug. "He's dead."

"God rest his soul," murmured the abbess absently. "But, see here, you are no ordinary fellow. A poet has the entry of all the great houses. You told me yourself you had made a song for the Provost's bridal and danced in his hall."

"That was before the college riots."

"But you must know some men of substance. Every clerk has friends in the Church."

"There is my guardian," said Villon, skipping pebbles across the brook.

"And who may he be?"

Villon told her briefly.

"St. Benoit," said the abbess thoughtfully. "They are under the jurisdiction of Notre Dame, if I am not mistaken. If your canon is acquainted with Thibaut de Vitry and Guillaume Cotin, the matter should be readily arranged."

Villon hooted. It was not strange that the abbess should know the names of these powerful ecclesiastics, whose wealth, the envy of many merchants, was secured by their high place in the greatest church in Paris. But somehow he expected her to be familiar with less subtle rogues.

"What are you hooting about?" There was a shade of annoyance in her husky voice. "Men break the sixth commandment every day in the week and twice on feast days. But it is a sin

65

to kill a priest. And it will take the good will of bigger churchmen than your little canon of St. Benoit to get you out of this scrape, my lad."

"I am thinking of the peculiar pleasure it would give Masters de Vitry and Cotin to make trouble for the ward of a canon of St. Benoit," murmured Villon, with a twitch of the lip.

"So that's the way of it." The abbess smiled too, an ugly smile. She was not unacquainted with such quarrels. "The big fish eat the little fish," she quoted the old proverb. "No matter. But what interest has this canon in you? Is he one of those who like very young men? Or is he perhaps something besides your father in God?"

Villon threw a small stone with a vicious jerk. He had misliked naming Guillaume de Villon to this woman who feared no one and respected no one. If she had been anyone but Huguette du Hamel he would have bidden her shut her mouth. But just because she cared for nothing but her own pleasure, she might choose to help him in view of last night's kindness. She was known to be generous to Baudes le Maistre.

"Aren't you chilly?" He pretended sudden solicitude.

She shook her head.

"The worst you will get," she pursued reflectively, "is probably banishment."

Villon felt heavy and empty all at once. Was banishment easier than hanging by the neck until you were dead? To have your name cried throughout the city as one to whom no man dared offer refuge under pain of forfeiting his property and his person! Was life outside of Paris, out of reach of the demoiselle Katherine, with none to applaud his verses, worth living at all? He could not bear it. Not even in such company as Huguette's when she was merry, and the road did not provide that often.

She chuckled.

"You don't seem so cheerful."

"Oh, I'm as cheerful as a crow over the gallows." Villon plunged his fingers into the brook to pluck out a minnow as a bird will dive for a dead man's eye. As quickly he let it drop back again.

"Then we'll imitate the crows and have a bite," said Huguette, gathering her skirts about her.

Villon helped her to her feet and drew her arm through his own. He had fallen into his old black melancholy, and it would be an effort to win back to the jollity of last night and the solace of Huguette's arms. His escapade amused her. She was willing to pay for her entertainment. But he could look for no help here.

It was a comfort to return to the kitchen, to see the coppers glowing like fire in the ruddy evening light, to smell the chickens browning on the spit, to note the great pitchers and the worn wooden cups set ready on the table. Huguette too seemed pleased at the sight, for she cried out gaily:

"Let us eat, drink, and be merry!"

"For tomorrow we dice, and may lose all," Villon finished with a wink.

Huguette laughed and took her place at the board.

Villon set himself to amuse her, as he had never labored to amuse Ysabeau. He told the abbess such stories as that wench would have relished, stories he could not have recited to Katherine de Vauselles, though the thought of Katherine swam hazily through the stream of folly on which he floated.

"What do you want to go back to Paris for, my little cabbage?" Huguette asked him, wiping the tears of laughter from her blue eyes. "Come with me to Port Royal. We'll treat you better there than they ever did at St. Benoit, I'll warrant."

"But how will Master Baudes treat me?" Villon asked.

"As I bid him," said Huguette firmly. "He is my lawyer, is he not? It is his business to legalize whatever the abbess chooses to do. And why should I not take you back, along with the wine and the wheaten flour and the raisins? We need some pepper too: you will provide that. Think," she cried, "it is little more than a month till Christmas. We celebrate Christmas royally at the abbey."

Villon burst into song:

*"News of Noel, now Noel let us sing.
New folk, cry God forgive us everything.
Sing we Noel for our new little king,
Noel, Noel, Noel!"*

"Oh," Huguette said scornfully, "we sing merrier things than that."

Villon did not doubt it, but he had a foolish affection for the ancient ballad. He insisted on singing it, despite all the abbess's protests, and made her join in the refrain. All the twelve stanzas: about Mary and Joseph and the ox and the ass keeping watch over the Baby. And the little bird who told the shepherds to look for the Lamb in Bethlehem. And the star in the east that guided the three kings, one carrying gold, and one myrrh, and one frankincense. And Simeon, who held his infant Saviour in his arms. And the priest who came to serve mass out of a vessel made of wood from the tree of chastity, saying: if you believe, God will snatch you up into Heaven; if you do not believe, you will go to hell by the gibbet. Villon found a perverse pleasure in chanting the childish verses as he sat in Perrot's fire-lit kitchen, his belly full of roast fowl and wine and his thin arm around the abbess's waist. He had always liked the refrain, with its play on words and the promise of everything and everybody being new. When he was a small

68

boy, the last stanza had suggested to him the windows at the Celestines: the streaming splendor where the blessed stood in the deep blue air of Paradise with the lutes and harps singing together, and, opposite, the damned. Now it was a grim reminder of the gibbets at Montfaucon and the dangling ragged things that hung there for the wind and the crows to part among them.

"Noel, Noel, Noel!" he shouted, as though his clamor could drown out his memories and his fears.

"Hush," cried Huguette. "Perrot will be coming to find out what the racket is about. Do you think I want to leave here without that girl's dowry?"

"I'll give you something better than her dowry," Villon vowed, homesick with the old tune and the drink and the suddenly renewed dread of not getting back to Paris, "if only you'll help to get me out of this."

"And what will you be giving me?" asked Huguette, laughing. It was evident that she did not believe him. But she liked him none the less for that.

Villon raised a hand to feel of the necklace hidden under his jerkin, but, thinking better of it, let his arm fall on the abbess's shoulder.

"I'll tell you another time. You're not going back to the abbey tomorrow."

"Not tomorrow," she admitted. "Very well, then. Come."

That night Villon slept. But he woke with the uneasy knowledge that he was no nearer home than before. Certainly as long as the abbess remained here at Bourg la Reine, there would be feasting and fun for both of them. But what more could he expect of her? And so close to Paris as he was now! He must drink quarts of Perrot's wine, eat pounds of his fresh pork, cozen Huguette into teaching him the lore that had enslaved

69

Baudes le Maistre, if he were to endure the torment of this nearness, this uncertainty.

As though in answer to prayer, Perrot found a day's business at the other end of the town. His man went with him. His maid had been called home to help at her sister's lying-in. Villon was left alone with the abbess. He could talk freely without fear of being overheard by the barber, whose simplicity he was beginning to mistrust. He could play with Huguette at his ease, and so delight her with his wit and his prowess in the field of love that she must want to help him.

But could she? He would find no worse ambassadress to plead for him in high places. His one hope was in her shrewdness. She had wriggled out of just such tight corners, unaided, the abbess of Port Royal.

Perrot set off in the grey of the morning. By nones the rain that had been threatening all day was beating heavily against the tiny windows and hissing in the chimney. It had never yet been so snug and cosy as now, when the abbess sat before the fire with a mug in one plump white hand and the other beating time in the air to the drinking song that Villon was teaching her, with plenty of japes to season it.

And all the while, through his joking, for all his comfort, ran a thread of sombre thought. For there was nothing like a good drinking song to bring you close to the pit of death and the beating heart of life. There was nothing like drink (and a barrel of oysters, such as Perrot could not provide, alas, to give an edge to your thirst) for quickening lust. And lust satisfied was death in little. The moment when the wine glowed sharpest, ran most sweetly down the throat, sang in the veins, with soft smooth hand in strong hard hand, eyes brimming with laughter clinging to brimful eyes, in that moment life throbbed, winging out of time and pain, birdlike and fairer than any

70

promise of the resurrection. But here was not Katherine, only Huguette du Hamel of Port Royal. Here dread of tomorrow crawled over present peace like a louse.

The abbess drank off the last of her wine, set her mug on the floor, and, leaning over, tweaked Villon's ear.

"Tell me, Villon, how is it you are not in the Church? A clever child like you!"

"Would you like me better if I were?"

"I don't say that. But for your own sake. Why didn't you make something of your chances? Become one of the athletes of God?"

"I had rather be one of the athletes of Venus."

Huguette laughed and shook her head.

"It wasn't that sort of churchman you meant. I know," Villon grinned. "You think I might have lived on the fat of the land like de Vitry. No. That's not my sort. If I were a skinflint, I would not be so skinny. Besides"—he stroked his scarred lip—"you forget the doings at the University when I was there. If Pierre de la Dehors had had his way, I'd not have got my degree at all."

"And who may Pierre de la Dehors be?"

"The Master of the Butchers' Guild. The students fought the townsmen with butchers' hooks, you may remember."

" 'The students are the worst,' " quoted the abbess, smiling.

"And why not? Women don't understand."

"What don't women understand?" the abbess chuckled. "That men need women?"

"They know that right enough. It's their business. But they don't know what it means to be a student. God, when I remember! Sitting in the straw, shivering in the cold air of early morning, while some ambitious whippersnapper drawled out a lecture on universals and—what was it?—accidentals. You could stop him by hissing and groaning and throwing things at him. But every class was the same: dry as the sands of Egypt. You'd think, to hear them, that they wanted you to suffer like the desert Fathers they were always quoting." Villon wetted his throat as though the mere memory tickled his thirst.

"So you cut classes, when there were any to cut. And cut your chance of preferment."

"And cut my lip to spite my face," he joked.

"Money is power, Villon. And how is a clerk, outside of the Church, to come by it? It's not as though you belonged to the merchant class and could make your millions in trade like another Jacques Coeur. No, my friend, I am afraid you will never be rich."

"Would you like me better if I were?" Villon repeated, wanting to hear no more reproaches such as came with bad grace from Huguette du Hamel's lips, wanting to kiss and forget.

The abbess's blue eyes glinted. Villon did not doubt that she preferred a rich lover to a poor one. If he had, her next words would have taught him otherwise.

"You are rich in wit, Villon. And I think, my dear little cabbage, you are hiding something from Huguette. What was it you promised me yesterday that was better than la Girart's dowry? You have not forgotten, I hope."

Villon would have cursed but dared not. A hundred times he had imagined how Katherine would look, what she would say, when he presented her with the necklace at last. He had no wish to lose it to the abbess. But if it would buy his return to Paris, to Katherine herself . . .

"I would give you the bells of Notre Dame," he lied generously.

The abbess chucked him under the chin.

72

"But you want something more in exchange than you have had from Huguette already." The shrewd blue eyes were not so clouded with drink but that they could look into this vagabond's heart. "Well, why not? I have nothing to lose by it."

Villon embraced her.

"Do you mean it? Will you help me?"

"You are a fool, Villon. It is all as simple as Perrot's face."

"What? What am I to do?"

"What am I to have for telling you?"

Villon fumbled in the breast of his jerkin. He drew out the necklace and laid it, his heart sore, his fingers trembling, in Huguette's plump white hand.

"Ah!" she sighed. "Yes. This is prettier than the bells of Notre Dame."

"Will it bring me the keys to the gates of Paris?"

She poured the necklace from one palm to the other, watching the stones gleam in the firelight.

"Perhaps."

"For God's sake don't say 'perhaps'!"

He had nothing further to offer. If this were not enough, he was lost indeed. Had she spoken only to tease the gift out of him? Was she a blacker devil than even she was painted?

She wagged her head wisely and slipped the chain into the wallet that hung at her girdle. Villon followed it with greedy unhappy eyes.

The abbess smiled contentedly.

"That was well done, Villon," she murmured. "Now let me see. Do you write two letters."

"Yes."

"Address one to the chancellery in the name by which they know you officially."

"François de Montcorbier—my father came from that place. He was a farmer there."

"Good. The second letter you must direct to the Great Council, which is now at Berry with the King."

"How do you know that?"

"Ah, my dear, trust Huguette." She winked at him. "But the name of the farm your father worked she does not know."

"Des Loges."

"You will sign that letter Master François des Loges, otherwise called Villon."

"Yes," he responded obediently, and sadly, for he could not at once cease thinking of his lost treasure.

"One or the other, and with good luck both, should bring you a letter of remission."

"Yes, but how . . ."

"I am stopping in Paris on my way back to my precious abbey. I shall carry your letters for you, my lad, and see that they are safely delivered into the proper hands. Now am I a good friend or am I not?"

"You are a darling!" he cried, embracing her more fiercely.

"Stop, stop! You forget what else I am besides," she warned him.

"Oh, you are the abbess of Port Royal, and I am a presuming master of arts. Forgive me, madam, and remember the proverb: the students are the worst!" he grimaced.

"And so you will not be coming back with me to Port Royal," she murmured, her blue eyes bright with laughter again. "When you see your Katherine again—that is her name, is it not?—will you tell her whom she has to thank for the sight of you safe and whole?"

Oh, she was capable of cruelty, the abbess of Port Royal. Villon sat silent, a muscle in his cheek twitching.

"Never mind," said Huguette. "Come, fill up my mug again, and we'll drink to our bargain."

He obeyed, caught again between the old pain and the excitement of this promise of freedom.

The abbess lifted her mug, smacked her lips, and patted her wallet.

Villon almost choked over his own drink. He did not speak but, sitting down, pushed the dishes away from one corner of the table, crumbed it hastily, and, drawing out a clean sheet of paper and a quill, dipped into his inkhorn.

"To the chancellery?" he asked like a boy at his lessons.

"Yes. The worst you will get," repeated the abbess cheerfully, "is banishment."

Chapter Five

Villon bounded down the attic stairs. For the first time in months he had a smart feather in his hat, and his suit was without stain or patch. He felt taller. It was the measure of his well-being. At the sound of his rapid feet on the boards, the canon called out to him to come in. Villon could have cursed with impatience, but he was too happy to curse. He was on his way to meet the demoiselle Katherine.

Guillaume de Villon was sitting beside the fire, one hand held out to the blaze, a tall ruddy old man with little of the priest about him but his tonsure and the light, inquiring and forgiving, in his brown eyes. He was not alone. Opposite him, his back to the hearth, sat a grizzle-bearded, long-nosed, frowning man in a furred mantle, Villon's quondam employer, the banker, Guillaume Perdrier.

He nodded to the young man with a look of distaste. Villon responded with an uneasy smile. They had not parted on the best of terms, those two. Guillaume Perdrier had been persuaded by Guillaume de Villon to give his ward François a clerk's job in the counting house. François had repaid this kindness by introducing Perdrier's sons to the choicest taverns and gaming houses in the city. Perdrier could scarcely have been ignorant of his former clerk's absence from Paris. He was by no means pleased to see him back again.

Villon glanced away quickly.

Near the door, turning his dirty cap round and round in his hands and looking as though he would like to creep into it and hide there, was a little fellow whom Villon could not place. But yes: he was the tenant of the canon's house at the Sign of the Lantern. One would need Diogenes' lantern to find the rent of it: the rascal had not paid it these seven years.

The poor tenant hunched himself in an awkward bow and shuffled his feet. Guillaume de Villon smiled at his ward encouragingly.

"There is a small matter of business to settle. You will not mind waiting?"

Villon shook his head. God, how he minded!

Master Guillaume turned to Perdrier, sucking his cheek meditatively in the way Villon knew so well.

"Let us have it straight," he said. "If this good man does not pay what he owes you, Perdrier, you will have him thrown into prison. He will have leisure to repent of his sins there, I do not doubt. But, though it is well that he should save his soul, his repentance will not put money in your wallet."

The canon threw a quizzical glance at the banker from

under his shaggy brows. Perdrier pursed his lips. The poor debtor peered over his cap at the canon. In the silence of the one there was misery, in that of the other a grim impatience. Master Guillaume measured these justly during the pause.

"*Radix omnium malorum est cupiditas*. The love of money is the root of all evil." It was the motto of the house of Burgundy. Perdrier served the house of Orléans. The canon was fond of his little joke. He went on, smiling with a genial disingenuousness that was too easily seen through. "If I release our friend here from the rent that he owes me, he should be able to pay his debt to you. But I must not be guilty of cupidity. It is a contest, Perdrier, between us two as to which of us shall sacrifice . . . not the money that is owed him but the satisfaction of his conscience in not pressing too hardly for that money." He paused again, sucking his cheek as before.

"You are pleased to jest." Perdrier was curt.

"It is no joke to have a bad conscience," replied the canon. "You would know if you had suffered that way. It is like the gout: only those sympathize with the pain who have endured it. Well, that decides me: you shall endure it! You shall be the man who gets his money, and I shall be free of the sin. Is it a bargain?" The canon's eyes twinkled. Perdrier rose.

"Yes," said the canon. "But wait just a moment. Our friend has already given me the rent, you see, so I must turn it over to you. He will repay me in due time."

He too got up and crossed the room to a cabinet, which he unlocked. Opening an inner drawer, he took out a purse, and handed its contents over to the moneylender.

The tenant continued to turn his cap round and round in his stubby dirty fingers, looking everywhere but at the two old men. Perdrier's annoyance was swallowed up in pleasure at getting his money. Villon's impatience to meet Katherine was checked by his amusement at the transaction. He let out a guffaw that made Perdrier redden with rage and startled the poor debtor into dropping his cap.

"I shall bid you good day," Perdrier snapped. "But let me tell you that the next time yonder Master François has need of pence to pay his debts he will not find employment at Number Seventeen on the Grand Pont. He makes too much of a racket." The banker bowed grimly and made his exit.

"Oh, Master de Villon, but—but I did not pay you—and—" Stammering, the bewildered tenant poured out a jumbled story of his misfortunes and his gratitude and his hopes till the canon raised a hand to dam the flow.

"Come, come," he said drily, "I have waited for my rents from you for seven years. If you were to pay me now, I could not bear the shock: I am getting old."

The man was crying with excitement and relief. His wife, his children, the sickness, the job he had hoped to get and lost . . . The story began all over again.

"Wait." The canon went again to the cabinet and took some coins out of the drawer. "I was going to raise the rent this last quarter," he said. "But, since I did not get it anyway, you might as well have the difference. Perdrier won't miss it," and he thrust the money into the man's square-fingered hands.

The tenant looked at him, bewildered by this crazy arithmetic, and then stammered helplessly:

"May God bless you! May the Holy Virgin have you in Her keeping! St. Joseph . . ."

"Amen, amen," interrupted the canon. "There is no interest on gratitude. The Church was ever against usury. Now be off with you. And see that you get a good apothecary to your wife."

At last the fellow was out of the door, and the two were by themselves. Villon shook his head, grinning. But he regretted the purse of money. He could have used some of it himself. He watched the canon lock up the cabinet and tuck away the key.

"Forgive us our debts as we forgive our debtors," he murmured. On that count, the canon should find a soft seat in Heaven.

"That's what Sermoise said." Master Guillaume glanced at his ward.

"Sermoise?" The name chilled Villon.

"Just before he gave up the ghost. That was what saved you, François."

Villon looked at the canon, who was sitting in his old chair, looking at the floor.

"I thought it was all your doing."

"I could have done nothing if Sermoise had not been afraid of hell-fire: he gave you his free pardon, hoping that God would take pattern by him. Poor fellow!"

But Villon hated the memory of the dead priest. If it had not been for Sermoise, he would never have had to leave Paris. He would not have suffered hunger and thirst and black loneliness on the roads. He would not have been jailed for a thief. He stood frowning into the fire, wondering if the canon was going to read him a lecture or give him leave to go.

The canon looked up with a sigh. For a moment he had been back in the gloomy sour-smelling prison of the cloister, where Sermoise had been carried and lay, clamped in his pains as in a machine of torture, terrified, caught in the grinding vise of remorse. He had seen the wounded priest's face with globules of sweat on lip and forehead, heard his groans punctuating the recital of the familiar syllables: My Blood, which is shed for you, and for many, for the remission of sins . . . But deliver us from evil . . .

"Lord, have mercy on us," the canon murmured to himself.

80

Christ, have mercy, echoed Villon silently, thinking again of Katherine. Could he go now?

"I saw Master Ferrebouc this morning. He would like to have that piece of work he gave you in a fair copy by tomorrow night. You will not disappoint him?"

Devil take it, thought Villon, he had almost forgotten. Copying always annoyed him. It was a job for men who knew the alphabet but not for your true man of letters. And he was set to copying what? The verbiage of the lawyers, who wrapped their meaning in long words the better to conceal it. You might earn a dinner by such a job, but your appetite would be gone by the time you sat down to it. As if language were a dead thing. The fishwives knew better.

The canon knew the sullen look coming into the lean dark face. Poor François! Would he never learn that life was not all made up of moments when the blood danced in the veins and the heart leaped like those flames? Why could he not take the drudgery with the rest?

"Well, you have business elsewhere now," said the canon. "And I must go to see Etienne about the last meeting of the chapter. Notre Dame is after us again." He got up and laid a hand on Villon's shoulder. "Copying decretals is not the worst thing in the world, my son. And wenching is not the best. But I suppose you are too young to believe that." He gave the bony shoulder a pat. He hoped François would be happy for a few hours. Then perhaps he would learn to be good. Villon winked and turned away.

But he was not merry as he ran down the canon's stairs to open the red door that led to the courtyard.

Suppose Katherine had gone! Suppose she had never come. It was late. The bells for nones had long since rung. The streets were empty and cold. He ran most of the way. As he neared the Holy Innocents he slowed his pace to a stroll. She must not catch him running to her. He must not be breathing fast when they met. He fixed his hat more jauntily on his head, straightened his belt, stared greedily about.

He found bitter fun in the fact that the cemetery of the Holy Innocents was one of the liveliest places in Paris. The hammering of the iron-founders resounded against the very walls of the charnel house. Circling the tombs men and women paraded, pricing the gloves and shoulder knots, the missals, the drapers' stuffs, the little cakes exposed for sale in the stalls, sometimes on the stones that covered the dead. There were good *bourgeoises* cheapening finery, gallants taking chaff from the salesgirls, clusters of idle folk around the preaching friars stationed here and there in the cloisters, stragglers with bad consciences about the priests receiving penitents, prostitutes with sharp smiling faces strolling about on the lookout for customers. For a nasty moment Villon, regarding the show, imagined that the pursy ecclesiastics, the preoccupied housewives, the clerks and messenger boys who kept brushing past him might stiffen as he watched into the frightened figures pictured along the walls of the cloisters, and the gay busy scene change to a clacking Dance of Death. These people, each of them intent on his private pleasure or his own business, the knight chucking the girl under the chin, the pimpled apprentice hopefully buying his salvation, would soon be such a collection of yellowing bones, such a dusty porridge as gave the gravediggers steady work. He glanced toward the wooden galleries crammed with fragments of skeletons exhumed to give place to fresh corpses and hastily looked away.

There was no sign of Katherine. He took up his station again near the booth of Blanche the Glover, where a group of plumed and velvet youths stood laughing at her rough jokes. A blind man with prayers to sell roared in competition. Villon pulled the fellow's sleeve. "I'll will you my spectacles," Villon promised him, "so you can tell the honest folk from the sinners hereabouts." But the joke tasted flat on his tongue. What good were his own eyes that could not find his demoiselle?

Suddenly the late-afternoon sun shone with startling brilliance, the February air grew warm, the dull distant clanging of anvils, the droning of priests, the noisy chatter at the stalls changed to a kind of music. He saw her.

He stood still a moment watching her approach. She was taller than he remembered (he straightened his shoulders). She wore green velvet, a treacherous color, but under her heart-shaped headdress the smooth face was lovelier than ever. There was fur at her throat and down the length of her bodice. He longed to touch it. And the curve of her cheeks that were meant to be kissed and kissed. His eyes clouded, and little lightnings played along his limbs.

She did not see him. She was looking up at her companion. It took Villon a moment to place the man. It was Noel Jolis, the brother of the shrew whom Turgis the taverner had married, and himself an agent of the old master grocer, Jehan de la Garde. He was not a bad fellow, Noel Jolis, though quick-tempered like his sister. Behind walked Katherine de Vauselles' maid, Marthe, a plump girl with soft eyes like a cow's, but hers were blue. They met Villon's, and Marthe reddened and looked foolish.

Then Katherine saw him. She gave a little skip, like a child, as though she would run to him. Was it Noel who pulled her back?

They were face to face. Neither spoke. There was only a long look between them, the hunger of months to satisfy with a look. Katherine dropped her eyes first, flushing. Noel broke the silence.

"You're quite a stranger, Villon. They've missed you at the Pine Cone."

Was Noel reminding him that he had a debt to settle with his brother-in-law?

"How's the grocery business?" Villon asked. "I didn't know it took you into this part of town."

"It was the demoiselle de Vauselles who took me here," countered Noel. "I had to carry a message to her aunt for my employer, and we left the house together."

Villon wished Noel at the devil, wondered why Katherine submitted to his company and how they should get rid of him. It was all her aunt, damn the woman!

"Here, don't we want some almond cakes?"

Katherine shook her head.

"Cheese tarts then."

"I have errands to do," murmured Katherine. "I promised my aunt . . ."

"A busy lady, your aunt. What with visits from Master de la Garde's clerk and—by the way," Villon broke off, "she isn't buying spices wholesale, your aunt?"

"She may be selling sweets retail," said Noel with a short laugh.

Katherine looked suddenly frightened, and Villon's quick wits fumbled at Noel's meaning. He knew only that he had not seen her in something like a year and that this meeting would be vain if he could not have her, for however brief a space, entirely to himself.

"Marthe will attend to the errands," he said hastily. "And Noel shall go along with her to see that she is not cheated."

84

Noel grimaced. Marthe waited, flushed and open-mouthed. Katherine put her head on one side.

"Would you, Noel?" she asked gently.

Noel demurred, and obeyed.

At last, wonderfully, among the crowd that flowed about the stalls, they were alone. Villon, with a hundred questions to ask her, a violent urge to dazzle her with his wit, to overwhelm her with his strength, was dumb as a fish. He seemed to have stepped out of the body of François Villon, master of arts, poet, and playboy: he was a serf, a thing, for Katherine to use as she would. A contented serf, a happy thing.

In her presence, delight, mounting, washed his soul clean of malice. Christ could do no more for him.

Carefully he studied the smooth brow, the downcast lidded eyes, the curves of the face, the soft seldom-kissing lips.

"You have been long away."

"You missed me?"

"I didn't miss the quarrels with my aunt," she laughed.

He damned her aunt again silently.

"I cannot live without seeing you: you would not be guilty of murder."

"One can buy remission of that sin too."

She knew then. Or was it a chance shaft? If she knew, did she think any the worse of him? He shifted quickly, looking straight into her green eyes.

"I used to tell you that there was no more beautiful lady in Paris. Now I tell you there is no more beautiful lady in all France."

"You have made a pilgrimage through France?"

"I've been about a bit," he bragged.

"Oh, I should like to be a man and see the world!" It was not the first time she had said so.

85

"Paris is the shining hub of the world, my dear. The rim of the wheel is always in the mud."

"There is plenty of mud in Paris," she smiled.

That was true. But he would have agreed with her equally if she had called the February sky above them a brass bowl or the fat monk near by a Cupid.

"We can't talk here," he muttered. "Come."

Wordlessly she allowed him to lead her out of the busy section of the cemetery to a deserted corner of the cloisters.

"I don't mind these folk." Villon tossed his head toward the bursting charnels. "They won't blab."

She wrinkled her nose. It was damp here, and there was an evil odor.

"You should have a sniff of Montfaucon," Villon told her. "This is roses and violets by comparison."

"You were going to take me there once. Do you remember?"

It had been during the college riots. He had not risked it. But did she still want to go? She nodded, her lips pursed in a queer little smile.

"Then I will take you," he vowed, adding, with a swift tenderness that none but Katherine had ever had from him: "Oh, my sweet, how you perfume even this place!"

Suddenly he could bear it no longer.

"Don't be afraid," he whispered. "They won't betray us." Katherine looked at him wonderingly, but his black eyes were on the loft above them and he was crying to the bones crammed there: "Tell no man, if ever you did this!" He held her tight, tighter. Pressed against him so, she cried "Oh!" He loosed her a little. She had not answered his kisses. Now it was for him to stare at her, his eyes blazing, his body burning, his heart hammering.

"What did he mean, Noel, when he said that"—Villon choked and stammered—"that your aunt was selling sweets retail?"

Katherine shook her head with grave pleading sweetness.

"Please, François. Not now."

"You are the only sweet thing in that house," he said harshly. "Katherine. For God's sake! Have you ever seen Jehan de la Garde?"

"Not yet," she breathed.

"And you would—but no. I will not believe!"

"Do not," she cried quickly. "It is not so. It is just Noel's talk. He is a gossip like his sister."

"What do you know of his sister?"

"Only what you have told me." It was all she knew of Paris except for the churches and the shops.

"But he would not dare to talk so," Villon insisted, "unless —"

"Hush!" she laid a long finger on his scarred mouth. "Let us not speak of it." She did not say: it is a long way off, it may never happen, there is a God in Heaven to whom we can pray.

He did not say: we must speak of it; it cannot happen; Heaven is where we are now, and Hell where you may put me.

In the midst of his misery he remembered that she loved him when he was merry.

"I shall carry off your aunt some night like the Pet-au-Diable and set her up in the courtyard of the University for a monument to sainted chastity. The students will dance around her and crown her with rosemary for memory's sake."

Katherine had a small high peal of laughter for that.

"You are a dear sometimes."

"You are my dear at all times," he retorted. "But, since you kill time betimes when I see you, it is high time you opened to me that heaven which will make me know I am beyond time's claw."

She laughed again, not looking at him. But then:

"Marthe will be coming back. She will not know where to find me."

"Not yet. Sweetheart. Tell me when I shall see you again."

"Ah, François, I do not know."

"But I know!" his black eyes brightened. "You are a brave girl. And tall enough."

"What do you mean?"

"My tunic and hose would just fit you. Would you truly like to see Montfaucon?"

She seemed at once frightened and thrilled, like a child at a play, unsure that the smoking mouth of hell with its lively demons might not be real, yet eager to see more.

"Listen. We shall have to wait for a warm night, but this is the mildest February I ever knew. I can send you word by Marthe unless you would rather have it by Noel," he grimaced. "She will bring you a proper suit. It is less than a cat's leap from your balcony to the garden."

She clapped her hands.

"Oh, François! Do I dare?"

"If I dare love you, you dare this."

"It is not the same."

"But you will?"

He had kindled her as he knew how. There might be joyful mischief for them yet in spite of her aunt and the master grocer.

"Perhaps I will," she whispered. And then, aloud, looking away: "Here is Marthe."

It was the signal for leave-taking.

88

Reluctantly Villon walked with them toward the gates. He had to bear Noel's company too.

Dusk was drawing in. Some of the vendors were already shutting up shop. The preachers were retiring. Soon even the blind man would stop bellowing and creep away. The cemetery would be emptied of all but the dead under the stones, the bare silly skeletons piled hugger-mugger in the charnels.

Life was short and nasty. There were only these snatched moments like a brief candle in the enormous dark. A small flame that leaped and shone and made your fingers glow red when you cupped it, though you saw the bones in the flesh then too. Oh, Christ.

Villon must spend the rest of the week seesawing between hope and despair: hope of seeing Katherine for an hour, despair at the thought of losing her forever. This misery sharpened everything like a sentence of death. There was no relief for him but in scribbling verses. Whether he waited for his companions in some tavern or sat hunched unhappily over the manuscripts he was copying for Ferrebouc, he would be turning tunes over in his mind and fitting bitter thoughts to sweet rhymes.

The papers in connection with the reversal of judgment against Jeanne of Orléans were still occupying the pontifical notary and his clerks. By now the lawyers were on the side of the bankers who were on the side of the King whom Jeanne had set over all France. Villon was not disturbed over the fact that what the Church could do the Church could undo. He wished only that he might have known that odd creature, virgin, witch, or saint. He would nibble at his quill, thinking regretfully of all the wonderful women he was never to know because he had been born too late. And then he would think of Katherine, and the black eyes that had been staring blindly into the past would shift restlessly to search the February sky. When would the weather change so that he could compel his demoiselle to keep the half-promise she had made him?

The change came early in April, denying winter with soft insistence, luring the canon out into the close to admire the willow buds and talk of the Easter feast, thickening the traffic on all the bridges and the bustle at the quays, setting the children to dancing in the streets, and drawing the crippled beggars out of their holes to cry alms from citizens made tender by these tender gusts.

Villon had but to breathe the morning air to send Ferrebouc's affairs to the devil. This was no season for slaving over tedious parchments. He passed the notary's door with his nose in the air and set off for the Petit-Pont.

You could scarcely see the barrows for the crowd of buyers milling round them: housewives before the butchers' blocks clucking over cuts and prices, shabby students begging the tripe vendors for an extra bit, kitchen boys from the Cordeliers buying fat geese, for one must feed the poor, thought Villon wryly, and who so poor as the Mendicant Orders? The stuffy odor of fowl mixed with the cold smell of fish. Underfoot the bridge was slippery with blood and bright scales. Villon paused to listen to a herring seller who was bawling hoarse oaths after a clerk who had given her a bad coin.

"May your mistress run off with a tomcat who'll eat the herring for you, they were rotten anyway, God grant the bellyache they'll give be your own entirely!" she shouted.

"Go it, my girl," Villon urged her on. "You have the tongues."

The stir and drama on the bridge more than made up for the stinks. The raw salty language of the women delighted him. There was no savor of it in all the books clamped to the walls of the Sorbonne. Let them hang there then like chained carcasses.

Turning away, Villon almost ran into Jacques Raguier, for once not drunk, but very jolly. There was to be a grand party tonight at the Chartrain mansion. René would be there, and half a dozen good fellows. Surely Villon was going?

So René was in town again. And making overtures to his rich relatives. It would do Villon no harm to be seen in those quarters either.

He must find Marthe and give her a message for her mistress. Or, better still, meet Katherine herself at the hour when she would be coming from mass.

But first he went back to the Red Door, leaped up the steps to his attic room, and began turning his small wardrobe upside down. He wanted a suit that it would not too much shame his demoiselle to wear. He found one that half-pleased him at last, and, with the queer-shaped parcel under his arm, ran out again to take up his station near the door of the Virgin, by which his lady came and went.

But Katherine did not come. Villon strolled back and forth, hugging his odd parcel, pretending an interest he did not feel in carvings he had seen ten thousand times, cursing himself for a fool, praying that she would emerge from the scented, candle-lit interior into the fair light of day. Suddenly he skipped forward. There was Marthe, her yellow hair blowing into her face as usual, her pale blue eyes wide, and her mouth hanging open.

Villon seized her arm.

"This is for the demoiselle Katherine. Tell her, tonight at vespers. If you meet Noel Jolis do not say that you have seen me. Do you understand?"

"Is there a letter?"

"There is the message I have given you: tonight at vespers.

And if you meet Noel Jolis he is not to know you have spoken with me."

Marthe nodded, took the package from him, and smiled and flushed as Villon pressed a few coppers into her hand. He stood staring after her until she disappeared. Then he swung about in the direction of the Mule.

Chapter Six

He did not believe that she would come. He could not believe that she would disappoint him. Never had a night been so soft, so chequered bright and black—the moon came and went in a drift of clouds—so quick with rumors of spring. Villon paced back and forth before the house of Mademoiselle de Vauselles, glad as a thief of the covering dark, his ears pricked for the noise of a creaking shutter, the velvet plunge of a cat leaping from the wall, the church bells that would tell him another hour had gone by.

She must come soon.

She was not coming at all.

He peered up at the balcony with eyes like a magnet to draw her forth. He thought he detected a slight figure moving there. He ventured a low whistle. There was no answer.

But now!

"Jump!" he whispered, and held out his arms.

He caught her, his own heart thudding so that he did not feel the beat of hers against his breast. He set her on her feet without a kiss. They must run for it and swiftly.

They turned two corners before he stopped her, panting, and seized her in a short laughing embrace. Then he held her off at arm's length, trying to survey her in the dark.

"How does it fit?"

"It's a bit tight in the waist, but I managed. You are thinner than I!"

"It is the law," he reminded her, "for lovers to be thin and pale."

"Where are you taking me?"

"To the Chartrains. You remember René de Montigny—old Etienne's nephew?"

But certainly. Villon had more than once boasted to her of his friendship with the scion of the eminent de Montignys, son of the late lamented Royal Pantler, nephew of a canon of St. Benoit, kin to the biggest financiers in Paris, and, though this Villon had hidden, employee of the master criminal who went by the title of the Great Khan. As Katherine nodded, Villon half wondered if his friend would supplant him in the eyes of his demoiselle. Beyond the lustre of the de Montigny name, there was the charm of his wicked reputation; he was handsome, too, and gently bred.

"His sister," Villon said, putting this thought from him, "i holding a feast tonight. We shall be of the company."

He pressed her arm.

"It's an adventure, sweetheart, eh?"

She could not deny it. They had not dared to light a lantern until now. It was a mad adventure. If her aunt should discover that she was gone! If her uncle, the canon, should ever learn of it! If Noel Jolis should have this tale to carry to the master grocer! But was it not precisely to escape the master grocer that she was here? Or was it just the smooth tongue, the fierce

94

urgency of Master François Villon? Whatever had brought her here, she was out in the streets of Paris at night, with no guardian but Villon, no servant but Villon, none between her and the unknown but Villon—himself, she felt as never before, dangerous and unknown too.

When they had reached the Chartrain mansion, passed the scrutiny of the Chartrain servants, and were mixing with the company assembled in the Chartrain hall, her heart beat more quietly. She was a little unhappy, Villon recognized, because, costumed as she was and introduced as Master Pierre de Bouteiller, there was no possibility of her dancing save with a girl like herself, and she had not Villon's talent for play-acting. But she took in happily the rich room, the great thick candles that lighted tapestries and furniture, colored satins and glittering gems, the music and the laughter. Villon pointed out the notables to her: the de Canlers, the Braques, the de Bonesles, and the de la Marches, names that spelled the weight of the law and the mastery of money. That stout lad who chimed with sequins when he moved was Sire Charlot Taranne, whose father had helped the Duke of Orléans ransom his brother from the English. There were sharp-faced parliamentarians and cold-eyed financiers, all befurred and bejeweled to fit their station. And there were their wives, parading in gowns that copied the fashions of the Court.

Villon hoped that the demoiselle Katherine would be impressed, if not by the sight of this assembled wealth and power, then at least by his own ability to present it to her. What could the master grocer do more? Glumly Villon answered his own question. Master de la Garde could take her from the modest de Vauselles house and let her queen it over the burgesses of Paris as Jeanne Chartrain queened it here. She could have Persian velvets to her back, pearls from Ceylon about her throat, Venice glass on her table, and even a little black boy to fetch and carry for her.

She stood beside him, munching a candied fruit and eyeing the wives of the lawyers and bankers gathered about Jeanne Chartrain. Was that what she too was thinking?

"Where," she whispered, delicately licking her fingers, "where is de Montigny?"

So that was what she was thinking! Villon grinned. But of course: she could see the bourgeoisie, if not such important members of it, any day in the week. But how should she lay eyes on one of the Companions of the Cockleshell? Not that she knew René for a thief and a murderer any more than she knew the whole truth about the man at her side.

"We'll find him," Villon assured her, taking her by the elbow and steering her through the crowd toward an adjoining room.

There was a card game, and there was de Montigny, his slim pale elegance that of a courtier, but his eyes never still and his shoulders twitching with repeated shrugs, as though he felt the tickle of a knife between them.

"That's René," said Villon. "But you can't meet him now. He's not one to disturb in the midst of play: you had better snatch a mouse from a cat's jaws."

He would have moved closer to the card table, but a little knot of men talking near the doorway stopped his passage. He recognized one of them, a man with the girth of a wine cask, the eyes of a fish, and cheeks ruddy with a network of veins that proclaimed good living: Denis Hesselin, master of the guilds of Paris.

"I tell you the two cleverest men in all France are the Great Khan and Jacques Coeur."

Villon wondered if René had heard. He must have made a

pretty haul for the Great Khan, or he would not be playing for such high stakes in his sister's house. But René gave no sign.

"Jacques Coeur isn't in France: he's on one of the Greek islands—very sick."

"He'll recover, no doubt. There's no medicine like gold. They say he was worth more than twenty-five million. What I want to know is what's to become of the small merchant?"

"My dear friend, there's no room for the small merchant. How are we going to find markets unless we organize our corporations on a grand scale? As we are doing," said the master of the guilds with satisfaction. "Don't forget"—he tapped his companion's silken sleeve—"we have the journeymen's associations to fight, and we're not placed as Coeur was, after the war, with the peasants flocking to the towns, ready to work for next to nothing."

"You have them in hand, Master Hesselin. If it isn't one fee they pay you, it's another. The right to work doesn't come cheap in Paris. But there are plenty of poor peasants even today. This system of pasture-farming does them no kind of good. Take any little tenant farmer here on the outskirts: he has a dozen children to feed, they breed like rabbits, and he'll sell his soul for an advance—it needn't be in money, he'll be grateful for truck. Wages are low, especially for the 'savage' who hasn't joined the association. He gets into debt before he can turn round. And you've practically made a serf of him."

Hesselin drew up one corner of his mouth in a grim smile. Villon felt the pale eyes rest on him a moment and, dismissing him, turn to his companion. But a beardless youth in a suit too tight for him could not occupy the attention of the master of the guilds. Villon was amused to think how differently Master Hesselin would behave if he could penetrate Katherine's disguise. He was also conscious of his demoiselle's uneasiness at

97

being measured by that appraising glance and of her bored indifference to Master Hesselin's conversation.

There was an angry shout at the card table. Villon saw René, with that look of suppressed triumph he knew so well, gathering a heap of ducats in his long clever hands. Would there be a quarrel? The master of the guilds, looking amused, moved nearer, his companions following deferentially. René stuffed his winnings away and, giving his small habitual shrug, said something Villon did not catch.

For answer, one of the players flung away his cards. One of them caught Montigny on the cheek. He rose, with an oath, his hand on the dagger at his belt. Before he could draw, the others pressed round him.

Katherine seized Villon's arm. Her green eyes shone enormous in the pale oval of her face. He knew then that he had been mad to bring her.

But this was no cheap tavern. This was the mansion of Robert Chartrain. The tumult at the table was smothered. A servant came in with a tray of drinks. The players resumed their places.

All but René, who was standing beside Villon, brushing off his sleeve as though he would brush off the touch of the men who had held him back.

Villon answered lightly the unspoken question in his friend's eyes.

"We're admiring the apes and peacocks."

René shrugged. He had come here tonight only because he might want his brother-in-law's help. He must not let them think him utterly lost. When it was safe for him to show himself, he must appear as one of the de Montigny clan.

Villon was praying inwardly that Katherine could hide her identity from René's penetrating eyes. He was grateful that his

98

friend was inattentive, still annoyed by the issue of the card game. Sulkily René accepted the strange youth as Master Pierre de Bouteiller, a distant relative of the canon's, lately come to Paris.

Villon murmured that he had promised his guardian not to offend the innocence of his young charge, who would like, he added, to see the sights of the city. René was as bored as Villon by the wealthy citizens and powerful nobles whom his brother-in-law entertained. But he had nothing to offer by way of diversion. Unless they were to visit Montfaucon?

Such an adventure smacked of their green days at the University. The neighborhood of Montfaucon was not attractive to a man in the pay of the Great Khan. It was the haunt of petty thieves, small-minded sinners. The greater stayed away until they were drawn thither by a halter about their necks. Unless de Montigny had an appointment there with one of the Khan's underlings? In that case, the danger of taking Katherine would be too great.

Suddenly Villon turned so that she would not see what he saw through the doorway. A stout figure in dark blue velvet, the master grocer, Jehan de la Garde.

"Come on, René," he urged. "Let's get out of here."

"And where," drawled de Montigny, "will we get girls? It will be dismal for Master—er—Pierre if we are to have a cock party."

"I hadn't thought of that," said Villon. But it was a lie. He had thought of everything instantly. He had imagined the awfulness of the hour and the scene, once they reached the gibbets, the contrasting gaiety of the cronies he would carry with him, the excitement produced by the wine he would induce her to drink, all combining to throw Katherine into his arms. Unless his demoiselle were so disgusted by what she would see as to cast her impossible lover from her forever. At this moment, with Katherine actually at his side, disguised in clothes he himself had worn, and Jehan de la Garde in the offing, he would risk anything.

"We can pick up some girls on the way," he pleaded. "It's a perfect night. You aren't afraid of the place, are you?"

De Montigny shrugged, frowning. His eyes slithered about the room. There was nothing René de Montigny was afraid of excepting poverty and boredom.

"For Master Pierre's sake," Villon begged. His arm was in Katherine's. He could feel her trembling, with excitement and perhaps with dread. "You know whom we're likely to meet there," he added below his breath. "We can't go this way. We need someone else who can talk the jargon."

"You've a tongue in your head," said de Montigny.

"You taught me all I ever knew," Villon flattered him. "If they began to make trouble, they'd kowtow to you."

"There'd best be more of us, in any case," de Montigny admitted, glancing about. "What about your friends there, Charruau, Robert Vallet?"

"Charruau's too fine for that sort of thing now. Vallet's under his wife's thumb: he won't come." Villon's eyes brightened. "I didn't see the Perdriers before. Is the old man here?"

"D'you want to invite him?"

Villon made a face.

Luckily the old man was home in bed. François Perdrier was not eager for a jaunt in de Montigny's company, but his brother Jean would follow any suggestion of that devil of a clerk, Villon. François must come if only to keep an eye on his reckless brother.

"Fetch your cloaks. With this moon, we need no lanterns. Come along!"

There was a press of people in the next room. Villon cupped Katherine's elbow in the palm of his hand and hurried her forward. Halfway through the crowd she stopped so short that Villon almost stumbled. Her eyes were on a tall stout figure in dark blue velvet that blocked their path.

"Never mind him. You are with me," Villon whispered, angrily.

They moved on. As they came up with Master de la Garde they were jostled so that Villon's elbow thrust against the big man's diaphragm.

"Where so fast, my young sir?"

"To put pepper in my porridge," retorted Villon rudely.

The master grocer drew himself up, the more savage for not being able to find a retort.

"He would like you to have it hot—but not in your porridge," murmured Jean Perdrier, who was just behind him.

"Forgive me, sir," murmured Villon, twinkling. "I meant no offense. I have you to thank, I believe, for my sugar and my spice. It would be churlish to be ungrateful."

He got Katherine away before Jehan de la Garde could think of a reply to this unintelligible boor.

"My spice and my sugar," Villon whispered in her ear.

He was drunk with joy for no good reason. Unless it were that he had sauced the master grocer in the presence of his demoiselle. And she fairly tucked under his lean arm, on the way to stranger adventure. He had always longed to astonish her. Tonight he would show her unforgettable things. And she would admire him as she could never admire that old purveyor to cooks and chemists. Villon could not share Katherine's days. Then he must show her the seamy side of his own. If he had not yet persuaded her to happiness, he might shock her into taking what he alone of men could give her. There was a luxury in horror that François Villon would never find stale. This it was that seasoned life, gave it a value the priests did not understand, though they preached hell-fire and damnation to eternity.

It was a long journey to Montfaucon. Jean Perdrier begged them to stop at a tavern: they had not even a basket of wine with them. But Villon cheered them and speeded them. It was late. They dared not keep the canon's young relative out too long. They would have their wine after they had shown Master Pierre what there was to see—something not to be viewed in the provinces, certainly. On such a fine night there might be other parties at Montfaucon with whom they could perhaps go shares. It had been done before, eh ho!

As they approached the monstrous structure and the queer smell of the place assaulted Villon's nostrils, he fell silent, wondering how his lady would receive what was to come. She was walking lightly and steadily beside him like the boy she appeared to be, sometimes breaking into a song, which sounded sweet and eerie in the moonlit loneliness. He asked himself why René seemed so anxious to press on. Whom did he plan to meet? Why had he invited their company? It was too late to draw back now.

The moon retired behind clouds as they mounted the hill, so that the appalling masonry with its huge stone pillars and wooden beams was momentarily hidden. Nothing but the foul odors drifting toward them told of the ragged bodies swinging there and the central pit filled with fragments of what once were men. Katherine held her hand to her nose, glad to cling to Villon's arm. His head was lifted, like a hound's listening. It was not for the hoarse metallic noise of the crows or the clank of the chains: there were human sounds on the heath, rough voices, a woman's drunken laughter, the sound of stone jugs knocking against each other.

Villon halted. Katherine stood beside him, alert, troubled, waiting. Jean Perdrier cried: "There's our wine, thank God!"

Villon shook his head. He was watching René, who moved like a cat about the heath, evidently looking for someone.

"They must have plenty to drink," said Jean Perdrier. "Even if it's poor stuff, I'm damned thirsty!"

"Let's go back," whispered Katherine, tugging at Villon's sleeve.

"Go back! Now? We've just got here. You haven't seen anything yet."

Jean Perdrier chuckled.

"Oh, come, they haven't such queasy stomachs in the provinces, have they? We'll get them to give us a bottle or two, and you'll be another man."

Villon noted with pleasure that Katherine could laugh at that.

"Get Villon to talk to 'em," Perdrier continued. "He knows their lingo, or says he does."

"They don't want our company: three girls to four men."

"We don't want theirs," said Villon hastily.

René had vanished. Whatever he was about, it was none of their affair. Nor did it concern the party on the slope.

"Listen," whispered Villon eagerly. "It's too dark for them to see us. We'll make a rush for them. Scream and grunt like devils out of hell-mouth: you've done play-acting before. You've only got to follow me. Flap your cloaks and yell. They'll think we've come to fetch the souls of the fresh fruit up there," he nodded toward the gibbets.

Jean Perdrier muttered, "That crazy Villon!" with more delight than scorn. François Perdrier repeated: "Crazy."

"You stop here," Villon bade him, "and look out for Master

Pierre. He's never seen a good show, he wouldn't know what to do."

Katherine murmured, "Oh," and held her peace.

Before they could protest Villon leaped forward hurrooing like a veritable fiend, capering, and making horns with his fingers. The noises that came out of his throat were wild enough to scare the dead. Jean Perdrier shouted as savagely if not with so devilish a note.

The group of revelers on the heath started up howling. Before Villon could come up with them they had run away, not daring to look back. Only one of the girls, literally frightened sick, lay on the ground moaning, a jug clutched to her bare breast and the wine spilling out. The prostrate form reminded Villon of a huddled figure he had seen in childhood lying on the street dead of the plague.

"Hi! Come ahead!"

He ran back, caught Katherine by both hands and danced her round and round. Jean Perdrier had a jug at his mouth and was satisfying his thirst.

"What a feast, eh?" he said, putting it down and peering eagerly at the food laid out on the ground.

The departed ruffians had evidently just begun their supper when Villon had scared them off. There was a great pasty, a couple of cold fowl, a flock of sausages, and a small tub of: "Oysters! As I live and breathe!" Perdrier gloated. There were crisp rolls, too, cakes, and abundant wine.

"Did my sister provide so poorly for her guests?" De Montigny had come back, alone. Had he met his man? Villon watched him indolently slicing breast of chicken and eating it from the point of a small dagger.

"We were late for supper," he murmured appeasingly. "The night air gives you an appetite."

104

The terrified woman on the ground, seeing these presumptuous devils attack with such good will the food that mortal thieves had provided, stopped moaning and sat up.

"Don't go," said Jean Perdrier, his mouth full. "There's plenty for all of us."

"I won't then," she muttered, wiping herself, and reached for a sausage. "My God!"

"Not your God, our God," Villon corrected her, "Who provides loaves and fishes—rolls and oysters—a tasty pasty, a chicken for picking, all we need for a splendid feed, and jugs enough of the proper stuff. Hand over that, Perdrier, by Bacchus! are not our throats as dry as yours?"

"It's not so bad," admitted François Perdrier grudgingly, munching. "They must have robbed a decent rotisserie."

His brother winked at Villon.

"Your friends won't be coming back to fetch you?" he asked the woman.

She cursed them for answer.

"What's your name, my sweeting?"

She seemed doubtful whether she should reply to de Montigny's question. They were not devils. They were certainly not sergeants. But who could tell what mischief they might do her if she gave them a handle.

"He only wants to know so he can remember you in his prayers," Villon jested, grateful that the whore's language was unintelligible to his demoiselle. He must get her away quickly.

"They call me Denise," the woman laughed. Even in the dark she could tell that some of these intruders were elegantly dressed. "Jesus, but you had me scared! I'm glad to be rid of that lot, though. They're no gentlemen."

"No?"

Denise stared at de Montigny.

105

"Have a drink."

"Sure."

She threw back her head and drank, wiped her mouth with the back of her hand, and laughed again.

"You've all got a thirst, but there's enough to go round." She gestured suggestively. "Trust Denise!"

Villon drew Katherine aside.

"What do you think of it now?" he whispered.

He did not mean the rude picnic and the giggling harlot, nor yet the wonder of the spring sky changing overhead. He was looking, he was asking his demoiselle to look with him at the fearful mass of Montfaucon: the thick masonry upholding the tremendous stone pillars and the wooden beams whose burden dangled like ill-wrapped bundles. The stonework, the iron chains, heavy as the weight of eternal damnation. And the shredded corpses, meagre, pitifully small, preyed upon by the wheeling crows. Villon felt them stare back at him from eyeless faces, grin back at him from lipless mouths. And Katherine at his side, warm and young, his living love. He was mad to seize her in his arms, crush her against his breast, feel her breathing quick and short. Surely he was dear to her now, as she to him, facing the dead in the dark.

"Hey, dearie! Have another oyster," Denise coaxed. "Nothing like 'em for making a man of you."

She looked closer.

"Why, it's a beardless boy!" she giggled. "How is it your tutor lets you out so late?" and she turned away.

"I wish," Katherine whispered with a low frightened laugh, "they would make a man of me."

Villon shook his head.

"What would I do then?"

He drew her off, his arm flung across her shoulders, to be

106

out of earshot of de Montigny's sullen pleasantries, Denise's loose laughter, the contention between the brothers Perdrier. Behind a clump of shrubs they halted.

"Ugh! The smell."

It was the odor of death.

As though to shut it out, Katherine buried her face against Villon's breast. He knew, holding her, the monstrous horror of the scene pressing upon her closed eyes, the shrill voice of Denise, the shouts of the men, crossed by the hoarse noise of the crows, hellish in her ears. He was mocked by this shivering, appalled embrace and by the night, large and soft about them.

He joked, to comfort her, he rocked her in his arms, like a child, he held her closer, slowly teaching her the measure of his strength, till she was quiet, acquiescent, giving, faintly, pressure for pressure, kiss for kiss. They stood locked together against all the evil of the world, locked against every misery of body or soul, locked against the vileness of the dead and the living, against the cruelty of time and the terror of eternity.

Suddenly Villon was conscious of one at his elbow. His arms dropped. Katherine gave a little cry. It was Jean Perdrier, half-dressed and half-drunk. Villon suppressed an oath. He had been flung headlong from Paradise, like another Lucifer. As in a dream he heard Perdrier crying after him: he had knocked him down. It was like something lived through once before. He was running the way he had run from the fallen priest on Corpus Christi night, only this time he knew the man he had struck would live to do him hurt, and he was not fleeing alone. He was stumbling downhill holding tight to Katherine's little hand.

Chapter Seven

He had loved her now these three years. He had held her in his arms three times. But this last time was different. She had almost surrendered wholly there in the presence of the dead, and of that damned Jean Perdrier who had parted them.

Her adventure had not been discovered. That Villon knew from a message sent him through Marthe. He wished bitterly that it were not so. Then she would have to come to him. He built fantastic castles for them to dwell in with rooms furnished, now like his attic at the Red Door, now like a grand chamber in the house of some rich patron of the arts. Nothing was too absurd, nothing too outrageous.

Meanwhile, he was kept with his sharp nose to the grind-

stone, working for Ferrebouc over the case of Jeanne of Orléans: if they finished it by midsummer they would be lucky.
De Montigny had left Paris on private business. There were
times when Villon wished he had gone with him. For Katherine was not to be seen.

Something had roused her aunt's suspicions. The watch kept
over his demoiselle had never been so close. He could not get a
message to her, and, when he saw her on her way to or from
church, companioned by her aunt or by Noel Jolis, she would
look at him with eyes that told him nothing.

Here was a dull joyless season. The birds that woke him in
the morning, the sticky buds in the court below, the soft rains
falling through the afternoon, all the tender reminders of
spring, only made it worse. And the occasions for happiness
that he must miss! There was the Fair of St. Germain, at the
Halles. He imagined himself moving beside Katherine among
the booths under pennants flying as at a tourney, studying the
latest style in gloves and shoes, in mirrors for the girdle and
trinkets for the throat, making her prouder of her beauty than
the great ladies borne in their litters along the crowded ways;
pointing out to her the foreigners: Florentines and Genoese,
even Mussulmans and Jews in their curious garb, and elegant
Venetians come to inspect the Paris furreries that rivaled their
own. He fancied her laughing with delight over the mounte-
banks and dwarfs, the curly-headed blacks from Egypt and
flat-eyed yellow men from far Cathay. Palm Sunday passed,
the Fair closed, and Villon's one visit was in the company of
fat Tabary, whose sole stupid virtue was to pay for his entertainment.

He brooded over the lost night at Montfaucon. The present
balked him, the future eluded. Sitting on his high stool at the
notary's, mending a quill, he found himself living backward

till memory halted at his first encounter with his demoiselle. It was in the church of St. Benoit on just such a day as this. He had gone to hear the Easter sermon, in gratitude to the canon for extricating him from a scrape he had since forgotten. His restless eyes, skipping over the faces of the parishioners and the chapter members solemn in their stalls, had met the eyes of a stranger, a girl. She had turned away, but his steady gaze had drawn her, compelled her to face him once more. There had been no scar on his lip then. He had looked keen though not handsome, arrogant though not noble. His bright black eyes had stared searchingly into hers, that were, he thought afterward, those of some creature out of Faery.

It was only afterward too, that he considered, meditatively, her other features: the arched brows, the tender curve of the cheeks, the tantalizing short red upper lip. He had tallied her loveliness with the ideal beauty of his boyish fancy: eyes not green but black, skin not olive but white, long slender fingers, like her own pointing upward, a narrow waist—that she had, and a round thigh—surely, there was perfection under her silks! But while the priest's voice droned on, an old canon coughed, and the light fell rosily from the painted window across his psalter, he had been conscious of nothing but her eyes returning look for look. Silent asking, silent answer, so complete it seemed they must rise at once and move together, hand in hand, out of the candle-lit church into the resurrection morning.

He threw down his quill and clasped his head in his hands. What had François Villon to do with a little bourgeoise, who was no more an Héloïse than he an Abélard? He had found out about her easily enough: she was the orphaned niece of one of the wealthier parishioners of St. Benoit, related to one of the canons, too, new-come to Paris with her green eyes and her dowry in search of a husband. Green eyes and green ways: she was but a child. And he loved her. He had loved her these three years, he repeated to himself, drawing his scarred mouth down at the corners. He had held her in his arms three times.

He raised his head. One of his fellows was standing at his elbow with a bunch of papers.

"Wouldn't it make you puke? First they hand her over to the Goddams, and then they turn themselves inside out to prove it was all a mistake, as though you could seal a head on its shoulders again with a bit of red wax from the notary's!"

Villon said drily: "You'd better not let Ferrebouc hear you. You'll part with your own head."

He stood up. He could bear it no more. The elaborate Latin reminded him of the uncomfortable hours he had spent cramming at the University. The thick black ink strokes, the careful legal script irritated him with its solidity: at least a poem had margins that gave your eyes a rest. He was stiff from leaning over the desk. The notary's room seemed oppressively airless. He cocked an eye in the direction of Ferrebouc's sanctum.

"He's not in, is he?"

His fellow clerk shook his head.

"Chapter meeting. Some trouble with Notre Dame again. He won't be back till vespers."

"Neither shall I."

"Eh?"

"I do hereby declare and affirm that several fine and notable hours of this day, if they be not immediately employed to the advantage of Master François Villon, scholar and master of arts of the University of Paris, will be an irreparable loss to the said Master Villon. He, therefore, seeing that the hours of the day are scarcely sufficient to provide for his pleasure, has, after long and mature deliberation . . ."

"For God's sake, what's this?"

"Has, after long and mature deliberation," Villon pursued steadily, "and for the evident good of his soul, freely and willingly consented and agreed to employ them, *videlicet,* the remaining hours, as profitably as possible. Agreed, confirmed, ratified, approved, and authorized by Master François Villon, with his letters engrossed and duly signed with his seal."

The legal jargon came as trippingly from his lips as though it were dance music. His fellow clerk hooted. Villon did not stay to hear his retort. He was off, out on the street, in the fresh spring air that would blow away the smell of ink and parchment and blow him to a sunnier, gayer part of town.

The Fair of St. Germain was over. But the Gingerbread Fair had only just begun. It was as good a place as any to forget the dull task from which he had run away.

The Fair was not so elegant as its predecessor. There would be no foreigners here except for the dark-faced Greeks one saw everywhere. Since the fall of Byzantium, the city was overrun with refugees, fleeing from the Turk. But there was the stir of a jolly crowd pushing past booths filled with gewgaws and gimcracks, the shouting barkers, the dwarfs and the giants and the cages of mangy animals. There were quacks with precious simples plucked on moonless nights and pardoners with holy relics from far places and moving wooden figures that worked by ingenious machinery. On one corner a knot of people were gathered before a dumb show: he could see the actors' striped hose twinkling on the platform above them. There was music, flutes and strings, drowned by screams and laughter where three huge blind beggars with clubs were whacking each other, trying to kill a pig they could not see and making the crowd howl with joy as they struck, not the pig but one another, on the shin, on the shoulder, on the head. And there was the warm spicy smell of the booth that gave the Fair its name, where brown and gilt cakes in a dozen fancy shapes drew the children like flies to the honey pot. This was the place to meet Ysabeau and Denise, unfrocked priests, and slit-eared Companions on the lookout to slit purses.

But Villon had said good-by to all that except as he could show it to Katherine, the strange dark side of him so fascinating to a little bourgeoise. Ah, she was not that! She loved danger no less than Villon, nay, more. If he were not a coward, he would have her now. She was not afraid of anything. Had she not risked all to come to him? She was only keeping from him to prepare herself to escape forever the stupid bondage of her aunt's house, her aunt's plans. It must be so. And Jehan de la Garde? God grant him a crutch in his old age to mix mustard with. Katherine would never consent to that alliance. And his creature, Noel Jolis? A flea that bit and jumped away and bit again, but only a flea, to be seized and crushed.

"My purse! They've stolen my purse!"

The shriek was taken up by the crowd milling around the dumbshow.

"Stop thief! Stop thief!"

He was gone, of course, whoever he was, a pickpocket, a cony-catcher, the sort that fed on careless pleasure seekers like these. Villon caught himself about to dart away as though he were the guilty one. He had done nothing. He had a twisted smile of regret for the lost opportunity.

He pushed restlessly through the crowd from one booth to another. What had he come here for? To watch blind men battering each other for a prize pig? To gape at a mechanical representation of the Trojan horse? To win a piece of fake jewelry at an archery contest? To buy a fairing for his love?

There was nothing on show that would please Katherine.

113

Her taste was more fastidious. God, he had thought he knew poverty when he was a child with a grumbling belly, when he was a student who gambled to buy his books and tutored fools to pay for his sprees. He had been rich then, he had wanted nothing then, there had been no Katherine then.

"Why, if it isn't Villon!"

"Come on, Villon, let's have a try at the quoits."

"Are you alone? I want a drink."

It was Jacques James, the eternal fiancé, Jacques Raguier, the eternal drunk, and Thomas Tricot, the merry little priest who had taken his master's degree with Villon, and, eaten up with admiration of him, sang his parodies of the hymns with a verve the originals could not command. They were so glad to see him that it was evident they were as bored by the Fair as himself. But no: it was only that they loved him. James was waiting to be asked when the wedding would be—was it the fifth or sixth time he had formed a new alliance? Raguier had discovered a tavern where the wine was better and cheaper than anything at the Pine Cone or the Mule, and, since they had found Villon, they wanted no better company. Tricot had heard a tune that was crying for such words as only Villon could write.

They would go to the tavern. They would hear the story of James's latest bride-to-be. They would tease him until he would see for the fifth, or was it the sixth, time that it was better to burn than to marry, however many *pro forma* objections Tricot might advance. They would drink to the lady and to the twelve joys of marriage. Villon thought how this was the one folly he had not contemplated. They would applaud Raguier for having found so fine a place to drink in. They would even commend Tricot for having entered the Church, which provided such good tunes for bawdy words. Villon thrust an arm into the little priest's and another into the prospective bridegroom's, and bade Raguier lead on. Their joyful shouts on seeing him had ministered to his self-esteem. He was able to see himself again as the swaggering scholar, a thorn in the flesh of his masters, a jewel in the crown of his fellows, the fun-loving, lute-thrumming, mischief-making wit.

The chosen wineshop appeared to be in the neighborhood of Notre Dame. It was impossible not to admire that edifice, however deeply Villon hated the power for which it stood and in which he had no share. Its massive grandeur bulked huge above the scurrying figures in black and brown, members of the higher clergy in richer colors, nuns in voluminous gowns with great hoods and white wimples, and a scattering of fine ladies, their trains looped over their arms, their headdresses dwarfing the gallants who held them in laughing converse, and the blind or crippled beggars, like images of the seven sins, who were always crouching at the doors. Villon swept off his hat as they passed and burst into mocking song. Limping down the steps came old Thibaut de Vitry and Guillaume Cotin, and it seemed to Villon that de Vitry knotted his thick grey brows at the sight of him. He interpreted the old man's frown in his own way: the canons of Notre Dame had to keep their cloisters clean; why must they be vexed by the rubbish of St. Benoit? The feud between the little church and the great cathedral was not Villon's affair, but he resented rich domineering old men wherever he met them. He could not see them without wanting to spit.

Tricot tried to silence him. But it was not the little priest's timidity that abruptly shut Villon's mouth. It was the unlooked-for glimpse of the demoiselle Katherine entering the

Door of the Virgin. There was no one with her but Marthe. With a quick movement Villon disengaged himself from his companions and leaped up the steps and away.

"Where's he going?"

"Not to say his prayers."

"Wait. He's playing some trick. You'll see."

Villon's reputation for japery stood him in good stead. They hung about a bit to laugh with him over the outcome. Then they got tired waiting and sought cordial solace elsewhere.

Once within the cathedral Villon made brief devotions before the Blessed Virgin. But it was such a prayer as he might more readily have said in the temple of Venus.

"Holy Mother, if You would save a miserable sinner, give him a glimpse of his lady. For Christ's sake, Who died to save sinners." He crossed himself and rose, peering about for Katherine. Blessed Mother, there she was! His heart was filled with exultant thanksgiving.

At once he was at her elbow. The pigeons croodling about them as he walked beside her onto the steps might have been Venus's doves. The air seemed to smell of violets.

"Marthe"—Villon fished in his wallet—"we shall want cheese tarts."

Marthe giggled. It was the old story. Katherine laid a hand on his arm.

"No. We shan't. Marthe, Master François will see me safely home. You have other errands. Or no: you will wait for me at the parvis. There is—" She stopped, wanting invention.

"There is a blind man near the west portal with prayers to sell that will get you into Heaven faster than I can swallow oysters. Here." Villon pressed a piece of money into the servant's broad hand. It seemed to him she would never be gone.

At last they were alone. The clerks and monks and burghers

passing to and fro were insubstantial as air. Nothing was real but Katherine, alive and alight beside him. His dear love. And the piece of lead he had been carrying in his breast was magically melted. Spring was here in very truth. The sun shed warm glory on buttress and paving stone. The pigeons crooned in music.

"Come."

She came, with little running "oh's" of laughter, her soft hand in his. They were together again. They were happy again.

There was a place he knew, down by the river, that was always deserted except for a passing boat or a boy fishing. At this hour there was not even a boy. There was only the sun on the water, and the bushes in leaf, and Paris with its fairs and taverns, its schools and churches and notaries' chambers, its solemn shopkeepers and quarrelsome knaves part of a forgotten world.

They spoke in whispers though there was none to overhear. Brokenly, with so much to ask and to tell. No, they had not found her out. Yes, she was well and content. How not be content, with Villon cracking jokes as you crack almonds at a feast and looking at her as though she were the feast and he would devour her with his black eyes. No, she had no plans at all. But—

She could not bear the question he did not ask. He could not bear to think of her answer. It was not Katherine who had the disposal of her fate. Certainly it was not François Villon.

"Sing 'Noel' and it's sure to come," Villon punned on the old proverb.

Katherine shook her head.

"You must not mind him. He is not amusing."

"That is why I mind him: because he is serious."

Villon would compel her to speak, to say what she would have given her right hand, that he held in both of his, not to say, what he would have given his hope of Heaven not to hear. She tried to put him off.

"It will come to nothing. I have not enough of a dowry. See how lucky I am!"

"God dowered you, sweetheart, with what you see in your mirror. That is enough for any man." Villon took one hand away to lift the glass that hung at her girdle and hold it so that she might look into her own eyes.

"A beardless boy," she murmured at the reflection, smiling. "What did your friend Perdrier say afterward?"

"I have not seen him since, damn him," said Villon, letting the mirror drop back into her lap.

"Don't say that. Perhaps he saved me from—being damned," she breathed.

"You would not say that if you loved me."

"Ah, but I do love you."

"You do not know what love is." His voice roughened. He was not looking at her but at the river, unseeingly, with fierce brooding eyes. He had let go her hand and was clutching the grass beside him as though he would tear it up by the roots, as though he would tear the world apart in the misery that swept over him. "But I can tell you. It is an ache in the veins by day and by night. It is the heart of you crying like a flogged child. It is a craving, like hunger when there is no crumb of food, like thirst when there is neither wine nor water. It is wanting to see Katherine, to fill your eyes with her, though she never look at you in return, to look at her continually. It is wanting to hear Katherine speak, though she say but two words and those words cruel. It is wanting to touch Katherine, with the tip of your little finger even, though you would cover her with your whole body if you could. It is being reminded of Katherine at every corner, having her come between you and every com-

118

panion, between you and your book, between you and your
dinner, till you cannot talk or work or eat, and cannot ever
rest, because, though she will not lie with you, she lies with you
every night in your thought, and there is no shame in it but
neither is there any joy. It is saying Katherine, Katherine, over
and over and over like a Hail Mary, as if the naming of her
name would make her real, bring her close, save you from the
horrors of this nasty world and all the terrors of death and hell.
Katherine!"

He turned to her at last, with such a look in his sharp face
that she took it between her hands and drew it down to her
breast. And then his arms were round her, and he was holding
her in a blind embrace, his wrenching fear, his jealous hate
slowly stifled against her heart. He was lying with his shut eyes
pressing against the stuff of her bodice, his hands clutching the
soft slenderness of her, knowing her love so much less than his
passion, yet stilled and eased, his pain fading out in the peace of
her immediate presence until he tasted slowly all solace, all
delight.

She remained quiet, trembling a little only. He lifted his
head. He raised himself to seek her mouth. Her own eyes
closed, and the yearning pity he had stirred changed to the
image of his desire. Half in fearful wonder, half in aching joy,
she gave herself to her lover's mastery.

He helped her up, brushed the leaves and twigs from her
skirt.

"Did I frighten you?" he whispered.

She was weeping, but she did not admit that she was
frightened.

"Now you are truly mine," he told her, proud and fulfilled.

She smiled at him through her tears.

"I hurt you."

"Yes."

"You are sorry."

"Yes."

Ah, she should not have said that!

"Sorry," she repeated, "that you must take me back. Marthe is stupid, but I am afraid—"

"You said you were not afraid."

"Not of you."

"Of what then? Of what a servant will think?"

She did not answer but took up her mirror and studied her face.

"You would not notice anything?" she asked hesitantly.

"You were never lovelier."

"But—I thought—I do not really look different." She seemed surprised.

He laughed at her.

"Oh, come! We must hurry. You must make up some story. You will be able to, won't you?"

"Katherine! When will I see you again?"

She seized his hand and pulled him along.

"I will send you word by Marthe, or by—Noel, perhaps," she said breathlessly.

"I do not mind even Noel now."

It was a lie. She had no right to name Noel Jolis. She might as well have named his master, Jehan de la Garde, for whom her dowry was, he prayed God, too small.

Hurrying his demoiselle back to the parvis, thinking up some tale to keep Marthe quiet, Villon was no less proud of his victory than fearful of a future that could never be as happy as this unrepeatable surrender.

Chapter Eight

The next morning Villon thoroughly astonished his fellows at Ferrebouc's. It was not that he whistled over his work. It was certainly not because of the sheets he spoiled scribbling verses when he should have been comparing decretals. But the man undertook tasks that he could have shoved off on other people. He spoke with respect of his employer, as one hoping for, nay, trusting in, due advancement. He labored when he should have been lunching, and, though he was as full of jokes as an egg of meat, they were none of them bawdy. It was impossible to understand what had come over him.

Ferrebouc, however, was lacking in admiration for his reformed clerk. The whistling annoyed him. One of the spoiled sheets, coming under his notice, offended his feeling for economy. Villon's respectful tone was, he could only feel, a bad joke. And Villon's absence the previous afternoon left him without a copy of a certain piece of evidence that he wanted at once. He had taken in this noisy careless clown to keep a University man from disgrace and out of friendship for the canon. But it was trying kindness too far to keep him.

Villon did not plead with the notary. Ever since their University days Ferrebouc had looked down on this young sprout, some six years his junior, who preferred singing songs round a stolen stone to sticking to his books. Ferrebouc had been coming up in the world with a steadiness that put the poet's career beneath contempt.

Villon had never needed a job so badly. He wanted money to give Katherine the trifles that would pleasure her. He wanted work to steady him in the exhilaration that her gift of herself had brought him. He could not waste himself in the drinking and gaming that had filled his days and nights when his suit had seemed hopeless. He had the happiest reason to keep clean of the brothels.

He had nowhere to turn. He could not go back to Perdrier's. The old man would have none of him. And he had no wish to beg of Jean or of his smug younger brother, even if they had been likely to grant him favors. Colin had damned him for a fool because he would not share the easy risks he took. If Montigny were on the spot he would have a way out. But Villon had determined that he would not go Montigny's way, would keep clear of Colin's gang.

There was always the canon. He had labored with Ferrebouc to grant Villon this berth. Now he must swallow his disappointment and set to work all over again. He thanked God for the old man.

The canon sucked his cheek meditatively and said he would see. It was not easy.

The tutoring jobs that his patient efforts at last secured were better than nothing. But they paid poorly. Villon's learning was rusty, and he was not inclined to polish it. The lessons in astronomy reminded him that he had been born under an unlucky planet, and instead of instructing his pupil in the constellations he would discourse with rich and humorous fantasy upon his star-crossed life. Rhetoric was an excuse for reciting his own verses, to the detriment of Virgil and Ovid. There was, moreover, keen competition from the Greek refugees in the teaching of the classics. Villon began to nourish a sincere hatred for the Greeks. He was no savant. He was a poet. A privilege for his pupils to be taught by such a master. But they were a stupid lot, concerned only for the dry bones of learning that would get them into the University, not for the lyric line fresh as a leaf from Apollo's tree.

His glimpses of Katherine were few and far between. Stolen interviews, never long enough to permit a repetition of his brief happiness. There were no presents for her. Neither was there any mention between them of Jehan de la Garde. The image of the master grocer haunted Villon's nights. He avoided the Pine Cone, not only because he was short of money and credit, but because he feared to meet the taverner's brother-in-law, Noel Jolis, with his businesslike ways, his loud self-importance, like that of one of the messengers of the realm, his reminders of the man he served and the girl with too small a dowry. Was it too small surely? And, if it was, why did Villon continue to meet Noel in the neighborhood of the de Vauselles house?

Villon had one pupil who showed some wit. He was strongly tempted to throw the books on the floor and teach the clever child without them. He taught him—card tricks. Discovery

123

was slow but inevitable. Villon was kicked out of the house and bidden never show himself again. Word was passed on to the fathers of the other young hopefuls in his charge. The canon was besieged by angry visitors.

"Why did you do it, my son? The boy would have learned those tricks soon enough without your help," the canon smiled reproachfully.

"Ah, but never so well," Villon retorted. "In such matters you cannot begin too early."

"You may be right. But that is not why his father engaged you."

"His father engaged me because you insisted on it."

"I shall never insist again."

Villon looked sharply at his guardian. If he meant it, there was small hope for Master François. But his next words were full of comfort.

"What are we going to do now?"

Villon studied the canon. The old man was sucking his cheek reflectively, his fingertips placed together in the shape of an arched church door, his brown eyes anxious and inquiring. He was a good old man. His goodness irked his ward often enough. At this moment it filled him with compunction. Villon could not help him, who was trying so earnestly to help his careless son. And yet, if the canon had been stricter with him at the beginning, he might now be a person of importance elsewhere than in tavern circles, a man equal and superior to Ferrebouc, as well off as any Perdrier. It was really his foster father's fault. And that of his true father, who had begotten him in the wrong month so that he was born under Saturn: there was no hope for such as those. All the arguments at the University about free will: they meant nothing. A man was governed by his

124

star. His life turned with the wheel of fortune. It looked as if poor François would be broken on that wheel. He passed from pity for the canon to an immense pity for himself.

But what! He was no ordinary man. He could match any poet in the realm of France. He did not doubt he could outrhyme the Duke of Orléans. He belonged at Court, not in some scrivener's musty anteroom.

But there was Katherine. He could not leave her now.

"You must let me think a bit," said the canon slowly. "I shall be seeing André Courant when he returns from his mission to Anjou. He may have something to offer. I will look round. Meanwhile, why don't you go to the rue de la Parchminerie and see about a copying job? You are bound to pick up something."

Sell his fingers. Well, it was no worse than selling his brains. Oh, if only he had been born rich! He would not have to play the tradesman then. He could have Katherine then and laugh at her dowry. He shrugged.

"You couldn't let me have a trifle for my purse? It's easier to get a job if you don't seem to need it, even with the copyists. Treat 'em to a drink—one good turn deserves another—"

The canon smiled quizzically. It was the old François. But, though he was not fooled, he gave him some money. He gave him too the blessing he had not asked for. With a new lightness in his heels Villon ran down the stairs and out of the Red Door into the street.

Perhaps he could get hold of Marthe and arrange a meeting with Katherine. She would lament the loss of his job, but she would comfort him too as only she could. He whistled joyously, tasting in imagination the sweetness of her pity.

Marthe was nowhere about. Villon stopped whistling as he

trudged on. Happy without cause a moment since, he was back in the dumps. Someone jostled his elbow. A fat face leered into his. Tabary.

"Hey, I thought I'd find you. Colin ith back."

"What's that to me?"

Tabary giggled defensively.

"I'm thorry," he lisped. "I thought you'd like to know. He hath thuch a thtory . . ."

"He may have the epic of Troy for all of me."

"But he'd like to thee you. It'th important."

"What's important?"

"I don't know what it ith egthactly. But he told me to find you. He'th at the Pine Cone."

Villon shrugged. Very well. Colin could not persuade him to get on the wrong side of the law. But the canon had given him money. He might get up a game and win a little more.

"See here, Tabary, is Robin's brother-in-law there?"

"Noel Jolis? I don't know. Do you want to thee him?"

"I want to see him . . . in hell. Come along."

When they reached the Pine Cone, Colin had gone. Tabary lisped excuses. He looked about for the taverner: he might have some message. But Turgis was not to be seen, and Tabary was not the only man afraid of Turgis's wife. She marched on them now like an army, a plump blonde woman of thirty, who might have been pretty if she had not been so old and so mean.

"What will it be?"

"Beaune," said Villon.

"Beaune," repeated Tabary with a surprised giggle.

"Show me the color of your money."

"Show her, Tabary."

Tabary looked blank. He couldn't afford Beaune—not the

sort Villon had learned to drink at the Red Door. Aside from his ward, this was the canon's one indulgence.

"Well?"

Tabary reddened and drew out his wallet. He could not afford it, certainly. He dared not confess this to Villon. Villon would not spare him: he had a tongue like a knife, that man. The funniest *farceur* in the realm of France. It was a privilege to ruin yourself for him.

Tabary had an inspiration. After all, he had the money. He had been collecting his mother's rents.

"Let me go out and buy thome hot meat. We'll eat here, while we're waiting for Colin!"

"I'm not hungry."

"Oh, but wait till you thee what I'll get!" Tabary was gleeful. He was afraid of his mother. But he would try to forget that. If he could make Villon think well of him now! He had not had the poet to himself in all the months since his return to Paris. He looked at Villon with anxious expectancy. "Would you rather have pigeonth or roatht pork?"

"Anything but crow."

Tabary grinned. "I'm not going to thteal it," he confided in a whisper. But perhaps Villon would think better of him if he did steal it?

He moved off to the rotisserie with a lagging step. He was always being reminded that he was no match for the others. It hurt him.

Villon did not look at Tabary. His eyes followed la Turgis as she served some students who were dicing at a corner table, turned quickly to box the potboy's ear, and then stood gossiping with a pair of priests who were paying their score. She tossed her head toward Villon. They glanced at him, and the

127

younger one smiled as he looked away. Villon put his hand to the dagger at his belt. But just then Tabary came through the door, a comic figure, his fat face puckered with anxiety in spite of his smile, a long loaf like a staff thrust under his arm, and his stubby hands occupied with a whole steaming fowl.

La Turgis hurried across the room to help him set down his burden and, as she did so, laid a hand on Villon's shoulder.

"Maybe you want to quit Paris again, Master François? Those priests have done you no hurt. It was one of your own jokes I was telling them made them laugh."

She was lying. But the two priests had slipped out, and one did not quarrel with Robin Turgis's wife. She brought the young men their Beaune. Tabary carved with gluttonous delight. Villon looked on and said nothing. He ate little. Tabary was distressed.

"Shall I get thome green thauthe? Or more muthtard?"

"Get every condiment on the calendar, man. Spices are no help to such fat meat as you."

"Not for mythelf," giggled Tabary unhappily.

The tavern was filling up with thirsty men in haste to eat and drink and be off. Colin still did not come. Robin Turgis showed himself at last, looked inquiringly at the remains of the fowl and the wooden mugs on Tabary's table, held a short colloquy with his wife, and, shrugging his shoulders, gave his attention to other customers. Villon continued to sit there, the black cock, he thought, turned into a broody hen. The wine had swollen his melancholy. He kept thinking of Katherine.

La Turgis asked Tabary to settle. She wanted their places for another couple.

"Letth go," murmured Tabary sadly. The feast had not been a success. And he had no right tale for his mother. "Maybe Colin'th at your plathe?"

128

"Go to the devil, Tabary, you may find him there."

Tabary flushed. He had tried so hard to please.

La Turgis nudged Villon.

"You'd best move on."

"He paid the score, didn't he?"

"He paid for this wine, not for what you drank last time," she reminded him sharply. "You're done with your wine."

"I'm not done sitting here."

"I wonder you take pleasure in it, with your bony haunch."

"I should have such a plump cushion for a seat as your brother Noel, eh?"

"He hasn't worn himself thin running after a lady too fine for him," she retorted.

Villon saw with peculiar distinctness the sharp blue eyes, the mean thin lips. He jumped up, threatening her. She shrieked. Through the clatter of dishes, the clank of tankards, the low rumble of talk that filled the tavern, rang shouts of pleasure at the prospect of a fight. Turgis pushed his way across the room. Tabary backed off, terrified. Villon ducked and ran.

He did not stop till he reached the bridge, and found himself among the noisy press of vendors and shoppers and passing clerks who cursed as they dug their way with shoulders and elbows through the crowd. He looked about him in dull amazement. What was the use of all this buying and selling? What were they in such a hurry about? Why should a man want to eat tripe or capon, to joke with his friends or quarrel with his enemies, to say his prayers or cheat at cards, to write a poem even? Katherine. Katherine to be married to that putrid old man, that damned stinking chandler, that, that . . . No. He must see her. She would deny it. He would find her. She could not do this to him. After all, François Villon was not nobody.

129

Was he not? What had he to offer? Oh, but she was his. She had proven it once. She would prove it again.

He must see her, speak to her. This was the hour and the place to find Marthe. She would carry a word for him. Marthe! There she stood, with her yellow hair blowing into her face as usual, her eyes wide, and her mouth hanging open.

Villon stood beside her panting.

"The demoiselle Katherine. Where is she?" He could hardly bring the words out of his dry mouth.

"Oh, Master François!" she stammered and flinched.

"Well?"

Even in his misery Villon could see that she looked frightened.

"I must see her."

"You can't, Master François."

"Why not? For God's sake, girl, what's up?"

Villon could have struck her.

He could scarcely make out her muffled answer. But he caught the words "marriage contract."

"Ah, Master François," she wailed, "didn't you know?"

Villon was overcome with such black nausea that he gripped Marthe's arm so as not to fall down there on the bridge among the entrails and the fish heads. He had always known. But he had never believed. A thief knew he must hang. But he did not believe it, not when he was being jolted along in the cart on the road to the gallows, with the hangman striding cheerfully behind. But when the rope was round his neck? Villon's scar pulled at his lip as he grinned sardonically.

There was a crushing weight in his breast as though his heart were being strangled by iron bands. It was difficult to breathe. Like an automaton, one of those comic figures they paraded at festivals and fairs, that moved as you pulled the wires, he walked woodenly away, leaving Marthe standing there, staring after him with wide fearful eyes.

He found himself sitting before a table with a cup of wine before him and a blowsy mountain of a girl standing over him. His eyes fastened on her puddingy breasts that shook when she laughed. She was laughing now.

"Good Lord, Master François"—her voice was shrill but her tone was kind enough—"you look as though you'd be hanged tomorrow. Drink it down, it'll put some heart into you."

Villon looked up from the great breasts to the little blue eyes twinkling in the fat childish face.

"Who wants a heart, Margot? That's only bait for bitches."

The fat girl sat down heavily beside him and began stroking his arm.

"Come, Master François darling, drink your wine," she coaxed. "You don't need a heart to love me."

"No, only money. That's all any of you want. That's why I'm no use to you."

He looked round at the other girls who were standing about, half-dressed, yawning or examining their own bodies with the professional's endless concern for his tools. One of them had a green and purple bruise on her arm, and was touching it tenderly and cursing the man who had given it. A dirty child ran in from the street, shouted: "Any mustard?" and ran out without getting an answer. Fat Margot patted Villon's hand.

"You're of use to us, my little cabbage. You've got what we need more than money. Do you think"—she sighed, and her red-veined cheeks curved in a smile that invited the girls' corroboration—"do you think we make money at this trade? Good God, the taxes on salt alone, and you've got to give 'em salt to make 'em thirsty. . . ." She broke off to turn her small bright eyes on a girl who was coughing in a corner.

"It's not a healthy trade," said Villon. But then, they were soon quit of it. They didn't last long.

"Take some wine, dearie," the fat girl advised the cougher, "and get done with it. This is no hospital."

"It's as filthy as one," complained the girl with the bruised arm.

"Do you sleep six to a bed here too?" grinned Villon.

The girls laughed at that, but Margot sighed.

"They can't make enough here," she complained, "to keep 'em in chemises."

"You mean they can't earn enough selling hats or sausages, or making tapestries. I'll wager they work harder at night than they do by day." Villon didn't give a damn when they worked or at what. But it relieved the pain in his chest to talk.

The fat girl leaned toward him confidentially.

"And you can't earn enough with all your book learning, my little cabbage. Or your billiards and your card games. There's no making a living at that. Nor at writing farces either, though there was a man here from Angers the other night who said it was as good to be a playsmith as a goldsmith in that town. But if that's so why did he come to Paris?" She gave a short triumphant laugh.

It was true, thought Villon. There was no money in any of those games. Or if there was, a week's profits paid for a night's entertainment. The good bourgeois who went shrewdly about the business of selling his wine or his silks or his groceries—Villon's cheek twitched—could have houses and lands, a good dinner at his own table every day, and after dinner a woman of his own to pet and be petted by. He made the priests rich too, saying masses for his soul when he was dead. But your gambler, your playboy, your poet who was no gentleman but lived by luck and died by chance, or treachery more likely, must

132

sleep in a dirty brothel and die in a dirty halter, and none would profit by it but the birds that ate his eyes out.

"Why such a groan, little one?" Fat Margot pulled Villon's ear. "You don't listen at all."

"Repeat," said Villon dully, as though he were rehearsing a player in a part: it was her mention of Angers that made him think of that, he had never been further from writing farces than at this moment.

"Listen, then," she ordered. "Here is this house of mine. You can see for yourself what it is now. But, if the right sort were to come here, the girls could give up working in the shops altogether, and I wouldn't be going grey over my taxes, not to speak of all I have to pay for protection. Ah, my little cabbage, if that provost of ours were like his father-in-law of blessed memory, it would be another story. But those good days are over. We must think what it is best to do." She folded her fat arms and looked at Villon tenderly, as though he were good to eat.

"Well?"

"Why, my heart, it is simple. You are a clever fellow. You will not deny that."

"I will not," Villon admitted, but in a toneless voice that made her cry out at him reproachfully.

"If only you did not always make up songs about the dead," she said then. "There are plenty of us hale and hearty, may the good St. Mary of Egypt keep us that way a long while yet. But God knows I don't care what songs you sing so long as they listen to you."

Villon pushed his stool away from the table.

"Damn you," he said, "why can't you speak plainly? What do you want?"

"How he rants! That's the poet of it, eh? I couldn't speak

plainer, dearie. Here is this house, I said. And me. You know me, Villon. They like me well enough. They think I'm good-natured because I'm fat. Well," she chortled, "look at me, Villon. Like a prize sow. Only I don't get any prizes. That's where you come in, dear heart. You get 'em for me. You're so clever!"

"Clever enough to be Fat Margot's pimp!" Villon slapped her face. She gave an outraged cry and then sat staring at him with her hand at her cheek. He had dropped his head into his arms and lay across the table heaving with sobs.

He had nearly slapped la Turgis too. He could only hit women when he should be murdering men. He gagged with self-disgust.

She took her hand from her cheek and began patting him on the shoulder.

"You're sorry, eh? Hush, then, dearie. I forgive you."

He was sorry enough, but only for poor François. The sobs tore at him as though his agony were apart from himself and he could not control the noise it made, the wrenching movements of it. Desperately he forced his shoulders to stiffness, forced the tearing thing in his chest to silence. He straightened up and looked at Margot. He was still suffering, there was a pain in his heart like a leaden lump, but he had his wits again. He managed a haggard grimace.

"How much was the show worth?"

The little eyes in the fat face blinked at him uncomprehendingly.

"I made you feel something, didn't I?" Villon demanded. "I moved the mountain. What do I get for it?"

The fat girl shook her head.

"What a poor rogue you are, Villon!"

"Make me a rich one," he retorted, and then, with wheedling

earnestness: "Save me, you're a good-hearted girl. Give me a couple of guardian angels."

"Angels! Gold, you mean."

"What is purer than gold, Margot? Besides, the coins we call angels also have wings."

He would make what he could out of her. He was in no mood to look for a job now. And he had not enough credit for drink.

"What do you take me for?" she asked. "Do you think I am made of money?"

"Of tallow more likely. If ever they burn you for a witch, Margot, what a light you will give!"

The fat girl crossed herself hastily, though she chuckled.

"God save us, what are you saying? I, a witch! They will sooner hang you for a black devil."

Villon got to his feet.

"I am going to church, Fatty. Shall I say a prayer for you?"

She blinked at him incredulously. Villon going to church? But he had frightened her with his talk of burnings.

"You might as well," she said slowly.

"How'll I pay for it?"

"Here."

She rose and lumbered up the stairs to fetch the price of a prayer. He had not even paid for the wine she had poured for him.

"You live on credit, Villon," she sighed as she put the money in his hand.

"I would love on credit too if I had time," he answered.

It was no lie about church-going. But it was not to say his prayers. He had left Marthe without a word. He must see Katherine. For once he could not imagine their meeting. Would he make her a scene before the assembled parishioners or more publicly in the parvis? Strike her—as he had struck Fat Margot? Crawl as he had crawled to her in the old days before he knew she loved him? She did love him. She had said it. She had proved it. Ah, how?

He turned on his heel without a farewell.

Fat Margot stood staring at the door that closed behind him, seeing the lean figure, the sharp grim face long after they had vanished. You don't build up a business that way, Fatty, she told herself. Would he really buy a prayer for her, or did he want her money for some other girl?

Chapter Nine

Villon made for Notre Dame and stood awhile before the Door of the Virgin. But Katherine did not appear. Why had he imagined that she would? He rushed back to St. Benoit. She was not there. He made for the de Vauselles house, hoping against hope that Marthe would be coming out on some errand, that his demoiselle would show herself at her window, on her balcony, debating with himself whether he should demand admittance to her, cursing himself for a fool, sick with rage and pain.

When he turned away at last, it was to make for the Mule. The canon and Fat Margot between them had supplied him with sufficient money to get thoroughly drunk.

He almost tripped over a figure crouched near the door, its clawlike hand extended for alms, its thin hoarse voice lisping over and over and over:

"The blessed Virgin will reward you . . . The blessed Virgin will reward you . . ."

"For helping an accursed whore?" asked Villon, and dug

into his wallet for a coin. It was the old woman's good luck that he was wretched, self-pity made him pitiful.

As he bent over her, she put her skinny hand with the long nails on his wrist and pulled him toward her so that her wrinkled face grinned at him like a death's-head and he smelled the bad breath coming from her toothless mouth.

"Buy me a drink," she lisped. "There's a sweetheart!"

It was as though the dead were begging him.

"And then you'll ask me to go home with you?" Villon joked her.

The old bag of bones giggled in response. He helped her to her feet.

"Come along," he said.

A proper piece from the cemetery, thought Villon, sitting across the table from her in the half-empty tavern, watching her gulp her cup of wine. She spilled a little. Her lips trembled over their bare gums, and she wiped her chin with hands that shook. He noted the thick veins, the swollen knuckles.

"Thanks, darling. You couldn't spare another now?" she besought him.

Villon called for the potboy. The blessed Virgin might not reward him, but the old whore would pay him with her story. She reminded him . . . Of what in God's name did she remind him?

"Did you ever hear of the *Romance of the Rose,* granny?"

She puzzled, her lined brows folding into a hundred wrinkles, her rheumy eyes searching his black ones. At last she nodded and showed her gums in a smile.

"Nicholas used to read it to me," she lisped. "Oh, eh, before you were swaddled, I guess. Nicholas used to sit me on his good knee, he was lame, you remember, no, you wouldn't remember, but he would sit me there . . . and he would read to me, it would heat him like wine, that book . . ."

"He never read you the lament for old age, I'll wager."

"Nicholas was a young man when he died." She drank carefully.

"Was he good to you?"

"Yes. He was good to me. Those were good days, but I didn't know it. I was a beauty, young man. I was a great beauty."

Villon looked at her. Her hair was frowzy, what remained of it. Her skin was the color of old parchment and wrinkled like a rotten apple. Under her scanty eyebrows her irises were pale as dirty dishwater. His eyes stripped her: he could see the shriveled breasts, the shrunken thighs, the skin spotted with yellow blotches and purple. She had been some man's joy once. This Nicholas. He had burrowed his face in her breasts and dreamed of paradise. In those arms he had found solace for all the misery of life, for the pain of death. Villon leaned over and pinched her ear. The ear-laps were pendulous and furred with age but still soft.

"Tell me about Nicholas."

"Nicholas d'Orgemont. He was a canon of Notre Dame, he was." She giggled. The drink was warming her.

Villon had heard that name. Master Guillaume had had a story. . . . D'Orgement had been convicted of cheating on his taxes and had been thrown into prison and died soon after. But that was in time out of mind. All that was left of it was what this hag could remember.

"Canon of Notre Dame," she repeated. "We used to live there, in the cloisters. Nicholas arranged it. It wasn't allowed, but he could pay for his pleasures."

"Did you love him very much?"

She shook her head. "You give me another cup of wine, and I'll tell you. I know more about love than is written in all your books, darling."

He obliged her. It eased him strangely to be sitting in a corner with this piece of the past while the young whores drifted in with their men and the familiar noises floated to him across the room: the iron poking the fire, the bawl of the taverner, the clatter of dice, chatter and curses and shrieks of laughter, and the broken twanging of some instrument.

"And when Nicholas died, did you go on living at Notre Dame? There are plenty of canons there who can pay for their pleasures," Villon prodded her.

"No fear o' that. I took up with a better man. Not a limping old stick."

"So Nicholas was an old stick?" Villon laughed sardonically. This from the mouth of a skeleton. "What was his successor then?"

She sat silent, nodding her head as though before an image that she recognized, as though she were saying: Very like, it is very like.

"Ah, he was a blade. He was strong as an ox." She mused, sucking her gums. "He didn't mind beating me. Sometimes when I look at myself and the spots of old age on me I think of the bruises he'd give me. I used to cry over them. As though that were something to cry over! H'mm." She sat, shaking her withered head, forgetful of her host. "I'd pleasure him," she lisped. "There wasn't a girl in Paris like me. I'd pleasure him."

"Did he keep you well?"

"I kept him, darling," she grinned. "I took up the trade of armouress. There wasn't any tax on armour in those days. And the young men were crazy for Italian work. We'd palm off the

German helmets on them and make a neat profit. And if I couldn't sell one thing"—the rheumy eyes peered lewdly at Villon—"I could always sell another. The beauty that I had then!"

Beauty. Fine grey eyes. Clear skin. And a chin cleft with a dimple. Soft hands. Small breasts. Firm thighs. The little garden of delight. This wrinkled speckled thing, glad to crouch beside a heap of burning garbage in the street. Had once great beauty. And a lover's joy.

He looked at her with unbelief. She saw it. Her pale eyes blazed. She clutched the edge of the table with savage claws.

"Oh, God, Christ! It's true! You'll never believe it to look at me the way I am now. But I had the greatest beauty in Paris those days. Damn you, it's true." She sat shuddering with rage and pain.

He watched her. It was like a play.

"Finish your drink," he said. She obeyed mutely.

Suddenly in the far corner of the room, a stool fell to the floor, and above the tavern noises a girl's voice screamed:

"Take your filthy money then. I don't want it!" They heard the crack of a slap.

The old hag started up as if out of a dream. She lifted a skinny arm—a melancholy fury, a warning Fate.

"Hush then!" she shrilled in her hoarse lisp. "Don't you cheat yourself, girlie. His money's no worse than the others'. It'll do you duty in your gutter days. Take it. Don't swindle yourself, like me."

They laughed at her. The young whore shouted with the rest, restored to good humor by the diversion.

"Do you cheat the grave, fair armouress," Villon grinned darkly, "to tell them this?"

She dropped back to her stool and huddled there, wiping her mouth with the back of her shaking hand.

Villon scarcely saw her. Her pain, her rage possessed him. The rheumatic creature by his side, with her biting memories, was only semi-real. He was seeing the young beauty she had been, the careless humorous passionate girl buried in that shriveled spotted skinful of bones. The grief, the anger, the longing were making a mingled music within him.

Troubled by his abstracted air, the old woman leaned toward him.

"You aren't angry, darling?" she coaxed in a harsh whisper. He pushed her roughly away.

"Yes. No. Get out!"

He flung some coins on the table and got up.

She stumbled after him through the noisy steamy room. At the door she caught up with him. Her claw was on his sleeve, her shrill voice in his ear, her foul breath in his nostrils. Furiously Villon flung her from him. "Damn you! leave me alone!" he shouted. He must get back into the swing of it again; he knew what he would call it: the "Ballade of the Beautiful Armouress."

Back to the Red Door, up the stairs to his attic.

He sat there in the twilight, hugging his knee, swaying back and forth to the tune in his head, filled with bittersweet anguish. Only when the song began to make words for itself, he began feverishly scribbling.

> It seemed I heard that She complain,
> The beauty, once an armouress,
> And thus she spoke in her distress:
> "Ha! brutal Age, foul wretch, why press
> So promptly to your victory?

Who holds me back, what foolishness,
When one quick thrust would finish me?"

He finished as the bells rang vespers. It was good. It would want polishing before it was perfect, but it was very good. The pressure of his agony was lessened. When you were sick, the surgeons bled you, and the disease was sucked up by the leeches. Poetry too was a kind of leech that sucked away the bad blood of too heavy sorrow. Go to, Villon, he thought, you can bleed yourself.

Something of his old swagger returned as he repeated the lines to himself. He would have liked to show it to the old hag. She would hate it, but she would know its terrible truth. By God, he would show it to her.

He went back to the Mule. She was gone, of course, long since, and there was no one in the tavern fit to appreciate what he had done. He must show it to somebody, win the praise he needed as never before. He thought of sending it to Katherine. For she would come to that end, too, if she lived long enough. Even Katherine de Vauselles. He smiled horribly. And made for Fat Margot's. She would hate it, too. She deserved better payment for the money that had bought their drinks. Hell, what did he care! She would understand his song and praise its power with her curses.

There was nobody there but one of the children that were generally underfoot. Fat Margot never got rid of the brats. She could have taken them to be exposed to the mercy of charitable folk where the abandoned infants lay at Notre Dame. But she was too lazy. The dirty little thing minced up to Villon and lifted her skirt as she had seen the big girls do. Villon ignored her.

He did not really see her. He was seeing Fat Margot as she

listened to his "Ballade of the Armouress." He was thinking of the song he might make against Katherine to the same tune.

Fat Margot came back in a moment, and a strange man with her. She tossed Villon a word and a laugh, and the two disappeared up the creaking stairs. Villon was not sorry the pair had come. He misliked being alone. He could hear them up above him.

But the terribly familiar sounds inflamed his rage, his pain, his balked desire. For a long time he could do nothing, though the old hymn to which he had begun fitting the savage words against his demoiselle went on and on in his head. When he had finally forced himself to finish he bounded up the stairs and began serenading them with the new song he had made. The man came out half-dressed and wanted to know if the poet were making game of him. Margot came heavily after.

"Are you his love?" she asked laughing. "Or am I?"

"It's about a woman who sells herself and the man she makes a fool of."

"Villon's only thinking of himself," said Margot, "and that's a fact. But he's grand at songs. This one is fresh as tripe. You should be proud to assist at the birth of it: he's a great man, Master François!"

In the midst of his misery Villon took pleasure in the fat girl's praise of him.

"Let's all have a drink," she coaxed. "There's nothing like wine to christen a new song."

So they drank. One did not get good Beaune at Margot's, only cheap thin wine. But Villon was past caring for that. He was drunk already, on pain and poetry.

The evening was wearing on. Two of the girls came in, com-

panioned by a couple of students, and were made to sit down
and listen.

"It's a pity," reflected the fat girl, "that your demoiselle can't
hear it."

The words chimed with Villon's thought. Katherine must
hear it. It would wipe the slow smile quickly from her face.
It would make the red creep up to the tight bands about her
forehead. She would be forced to think of François Villon then.
She would not pity him. She might hate him. But she would
not forget him.

He plucked at the strings of a lute that he had picked up.
"And why not?" he asked.

"Let's go!" cried one of the girls.

"Here! Not so fast, my pretty." The student she had brought
with her pulled her back onto the bench and put a possessive
arm around her. She laughed and bit his ear.

"It's too early for serenades," the other girl said. "Why don't
we show the boys a good time, and then we'll all go?"

Fat Margot shook with laughter, her cheeks like shrimps in
aspic.

"Go along," Villon agreed. "I can wait."

I can wait now, he told himself, as they shrieked and buf-
feted each other at the thought of the fun ahead. It was yesterday that I could not wait, he thought, as they left him.
Because a man dies—of a knife-thrust got in a stupid joke, of
a rope necklace too tight for him, of a misstep in the dark, of
the pox, of the plague—a man dies, and then it's all over: the
play and the funning, the drinks and the music, the jousts and
the dances, and the kissing. A man dies, suddenly. Yesterday
he could not wait. For fear death would seize him before he
saw her again. Before he had her again. He would never have

her now. There was nothing to wait for. Nothing to make up for the shames and cruelties he had swallowed but the sharp ecstasy that was denied him forever. He broke a lute string with a sad twanging sound, flung the instrument from him, and sat staring at the wall where a soiled scrap of arras, Fat Margot's pride, showed Sheba holding court with Solomon. Save for their shabby majesties, Villon was alone.

Fat Margot reappeared, lit a candle, and sat down to mend a child's garment by its light. The girls began to drift in, Jehanneton, the milliner, Blanche, from the shoemaker's shop, Guillemette, who had gotten the arras cheap from the tapestry factory where she worked.

They greeted Villon with laughter: had he spent the whole day there? That was as dull as minding shop: he'd have no news for them. Oh, but he had! Margot assured them, chuckling: trust Master François for that. He might try to palm off worthless old coins on you, but he'd always pay you in new songs. The girls lounged about, pleased to be entertained.

Villon picked up the lute from the floor and rummaged in a disordered cupboard for a string to replace the one he had snapped. While he was adjusting it, the students came down and demanded to be shown some fun.

They would all accompany him to the de Vauselles house to hear the serenade. The girls were delighted. Villon, in spite of the heaviness in his chest, felt a flicker of pleasure at the notion of an audience. But Fat Margot asked what her customers would do if they found the house deserted. Besides, she argued reasonably, if the whole crowd of them came trooping along, they would have the sergeants after them in no time, and Villon could sing his song in jail where his demoiselle would never hear it. Let him go along, and come back to report to them on his success. They would celebrate it jollily enough.

The others sulked and complained, but the fat girl was not to be moved.

Villon was content. He saw himself standing in the shadow under Katherine's window, strumming a love song that she fancied—it was said to date from Abélard's day—saw the casement open into the dusk as she leaned to listen, and then, then the tune would alter, the words would come differently.

She had never had anything but sweetness from him: she would taste the bitterness he knew. She had felt nothing fiercer than his brief embraces: she would learn the sharpness of his malice. It was just. Her heart was of stone. He would give her stone for stone, hurt for hurt. He was horribly content.

So he went, moving unhurried through the streets, wretched and eager. So he came, in the dark, to the familiar house, to the familiar window, behind which he could see a glow as of candles that meant she must be there. So he stood, in the shadow, touching the strings.

He began to sing. The casement opened as he knew it would, but the face that showed was Marthe's. He sang on. Marthe vanished, but the window remained slightly open. The song was tender. It plained, it praised, it drew, at last, to the little lighted square that looked out upon the black street, Katherine. The candles behind her were snuffed that she might see him more clearly. She leaned against the frame, listening, one hand on the sill. His own hand made a discord. He began again savagely, the other tune, the hymn tune, but the words, his own, fit for the devil's mass. Before the first stanza ended she cried out as though she had been struck. In another moment the casement was slammed to. The candles were lit again in that room. Other windows opened, in houses flanking the de Vauselles house and across the way. Heads were stuck out. There were catcalls and laughter. When he struck the final

arpeggio, a chorus of amused and indignant neighbors had
thrown the street into a small uproar.

Villon slipped away. No one had touched him. He had punished her as she deserved. But there was no satisfaction in it.

He was reminded that he had never seen her deeply angry,
never seen her weep. He told himself with faint surprise that
he did not truly know her. He knew only that he loved her.
With an effort he visualized that face, which he had so often
compared to a garden, grown strange and ugly with sick pride.
She would look hateful. She was hateful. Villon laughed at
himself. Ovid had never sung a metamorphosis like this. But,
if she summoned him, he would go to her, running.

He did not return to Fat Margot's. The Mule was nearer.
He would have his song sung all over Paris before he was done.

He spent that night as he had spent so many nights, drinking
and singing and drinking again, paying for his drinks with his
jokes. He made up a short farce, acting all the parts himself,
naming no names, giving the characters allegorical titles:
Cupidity, who spoke in a deep voice and had a twisted nose
made out of paper (Katherine's aunt); Lechery, who was a
dealer in mustard but never had any for himself when he
needed it (Jehan de la Garde); Pandar, stolen out of a foreign
story but featured, for Villon, like Noel Jolis; the Rose, who
was Katherine herself; and Everylover: a poor brilliant poet
to whom the Muses brought fame and wealth and to whom
Venus would have granted the Rose, but that he said it was
cankered and gave it to the grocer to wear at a guild banquet.
Villon almost forgot his pain in the excitement of pointing the
repartee with punning rhymes.

They started gaming. Villon played with what was left of
the money the canon had given him, but he was careless and
soon lost his few winnings. In the end he had to leave his

dagger in pawn. The weight of misery began dragging at his heart again and could not be thrown off. He stumbled home late, fell into a thick sleep, and opened his eyes to the sound of church bells, a headache, and the dim consciousness that despair would gripe him as soon as he was broad awake.

He did not rise. There was nothing to get up for. He was half grateful for the nausea that distracted him from his other torments.

It was nearly noon when he dragged himself out of bed and began to dress slowly. He hunted about for his dagger, and only after some minutes remembered with irritation that he had been compelled to leave it at the Mule the night before. On the wall hung a long sword too clumsy to wear. Well then, he would go out unarmed. By God, what did it matter? Fat Margot's favorite oath. He would go to her.

With an embellished tale of his triumph over the girl who thought herself too good for him. Fat Margot would lap it up. She would give him credit, too. The Mule was closed to him temporarily. So was the Pine Cone.

He dragged himself down the stairs and closed the Red Door behind him with a bang. The air was fresh and sweet. He breathed deeply. He was all right. But suppose he met the demoiselle Katherine? He spat. She would be the one to flinch and blench. By God, he was all right. He would go to Fat Margot.

Chapter Ten

The fat girl's place was deserted at this hour. She could give all her attention to Villon. He wanted it badly. She fetched a herring to cure him of the brown taste in his mouth and wine to wash away the taste of the fish. She roared over his malicious verses until the tears came into her small blue eyes. She flattered him to the top of his bent. What could this whore's praises mean to François Villon? Not a good goddamn, he told himself, lapping them up shamelessly.

"When you're hungry, a herring's as good as salmon, eh? It's the same with me, Villon. I know you cannot pay me. But if I can't get money from you I will take something else."

"My dagger? But I haven't it with me." He launched into ribald puns that made her shake with laughter.

He was killing, that one, she thought, as she rubbed her cheek with the back of her plump hand. You could never be dull with him. Sobering, she leaned over him, her small blue eyes bright with purpose.

"Well, Villon, how about it?"

He shrugged.

"What's it to you," she urged, "to carry a trayful of drinks, if the crowd is watching you, waiting to hear what joke you'll crack next? They'll clap your songs as no actor was ever clapped in Paris or Angers. You'll bring me custom, don't fret, and you'll have an audience, by God, the right sort. Think of it, Villon."

He was thinking. He pinched her round arm above the elbow.

"What would you pay me, Fatty?"

"By God, Villon, what should I pay you? I offer you food and lodging and the jolliest audience in Paris. What more do you want?"

"The fattest girl in Paris."

Margot's face sharpened with triumph as she embraced him.

"Then it's a bargain, my little cabbage. You'll never be sorry, you'll see!"

Her joyful exclamations were interrupted by the entry of a couple of students. Before the fat girl could welcome them, Villon was at their table, arms akimbo, black eyes challenging.

"What will you have, gentlemen? A jug of wine, bread and cheese? Or will you wait for the ladies?"

The deferential tone contrasted comically with his impudent air. The polite words that issued oddly from the scarred mouth were followed by a broad joke.

The pair laughed and gave an order.

"He is good, eh? He is wonderful, my Villon!"

"Your Villon?"

Margot nodded, and winked one eye.

"Come tonight, when there is a crowd, and you will hear him. Do not tell me you do not know Master François Villon. And you from the University."

"Of course we know him, Fatty. But he wouldn't play potboy for you. That is not the poet!"

"You are right. This is not the poet," Villon grimaced.

"Ah, Villon!" cried Fat Margot with angry reproach. "When I have just set you on your feet. Is it fair?"

"See here, you aren't really Villon, are you?"

"Whom Fatty has just set on his feet, as you heard, both feet stuck fast in the dirt."

The two young men stared at him with a mixture of astonishment and disbelief.

"The fellow's a liar."

"So's Villon."

"All right. If it's he, he'll be able to recite some of his own verses. But I'll wager you my new gloves that it's a hoax."

"The gloves with the fringes?"

"Yes, against a clean copy of his best ballade."

Villon regarded them with moody eyes. They spoke as though he were not there. Fat Margot was hugging herself with laughter.

"If you're truly Master François, recite the song against Katherine what's-her-name," shouted the student who had pledged his gloves.

"Of course he can sing that one. Everybody knows it by now," cried the other.

"No." The fat girl had an inspiration. "Recite the awful

verses you made about the old hag of an armouress. No potboy has them by heart."

Villon's eyes were two coals in his scarred face. He would let them have it. He would never do a better thing.

"It seemed I heard that She complain,
The beauty, once an armouress . . ."

The scar on his lip affected his speech slightly, but he spoke the poem clearly, in a low harsh voice, from the soft beginning to the cruel end. They would never forget this, wager or no wager, gloves or no gloves. The boys lounging at the table before him would be telling their grandsons, fifty years hence, how they had sat in Fat Margot's place one autumn afternoon back in 1456 and heard the poet, François Villon, looking like a villain, with the voice of a fallen angel, recite his own stanzas on a broken whore. He would be remembered. In all his wretchedness and filth and damnation. He would be remembered in all his glory.

He stopped.

The student who had lost his bet gave Villon a look of bleak incredulity. Fat Margot waggled her head, crying:

"You believe me, now, eh? Come tonight, and you'll hear more. Something jollier, what, Villon? And tell your friends. It'll be a treat!"

That was what he wanted, she thought, watching the sullen face, that had brightened so strangely as Villon felt his own power, twist into the old sardonic grin. Praise is meat and drink to him, she thought. And I'll make him happy. That skinny carcass of a Vauselles doesn't know how. He'll forget her. By God, I'll make him forget.

Villon heard her thoughts as though she had spoken them aloud. By God, could Fat Margot do that? Whether she could or not, what was there left for him? He turned toward the door.

"Where are you going?"

"Home. To fetch my gear," he muttered.

"You hear him? Now do you believe? Don't forget to come back!" she shouted.

He wanted to get out. He did not want to go back to the Red Door. He flinched at meeting the canon, at meeting his reproachful look, at being reminded of the jobs to be had in the scriveners' quarters. Villon a proper clerk. There was no reason for him to turn respectable now. How explain that to the canon? He might as well sing him the song against the demoiselle Katherine.

Why couldn't he put her out of his head as he put her out of his heart?

If he could see her, just once. To flout her to her face. To remind her of what they had shared, the happy days, the sacred hour that she had soiled forever. To give her a present to remember him by when she was Madame de la Garde. A full purse, that was what she wanted. His own was empty. Had he nothing to offer? He was short and lean and ugly, with a scar across his mouth. But more than one girl had liked his black eyes. Was it nothing to be young and quick and strong? Was it nothing to be a keen wit on the way to being a great poet? It was nothing if you had nothing.

"Hi! Villon!"

He turned at the rough voice hailing him. Robin Dogis, arm in arm with Roger Pichart.

"Where are you going? How about a little game?"

He had nothing to play with. But there was no need to tell them that.

"Not at the moment. I'm busy."

154

"Haven't got a job, have you?"

"Maybe."

"A job! Well, it's one way of making a living," said Pichart. "That was a damn funny song, Villon. Hutin was telling us —he was at the Mule."

"Not so funny as the girl's face when she heard it, I'll bet."

Villon had a miserable smile for that. He might make mock of Katherine if it pleased him. He might publish his wrongs all over Paris. But there was a relish of bitterness in hearing it from his scoundrelly friends.

"Aren't you afraid she'll pay you back? She can have the law on you for defamation."

"And what about my lawyer?" asked Villon arrogantly.

"Your—?"

"If a dead peasant girl can have a lawyer, why not a living poet? It's a toss-up between Ferrebouc and André Courant."

They knew Ferrebouc's name but not that of King René's solicitor. They hooted nevertheless.

Villon escaped from them at last. He turned down the rue St. Jacques with a light step and a heavy heart. Katherine would never have the law on him. He knew her better than that. Christ, he didn't know her at all: to dismiss him without a word. To let herself be seduced into this marriage contract for the sake of beastly bourgeois notions of prudence and decency! Oh, she would be comfortable, she would be rich. And she would be wretched, God help her. Could de la Garde's moneybags weigh enough to balance Villon's passion? And he, how could he go on, knowing he had lost her forever?

He did not enter the Red Door. He could not go home. His room was, like every familiar place, horrible to him, with its reminders of the days, so close behind, so far away now, when in spite of everything that threatened him he had felt secure,

155

proud and at peace in Katherine's tenderness. He damned her again in the foul words of the gutter, but he could not tear her out of his thoughts. She drew him still. His dear, his false sweeting, his pitiless love.

He dragged himself around the corner and toward the de Vauselles house. She might be emerging from the door at this moment. She might be on her balcony, or at her window, looking out. How would she look at him? What would she find to say?

The door was indeed opening. Villon looked sharply. The person coming out was not the demoiselle Katherine. It was a man, with a brisk air about him and a thick stick in his fist.

Villon turned rapidly on his heel. He was not quick enough. Noel Jolis had him by the shoulder. Villon reached for his dagger. He remembered: he had no weapon on him.

There was a stinging sensation across his shoulders. He stumbled and fell into a heap of rubbish.

"That's where you belong," shouted Noel, "in the dirt!"

Villon scrambled up. He had nothing but feet and fists with which to defend himself. He tried to kick, to strike, to bite. Noel was too strong for him. One heavy hand held Villon fast. The stick came down on his back, hard, again, again, again. He howled. There was no respite. He was being beaten like dirty linen. He struggled. His jerkin ripped open. Noel tore it wide. Villon's curses came in gasps. The stick fell across his bare skin like burning wires, like hot needles. He was sick with rage and shame. Noel was beating him like a schoolboy. Up above, the neighbors' shutters were opening, heads were peering out, the same shutters that had opened last night to let them hear his song against Katherine. Now these good people were witnessing her revenge. A crowd was gathering. There was whistling and crows of laughter. At him, François Villon, the wit, the poet, the pride of Paris! Christ, the outrage! He would never live it down. He was blind with fury, sobbing with pain. As though it were another creature in his body, he heard himself cry out.

"Noel, Noel, stop!"

Katherine's voice. She was seeing him flogged. Had she arranged it? He struggled fiercely, in vain.

"Stop!"

She pitied him. He spat on her pity. He reveled in it.

"Be quiet!" A deeper voice, more like a man's, old Madame de Vauselles, her bitch of an aunt.

It was not Katherine's doing. But she had allowed it. She had witnessed it.

Villon grunted, working to free himself from Noel's clutches. He crooked a knee around Noel's ankle. A rapid jerk, and Noel sprawled in the street. Villon made a hoarse gasping sound, the nearest he could come to laughter. Noel stumbled up. The stick came down again heavily on Villon's burning back. He fell. He did not rise.

"Have you had enough?"

Villon groaned, sick with physical hurt, too sore-hearted to speak.

Noel dusted off his hands. He had suffered nothing worse than some kicks on the shin, a bruised elbow, a scratched cheek. The crowd roared at his triumph.

"You'll sing out of the other side of your mouth now!" grunted Noel.

He walked off. The jeering crowd melted away.

Villon lay moaning, his clothes in tatters, his back crossed with burning wounds. It was finished, all but the fire in his shoulders, the black fury in his heart.

They would not laugh at his jokes any more. He was himself a joke for them to laugh at. He heard them as they called to each other before closing their windows on the show that was over, before strolling off to spread the tale of his disgrace. Not one stirred to lift him from where he lay. Not one spoke a word to comfort his misery.

"Oh, Holy Virgin!" Horror and tenderness were in the voice that roused him from his anguish. For an instant he thought it was Katherine. The whipping had turned his wits. It was only Marthe.

He groaned more loudly, hungry for pity, while he mocked inwardly. The silly fool. He would have laughed, if he had been in her shoes. To see a man thrashed like that!

She put a large trembling hand on his shoulder.

"Come into the house, Master François," she whispered. "I'll poultice it, Master François. They won't know." Her words came in spurts, like wine from a narrow-necked jug.

"In there?" Villon, risen, his hands over his wet eyes, would have shrugged. The movement made him cry out again.

"Oh, Master François!"

Had Katherine sent her? Would she nurse him after this? He could still hear her voice crying, "Noel, Noel, stop!"

"This way."

He had to lean on Marthe. They were using the back entrance. Would Katherine be waiting for him? He writhed inwardly. He hoped, sickly, that she would—that she would not.

In the kitchen there was a fire going and a black pot bubbling on the hob. A short wrinkled serving-woman was stirring something in a wooden bowl. She laughed toothlessly as Marthe brought Villon across the threshold.

Marthe looked at her like a frightened rabbit. The old creature said nothing.

And Katherine?

"Here. Master François. If you will give me your shirt. Oh, holy Virgin!"

There was a pot of grease on the table ready to lay on his raw back, and a heap of clean rags. Katherine must have given orders. Where was she? Marthe moved clumsily, but her touch was surprisingly gentle. The old servant kept grinning and nodding and making little whistling noises through the gaps in her rotten teeth. She reminded Villon of the beautiful armouress. That was good work. When he did that, he was good. Pride revived a moment and died again.

Marthe tried to give him ease, afraid to touch him, eager to touch him, to comfort him, to come closer than she had ever dared. Villon was quiet, savoring the bitter taste of his shame, thinking of Katherine, how soon she would come, what he would say to her, what she would say, and do.

Suddenly Marthe stood stiffly away from him, her hands at her sides, her big blue eyes wide with terror. There were steps in the passage. The old servant chuckled, "Hey, hey, hey!" Marthe glared. She gripped Villon and almost lifted him bodily from the bench.

"This way," she whispered, with a half-angry, half-beseeching glance at the old cook. The woman wagged her head and sucked her withered lips in silence, but Villon noticed that she hurried to hide the grease-pot and the rags.

As the door closed he heard behind them the masculine voice of Madame de Vauselles. The twisted nose had sniffed something odd. Panicked, Marthe pulled Villon after her up a flight of narrow stairs, thrust him into a dark hole with a bed in it, and left him.

He lay down on the bed, the straw mattress rustling under

159

him. After ages of blind pain he opened his eyes. Slowly the furniture took shape in the dimness. He made out a chest against the wall, a wooden crucifix above the bed.

He had not noticed the bells. It must be after compline. He was too sore to move. He lay on his stomach on the straw mattress, his fingers locked under his closed eyes. He pricked his ears at every sound, the creak of a board in the old flooring, the gnawing of a mouse behind the wall. The time was endless. He thought of trying to get up: if he should meet the lady with the twisted nose he could give her as good as she gave and better. But the faint impossible hope that he might yet see Katherine kept him lying there. And the pain. He could feel the thumping of his heart. His back burned and throbbed. Christ, would she come? Would she never come? He climbed down from the bed and knelt awkwardly before the crucifix.

"Holy Virgin, Mother of God, look down upon Your servant, François Villon, this night. Grant him, a miserable sinner, Your divine mercy. Put it into the heart of the demoiselle Katherine to come to him, to speak with him. Blessed Virgin, in the name of the Father, the Son, and the Holy Ghost. Amen." He paused. He added in a passionate whisper: "For Christ's sake!" He sighed deeply, groaned, crossed himself, and got up. He heard footsteps. So soon? His prayer was answered so soon?

The door opened with a squeak. Katherine! he shouted wordlessly. It was Marthe.

She had a cup of wine in one hand and a plate of food in the other. She set them on the chest and then touched his arm with the possessiveness of one who had tended him. She was out of breath. Did it go any better with him? She had tried to come sooner, but the demoiselle Katherine had kept her. No one guessed that he was here.

Then she was not coming. She had not tried to help him. It was all Marthe. Only Marthe. He cursed, his eyes full of tears.

She lit a candle stub so that he might see to eat. He tasted the wine. It was good. Even in his misery of body and mind he could savor it. He could not touch the meat and bread. Marthe stood and watched him. As he pushed away the cup, the candle flame, that had been fluttering crazily, quivered in its pool of tallow, and went out.

Villon could hear Marthe breathing. Without looking at her, he could see how she stared at him through the dark, her mouth open, her eyes enormous. He wiped his mouth with the back of his hand, drew her toward him, unresisting, a warm frightened yielding armful. He could not see her face, but he could imagine the look in the wide blue eyes.

"Oh, Master François!" he mocked her in a falsetto whisper.

She pitied him, not like Katherine. He wished he were not so sore.

She would have given herself under the eyes of the crucified Christ above the bed. The straw rustled as he drew her down to him, lying carefully so as not to touch his burning back, one hand thrust above his head, the other thrown across her soft panting breasts.

Damn Katherine!

"Marthe," he said in a low voice, "Marthe, do you love me?"

"Oh," she sobbed softly, "oh, Master François!"

Chapter Eleven

Marthe did not know how to tell him that he must go. The
old cook would not betray her. But there was no guessing when
the crooked nose of Madame de Vauselles would sniff something suspicious. And Katherine?

Villon, creeping down the dark stairs at last, trying not to
groan, thought of showing himself to Katherine. He had
known what to do when she cast him off. But how did a man
revenge himself on a woman who had seen him thrashed? See
your lawyer, Villon, he told himself wryly. And let himself
out into the night.

He limped back to the Red Door. He did not want the
canon's nephew, Flastrier, dressing his sore back. He did not

want the canon probing for nonexistent wounds in his ward's conscience. But he could hide in his room till his wounds were healed. And think. Christ, if he could only stop thinking. He was too sick to make a poem.

He rose at last and made for the Mule. For a little it seemed that fortune was with him. He struck a set of innocents. He let their winnings pile up. Then, when they were happy and reckless, he began trying his tricks on them. He had just evened the score when in walked Pichart and struck him jovially on the back. He could not bear the pain. Flinching, he nearly dropped his hidden cards.

He could have killed Pichart. Instead, he invented a lie about an appointment elsewhere and cleared out before he should be discovered. He limped down the street. It was tough going. And where should he go?

Where he was welcome. Three women would smile to see him. Marthe. His mother. Fat Margot.

She was standing in her doorway. On the lookout for customers?

"Well, how are you, dearie?" She followed him inside.

"Rotten." He sat down gingerly on a bench and glanced about. They were alone.

"What'll it be?"

"White wine and oysters, Fatty, to start with, roast capon with liver sauce, and fresh almond tarts, and a couple of custards flavored with Spanish wine."

"You know how to order a meal," she said, not stirring.

"I am a Master of Arts. The art of ordering is also taught in the Schools. Well, why don't you fetch it?"

"Where's the money?"

"In the coffers of the College of Navarre."

"Maybe you can get the beadle to open them for you," she laughed.

"Laurens Poutrel? I'll have a long wait. You'd better bring me some herring in the meanwhile and a mug of beer."

"And where's the money for that?"

"Don't you think of anything but money?"

"Not the way things are now." She glanced down at him, and her eyes brightened. "I'll fetch it," she said. He couldn't pay. She had never seen him look so wretched. Everyone knew how he had been beaten by Noel Jolis. They were glad of it, most of them, hating him, fearing his malicious tongue, jealous of his fame. They were glad of the chance to laugh at him. But this was her good luck. His wallet empty, his clothes in rags, himself a jest in his old haunts, he should be glad to creep into any corner that would give him shelter and a morsel to eat. But she must cheer him up first, get him in a mood to listen.

"You wait," she muttered. "I'll take care of you, Villon."

She sat with him while he ate, watching him as he tore at the loaf, washed down the salt fish with thirsty gulps.

She didn't know why he should excite her, the little black-eyed runt that he was, with his scarred lip. But when he told his stories, when he sang those terrible songs of his, you forgot how he looked. The voice on him! The mimic he was! Suppose he was short: he was well made, though, fine-boned and graceful. More like a boy than a man, except for his crooked lip, his snapping slithery eyes. He, caring only for that fool of a Vauselles! He must feel different about her after the beating she got him.

"It's a pity you didn't come back that night, Villon."

"I was busy."

"Finish your business?"

"Maybe."

"You want a change, Villon. And a chance. Why don't you let me give it to you?"

"You!"

"Yes, me. You made a hit with those students the other day. They came back to find you. They wouldn't be the only ones. You stay here, you'll draw the biggest crowd of any house in Paris. You'll be famous. You'll make Fat Margot's place famous. Why, what more do you want? You'll have your dinners, as good a bed as you get at the Red Door, and you'll be glad to go to bed too."

"And glad to get up again, Fatty?"

"By God, has anyone made you a better offer?"

"I'm trying to decide between a bishopric and being secretary to the Duke of Orléans."

"While you're deciding, sweetheart, you might as well stay at Fat Margot's. I need a potboy."

"You need everything that begins with a 'P': a potboy, a poet—and a punch!"

He jabbed her, but not too hard. After all, she had fed him and he owed her money.

"By God, Villon, ain't you ashamed?"

"No!" he shouted. "And, to prove it, I'm staying."

"Ha! I knew you'd come round. You're a smart one, Villon, and no mistake. Wait till I tell the girls!"

Villon began the evening with a tray in his hand. He ended it sitting on a table singing ribald stanzas against the enemies of good living in the cloisters across the street.

Fat Margot had not been mistaken. His name was known at the University, and in less respectable haunts. His story was known, and there were those who came to settle a wager as to whether he had been beaten to death by Noel Jolis.

Before a month was out, they were clamoring for him at every table, demanding another song, a verse on the crony across the room, a joke pointed at such worthies as his former patrons, the banker Perdrier, the notary Ferrebouc. He was good at that. He would have liked them to see him, capering about, slapping the girls on the buttocks, or staring meaningfully into their eyes while he cracked broad jokes for the ears of their companions. He thumbed his nose at his quondam employers with every jest aimed at the third estate, which he mocked even more readily than he mocked the pursy canons of Notre Dame.

What he had once done for the sheer fun of the thing when the mood was on him, he now did for the sake of such food and shelter as Margot gave him. No, for the sake of poetry.

He could not write verses when he was bored. He needed an ecstasy of joy or misery. He had known the first briefly with Katherine. He would not know it again. He knew the second as he knew his own bony hand, the fine black hairs between the knuckles, the strongly etched lines on the palm.

He had started a lovelorn ballade, an acrostic weaving his name with Marthe's, to make Katherine writhe when she saw it, as he meant that she should. Save for that, he had composed nothing for weeks but coarse quips and rough jingles. But he was not afraid the well had run dry. As the glowing autumn evenings turned to the bleak rains of early winter, his audience responded more mechanically to the jokes that ceased to be quite so funny. Margot's demands on him mounted, and with them his distaste for the ugly routine of which her caresses were a part. But Villon had his consolation. The hollow nastiness of his nights and days was feeding the horror and the grief that were the source of his songs. He would avenge himself on his life by showing it for what it was.

Waking in his frowzy bed one afternoon, he sat upon one elbow to see Margot standing over him, a reflective look in her small blue eyes.

He yawned and stretched, wishing her at the devil.

"Villon," she said in her soft fat voice, "I have been thinking."

"What with?" he asked carelessly. "Your belly?"

"Eh, Villon, with what should I think?"

She sat at the foot of the bed, and he lay down again, his hands clasped above his head.

"You saw how it was last night," she said. "We're not doing the business. And the sergeants will have to be buttered tomorrow: the Provost is after us again. If only you could get round him. His wife thinks you a great poet, Villon. Or was that another of your jokes?"

"I made a song for her wedding day, if you call that funny. What do you suggest, Fatty? That I pay my respects to Ambroise de Loré and ask her to see that her husband goes easy on the brothel keepers, in memory of her epithalamium?"

"It was different," said Margot mournfully, "when her father was provost."

"You were a virgin then, Fatty. It was very different."

"That must have been longer ago than I thought," she said seriously. "But, by God, Villon, what are we going to do?"

He grinned lazily and said nothing.

He did not need the fat girl to remind him that things were getting worse instead of better. If trade was dull for the small shopkeeper, it was worse for Margot's sort. The Companions could always be counted on to come around, but they were dangerous customers. If they didn't pay in counterfeit coin, they were likely to get you into trouble with the sergeants. The apprentice burdened with heavy fees looked for the cheapest pleasures he could find. The students had longer than ever to wait for remittances from home. The bourgeois busily amassing a dowry of a thousand francs for each of his little daughters thought twice before he crossed the threshold of a brothel. One might as well live in Bohemia, where the monster Huss had shorn even the Church of its wealth and power, where no man owned more than another, where, they said, no man had anything for himself, not even his wife.

The girls complained to Margot that, instead of love-making, they must listen to stories about shops that had closed their shutters for good, about factories that had moved out of Paris because the peasants, many of them poor tenant farmers, were glad to take wages the city worker would spit upon.

When Villon saw that the crowd at the tables was made up chiefly of burghers out for a good time, he would poke fun at the fat bankers, the great drapers and mercers, all straining to imitate the fallen Jacques Coeur, with his twenty-five millions. But lately the laugh that greeted his jokes would be followed by glum mutterings about the state of the small merchant, squeezed between the powerful corporations that owned their men as they owned their mills and the journeymen's organizations that crowded out the wretched "savage": the independent workman. It was plain that the rich were getting richer and the poor were getting poorer.

"Yes, you may groan," cried Margot, her eyes blazing with sudden rage. "Where are all your fine friends, anyway? Your Vitrys and your Montignys and the rest? What use are you if nobody comes to listen to you but fellows who must pawn their breeches to pay their score! What good are their dirty breeches to me?"

Villon cracked a ribald joke, but she did not laugh.

"And you lie there!" she cried, "like a fine gentleman, a lord, is it, or a duke, maybe. You . . ."

"See here, Fatty"—he sat up at last, his eyes glittering—"do you want me to get out? I've a tongue in my head, you may remember. I made your place known with it. I'll get out if you like, and I'll make your damned place better known."

"No, no, Villon. You do what you can, I suppose. Only, I am worried."

Villon fell back on the bed relieved. He had no wish to get out. Where should he go?

"What do you think I came here for? The soft bed? The fine wines? I came because I thought I could get some writing done and show you a favor at the same time. I'm not above doing a girl a favor. But you give me no rest. It's Villon, here, and Villon, there, fishing the flies out of the milk and cutting the maggots out of the cheese and playing the clown between-whiles."

"But we've had good times together, Gogo," Fat Margot reminded him, dimpling and stroking his legs beneath the coverlet. She studied the thin sullen face, the bright black eyes, and, leaning across him, bent to kiss the scarred mouth. He mustn't be angry. He mustn't go.

"You are so clever. I thought you would tell me what to do."

"Do?" Villon pushed her away. "Do what you know how to do, you fool. Go after the trade. You haven't been out of the house since I came into it."

It was what she had been thinking. But she had hoped he would say something else.

"Maybe you're right," she conceded. She got slowly to her feet. "Maybe I'd better . . . But if the sergeant comes this afternoon?"

Villon shrugged. Fat Margot shook her head despondently.

"And you won't forget to fetch some pears and apples? And

we ought to have more firewood. And the big kettle needs mending: it leaks."

"Anything else?" he asked drily.

She was busy with a bit of cloth and a paintpot and did not answer directly.

"Yes, Gogo," she murmured. And paused. She was about to beg him to stay away from the other girls in her absence. After all, he might be expected to be faithful to the one who kept him. But, turning toward the bed, she saw the malice in the sharp black eyes fixed upon her, and she bit her lip as her own eyes hardened.

"Maybe you want me to make a poem about your sweet face."

She smiled incredulously, not heeding his tone.

"Yes, Gogo!" Perhaps he was really fond of her. And it would keep him busy while she was gone. She returned with zest to her make-up.

He had said it in jest. But when she seized on his words, he began to wonder if there might not be something in the notion. The next day, when she interrupted her embraces to ask for the poem, he put her off with a sneer. But he kept thinking of it.

Her absences gave him leisure to think. Her complaisance fed his hatred of her, of his condition, of himself. Her fondness fed his cruelty. He helped her, as before, fetching wine for this party, fruit and cheese for that, joking the guests now and then, oftener moving in sullen silence, for it was not his jests that they depended on now so much as Fat Margot's excursions. She would set out for the Holy Innocents or for the purlieus of Notre Dame near by, where she glorified her moth-eaten furs and false jewelry by the clever tricks of her round, highly colored face, her soft plump hands, her fat honeyed voice. She was not always successful, and, when she came back to him empty-handed, Villon turned ugly.

He could not stick it much longer. He would not go back to the Red Door. Some rumor of his ward's situation, if not full knowledge, must have reached the canon's ears. He was able to forgive murder sooner than self-murder. Villon wondered restlessly where René was keeping himself. He might know a way out. Colin had shown up at Fat Margot's once or twice, but always when it was too crowded for them to have a word. There were worse things than belonging to Colin's gang. The risks were as high as the gallows. But you lived high, too, if you weren't caught. A foul whiff from Montfaucon on a hot summer day filled Villon's nostrils, though he was shivering in Margot's fireless room of a wintry evening.

"Well?" he said abruptly.

The fat girl had come in, rousing him out of his miserable reveries.

"Nothing, Villon," she quavered, footsore and dispirited.

He was seized with a choking hatred of her soft fat voice, her small blue eyes, her dimpled painted face. He punched her, his nail inadvertently scraping her lip.

Her little fist flew to her face, and she retorted on him with curses. The elegance assumed for the street contrasted oddly with her attitude as she stood there, a round breathless fury, with a scratch beneath her snub nose, shrieking to heaven.

"Shut your mouth, you demon!" shouted Villon. "And give me your jacket. It'll fetch something." He had his hand on the fur.

She tore it out of his grasp.

"No, by the death of Christ, you'll not!"

"Give it here. I want to eat," Villon growled, though he was too angry for hunger. "And not the slops in your kitchen either."

"No, I say! What'll I wear when I go out?"

"What'll you wear?" he repeated maliciously. "Never mind. Just show 'em your phiz with Master François' signature on it."

She snatched up the mirror at her girdle and rushed to the window to examine the damage.

"You devil! See what you've done!"

"We're a pair, Fatty," said Villon. The good rat to the good cat, ran the proverb. The vile rat to the vile cat, then.

She turned round, facing him. Her eyes were as hard as ever, her painted cheeks streaked with tears but beginning to dimple again.

"Eh, Villon, you and I," she said. "Antichrist!" But the anger had gone out of her voice.

He could beat her, he could rob her, he could mock her intolerably, but she must have him still, the little black-eyed runt. All the sly charm that was her stock-in-trade was summoned, was heightened, for his benefit. Her dimples deepened. Her blue eyes shone.

"Gogo!" she murmured hoarsely.

He threw her a sardonic glance and reached for the jug, more than half full of wine, on the floor beside him.

"Here, don't be greedy," she cried, "give us some."

He handed the jug over in silence. She emptied it eagerly.

"I'll get us another," she said. It was the usual end to their quarrels, the prelude to the usual end. She was gone and back in a moment. The fat girl could move quickly when she chose.

So they made their peace. Blows or embraces, it was all one. A monotonous horror from which there was no escape.

That night he refused to go downstairs. The place was almost

172

deserted, but, if it had been packed with a clamoring crowd, he would not have lifted a leg. He sat on the bed, in the cold, with nothing but a candle and a jug of cheap red wine for company, reviewing with bleak exactness the weeks that had just gone by, that would never come again: the running back and forth from the dirty cellar to the sloppy tables; the odors and the noises, the blows, the curses, the caresses; Fat Margot in her finery saying disconsolately, "Nothing Villon," Fat Margot hiccuping with rage, belching with drink; the sharp voice in which she cried "Gogo" when she claimed him; every vile intimate detail of existence here in this brothel where they'd set up house. He savored his disgust, he hugged his horror to him. Crouched, shivering, on the bed, not tasting the wine that he reached for to warm himself with, he searched savagely for words that would show the thing that was gnawing at him like a wolf. He would omit nothing, gloss nothing. He would give Fat Margot what she asked for: a mirror in which to see herself with the poet Villon beside her, the two of them together, wallowing in the same filth, here in this brothel where they'd set up house. This was his refrain that he sang with bitter gaiety to a fine old tune, swaying back and forth and cursing indifferently as he spilled the wine.

The candle was almost done for when he finished, and he had hard work finding a scrap of paper and struggling with the congealed ink. But it was finished. It was good. He gloated over the truth of it. And in the midst of his pride, he was sick with despair. Fat Margot had no more to give him, having given him this. What was there left for him? When she came up she found him sobbing drunk.

"You, Villon," she nudged him. "You are a fool. Are you crying for the moon?"

It was Katherine she meant, and he knew it. He cursed her, but she seemed not to hear him.

"You should have been there tonight. That Colin of yours came in, and a monk from Picardy with him. I didn't half like the looks of him. I don't know what kind of money he gave the girls."

"Colin?" Villon looked up, blear-eyed. "Did he ask for me?"

"Yes, my pretty. Don't fret: he'll be back. A bad penny always turns up again."

Fat Margot was right. Colin was back the next night, tight-mouthed and sly-eyed as ever, and Dom Nicolas with him, a red-faced man who spoke the jargon as though he had learned it at his mother's knee. Villon sat at their table, mum as an oyster. Colin did not try persuasion this time. He asked him shortly if he liked his job. Villon shrugged. If he could use a little money. Villon grinned. If he knew the College of Navarre well enough to find his way about the chapel at night. Villon nodded. There was a pause, during which the Picard drummed restlessly on the table and Colin eyed his friend with a suspicious sneer.

"What about René?" muttered Villon.

"What about him? He's not here, and we don't want him. He's a financier, not a craftsman."

"A craftsman, hoo, hoo!" the Picard roared.

"Wait t'll you see Petit Jehan at work. You'll know what I'm talking about," said Colin firmly. "Well, Villon?"

"No," Villon shook his head. He didn't care to see Petit Jehan at work. The whole thing smelled to him of Montfaucon. "No."

"Too queasy? Maybe you like it here better. All right. Stick to your lump of lard if that's what you want for your Christmas feast."

174

"God's body," muttered Villon. He had forgotten Christmas. It was just around the corner. And the New Year too. He couldn't meet it in this den.

"Tabary's in on it. For a lark. He doesn't know how much it'll get us. Neither do we. But it won't be a small sum. Of course," said Colin with cold scorn, "if you're afraid . . ."

Villon poured out some more wine for himself.

"We'll have"—he cleared his throat, swallowed some wine, and tried again—"we'll have to go through Saint-Simon's garden."

Colin allowed himself a tight-lipped smile.

"You'll show us, Master François," he said. "But first see that you make friends with the canon again. Let it be known that you're back at the Red Door. It's a better address."

Villon winked and nodded. But it wouldn't be so damned easy. He lifted his cup.

"Here's to a merry Christmas!"

Chapter Twelve

As he stuck his quill into the ink, Villon noted that the stuff
had thickened with cold. He held out his frozen fingers to the
candle flame. The booming of the great bell of the Sorbonne
had shaken him out of his self-absorption. He counted the
strokes. Nine o'clock. God knew he had need of God's mercy,
he thought grimly, as he made the sign of the cross. *"Angelus
Domini nuntiavit Maria,"* he muttered, *"et concepit Spiritu
Sancto. Ave Maria, gratia plena . . ."* Mary, full of grace, let
my ink hold out until I am done.

He drew the manuscript toward him. He was shuddering
with cold, and wretched, but a thing leaped and burned within
him like a candle in the bitter dark. He had only to polish off

the last few stanzas. What a legacy! And then he must be off into the freezing night to keep his rendezvous.

He bent closer over the page, smudged with old stains from the tavern table where he had started work and ill-scrawled at the bottom because of the stiffness of his fingers. He would put it all in, the sounding of the angelus, his muttered prayer, the congealing ink, the guttering candle. The date was set at the very beginning:

> *In the year fourteen fifty-six*
> *I, François Villon, clerk—wits clear,*
> *Bit in the teeth although it pricks,*
> *Free of the yoke, considering here*
> *A man's works need an overseer*
> *As sage Vegetius has taught,*
> *The good old Roman we revere,*
> *Lest all that labor go for naught . . .*
>
> *At the time mentioned, as you mind,*
> *Near Christmas, in the dead o' the year,*
> *When the wolves live on the wind,*
> *And men keep close at home for fear*
> *Of cold, hugging the fire's cheer,*
> *There came to me the wish to break*
> *Love's prison, where my very Dear*
> *Had held me in such sore heartache.*

They knew how she had served him. He had left her his heart, a pale dead thing now, a poor token, engraved with his ineradicable passion. A poet could give no more, a beggar no less. He had said he was going to Angers to forget her. That was half a lie. Did she think she was the only one who needed money? There were other ways of getting it besides selling your body. Ah, but he could not blame Katherine, he told himself for the hundredth time: it was the old woman with the crooked nose, whom may God damn, he thought, and went on rapidly skimming the blotted pages.

To Master Guillaume Villon: the bruit of my fame, my tents and pavilions. To Master Robert Vallet, poor clerk of Parliament (a good description of that fool of a financier): my underdrawers, held in pawn at the Trumelières tavern, to make a finer headdress for his lady. To Jacques Cardon, the merchant-draper: acorns from a willow grove, which is nothing, or maybe proper food for a hog, as well as a plump goose, a fat capon, and ten hogsheads of white wine daily, with a couple of lawsuits thrown in lest he grow too fat. To that nobleman, René de Montigny: three dogs (three-headed Cerberus at the gates of Hell if he chooses to take it so). To the Captain of the Watch: the Sign of the Helmet, with no vizor, so that he cannot see to catch miserable rogues. To the Bastard de la Barre: three heaps of straw to lie on while he pursues his amorous trade. To the Wolf and to Cholet: each a duck stolen from the moats toward dark, as in the good old days, and a long Franciscan's tabard to hide the booty, firewood too, and pease and bacon. And, out of pity, to three poor little shivering orphans, provision for this winter at least: firstly, to Laurens, Goussouyn, and Marceau, who have neither kindred nor goods (but who have kept the city in their usurer's gripe as long as I can remember), each a small share of my estate, or fourpence if they prefer. To two poor humble clerks—the rich and powerful Cotin and de Vitry—who sing so sweetly at the lectern (St. Benoit will relish this jest): my benefice from the University and the rent from the Gueldry house that no one has yet been able to collect. To the prisoners at the Chatelet: my mirror and the generosity of the jailer's wife. To the hospitals: the spider webs that curtain my windows. To the vagabonds who sleep under the stalls: a punch in the eye and a dog's death. To my barber: the clippings of my hair. To my cobbler: my old shoes. To my tailor: my worn-out clothes, fit for the ragman, all at less than they cost when new. To the Mendicant Orders: luscious and delicate morsels, custards, capons, and fat fowls, and the preaching of the Fifteen Signs of the Day of Judgment. To Jehan de la Garde, the master grocer (Villon's face twitched as he read): the Sign of the Golden Mortar and a crutch left by a worshiper at the shrine of St. Maur with which to pestle his mustard, with nothing but the itch of St. Anthony's fire to rack the fellow sent ahead to do me mischief (there was too covert a dig at Noel Jolis, but no matter). To Merebeuf, the draper, and de Louviers, the alderman and collector for charities: each an eggshell full of old coins . . .

Oh, there was nothing wrong with these legacies. They would furnish laughs for more than one evening, for more than a year. Villon had lived half his life over again setting these things down. Funny, how you packed a day's misery, a night's merriment into a single line, the ups and downs of a winter into a batch of verse.

Memory was a queer thing. The mind was a queer thing. They pretended to describe it in the jargon of the University. As though their crabbed Latin could trap the free-ranging spirit! Villon felt again the restlessness, the cramping sense of bondage he had known, shuffling the straw with his feet while the master droned on and on. There were scraps of it that, in spite of himself, he would never forget: the Estimative, the faculty of judging, whereby we achieve perspective, or judgment; the Simulative, the faculty of imitation; the Formative, the faculty of giving form to ideas . . . One could go mad and lunatic for months over such stuff. Villon dug into the inkhorn again, swearing as he ground the nib of his quill into the freezing liquid. There was matter for more verses in this, with a jab at Aristotle into the bargain.

He scratched away, then paused to reread the scrawled lines, in his content with himself caressing the old scar on his lip with the feathers that tipped his pen. One more stanza and he was done:

> *Made at the aforesaid date*
> *By the renowned Villon. Ah, me,*
> *He munches neither fig nor date,*
> *Dried black as an old mop is he.*
> *He's left his friends as legacy*
> *His tents and castles, every one;*
> *A few poor coppers yet there be,*
> *And soon these also will be gone.*

Eh, ho! It was finished.

Villon heaved a great sigh, shivered again, and grinned. There would be figs and dates in plenty, and pasties and tarts, and oysters and salmon, and capons and goose, sweet jellies, sharp sauces, red wines and white, songs and dancing, and at the end a gay girl on a soft bed, if it went well tonight.

The flicker of the candle drew his eye. The flame was running round the melted hillock of tallow like a frightened live thing, dipping and rising waveringly as if it were being hunted. The wick stuck up in the middle, black as a gibbet. The flame leaped, sank, quivered, died. It left a nasty smell in the nose.

Villon got up quickly and quietly, his hand on the knife at his belt. It was so cold that his cloak was wrapped close round his thin shoulders. Lie there, he said tenderly to the sheets hidden by the dark. You will talk loud enough yet for Paris to be listening.

But they must hold him no longer. He was late now. Swift,

silent, half afraid of himself in the chill blackness, he slipped out, down the stairs, with one ear cocked for the canon's stirring, opened the house door and closed it behind him so carefully the hinges might have been of velvet.

He looked up and down the street. It was covered with a light fall of snow that would make quiet going but would show footsteps too. He glanced upward. Thank God, a moonless sky. He need make no bones about going across to the Mule, but, as though he must practice secrecy, he walked lightly, moving in the shadow of the cloisters. He evaded the image of the Virgin where the votive lamp cast a swaying circle of light and looked about again sharply before he turned the corner.

Coming from the cold black street into the tavern, he was dazzled by the sudden warmth from the roaring hearth, the candle shine, the clatter of mugs and tongues. For a moment he thought they had gone without him. Then he saw at a corner table the lean short figure of Colin de Cayeux, with his black hair hanging stringily behind. Villon cast a quick look round. The others were all there. Tabary, looking fatter and more foolish than ever—he would be told nothing and given little more. Dom Nicolas, not in his monk's cassock tonight, his Picard face coppery as a harvest moon. Petit Jehan, wearing a short cloak, his dumpy fingers playing with his black beard as though they knew no shrewder work. Colin looked up, caught sight of Villon, and signaled. Petit Jehan seemed angry. Villon regretted that he was late. But he had had to finish his precious legacy. Colin would smooth matters over. The business ahead of them was not for an early hour in any case.

They had had their supper. Villon ordered some wine and helped himself to the cheese. His success with his poem, and the sharp December air, made him think himself hungry, but he found that excitement and dread killed appetite. As he ate he regarded Petit Jehan. The man fascinated him. Colin was not so clever. Yet even Colin had been scared off in the St. Mathurin affair by the barking of dogs. Villon wanted to tease the black-bearded little man by yapping like a hound, but thought better of it and finished his drink in silence. Colin gave him the wink and took Tabary by the shoulder. Dom Nicolas rose, Villon followed. Petit Jehan remained sitting at the table. He was to settle the score.

A low door in the rear led to the alley. They used that. There was a stench of ordure. A chink of light from the tavern door gleamed on a snowy pile of refuse and showed Colin's breath rising in frosty gusts as he whispered savagely into Tabary's fat face.

"You're blessed with a bad memory, Tabary. Whatever you see, whatever you hear, you'll keep mum."

"It's a hanging job," muttered Dom Nicolas.

"Shut up, you damned Picard!" And then, as though to re-assure himself: "It'll go smooth as oil."

Villon said nothing. He could pull a face, helped by that old scar on his lip, that would frighten the soul out of Tabary's body. But Colin turned on him next.

"It's nothing to put in a song, either, Master François."

Villon grinned nervously and tossed his head toward Tabary. "You'd better have him swear."

"By the body of God, Tabary, you'll hold your tongue?"

"By the body of G-GGod," stammered the fat young man.

"God save you else," muttered Villon with cruel sweetness. They started as the door opened on them. But it was only Petit Jehan.

"Come on."

It was silent going over the snow in the dark. Villon led

182

them. He had an odd feeling of its being some other man who was picking his way so carefully in the van of the other four. This was another thing altogether than the free feeds of the roistering collegian. It was different from the exploits with Jehan the Wolf and Cholet at night along the moats. Nothing to put in a song, Villon reflected. He mocked Colin de Cayeux. Strong you may be, he apostrophized him inwardly, and clever you may be, and admirably reckless, my dear friend, but famous you will never be unless François Villon puts you in a verse. Even if they make a hanging case of you, nobody will know or care by the time the rope is frayed. But if I damn you with a word, you'll be remembered, believe me.

Villon was no longer uneasy. The thought of the poem he had just made was emboldening as wine. The terror in Tabary's face chased away his own fears. Not that it was a simple matter to lead them, though he knew every step of the crazy way they were going. Night changed all the signposts it did not hide. He halted. God's birthday, had he taken them too far? No, that was the wall in front of the Saint-Simon house. Master Robert would be sorry, if he ever learned of it, that he had not been at home to entertain such visitors.

It was nothing to leap the low wall into the garden. Colin let them into the house as though it were his own. Villon would have given his little finger not to miss Tabary's face when Petit Jehan dropped his short cloak. Even in the dark you could tell that he had an armory of picklocks at his belt. Villon threw his own cape on the heap that Tabary was to watch. There was the ladder, as Colin had placed it two nights since. Once they had scaled the wall that separated the Saint-Simon house from the court of the College of Navarre, there should be no trouble. But four men humping themselves over a high wall, one after the other, even in the dead of night—it was a little past ten o'clock—must pray that the Watch was nowhere in the neighborhood. They did not leave Tabary alone without swearing him to silence again. But if, by evil chance, he were caught, he would stammer so in his terror, Villon reflected, that no one would understand him.

For himself, he had nothing to fear. They were careful workers, Colin and Petit Jehan. They had not let the sergeants get so much as a sniff of them when the dogs gave the signal at St. Mathurin. Yet, as he leaped from the top of Robert Saint-Simon's wall into the court of the College, the thrill that ran through his limbs was not from his jump, or the cold either.

Colin opened the window for them to crawl through. It was odd being inside the College at night. The familiarity of the place, especially after Dom Nicolas had lit their dark lantern at the lamp burning in the chapel, somehow increased the strangeness. Villon was glad he was not alone. Not that this was a job he could have handled. Colin cursed under his breath as he set the lantern close to the coffer. It was strongly bound with iron. Petit Jehan shook his head over the four intricate locks.

Villon stood guard with the Picard. Except for the hanging lamp above the altar and the lantern by which the other two were laboring, the place was in darkness. This was a blessing, but, as the time wore slowly on, it became oppressive. The noise of the tools as they pried at the heavy stubborn locks made the silence fearful. Restless, Villon left the Picard squatting on his heels, and strolled over to watch Petit Jehan. One did not see such a master craftsman at work every night. Colin looked up sharply.

"Did you hear something?"

Villon shook his head.

"I just wanted to see how it was going."

Colin's curse was hushed, and Petit Jehan clasped the tool he was using to his breast as the sound of a church bell boomed above them. Already the chimes all over the city were beginning to usher Christmas in, and only three locks had been forced. Petit Jehan's frowning forehead glistened with sweat, and his teeth were clamped so tightly over his underlip that it looked as though his black beard grew out of his mouth.

Villon paid no heed to Colin's anger. The last lock was giving. They raised the lid carefully. Within was a smaller iron-bound coffer, chained to the larger chest, and three cunning locks to be broken before they could come at what it held.

Colin cursed in earnest then. Petit Jehan worked furiously, in silence, merely holding out his dumpy hand to Colin for the tools as he needed them.

He smiled briefly as he wrenched the third lock out of place and with a sudden new gentleness lifted the lid of the inner casket.

Villon could have cried out. The money was not even in bags but stacked in neat piles as at a banker's. You could count it at a glance: fifty, a hundred, two hundred, five hundred crowns! Dom Nicolas had scrambled to his feet and come over to see. But they dared not stop to admire. By the clanging of the bells it must be close on midnight. The job had taken them nearly two hours.

Sweetly and swiftly the treasure went chinking into the bag Dom Nicolas held out to them. A hundred crowns apiece. But Tabary? Damn Tabary! Two crowns would pay him well for his services. He needn't know they'd taken in more than a hundred altogether. They were ready to go.

Dom Nicolas stopped them. What about the ambry near the chapel? The Picard ventured there must be not five hundred but five thousand crowns concealed there. Petit Jehan hesitated. He was worn out with his labors. But Colin looked interested. Villon glanced rapidly from one to the other. He was as tired as though he had done the master picklock's work himself. The clangor of the bells worried him. With that enormous noise they could never hear the Watch coming to surprise them. Let the ambry alone. They had enough. The others were not persuaded. Colin damned Villon for a craven novice. The Picard looked disgusted. Even Petit Jehan, yawning as he tucked his tools about his person, seemed to think they were making a mistake. Villon whispered to Colin with a grin: *"Radix omnium malorum est cupiditas."* It was years since Colin had seen the canon. Why should he recall him saying that, sucking at his cheek, his fingers arching as the tips met? But Villon remembered: his blouse stuffed with bunches of ripe grapes; Colin there too; and a furious vintner who had chased them to the Red Door itself; and the canon, with his grave voice and his deep chuckle, repeating: the love of money is the root of all evil.

"A hundred crowns is no trifle," Villon muttered.

Perhaps it was the bells that convinced them. They yielded. Back over the wall again, pulling the ladder after them. Colin holding the bag. Plucking their cloaks from the heap. And Tabary staring at them with saucer-eyes.

"Here's two crowns to celebrate Christmas with. Did you hear anything?"

"My God did I hear anything. You were gone half the night. I thought you were lotht," Tabary sighed, fingering his two crowns and then biting them anxiously.

"It was a damn nasty job." Petit Jehan shook himself all over. "Look sharp now. If you were straight with me," he snarled, "I'd get double the share of the rest of you."

"But we're not straight, my dear," chuckled Villon, shouldering Tabary aside while Colin counted out to each his part in the contents of the precious bag.

"One of us must be short. Who loses on Tabary's two crowns?" the Picard whispered.

"I do," said Villon quickly. "There's no glutton for money like a monk. It takes a poet to be generous."

"Are we never going to get out of here?" asked Colin.

Villon executed a noiseless caper and kissed his hand to the ladder in the dark. Colin had insisted that they replace it to avoid rousing suspicion in the morning. It was a beautiful ladder, a tall strong blessed ladder, a bountiful ladder, you might say, that led to such wealth.

"Good-by, my love," Villon whispered gaily, dancing after his companions like a mountebank. It was wonderful how a heavy purse put lightness in a man's heels. And the night alive with bells still sounding clamorously to ring in the Nativity. Christ! what a Christmas he would have.

> *News of Noel, now Noel let us sing.*
> *New folk, cry God forgive us everything!*
> *Sing we Noel for a new little King,*
> *Noel, Noel, Noel!*

It was a queer song for Master François Villon to be filling the White Horse tavern with on Christmas Day of the year of Grace, 1456. His black eyes darted round the table at Colin and Petit Jehan, Marion nibbling almonds, Jehanneton with her head on the Picard's shoulder, Blanche drinking from Tabary's mug, and Sidoine and Ysabeau on either side of himself. He winked at them in turn. Noel, Noel, Noel. A child's song. Except ye become as little children, said the Scriptures, ye shall not enter the Kingdom of Heaven. He was opening the gates of Heaven for them. The girls' thin metallic voices and the men's huskier ones joined in the refrain. They had known it from their cradles. New folk, cry God forgive us everything! Villon felt like a new man with last night's work behind him and the winnings in his wallet. God had something to forgive him now. But He was a master hand at that. He probably relished it as the craftsman Petit Jehan enjoyed picking locks, as a poet enjoys turning a stanza. When forgiving came a bit hard, like forcing that confounded strongbox, there was something to boast about. Surely the good Lord took pleasure in the task of pardoning a gallows bird. Villon was feeling high.

"Where do we go from here?" demanded Sidoine. A dancer's feet must ever be moving, Villon reflected.

"Angers is a good place," he observed. "There are more shows there than churches."

"You're not going there to write farces," Colin told Villon shortly with a sly look.

"Ooh, are you going all the way to Angers?" cried Ysabeau. "Reely?"

"Why not? I have an uncle there who is dying to see his famous nephew."

"Is he rich?"

"He's a monk. But something of an oddity. He could take lessons from Dom Nicolas here: the gold doesn't properly stick to his fingers."

The Picard laughed. "It doesn't stick to mine."

"But my uncle is a little foolish, dear Dom Nicolas. There is another inmate of the same abbey who has managed to get together five hundred times as much as each of us took in last night."

"Five hundred crowns?"

"That's the sum."

188

Tabary stared and flushed and pushed Blanche away from him. He stammered with indignation.

"Then you m-mmutht have g-got five hundred altogether. You t-tt-told me it was jutht one!"

"Jutht one—apiethe," Villon mocked him.

"One hundred for each of you, and two crownth for me—two crownth!" Tabary looked as though he might burst into tears.

"Shut up, Tabary. What did you do to earn more? Did you risk your fat neck?"

"I'll pay you back for thith, thee if I don't!"

"No you won't, my boy, unless you want to get jailed. They may get wind of the little affair at the Augustinians too. You got eight crowns out of that job."

"I thought this was Christmas Day," Villon said. "Peace on earth, good will to men—and women. Tickle him into a good humor, Blanche, there's a sweet girl!"

Blanche snuggled up to Tabary, but she looked cross: she would have preferred another companion.

"Fine doings, I must say!" Ysabeau eyed Villon sideways. If he had a hundred to spend . . .

"Oh, we're fine fellows," he assured her. "And you, my darlings, had better keep mum."

"Reely!"

" 'Reely.' Unless you like us better hanging up than lying down." Villon grinned.

"What d'you think we are?"

"Beautiful, beautiful ladies. The pride of Paris, the pretties of picklocks, the pets of poets. But do we not eat? Do we not drink? What manner of feast is this with half a goose on the table and the green sauce all gone and every damned jug empty?"

"What'll you have?"

"Beaune," said Tabary sulkily.

"Burgundy."

"I'd admire some wine of Arbois," murmured Ysabeau. "I do love the smell of raspberries in it."

"Arbois let it be. But is no one to call for hypocras?"

They all looked jollier at that. But Villon would not let them give the order until he had summoned the host himself. The man hurried over to the loaded table, surveying with satisfaction the platters of roast fowl and golden-skinned game, the gaping pasties running with rich juices, the custards and cheese tarts still waiting to be consumed. He had an interest in the rotisserie on one side of his wineshop as well as in the bakery on the other. Nor could he complain that they were not drinking.

"Tell me, my friend, how do you prepare your hypocras?"

The host smiled broadly and rubbed his hands together.

"With the very best spices, sir. You will get no finer hypocras in any tavern of this city."

"I believe you. But what spices?"

The taverner wagged his head understandingly.

"Cinnamon, ginger, mace . . . Oh, I assure you, the very best."

"How much cinnamon?"

"Half a pound. I pay six full farthings for it."

"And what sort of ginger?"

"White ginger."

"Not less than an ounce, I hope?"

"Indeed not, sir."

"No cloves?"

"Oh, yes, cloves, cloves."

"But pimento?"

"The finest pimento."

"You said nothing of sugar. Without sugar hypocras is undrinkable."

"Sugar of course. A pound measure."

"Fine white sugar, sparkling like the new-fallen snow and sweeter than honey dripping from the comb?"

"You have taken the words from my mouth."

"A remarkable mouth that let them fall to me. And the spices are fresh, you say, from no musty storehouse but straight from a ship that still smells of the East?"

"Fresh as butter."

"And ground to a powder."

"To a powder."

"Fine enough for these ladies' complexions?"

"I dare say."

"It was I who dared," Villon corrected him. "And the wine into which you mix them is set over a brazier and mulled and mulled and mulled and mulled. . . ."

"Yes, yes, thoroughly mulled."

"So I was saying. How long will it take you to prepare it so that it is hot in the mouth but not too hot, and sweet on the tongue but not too sweet, and good in the gullet, it cannot be too good, and quick in the veins like the frenzy of love itself?"

"A very little wait, and I shall serve you such hypocras . . ."

"But if the spices are not yet ground?"

"Oh, but they are."

"Then they cannot be fresh."

"Damn it, Villon, you've teased us enough. We'll have our wine and that quickly. And while the hypocras is heating you can serve us some Aunis, a good vintage, mind. The year forty-six will do." Colin was not a patient man, and, though the others were laughing, their mouths were watering too.

The taverner hurried off to fetch the order, relieved to be freed from the importunity of so knowledgeable a guest.

"Well"—Villon pinched Ysabeau's cheek—"you did not think I was so skilful a vintner, did you?"

"You sounded more like a grocer," said Ysabeau, for he had pinched her too hard.

Villon looked black as the devil at that thrust.

"You sounded like a poet," said Sidoine sweetly to soothe him. "Where's your lute? I want to dance."

Villon would have refused, but Sidoine thrust her brightly rouged smiling face into his, pressed her small firm scented breasts against him, and coaxed so tenderly that he ended by kissing her and pulling the lute from under his stool. The girls were instantly on their feet, but after one gay round Villon thrust his lute upon Dom Nicolas and swung Sidoine into his own arms.

She was an expert dancer. None of the other girls could match her. It was a perfect poem to see how she glided in the narrow space the tavern afforded, like a swan, like a twirling leaf, how she curtsied and turned and leaped as if she had wings at her ankles, and then, floating toward her partner, beckoned him gently with her tiny white hands (it was incredible that on ordinary days they dispensed sausages) waving like petals in a soft summer wind. Villon seized her and crushed her against him till her laughter turned to gasping.

"Thank God for hypocras! It has saved me from being pressed to death." For Villon released her at the sight of the taverner, importantly bearing the great bowl of spiced, steaming wine.

The others had already reseated themselves at the table, the girls leaning over the fragrant basin with little oh's and ah's of delight; Colin was waving the ladle, but Villon snatched it from him and gravely cut the steam with the sign of the cross. They all stared at him while he said grace, and Tabary mumbled an amazed echo of his solemn: *"Deus det."*

But the prayer ended with a wink.

"Poor little Jesus, He had nothing but mother's milk on His birthday. We have learned better in these fourteen hundred years."

"Fourteen hundred and fifty-thix," said Tabary.

"Always correct, my Tabary."

"Is it sweet enough?" asked the taverner, his hands on his hips, his face anxious and eager at once.

Villon sniffed at his cup without answering.

"And hot enough?" asked the taverner, seeing that the rest waited on Villon's verdict.

Slowly, solemnly, the poet waved his cup thrice in the air and set it to his lips.

"I hope hell is no hotter." He fetched a sigh of satisfaction. "We shall all be cinders else, and what will the devil do then?"

"I promised you the finest hypocras in Paris."

"It is not at all bad. How soon will it make me drunk?"

"Don't get drunk yet, Villon," cried Sidoine. "I want to dance again. And you must give us verses."

Did they really want him to recite? Perhaps they did. But were they worthy of his verses? They were, by God. And if not, when should a poet be expansive if not on Christmas Day? He was aching to hear them roar over his legacies. He took a slow sip of hypocras. And cleared his throat.

> *"In the year fourteen fifty-six*
> *I, François Villon, clerk . . ."*

He had forgotten them. And the threat of discovery. And Fat Margot, who had sent him to last night's dangerous work to escape her. And the beating that had sent him to Fat Margot. And Katherine de Vauselles . . .

"Near Christmas, in the dead o' the year,
When the wolves live on the wind,
And men keep close at home for fear
Of cold, hugging the fire's cheer,
There came to me the wish to break
Love's prison, where my very Dear
Had held me in such sore heartache."

His voice cracked. He cleared his throat again, winked at Sidoine, and pulled her to him. He would make them laugh yet. The bowl of wine was more than half full. Sidoine was the prettiest little piece there.

Chapter Thirteen

"Cry Noel: it comes round again!" That was a true word. Villon stared at the massed snowy clouds riding so gently through the autumnal blue and sighed. They reminded him of the drifts on the rue St. Jacques that had made the Christmas fires within seem cosier, the wine sweeter, the goose richer. He was near to another Christmas now, but not to the rue St. Jacques. The saliva ran into his mouth as he thought of the feast of a year ago. He spat into a ditch.

He felt fairly safe at this distance. He wondered where the wily Petit Jehan had stowed himself, and the Picard monk. He knew that, after the affair of the College of Navarre, Colin had made for Brittany. To Tabary he gave scarcely a thought. The fat fool.

Fear of the danger at his heels was less keen than anxiety as to what lay ahead. He had not committed murder this time. It was not Angers he was trudging toward, with its famous steeples and its all but Parisian whorehouses. His talk about the rich crony of his uncle had been an empty boast. He was approaching the little town where the dead peddler had expected to get rid of his stolen goods. Villon flattered himself that he would not get the worst of it again in dealing with a fence. A man learns. But the devil of it was that he had nothing on which he could get money.

Slouching along ahead of him was a tall man, lame, with a staff in his hand, and his hat, which sat oddly on his head, hung round with cockleshells like a pious pilgrim's or an accomplished rascal's. Villon walked faster to get abreast of the fellow.

The pair eyed each other askance. Villon muttered a greeting in the jargon of the Companions. The man replied in the same queer speech. By mute consent they turned in together at the tavern on the right and sat down at the same table.

While they waited for their drinks Villon studied the stranger. He saw now why his hat sat awry: he lacked an ear. Villon judged him to have been a soldier by trade who, since the peace between the houses of Burgundy and Orléans, had gotten his living as he could. It was easy to believe that a man would risk his neck rifling a coffer rather than face enemy cannon. Villon had never seen war, but the horrors of its aftermath that had haunted his childhood were more vivid than the memory of his last meal.

The stranger drew from his wallet a pair of dice and held

them in his hard palm as a jeweler holds the stones he promises to place in an elegant setting. Villon had his own pair. But he had profited more by Colin's instruction in the jargon than by what he had taught him about cogging the bones.

"I'll beat you at billiards," he volunteered.

"Ah," said the stranger, "I saw a fellow play billiards once, in Dijon . . ."

The drinks came. The stranger began describing the game. It had stayed in his memory because it had been so brilliant and because the player would never display his skill again. He had been taken with the other members of the Dijon gang and cooked to death in a vat of boiling oil as a counterfeiter. A hot end for such a cool one. Name of Turgis. Christopher. A taverner.

It was no new story to Villon. Christopher Turgis was the blackest sheep in Robin's family. Did the stranger know Robin too? If he had ever put foot in Paris, he must have had a cup of wine at the Sign of the Pine Cone. He had. He knew his way about Paris. He'd only just come from there. The Sign of the Golden Lion, near the prison, the Sign of the Mule on the rue St. Jacques—there was no street in the world like the rue St. Jacques—and the girls on the Petit-Pont, the stranger whistled. And there was one house, run by a girl as big as a barrel: he had spent a night in that house. He laughed. But she had failed him in one respect, had Fatty. She had promised to show him her pet customer, a devil of a fellow (Villon glowed), nothing much to look at, the girls said (Villon winced), but a wit, a songsmith who had no match (Villon nodded). He had even made verses in the jargon.

"I know whom you mean," said Villon. "He has a reputation in Paris. A University man."

"I thought he was one of us," said the one-eared man.

"He's one of us right enough," grinned Villon. "But he's not in the pay of the Khan—I'll vouch for that."

"He's in with Colin de l'Escailler's gang, I thought."

"Colin de Cayeux," muttered Villon.

"What's that?" the stranger asked with quick suspicion.

"God's body, a Coquillard is not so stingy as to use one name only. Tell me more about Fatty's pet poet. I make verses myself when I've nothing better to do."

The stranger spread his knees apart, set his great hands on his thighs, and shook his head.

"That's a trick I can't turn. I couldn't set two rhymes together if you were to hang me for it."

"They'll hang you for something else," suggested Villon. "But what about Master What's-his-name?"

"Ah, him," said the stranger. "Villon, they called him. Jehan Villon, or was it François? Never met him, you say?"

Villon shrugged.

"I may have been at Fat Margot's when he was there. Now you name him, I believe he's paid for my drinks once or twice, though he hated doing it. Yes, by God, and I've slept with his girl too."

"He didn't beat you up?"

"It was he that got the beating," answered Villon, wryly.

The stranger laughed.

"They were talking about some row over a woman. Fatty's crazy about this Villon herself. Said he was mixed up with a girl of the middle class—relatives in the Church, money, all that sort of thing. Fatty was singing some song about her," said the one-eared man. "She was to be married to a rich old devil, in the salt trade, if I remember right, but it came to nothing. He got sick of his bargain before the deal was closed."

"What d'you mean?" Villon had to hear it again. Katherine: not married? His heart jumped in his breast. Katherine, my dear, my love.

The stranger gave him a long look. Villon read what he was thinking: what's all this to you? It won't put money in your purse. I've seen oddities in my time, but never one of the brethren hungry for gossip as a woman.

"Damn me, are you sure?"

The stranger's battered face broke into a slow smile.

"Sure, Villon," he answered.

Villon glanced away. He had been strung taut as a lute string. By the quick inward sense of release, he felt how intensely he must have fixed the stranger.

He was happy, he was wretched. He was proud and ashamed at once. He could think of Katherine again without the burning misery that had inflamed every imagination of her married to Jehan de la Garde. Phoo! Villon wished the grocer pickled in one of his own salt tubs. But he could not think of her without pain. That night at Fat Margot's, the one-eared man must have heard enough and more of Master François. The wit. The songsmith. The lover cheated and denied. It must be a great thing for him to meet the famous man at last and to discover what a figure he was (nothing much to look at, the girls said): short and bony, black as a scarecrow and as weather-stained, with his scarred mouth and his sliding eyes. Villon blinked to hide the tears that filled them.

A man could play the melancholy lover among knights and ladies: it was the elegant old fashion to be dying of a broken heart, with Lancelot, it might be, smiling mournfully from the tapestry above the gilded couch and Alain Chartier's verses on your sad lips. But in a provincial tavern, to the noise of billiard balls, under the cold eyes of a one-eared thief . . .

Villon shrugged. He must find out the fellow's game. Profit by it if he could.

The stranger leaned across the table and put a heavy hand on his arm.

"Forget her. No woman's worth burning your fingers for. And don't go chasing back to Paris too soon. It's not healthy."

Villon's eyes lit with a question. The stranger nodded slowly.

"Montigny's swinging."

"René!" Villon grinned, but not with joy. "René," he repeated in a whisper.

"That same. They say his sister tried to get them to let him off. And she big with child. She didn't like to see the brat's uncle hanged before it was born. They finished him all the same."

Villon saw René, the blond, handsome, smiling face, the jerking shoulders, the long fingers with their trick of snapping whenever he thought of easy money, and when did he think of anything else? Villon saw him: the long hands that must be green shreds and the shrewd face picked of its eyes, black and swollen. God, it was strange to know he was out of the world. He had seemed older than Villon by a good deal in the University days, when the canon had smiled on his ward's friendship with old Etienne's nephew. Later on, the difference in years had mattered as little as the difference in birth. Old Etienne must be still alive, maybe his thin fingers were trembling over the canon's chessboard this minute. No more games for René. He'd loved gambling better than women. The chance of big money. He had financiers' blood in his veins. He hadn't had the luck, that was all. René.

"Come out of it," said his companion in a loud voice.

Villon glanced at the one-eared man and smiled again nervously. And took another gulp of wine. René hanged.

But Katherine. She was free. His face must have changed at this thought.

"That's better," said the one-eared man.

The door opened. A couple of young men came in singing at the top of their voices. They looked as though they belonged to a wedding party. They were followed by three older men, not quite ruffians. The one-eared man surveyed them and muttered: "By God, la Hire!" The last member of the group, a short blond man with a cast in one eye, nodded to him curtly. Villon guessed that he wanted to milk the youths without help. He squinted inquisitively at Villon. Villon stared back and then took in his companions.

The young fellows were not blind drunk, but it was clear the money in their belts would put them to the torture till it was spent. La Hire's comrades were a dark scar-faced man and a tall clerk who twisted the French tongue like the Goddams and must have come from overseas.

The one-eared man had seemed slow of speech and movement. But he was brisk enough in making Villon and himself free of the other party.

"Glic?" asked the one-eared man.

"Condemnade," said la Hire.

"Good enough."

The deck of cards la Hire had been shuffling was placed in the middle of the table. La Hire drew.

"What'll you have?"

"A queen," the boy laughed.

"No go."

La Hire drew again, asked the same question of the next

player, and gave another refusal. The Irishman made the first lucky guess. But when his turn came again he missed. On the third round la Hire was too busy scratching his head to look at him as he put his query. The Irishman demanded a king: a king turned up. On the fourth round one of the youths guessed right. On the sixth, at the Irishman's turn, la Hire blew his nose with his fingers, and the Irishman got the card he asked for. Villon was no longer in doubt as to their game.

He maneuvered it so that he should be the next to draw the cards from the deck. La Hire looked sulky, but Villon knew how to soothe him. At first la Hire failed to catch on. But when Villon scratched his head, the Irishman asked him, in that queer accent of his, whether he'd caught la Hire's fleas. La Hire took the hint, demanded a king, got a king, and squinted at Villon so that he burst out laughing. After that it was easy.

Villon had not hoped for such a windfall. Perhaps his luck had turned. Katherine was still the demoiselle de Vauselles. The one-eared man must have some good scheme up his ragged sleeve.

By the time the two boys had staggered off with too much under their belts to remember what had been taken from them, even la Hire was in a better humor.

They were all hungry, and the Irishman was commissioned to fetch a piece of pork and a fowl for their dinner. The one-eared man bade him bring along some apples and chestnuts for roasting in the fire. If a man wanted something hot and sweet at the end, he could take up with one of the girls who had begun drifting in. For himself, he would be content with a good dinner and enough wine to ensure a long night's sleep. He wasn't as young as he had been. Not like this one, he said, jerking a thumb at Villon, who grinned back at him.

There was little talk over their supper. But when they sat

before the hearth, waiting for the apples to brown and munching the mealy nuts, Villon listened sharply to the casual words of his companions. They must be planning something ampler than the fleecing of a couple of gilded youths. Who was la Hire? Where had the Irishman been working last? And the dark man, who seemed to come from Dijon: he maybe had a commission from the Great Khan himself. Had any of them ever had traffic with Colin, with René? They had not been mentioned in the presence of the young prodigals, but now the one-eared man invited Villon to drink a health to the hanged man's soul. The others pulled faces, cursed briefly. It was all in the day's work.

During the play Villon had forgotten René. The reminder irked him. He would see René's pallid face leaning toward him, his shoulders jerking, and then he would see him stretched on the gallows, stiff and monstrous. Villon thrust the sight out of mind. He came back to the thought of Katherine. He began to sing.

"That's a brave song," said the Irishman. "Who wrote it now?"

"A trifle," replied Villon proudly. "I did."

"By God, that's great. Sing us another, lad. I never thought to meet with a man of learning in this place."

"No more did I," admitted Villon, cheered by the flattering tone.

"I can turn a tune when I've a mind to," said the Irishman. "Did you ever hear of Sidelius Scotus?"

"I've heard of Duns Scotus." Villon winked.

"They were born in the same country, my poor green isles, and they both landed in Paris, but they were no more like than you to the Bishop of Orléans.

"Orléans?" asked la Hire.

"What of it?"

"Nothing." He shrugged. "I've a stepbrother in the Duke's service."

Villon pricked up his ears. The Duke's verses might not be as fresh as his own, but Orléans was nothing to sneeze at. If wishes were horses, that was where he would be this minute, instead of with this riffraff who didn't even know how to praise him properly.

"Good job?"

"Barber."

"To the Duke?"

"To his dogs."

They laughed.

"Sure. He trims the spaniels so they're fit to appear at Court. He can have it." La Hire grimaced. "There's nothing in it for us," he added.

"Wonder if he'd trim me," said Villon. They laughed again. But Villon was serious. The verse tourneys at Blois were famous. Why shouldn't Master François find a soft berth there?

"You don't know Sidelius then." The Irishman's patriotism was not to be quenched by the Duke of Orléans. He pointed a crooked finger at Villon. " 'Twas he gave a name to the sort of thing we should be hearing from you now: he called 'em saturated songs."

"Saturated songs." Villon savored the phrase. "Damn good." He wetted his throat. "How's this?"

It was his ballade on Jehan Cotart that he gave them: "Old Daddy Noah, planter of the vine . . ."

The one-eared man applauded mightily. Villon was his discovery. The Irish clerk began to match songs with him. The others, dolts who had never heard of Master François, were yet sufficiently mellowed to make good listeners. Three of them

204

had girls on their knees. The prettiest sat on the Irishman's lap and was jogged like a child to the music.

It was during a short pause, while the others were playing with the women, that the one-eared man took Villon by the elbow and drew him aside.

"See here," he muttered. "La Hire's all right. And the Irishman seems straight. But I don't trust the other. He may be in the pay of the Khan, but he may be in the pay of somebody else too. What do you say we slip off?"

"Slip off?" Villon had his eye on a girl, a slim black-haired piece who called herself Belet.

"Have you ever been to Bourges?"

"Bourges? It would take us more than a fortnight to get there."

"You've the legs for it. And you're smart. I could see that if I had only one eye," he grinned, pulling the stump where his left ear had been. "I'll let you in on a good job there."

"What's wrong with this town?"

"Nothing doing here now. We don't need to do more than ten miles a day. It's a sure thing." He began whispering rapidly in the jargon. Villon listened, but his eyes followed the little Belet. She was making love to the Dijon man, who looked as though he were about to fall asleep, and once she winked at Villon over his head.

"We go through Blois . . ."

"Let's take la Hire. We can see his brother, the barber: a razor wouldn't be out of the way," Villon sniggered.

"At the Duke's? I don't want any dukes. It's the bankers that'll butter our loaf. Maybe Jacques Coeur died in Chios last year. Maybe he was finished long before that. But a fortune like his, big enough to buy the Pope, don't vanish overnight. And listen . . ."

It sounded good, the plan of the one-eared man. But Villon hesitated. He had not forgotten René. He wanted news about the robbery of the College of Navarre. He was out of reach of the law here. Why take another chance? The one-eared man had mentioned Blois. The name stuck in his mind. If he had a letter to the Duke of Orléans! It would be softer living than any job in Bourges could bring him. And no risk. No risk, René, he said to his friend's ghost, d'you know what that means?

"What's the matter? Isn't it easy money?"

Villon looked at the one-eared man and looked away.

"Maybe I'll land in Bourges. Some day. Maybe I'll be sorry I didn't go in with you. But now—I'm for Blois."

"The Duke's?" cried the one-eared man. "What's your game?"

"Poetry." Villon was watching the little Belet and did not see his companion's face. "I was a thief before I was a poet. But Orléans doesn't know that. He doesn't know what a prince of poets I am, either. He'll find out."

"La Hire can't help you," said the one-eared man sulkily, "if that's what you're counting on. He hates his brother."

"Christ, man, do you think I want an introduction to the barber? I'll have a letter to the Duke in my wallet."

The one-eared man stared at Villon.

"Where'll you get it?"

"I can write," said Villon.

The little Belet had fastened her eyes on his, and at his snigger she laughed too, so that it was as though he were look-ing in a mirror at his own amusement.

The Dijon man lay with his head on the table.

Villon clapped the one-eared fellow on the shoulder with

another laugh for his sour look. Then he rose and strolled over to la Belet.

"Ah, troubadour!" she cried.

He grinned, but he did not see her. He was thinking of how he would phrase the letter to the Duke.

She touched the scar on his upper lip.

"Little rabbit," she murmured. "You can sing with that, little rabbit. Can you kiss?"

It was the devil to be harelipped. What would they think of it at Blois? You could tell it was no unlucky birthmark. A man could get a cut like that in a tourney, too.

"You're not angry," the girl coaxed, stroking his cheek.

He surveyed the others scornfully, the one-eared man, frowning into his cup, the sleeping drunk, the barber's brother, the Irish clerk. It was too bad if a whore thought him no better than they.

"It must be wonderful," she sighed, with honey in her voice, "to be a poet."

But a poet must be among poets, thought Villon glumly. He might make verses of dangling corpses like René and cheap pieces like la Belet, he might tell the truth about the whole damn show, but he wanted men who understood to listen and to praise. They might live soft as dukes, though Orléans himself had been an exile and a prisoner, in his best years too, but they'd know what he was after, the words, the live words, the sure music . . . If things had gone differently, if he'd not got that scar on his lip, that other scar deep in his soul, God damn it, if he'd not been tempted by Colin's fancy schemes, if he had not lost Katherine . . .

"Sweetheart." The girl was after him again.

He took her cup and drank. Nothing mattered. Not René.

207

Not Katherine. Not the money he had stolen from the College and spent. Not the money he had won tonight and that she was trying to get away from him. She'd get it, she'd get enough of it. Nothing mattered. It was all over before you could wink.

He seized her, threw her on the bench, flung himself upon her. Her slightness surprised him, angered him. He was all blind haste. But after, as he lay there, in a kind of appeased bitterness, strange luxuries blossomed slowly behind his closed lids. Dim memories of Anjou, of archery and laughter in hedged gardens, of a distant evening at the Provost's house, harping and dancing, dissolved into anticipations of Blois, like colors and shapes out of some jeweled Book of Hours. Suddenly the girl jerked away from him, coughing. He got up with a curse.

"I couldn't help it, it caught me, here," she gasped.

He didn't answer.

It was near dawn. The landlord would be coming with the score. The one-eared man had disappeared. The girl wanted money too. You couldn't hold it. Not the coin. Not the dream.

The church bells were at it again. The tavern smelled of wine fumes and staleness. He was sick with it all. He wanted fresh air, a fresh scene, God, he wanted sleep. He threw her some money. Too much. And staggered outside. He was filled with hatred and self-contempt. He sat down in the street, his dizzy head in his hands, a melancholy verse on his lips: "In the abyss of dolor sunk."

Where had he heard that? It was a line from a poem by Charles, Duke of Orléans.

Chapter Fourteen

He picked himself up with the determination to go to Blois. The Duke was a patron of poets. He was known to like peddlers, too. They said you could always get in at the castle with a pack of oddities, tricky little knives, rosaries with relics hanging from them, lute strings, and spectacles. Villon, glancing down at his stained suit, considered presenting himself at the postern gate as a packman. Yes, and then?

There must be someone in the neighborhood who would help him to be received properly. By God, there was the little Perdrier: Henri, who had turned moneylender like his father, set up shop in the town of Blois, and served the ducal house. He would go there, borrow enough to buy a decent outfit, get into the Duke's good graces, and—hurroo! his fortune was made.

It was not easy to convince the little Henri that the lean vagabond who demanded an audience of him should not be kicked out of the back door as quickly as he had slipped in at the front. Villon had to remind him how he had chummed it with his brothers when their escapades had been the envy of this younger son of the house of Perdrier. He named the Montignys familiarly (not René but his fine relatives), spoke intimately of his wealthy fellow-student, Charruau, of the King of Sicily's solicitor, André Courant, the Duke's friend, of Taranne, whose father had helped to ransom the Duke's brother from the Goddams. He managed to mix just enough truth with his prodigious lies to enchant the little Henri into believing more than half of them. His explanation of his present shabby state was simple: on his way to the castle, where he had been invited to take part in a verse tourney, he had been set upon by ruffians in a wretched inn, robbed of his substance, beaten, and left for dead. God alone knew how he had managed to get this far, where he knew he would find an old, a precious, a trusted friend. He could not go to his Grace like this. Even the little Henri had mistaken him for a beggar!

Villon wheedled a loan, at usurious interest, from the younger Perdrier, together with a recommendation to the best tailor in Blois. He had pretended to the little Henri that he knew everything about the castle. By the time he had done pumping the tailor he knew a good deal.

There was no verse tourney forward. There had been one, very magnificent, in the spring of the year. King René of Anjou had come on a visit with a fine retinue and such gifts as a king may present to the cousin of a king: gilded javelins, silver enameled goblets, Turkish knives, splendid horses. Villon recalled the visit he had paid to Anjou as a boy under Courant's tutelage, recalled the King's broad smooth-shaven, snub-nosed peasant face. He would not see it here: Anjou had returned home months ago, leaving behind his son, Lorraine d'Anjou, the devoted servant of her Grace. The Duchess had not been able to enjoy hawking and hunting and dancing with her princely gallant these last months, however. After seventeen years she was about to present Orléans with an heir.

"His Grace has been a father before," Villon reminded the garrulous tailor.

"Father of a gray-haired woman by now. Which will make this child remarkable, whatever it is."

"He must have been married out of his cradle the first time."

"They say the bride wept quarts of tears—to have to take a little boy for a husband. Richard II's widow, she was. She died in childbirth: that's why he's in such a fever about her Grace. Will you just raise your arm a little so I can measure?"

"But there was a second wife." Villon must get it straight as the seam on his new suit.

"Bonne d'Armignac: she brought him money and troops but no children. She died while he was in exile."

"You'd think he'd have gone back to Orléans, once his ransom was paid, instead of coming here."

"The castle couldn't stand the siege. You should see what the Goddams' cannon did. I come from Orléans," said the tailor, standing back to admire his handiwork. "It's a great town. They say"—he stepped up to Villon again and pulled at the puff of the sleeve—"they say that, when the Emperor asked the King which city he preferred above all in the realm of France, he answered: Orléans!"

"Yes," responded Villon quickly, "and then the Emperor asked, 'What about Paris?' And the King said, 'Paris is no city, it's a world.'" He paused. "I come from Paris."

"So?" The tailor was not impressed.

Villon began flinging questions again. What sort of man was his Grace? Generous? Thrifty? He was too old for tennis: was he fond of cards? Did he still hate the Goddams? He had been compelled to stay on their beastly little island for a quarter of a century—maybe he had come to like them, as, after a quarter of a century of beastly living, Villon admired life.

Well, the tailor explained, stepping forth and back again, yardstick in hand, one eye on his precious tray of pins, his Grace was careful with money. He'd had to pawn his shirt, not to mention his jewels, his books, his tapestries, his lands, to pay the ransom. Eighty thousand crowns when he got his liberty and twice as much again after he was out of England. And then there was that business of trying to get back Asti: he had no luck there. That was why he kept after his stewards, trying to cheapen the wines and the spices and the charcoal—you needed plenty with a household that had four-score people in service. He was fussy about food, too: never touched a morsel before he'd tested it for poison. He'd been on the lookout ever since his trouble with that Italian devil: Sforza, was it? But his Grace was kind too: there wasn't a Friday that he didn't wash the feet of thirty poor folk with his own hands and see them properly fed; he'd sent the tailor's wife some special fruit at her lying-in, and he'd sometimes pay the gambling debts of her Grace's ladies. The Duchess loved cards, she was a gay one, but not the Duke. His passion was chess: he had a Lombard champion up at the castle now who played blindfold.

"His Grace isn't much like his father, eh?"

"Louis of Orléans? Ah, him! He staked his own horse at

cards. They say he used to be ready for church at matins because he'd been up all night dicing. He wasn't home much. The Queen kept him in Paris."

And now, thought Villon, he's back in Paris, moldering in the chapel at the Celestines, with an empty brain-case and his left hand sliced off at the wrist: the Burgundians had made a nasty job of murdering him. And his son Charles was getting an heir from a niece of the house of Burgundy. The old feud had been interred to the chime of wedding bells. Villon grinned.

And frowned. He misliked the gossipy tailor's picture of the master of Blois: a deaf, ailing, timid man, who could not forget that he had spent the best years of his life in exile, an aging man, jealous of his young wife, impatient with new fashions in dress and verse-making, a man whose sense of comedy was confined to gentle whimsies, whose melancholy could never take the measure of Villon's giant despairs. But the birth of the child that the Duchess was carrying was bound to open his heart and his purse strings: there would be royal festivities at the castle. Christmas was coming to make greater cheer. Eh, ho! François Villon, though he must sit below the salt, was more than Charles's peer in poetry.

His fine suit and his forged letters won him entry to the castle. But he was not there two days before he discovered that it was no great matter to be a poet at Blois. Everyone wrote verses, the downy-lipped cupbearers and squires, the bearded soldiers and seneschals, the stewards and secretaries, old Master Jean Cailleau, the Duke's friend and physician, as well as the handsome young major-domo, Gilles des Ormes, the Duke's favorite, and his regular partner at chess.

Aside from that, the gentlemen and ladies of the Court did what men and women do everywhere. There was eating and drinking, gaming and lusting at Blois as in the streets and taverns of Paris. There were services in the chapel duly, and sometimes priest thrashed priest, just as at home. Villon relished the luxury, the royal elegance, but the perpetual ceremony disgusted him. He could accustom himself neither to the unctuous courtiers with whom the rich rooms swarmed nor to the dogs. Whether it was one of the spaniels looking for a caress or a greyhound approaching like one in ducal livery, he would back away. In Paris dogs were a menace. On the road they were fiends. He hated them. To revenge himself he would tease the Duchess's monkey or her fool, who, like the monkey, wore an iron collar.

Villon was keeping a circle of eager youths laughing at his sallies when a general movement greeted the appearance of a tall, heavy, somewhat stooped figure, his black velvet set off by chains of thick gold, his pale face wearing a look at once distinguished, affable, and a trifle strained. This was Charles, Duke of Orléans.

He smiled faintly, glanced about, singled out Jean Meschinot, the Breton soldier, de Villebresme, his ambassador to Hungary, and several ladies, with a gracious nod, and passed among the company like a proud ship sailing down the Seine, making a flurry among the lesser craft, or perhaps more like a sacred image in a Church procession, before which the crowd fell back with murmurs of reverence and hushed excitement, only the nearest priests taking it all too much for granted, though they made a show of due solemnity.

Villon was grateful when the signal was given that it was time to go in to dinner.

From his place at the lower table he watched all with a malicious eye, not ceasing to heap his plate with the delicacies that a troop of servingmen bore on elaborately dressed platters.

The bread masters and cupbearers, as befitted those who carried the materials of the Blessed Sacrament, ranked above those who bore the main dishes, a convention that seemed to Villon of a piece with the Duke's verses: all airs and allegory. His Grace was no great eater. He amused himself feeding scraps to the spaniels that begged, moist-eyed, at his knee and to the monkey that perched on his chair and kept trying to dip a long mauve hand into his plate. He spoke seldom and smiled only once. At the beginning of the meal they brought him a special little box—his Grace had a passion for little boxes—in which he kept his fork. In this toy he showed a child's pleasure. But he looked grave as he touched every dish offered him with a golden "test" clasped by a serpent's tongue. As a preventive against poison, the cup he drank from was of polished serpentine. The poor, thought Villon, with a crooked smile, must suffer hunger pangs from want of bread. The great, whose tables were loaded with carp and salmon, roast goose, stuffed peacocks, quince jellies, and cream tarts, starved themselves out of fear.

"I'll swear," Villon observed to his neighbor Fleury, the tambour player, "that chaplain yonder hasn't had but four draughts of wine since we sat down."

"He'll have precisely five," answered Fleury.

"How do you know?"

"For the five wounds of Christ. And he'll take the last in two sips."

"Why two?"

"For the blood and water that flowed from the side of our Saviour."

At last the meal was drawing to a close. The Duke was cleaning his teeth with two small silken cords. Sugared spices in silver dishes and great bowls of fruit were being passed. The chaplain helped himself to an apple. Villon watched him as he cut off a quarter of the fruit, laid it aside, peeled the remainder, ate it slowly, and then consumed the quarter skin and all.

"Explain that," he demanded of Fleury.

"What?"

"The apple."

"Oh, he always takes them that way. The three quarters he eats in memory of the Holy Trinity. The fourth in memory of the love with which our Lady gave the apple to the infant Jesus."

"But why doesn't he pare that quarter?"

"Because little boys eat apples skin and all."

Villon grimaced. More allegory. He was sick of it. That pious old man on the other side of the table put the clock back two centuries.

He had been glad to go in to dinner. He was relieved when the ceremonious meal was concluded. The company rose and scattered among the tapestried rooms for music, dancing, and games.

His Grace sat down before the chessboard. Young Gilles des Ormes stood by to help him against the Lombard champion. It was wonderful to watch this Juvenal Negro striding up and down, calling out his moves without a glance at the board. But the wonder soon palled.

Villon glanced about the hall with its knots of courtiers and ladies, a couple flirting over a curio they pretended to examine, the chamberlain and the comptroller wagging their scented beards over the necessity for exterminating the Turks, a group of ladies-in-waiting helpless with laughter as they teased a pretty page, the dancers in the farther room shouting: the Duke's monkey had got among the musicians and was solemnly plaguing the lutanist.

216

Villon moved from one group to another, his ears pricked to catch what they could.

"They took Byzantium. God knows where they'll move next. There's no man who hates the infidels more than I do. But I respect them: they're a power to be feared."

"Pearl buttons. And the sleeve slashed this way."

"It cost him his bishopric."

"I tell you the bankers had the barons in their fists. I'd give half my lands for a little ready money."

"So she said to him, if he would come after vespers . . ."

"Where should he send his son? A knight's not worth his ransom any more."

At the far end of the great hall, with a group of her Grace's ladies, stood Georges Chastellain and Olivier de la Marche. Villon was inclined to avoid them: they had not invited his collaboration on the masque they were composing for the coming festivities. But he crossed the room, hopeful of saying something to catch the attention of the keen-faced nobleman beside them: their patron, Pierre de Brezé.

"You don't want to play the Castle of Love." It was little Marie Blossette speaking, the one with the large dark-fringed eyes and the dimples that made deep creases in her softly colored cheeks. "That's so dull!"

Villon agreed silently. It was another of those courtly games that bored him with stale allegory. De la Marche suggested a debate.

"Oh, yes!" la Blossette dimpled deliciously. She paused only a moment for her topic: "Are men more constant than women?"

"No, no, we know what they will say. This is better: Which would you prefer: that they spoke ill of your mistress and you found her virtuous, or the contrary?"

Georges Chastellain demurred. Let them rather argue as to which lady is the more lovable, the foolish beauty or the plain-featured wit.

Pierre de Brezé glanced with a dry smile from the courtly poet to the dimpling lady-in-waiting. "You, of course, will speak for the foolish beauty."

Chastellain bowed acceptance.

None of the young men offered to speak against him. Here was Villon's chance to distinguish himself before de Brezé. He stepped forward.

"If your ladyships allow me, I shall be glad to argue on the other side."

"Good." Pierre de Brezé nodded and clapped his hands. "Chastellain, you shall begin."

As the ladies settled themselves to listen, the twinkling of their jewels, the rustling of their satins made Villon think of the tuning up of the Court orchestra. He turned quickly to face his opponent. The lectures at the University had never drawn the same attention from him.

Chastellain was not as dull as the moralizing verses with which he was setting the fashion at Blois, but Villon hoped to outwit him. At the same time he was wondering how he could avoid offending the ladies by a defense of homeliness, however witty. Above all, he wanted to hear de Brezé's approving laugh, to have the praise of that powerful nobleman. If de Brezé's patronage were added to the small stipend he received from the Duke, he would have enough money to silence Henri Perdrier's demands for a while, he could take part in a card game without fear of the consequences, he might even buy himself new gloves or a pretty dagger that would support the self-assurance of a Parisian nobody.

He joined in the applause as Chastellain came to his conclusion. His low bow to the little company before he opened his own discourse concealed the malicious spark in his black eyes.

He began by reciting the motto of the house of Orléans: righteousness and judgment are the foundation of Thy throne. Righteousness, he declared boldly, was on his side, and judgment in the gift of the ladies present: further, since they were as wise as they were lovely, he ventured to speak before them against the foolish beauty.

Villon could play the University man here. He proceeded, in academic fashion, to name all the fair women in history, whose folly had brought shame and ruin with it, from Helen of Troy to the damnable Queen Blanche of Navarre. He also mentioned Dido.

"We know that she was lovely, since the pious Aeneas yielded to her charms. But we know too that she could not hold him: ergo, she was a fool. His departure brought her to despair, and she threw herself into the flames. It was a death proper to a heathen, but one that only a foolish woman would invite. Nor should we forget who was Dido's rival—Aeneas deserted her for his true love: Italy! And Italy is still beloved for her intelligence, though she is not so fair as the fair realm of France."

There was a murmur of approval—or was it impatience?

Villon shifted his stance. It would serve his argument better to recite the names of those ladies, admired for their wit, though with nothing to be said for their looks. He found himself at a loss. Judith of Bethulia had got into the enemy's camp by sheer cleverness, but she would scarcely have triumphed over Holofernes had she been a plain girl. Delilah was shrewd enough, but a handsome wench into the bargain. The brilliant gifts of Héloïse were not remembered more than the beauty that had undone her learned lover. He wished himself back at home in some tavern where a brawl would have interrupted the debate before it got so far. Who cared for ugly women, however witty?

De Brezé had folded his arms and was tapping them with his fingers. Get on with it, Villon, he admonished himself.

"Granted"—he looked at la Blossette—"that beauty wins a woman her lovers. Intelligence gives her the bright eye and the sweet speech that keeps them. Having once snared a man by her looks, she binds him to her by her wit. If a woman is a beauty and a fool, you forget her appearance when she opens her lips to speak, and after she has spoken you look in vain for what formerly delighted you. But if she is plain and clever, once she exhibits her wit, you ignore forever whether her nose is long or short. Time, sweet ladies, that is the destroyer of nearly every excellence—that bows the straight back, digs trenches in the smooth skin, spoils the good mouth—time cannot injure wit. Like wine, it ripens with years, and while other graces wither holds its bouquet."

He thought suddenly of the old armouress. She had had beauty in her day. Who cared for her stories now? There is no hope for you, Villon, he told himself. But he must go on.

"The company will forgive me"—his black eyes swept them with a quick smile—"if I bring in a reference more usual at the University than at Court. But these accomplished ladies will recognize the authority of Aristotle.

"Man, said our philosopher, is engaged in an activity peculiar to him and not shared by the rest of creation. It is not mere life, which he has in common with vegetables. Even a cabbage head is alive. And if we set apart the life of nourishment and growth, and consider the life of sensation, that again man shares with his horse, his hawk, and"—Villon was about to say "his lice" but hastily substituted—"every dumb beast. There remains," he pursued, "yet another kind of life: that of the rational nature. We might say that beauty is the part of vegetables: witness his Grace's gardens, and of animals: witness his Grace's palfrey. But wit is the sign and token of reason, its exercise is a purely human activity. As reason raises man above brute creation to a place a little lower than the angels, so wit raises woman to the height of man and sets the lady born above the flat-eared peasant."

Were they listening? He must make haste to show de Brezé that he could moralize as well as the pious Chastellain.

"But we must not dwell too long on the notions of a philosopher who, however great, was yet a pagan. Think rather how the most perfect Lover that ever walked the earth, He Who spent His blood for us all, preferred the wise to the foolish virgins and made no question of their beauty."

La Blossette glanced surreptitiously into her mirror. This was not the way, thought Villon, impatient with himself. He was not in chapel but at Court. He dropped to one knee and held out his hands.

"Ladies!" he cried. "I have argued as though you were all old and ugly, and I desired to praise the only arrow left in your quiver, to flatter you into granting me the victory. But I am so dazzled by your beauty that I cannot fitly praise it, and so I have argued in favor of wit. Gracious ladies, in the end, it is neither the one nor the other that is the hope and help of your lovers in their secret need, and in the name of the Holy Virgin Who is Queen of queens and Mistress of us all, I throw myself on your mercy!"

Villon rose from his knee with a rapid glance round the little circle. These ladies, like summer fruits in silver, these gentlemen stiff as swords with jeweled hilts, how could he win their praise? And if he lost, the worst was not the blow to his pride, heavy though that would be, but the fact that de Brezé would remain unimpressed: there would be no ducats for poor François. It was a cruel thing to be penniless on the road. He doubted whether it was not crueler to be poor at Court.

"Prettily turned, Master François."

Villon bowed to de Brezé with flashing eyes and springing hope.

"What do you say, ladies? To whom shall we award the laurel?"

They disputed the matter with ready laughter. The ladies, Villon thought, were on his side, but the gentlemen counted among them Chastellain's collaborator, Oliver de la Marche, Blosseville, the scholarly young squire who had just added Chastellain's history of Burgundy to his famous collection of books, Jean Meschinot, who had matched Chastellain's five and twenty strophes on the princes of Christendom with five and twenty ballades on the same theme. None of them would care to distinguish François Villon.

None of them did. With a gentle word, a careless laugh, a glance, a gesture, they turned attention from Villon to Chastellain, and so skilfully that even in praising the Paris poet they managed to show him inferior to the lettered courtier. He was defeated.

But surely la Blossette had dimpled at him unmistakeably. Villon moved closer to her.

"You must have read the story about the ladies' argument as to whether the knight or the clerk makes the better lover."

"Yes?"

"You remember the decision they handed down was in favor of the clerk. But the story was written by a clerk. By the same token, I could not expect a lovely lady to decide in favor of a plain one."

222

"You have forgotten the Lovers' Code, Master François: virtue alone makes one worthy of love."

"I should have used that," said Villon quickly: "the virtuous are not noted for their beauty."

"For shame!" Her dimples creased her soft cheeks.

"The exception proves the rule. But I never got beyond the first article of the Code."

"Yes?"

"Marriage is not a valid excuse for love."

She laughed deliciously, and looked up, not at Villon, but at the young man who had strolled over to them. Gilles des Ormes, the young major-domo. Tall, and high in the Duke's favor, handsome, well-borne, a graceful maker of verses. With every reason for self-conceit. But charming. Beside him, Villon was sharply conscious of his short stature, his thin swarthy face with its scarred lip, the button already loose on the cuff of his new suit.

"And how did you fare?" The sparkling look, the dimpling cheeks were all for des Ormes now.

The chess game was over. Juvenal Negro had bested his Grace again. The higher laughter, the gayer music indicated that the Duke had retired. The harper was playing flourishes that made Villon prick his ears.

"I never heard that melody before. It must be a new invention."

Gilles des Ormes smiled deprecatingly.

"On the contrary, Master François, it is very old. It was composed for the song: 'Madame, I am happy now.' His Grace was my own age when he had the music embroidered in pearls on his sleeves. It took something like five hundred and seventy pearls. A pretty fancy!"

"A pretty sum," muttered Villon.

223

"If it is new tunes you want, you should have been here in the Spring, when René of Anjou paid us a visit. He brought his harper, Vaillant, along with him."

"To harp on the simple life?" punned Villon.

"It is unfortunate"—Gilles des Ormes' courteous tone was gently condescending—"that you missed the verse tourney."

"You do not imagine that I could have won?" asked Villon with mock innocence.

"It is not impossible," Gilles conceded. "The carpenter was mending the wells at the time. Not that we expected a siege," he smiled, "but they had fallen into shocking disrepair. The want of water gave his Grace the notion for a ballade: 'I die of thirst beside the fountain's brink.' He had us all turning verses on the same theme. If you care to see them, I can show them to you in his Grace's manuscript book."

"That would be charming," said Villon. But he was not charmed. He disliked des Ormes. He wanted to attract the attention and open the purse of Pierre de Brezé. I die of thirst, he was thinking, beside the fountain's brink. That was the Court, where you came in hopes because you were desperate, where you were a stranger in your own country, where you felt your strength and were powerless, where everyone welcomed you with exquisite courtesy and rebuffed you as firmly.

"If you will remind me, tomorrow, it will give me great pleasure to show them to you."

"It will give me great pleasure to remind you," replied Villon with suppressed venom.

Des Ormes bowed gracefully and moved over to join Chastellain, Blosseville, and Oliver de la Marche. The ladies, too, were stirring. It was late.

"It is a pity"—Pierre de Brezé was drawing back a chair for Marie Blossette—"that her Grace had to miss the debate."

224

"I think she suffered more in the autumn when she had to miss the hunt. We used to find her tarnishing her falcon's bells with her tears. It is God's mercy that she was confined at this season—what is there to do in winter but sit by the fire and wag your tongue?" She pouted prettily.

" 'Winter weather—fire, fire, summer season—drink, drink!' " quoted Villon. "You would rather be warmed within than without, eh?"

"Oh, but summer at Blois, Master François, you do not know how delicious it can be—boating and bathing, and supper and songs in the open!" Marie Blossette sighed wistfully.

"Everything is delicious at Blois, dear lady. Are you not here always?"

She shrugged, and dimpled.

"I did not really want to defend plain women, however witty. I had only to look at you, and my case was lost. I was lost."

"You are a courtier, Master François."

"A gambler."

"Oh! What do you play for?"

He leaned closer, with a quick glance round to satisfy him that the rest of the company had forgotten François Villon.

"What does any man play for when a lady is in question?"

"I thought you would teach me a new card game."

"I would do anything to keep us both from the eighth deadly sin."

"The eighth?"

"In the Schools they call it *accidie*. I have heard a hundred sermons on it by preachers who should have been damned for what they preached against. The common name for it is boredom."

"You are bored, too?"

"How can one be bored at Court?" asked Villon with half-concealed irony.

"You say that because you are a stranger. But it is always the same: the same gossip, the same dinners, the same services at chapel, the same games. I didn't dare play tonight: I have been having the same run of bad luck!" she smiled ruefully.

"That's serious," Villon commiserated her.

"Serious! When I owe everybody," Marie Blossette wailed. "But I shall have my revenge. You've heard of his Grace's new acquisition: Habano's *Treatise on Poisons?* Nicolas Astesano is making a copy of it, and he's promised to show it to me. I'll study it, I warrant you. Then I shall know what to do about them all."

Villon's eyes quizzed her.

"The furrier, I mean, and the jeweler and the fellow who cleans my gowns and furnishes me with pins and buckles. I can't possibly pay them. Ergo, I must poison them!"

He chuckled.

"Are not your eyes, my lady, deadly weapons enough?"

She shook her head at him.

"Perhaps I can help you."

Her dimples deepened in an incredulous smile.

"I know a few card tricks that might turn your luck. Let me show them to you."

"Indeed I will!"

"But," Villon lowered his voice, flashing his black eyes at her, "no one must know."

She looked at him doubtfully, still smiling. Her back was to the group of courtiers and ladies. He faced her and them, with one eye cocked to see that his siege should not be interrupted.

"You are not like the others," he assured her softly. "If you were not in her Grace's service, you might have ruled an abbey, you might have governed a kingdom. It is because you are too clever for them that you are bored at Court." Villon knew that you must flatter an ugly woman on her looks and a pretty one on her good sense. He hid a grin by stroking his scarred lip. "You remind me," he told her, "of my best friend."

"And who is that?"

"A poor poet, who is also my worst enemy. He has the keenest faculties of any man in Christendom, but there is one that he lacks."

She questioned him with arched black brows.

"Money: without which he cannot enjoy the others."

She laughed.

An elderly lady-in-waiting, Simonette Gazille, who had formerly attended the Duke's daughter, came rustling and glittering toward them. Marie Blossette turned.

"Are you coming, my dear? Her Grace will want you early tomorrow."

"At once. Good night, Master François."

"Good night, my lady." He gave her a sharp long look that she could not mistake. She was gone.

"Well, Master François," de Brezé said genially, "how are you recovering from your defeat?"

Villon smiled, looking after Marie Blossette.

"By preparing," he answered glibly, "for a victory."

Chapter Fifteen

Villon went to his room. But not to sleep. He kept his candle burning. He thought of Marie Blossette, the dark eyes large and alight with laughter, the smoothly colored cheeks softly creasing as she dimpled, the small white jeweled hands, the firm slender body under the fragrant silks. She had not smiled at him without cause. He was something new at Blois. Those sly eyes of his had seen things queerer than Moors and monkeys. The jokes that issued from that scarred mouth were rougher than those allowed his Grace's fool. Knowing nothing of hawks and hounds, and only so much of horses as he had learned by grooming them when there was no other way to get bread, he was set apart from the courtiers who surrounded her. They loved strangeness, these ladies who were willing to don the dress of a shepherdess for the sake of entering a world closed to the Court. Villon's odd look, Villon's wicked tongue must delight them. As they had delighted Katherine de Vauselles. He laughed sardonically, remembering. The thought of her still had power to do him hurt.

If she were here now! They had never been together in such a softly furnished room as this, with a fire glowing in the brazier and waxen tapers lighting the silken hangings, the polished woods, the burnished metal. With cups of mulled wine, sweet and spiced, to quicken the blood. With harp and flute sounding distantly to fit the broken music of their speech.

Her Grace, Marie de Clèves, her Grace's pretty lady-in-waiting, Marie Blossette, dreamed in their ignorance of the joys of the simple life. Mary, Mother of God, thought Villon, no treasure counts but living at your ease.

When François was a child, Master Guillaume, away from home on some church business, had left him one night in charge of a comfortable canon who knew his Ovid better than his breviary. The murmur of voices in the next room had not stirred the boy's curiosity until he heard a woman's laugh. He had got up, then, surprised and inquisitive. A beam of light betrayed a chink in the plaster. He had crept close to the wall and, crouching, peered through. At first he saw only the canon's broad back, but then his eye found and clung to a dazzling breast, the soft curves of a woman's body. He watched her as she leaned on one elbow to take a cup of wine from her companion. He saw them kiss, and then, startled by a sudden noise behind him—it was his book fallen to the floor—jumped up as though he had been caught. Long after his own candle was out and no more light came through the chink, he lay

229

awake, listening to strange sounds and imagining most un-canonical play.

He had scarcely thought of it since, but now the scene came back to him sharply. All the properties were here: the soft couch, the soft chair beside it, the brazier, the light, there was even drink on the table, for his Grace kept his guests most happily supplied—everything but a woman.

Villon grinned morosely. Either you were lucky in your fortunes or in your love. Some men had neither. No man could hope to have both. Except perhaps such a handsome, gifted, well-bestowed gentleman as the Provost of Paris, with his ex-quisite Ambroise de Loré, or so great a lord as René d'Anjou, who had recently taken a second bride, young and lovely as the morning. It was with her that the King had amused himself here last Spring, playing at shepherd and shepherdess, wandering across the pastures with a crook in his great fist, eating plain fare out of a basket, making love in the open like a peasant. Villon wished he could have seen them at it to mock them.

He imagined the King quoting with unction the old verses on Franc Gontier praising the simple life. A king might relish such a masquerade. And the Court would pretend he was right, that the serf's lot was a happy one, that the cheerful brute of a peasant could not estimate the great lord's responsibilities. While the town of Anjou groaned under its taxes like an over-loaded mule.

Villon, warming his hands at the brazier, looked back over the roads he had tramped to get to Blois, the hungry days, the cold comfortless nights. He hated the taste of a raw onion, the smell of sheepskin, the appalling solitude of the fields under a blank sky. He shivered, safe in this cosy room at the castle. No treasure counts but living at your ease. Damn it all, thought Villon, if princes praise the simple life—it was the all-powerful

Philippe de Vitry who had written the verses that Anjou moralized upon—let a poor devil speak up for luxury. Such as that nameless canon had enjoyed with the lady. Such as Master François could have known tonight if Marie Blossette were less difficult.

Villon paced up and down the room humming to himself. He did not need the brazier for the song that was beginning to warm his blood. A reply to Franc Gontier. Jean Meschinot had got ten crowns for his last dull verses. If Master François received as much for these, he might have more luck with Marie Blossette. But he must not think of that now: only of his rhymes.

He sat down, rejoicing in the fine Italian paper supplied by his Grace, in the smooth-flowing ink: it did not freeze in the horn at Blois. He commenced to write.

His candle was flickering low when he was done. He flung down the quill not caring how the ink splattered. It was good, whether de Brezé would like it or no, however they paid him. All the rich sensuality that they pretended to despise glowed and sang in these verses: the downy cushions, the burning brazier, the tender whiteness of the woman, the drinking, the amorous game and its fierce solacing end—he had written all that his avid senses cried for. And there, too, definite, plain as the snub nose on Anjou's broad genial face, all that the great lords offered instead: a stinking onion, a mug of milk, hedge-love.

Villon was impatient for morning. De Brezé must see this. It was worth ten crowns, surely. With money in his purse he could seek out Marie Blossette and woo her in earnest. "No treasure counts"—he rolled the refrain on his tongue, with the wine that his Grace had provided for a nightcap—"but living at your ease."

He slept well, and woke content. But when Gilles des Ormes, with courteous reminders of his promise, led him, late in the morning, up the three flights of stairs to the south tower chamber, he was not wholly at his ease.

Villon took in the company with his swiveling eyes. His Grace's secretary, Beaugency, was officially flourishing the keys to the chests that held his Grace's books. Young Nicolas Astesano was examining an old tome on physic so that he might compare it with his own work on Habano's treatise. Bending over another lectern was Blosseville, who spoke of books as less scholarly young men spoke of women, and handled them with the same luxurious delight. Before the fireplace stood Tignonville, her Grace's genial equerry, laughing over his own version of one of Boccaccio's stories, and beside him Pierre de Brezé, of the stern face and the generous purse.

"Magnificent!" cried Blosseville. His long white hands hovered over a binding studded with huge moonstones that held the *Hours of the Virgin*. "But this is only the casket for the true jewels: look!"

He was not wrong. He opened to an illuminated page from which the blue and scarlet capitals shone against the solid black script, the margins delicate with flowered scrolls in rose and yellow and green, faced by a set of miniatures that blazed like rubies and sapphires set in gold.

"Yes, that is a fine piece of work. But here is something more curious."

Blosseville turned half reluctantly to the volume that Beaugency brought forward.

"Arabic?"

"A copy of the *Koran*."

"You read Arabic?" asked Villon respectfully.

"No. Why should I?" Blosseville laughed. "Do you buy these things to read?"

Villon shrugged. He did not buy these things at all. But that had not occurred to Blosseville who was lamenting the treasures his Grace had parted with in order to assemble his ransom.

"It is his Grace's manuscript book that Master François desires to see," said Gilles des Ormes, observing that Villon did not fully share the bibliophile's excitement.

"I trust I shall have the pleasure of inscribing some of Master François' verses there before long," said Astesano politely. But the courteous words were also a reproach to Villon for not having produced something to be set down there.

"If we can inspire him," Gilles des Ormes smiled. "His Grace was asking me whether I had had the privilege of seeing some new work by Master François. I was compelled to say that I had not. You should not hide your talents here," he added gently.

Villon understood the reproof. He had done nothing to earn the stipend that the Duke offered him. They thought him lazy or helpless. Well, he would show them. He glanced at de Brezé. His lordship was listening impassively to Tignonville's chatter.

"Observe, Master François!"

Beaugency placed the manuscript book before him. A gorgeous thing, bound in red leather, rich to the eye, smooth to the touch, spicy to the nostrils. It was open at the verses written for the last tourney. Villon skimmed the pages rapidly. There they were in firm black script, one set of stanzas after another, with the name of the author set forth in a fine flourish: Master Jean Cailleau, Master Bertaut de Villebresme, Gilles des Ormes, Jean Robertet, and, head and crown of them all, inscribed as

233

always with a great FORTY for the year of his liberation from the Goddams and his marriage to Marie de Clèves: Charles, Duke of Orléans. His physician, his ambassador, his seneschal, the secretary to his neighbor, the Duke of Bourbon, his whole army of poets and poetasters had tried their skill. They were various, these ballades, and they were all alike. Each expressed the man who had made it, by some turn of phrase, some greater or lesser craft, each imitated the tenderness, the melancholy, the whimsy, the sweet trivial charm that were the stamp and seal of the Duke of Orléans.

> *I die of thirst hard by the very fount,*
> *Trembling with lovers' chill and lovers' fire.*

"Wait," said Gilles des Ormes, thumbing the leaf, "let me show you."

"I thirst no more," Villon read, "now is the fountain sealed; I am well warmed without the fires of love!"

He nodded. The trembling lover, the old man out of love with love. François Villon could speak for both. The shivering touch. The fever that burned like liquid flame in the veins. The longing—false as hell—to be rid of longing. But Charles, Duke of Orléans, fitting rhymes like a cabinetmaker, playing with whimsies as a child plays with sticks and stones, played at emotion too.

All those verses about Care, the thief of joy, and Thought in his cool shuttered room. That St. Valentine's Day poem, about Doctor Listlessness, who came to feel the old amorist's pulse in the morning and bade him turn back to his pillow again. The easy invitation to sup or bathe or go boating, as though a man need never ask how suppers were to be paid for or who would pull the oars. That was why the old troubadour complained that a song without music was like a mill without water. His master's pretty things needed lutes and strings to give them body. Empty comments on an idle day. They ground no corn. Of verse-making the tired gallant knew something. Of life, the great Duke knew nothing at all. The worst he had endured was leading a princely life in a foreign country and losing a fraction of his dukedom.

"You are charmed, Master François. So were we all. His Grace believes you could charm us too. Can you not give me something to show him?"

Villon looked at des Ormes with snapping eyes. If he could charm some money out of de Brezé, and compliance from Marie Blossette, even he might find exile endurable.

Tignonville, thumbing the manuscript book, interrupted with a chuckle.

"What's the joke?"

"A poem about a beating."

Villon's eyes flashed. He could write a poem about a beating that would beat all, he thought grimly.

"All on one rhyme," said Tignonville appreciatively. "And written like a grammarian. There's neat work for you!" He stepped aside for Villon to read:

> *Master Etienne le Gout, nominative,*
> *But recently, in manner optative,*
> *Desired, it seems, performance copulative;*
> *But failed of his conjuncture genitive.*
>
> *He doled out ducats, six of them, dative,*
> *That he might have his sweetheart vocative,*
> *Master Etienne le Gout, nominative.*
>
> *But he encountered an accusative*
> *Who seized him by his gown, thus ablative;*
> *Then from a window quite superlative*

He leapt, beneath the buffetings passive,
Master Etienne le Gout, nominative.

The wit scarcely made up for the want of music and the jerky metre, thought Villon.

"What's the story?"

It was old to them, but apparently they still found it funny. Tignonville slapped des Ormes with his great fringed glove:

"You tell. Oh, ho ho ho!"

"The verses give it perfectly," the young major-domo's voice sounded a hint of reproach at Villon's obtuseness.

"He's right," chuckled Tignonville. "It's all there. You see, le Gout had a rendezvous with a lady. Gave her six ducats, dative, to smooth the way. But his secret leaked out. He went to her room at the appointed hour. But just when he thought he was going to get his money's worth, he heard a suspicious noise. Discovered! He was no warrier, le Gout. He made for the window. His accuser (accusative, you remember) managed to get in a whack or two before le Gout jumped. But he left his gown in the other man's hands. 'Master Etienne le Gout, nominative!' Oh, ho ho ho!"

Villon laughed without merriment. He was recalling Noel Jolis' stick about his own shoulders. He was wondering what he could do if he had six ducats. Thinking of Katherine. And of Marie Blossette.

De Brezé was watching him with keen not unfriendly eyes.

"Perhaps you have something of your own to show us, Master François?"

Villon warmed to the Grand Seneschal. He patronized the noble stick-in-the-muds, but one might win his interest with a piece as fresh as it was vulgar.

"Perhaps I have."

236

With a Villonesque disregard of courtly manners he dropped himself into a chair, flung one leg over the velvet arm, and commenced.

Out of the corner of his eye he looked at de Brezé. The Grand Seneschal was stroking his beard. Was it to conceal a smile? Villon's voice was rich and musical, and edged with naughtiness:

> *"On softest down a fleshy canon sprawls,*
> *The room rush-strewn, the brazier alight,*
> *Mistress Sidoine beside him sweetly lolls,*
> *Her tender flesh perfumed and dazzling white:*
> *Thus to drink hypocras, or day or night,*
> *To laugh, to kiss, to toy, to take delight,*
> *And naked, skin to skin, to find relief—*
> *Since through a chink I saw those two appease*
> *Their bodies so, I've known: for quenching grief*
> *No treasure counts, save living at your ease."*

De Brezé sees the thing, Villon flattered himself: anyone must see it, it's as plain as the naked woman in the shows they put on at festival time; he's licking his chops over it, pretending he's above that sort of thing. Villon cleared his throat and went on:

> *"Would honest Gontier and his Helen call*
> *That life a sweet one? They would scorn it quite.*
> *They ask a stinking onion, that is all,*
> *A sop of bread in milk, the simplest mite.*
> *Their broth, their pottage, never tastes aright*
> *Sans garlic, that's their daily sup and bite.*
> *No offense meant, this is my firm belief,*
> *Let them lie under hedges if they please.*

What's better? Couch and chair? Confess, in brief,
No treasure counts, save living at your ease."

It wasn't the picture of the simple life that the prince painted, that Anjou admired. But it was true.

"They live on barley bread and acorn-fall,
Drink water all year round in wine's despite.
The birds from here to Babylon may call,
But not call me to suffer such a plight
One day, one morning, even. Get me right:
God knows, with honest Gontier I've no fight;
Let him and Helen live, if they'd as lief,
Beneath the briar bush on bread and cheese.
But for the simple life I hold no brief,
No treasure counts, save living at your ease.

Prince, judge the case, and bring us to accord.
Myself—and there is none I would displease—
When but an urchin heard it said, my lord,
No treasure counts, save living at your ease."

Villon sat quiet, only his black eyes and his rapid pulse alive, waiting for praise. Tignonville twinkled merrily but said nothing. Gilles des Ormes exchanged glances with Astesano. Beaugency was hovering over the books. Blosseville coughed deprecatingly. He must hope his patron shared his own disgust with the stinking onion and the poet's jaunty attitude. Damn it, thought Villon, didn't de Brezé know a good thing when he heard it? Here were great lords gathered. François Villon was only a clerk. But one who could write verse as no man had written it before him. He swung his leg impatiently.

"One can see that you have not much sympathy with the people, Master François," observed de Brezé, with his dry smile.

238

"No," Villon answered quickly, springing up, "I never was a peasant. You may say his life is pleasant. But I'd rather dine on pheasant, if your lordships are complaisant."

They all laughed then, and de Brezé struck Villon lightly on the shoulder.

"Here's that for your pains," he said and opened his purse.

"A thousand thanks, my lord." Villon stopped himself as he was about to bite into the coins to try if they were honest metal.

"Let us hope," Gilles des Ormes smiled at Astesano, "that Master François will yet give us something you can copy into his Grace's book."

So it wasn't good enough. In spite of Tignonville's jolly acquiescence, in spite of de Brezé's gift. Blosseville was helping Beaugency put away the Duke's treasures. The Grand Seneschal was leaving. They were all leaving. The exhibition was over. Des Ormes had an appointment with his Grace. They went off, Tignonville and Astesano arm in arm, chatting about a lame goshawk. No one asked Villon where he was going, what he had to do. No one invited his opinion on birds or horses, suggested a gallop round the park or a game of chess, spoke of meeting him again after chapel or after dinner. No one asked for a copy of his verses, not even de Brezé.

But he had money in his purse. He could meet Perdrier without flinching, though of course he could not pay him yet, need not, if he managed cleverly, pay him at all. He could seek out Marie Blossette and lose to her, if it meant winning her in the end. He would dare as much as Etienne le Gout, and be secret enough to escape a beating. One would do him for a lifetime, and a man must have some fun, even at Court.

He ran lightly down the second flight of stairs and almost bumped into two men from the village coming up. He had seen them about the castle before: Jean Lessayeur, the jeweler, and the upholsterer, Petit Jean. They must have come to put the finishing touches to the Duchess's bed of state: Marie Blossette had described it—the silk draperies were fastened with Orient pearls. That would be the least of the Duke's commands for the parade of his young wife's lying-in. It was a great night for the merchants of Blois when his Grace got his lady with child.

Petit Jean, the upholsterer, bore no resemblance to the black-bearded dumpy fellow in the short cape who had performed so skilful an operation on the locks a year ago come Christmas Eve. But his name reminded Villon uncomfortably of home. Where was Petit Jehan now? Call no man happy till you know his end, thought Villon, moralizing on the wheel of Fortune. Take Lessayeur, now, the Court jeweler. He had prospered since the fall of Jacques Coeur: his Grace's trade had not gone to Tours so often since. Would he make a finish like that mighty merchant?

Coeur had died miserably in Chios, and all his millions could not save him. Nor would have saved him, had he been luckier, from the death-sweat, the racked limbs, the laboring heart, the blackness before his eyes, the torture of the last choked striving minute. Where was he now? With the rest of the great and little dead, the popes and apostles, lords and princes, kings, clerks, peddlers, thieves. Where were they? The wind had carried them all away.

Moving hesitantly among the treasures in the great hall, Villon reviewed Coeur's history. He had owned half a dozen ships that plied yearly between Montpellier and Alexandria. He had been granted special permission by a papal bull to trade with the infidels, brought incense and perfumes from Araby, velvets and rugs from Persia, silks from Cathay, sugar and licorice and nutmeg from Egypt, pearls and rubies from India, pepper, cloves, ginger, and cinnamon from the isles. He had bought jeweled daggers in Turkey, and, it was rumored, slaves. He had employed scores of agents—three hundred was the figure commonly named—to carry on the commerce that raked in his moneys. And no one now so poor as this banker who had lorded it over the Pope, over the King of France. He had had his enemies: who hasn't? They had accused him of assorted crimes: making gifts to the Saracen sons of dogs, exporting silver alloy, wringing money from the King's tributaries on false pretences, returning a Christian slave to the Sultan, poisoning the chief lady in France, that Agnes Sorel who had been the King's mistress. He had been stripped of everything. The very day that Byzantium fell to the Turks he had gone through the shameful ceremony of making amends for his sins. And now he was less than the meanest beggar breathing: he was dead.

Villon would go that way, too: perhaps up aloft, like René de Montigny, with the hangman to hurry him and a crowd of wretches no better than himself to shout over his last kick.

He turned from the tapestry at which he had been staring with unseeing eyes to grin at himself morosely. What had got him? Was it because they had not praised his verses? Because he had met a man with the name of his accomplice in the affair of the College of Navarre? He was not in danger here.

If only he could find Marie Blossette, she might divert him from his stupid fears. He would make love to her as no knight had ever done. He would play the funster for her like any fool. It was the only escape. Except poetry. And they did not like his poetry at Blois.

He found her at last, before her embroidery frame, gathering her silks as she prepared to put her work aside. She looked up at Villon with a smile that made provocative creases in her smooth rosy cheeks. Her dark eyes shone at the sight of him.

The ladies who companioned her laughed banteringly. Villon could have sworn that he had been the subject of their gossip.

A thimble fell from her basket as she rose, and rolled away out of sight. Villon knelt to hunt for it. The other ladies were moving off with little laughs and backward glances.

Villon was slow. Marie Blossette might have signaled to one of the servants standing like waxworks in the violet and grey of the ducal livery, but she allowed Villon to conduct his hunt unaided. On hands and knees he glanced round. The ladies, he noted gratefully, had not waited. He stood up.

"You have found it?"

"No."

"Oh!"

"But I shall find it, I promise you. Your ladyship will permit me to bring it to you?"

She lifted her narrow eyebrows.

"I want to show you those card tricks, too."

"I should like that," she said with a little eager laugh. "Do you think I can win, then?"

"Every game."

"Oh, that would be wonderful! I have nothing to pay my debts with now."

"Let me help you."

"You?"

"Why not? I have not had my stipend yet from his Grace. But—wait. Shut your eyes and open your hand."

Smiling, she obeyed. He took de Brezé's gift from his wallet and dripped the coins into the rosy palm, one after another. Marie Blossette laughed and opened her dark-fringed eyes.

"You want me to be in debt to you, too, Master François?"

"Yes yes yes."

He dared to take her hand, to shut her little white fist on the coins. She permitted him, smiling.

There was a pause. The lady-in-waiting, tutored in how to behave in the company of dukes and duchesses, knights and lords, seemed at a loss for something to say to this black-eyed clerk. She dimpled as though his gift pleased her. She pressed her basket of silks against her little breasts as if his presence crowded her, though he was so slight a figure of a man, a person of no importance.

"Scripture tells us: an eye for an eye," said Villon. "Will not your ladyship look at me?"

She looked.

"Should it not rather be a heart for a heart?"

"Are you so bold as to rewrite Scripture, Master François?" The soft gay voice shook a little.

"Does it not also bid us love our neighbor as ourself? Here in the castle surely we are neighbors. Even if my room is not in the same wing with your ladyship's. Or is it?"

"I am in the west wing, on the second story." She dimpled again, blushing.

"The third door to the left?" he ventured.

"The fifth to the right," she breathed. She glanced down the long room at the servitors standing beside the arched doorway. "I must go," she said hurriedly. "Her Grace—"

"Forgive me for detaining your ladyship." He bowed deeply. Flushed, smiling, sighing briefly, she was gone.

Villon turned on his heel with a grin. He flung into the air and caught again a small thing he had concealed in his bony fist. It was a lady's thimble.

Chapter Sixteen

After vespers Villon slipped quietly upstairs. He moved circuitously so as to avoid the remark of the stiff figures in grey and violet who guarded the doorways and who always reminded him of wooden effigies. Three soft knocks admitted him.

His rapid glance took in the old-fashioned furniture—pieces that his Grace's mother must have brought with her from Milan—the silken curtains embroidered with the emblems of the house of Clèves, the ivory and silver and crystal toiletries, the picture of the Madonna and Child with the votive lamp shedding a soft flicker over its gilt and jeweled frame. His quick nose sniffed the fragrance of burning pastilles. Even Blois had not yet shown him such intimate luxury.

And la Blossette? She was standing with her back to the curtained window, her hands, so little for their heavy rings, fluttering over her furred bodice, her eyes with their long dark lashes bigger than ever in the rosy triangle of her face.

"Is it you, Master François?"

"I am not sure. It may be only a dream I am having."

"Did you dream that you found my thimble?"

"That too."

"And"—she laughed a little—"your cards?"

"Yes, my lady."

"Come, let us see what you can teach me, Sir Clerk!"

There was nothing Villon would not have taught her, and at once. But Marie Blossette had not quite forgotten that the court poets merely tolerated this off-scouring of the University of Paris, that the fascinating scar on Villon's upper lip had never been won in a tourney, that the mild affair her Grace had enjoyed with the Prince of Sicily and the amusing escapade of Master le Gout would never excuse the condescension of her Grace's lady-in-waiting to a mere master of arts, however compelling his black eyes and his edged tongue.

He showed her several tricks. He instructed her in one of the ruses of the Companions. He complimented her on her quickness. He looked deep into the dark-fringed eyes. He arranged the cards in the small white hands and pressed the perfumed fingers where the rings allowed. But if Marie Blossette had never before been gracious to a clerk, neither had François Villon tried to persuade kindness from a lady of the Court. He did not doubt she would yield. She feared that he would conquer. But not so soon.

She did not let him forget that there were ears in the thick walls of the castle. He was in the midst of a naughty story with which he hoped to excite more than her laughter, when she suddenly cried: "Hush!"

He had heard nothing. He did not care if he were discovered. But la Blossette felt differently. She pushed him behind a heavy satin curtain. But it was only the wind in the chimney.

Nevertheless she went to the door.

"Oh, my dear friend!"

245

"I was wondering what had become of you." Villon recognized the voice of Simonette Gazille, the old lady who had been in the service of his Grace's daughter by his first wife. She swept into the room and sat down in his place. "What are these?" She had caught sight of his pack of curious cards.

"I was amusing myself before going to sleep." Marie Blossette imitated a yawn. "Has her Grace asked for me?"

"No, dear. But I did want a word with you."

Villon heard the small noises that meant she was settling back in her chair.

"I shall not stay long. Though Heaven knows you do not need a beauty sleep. And I am too old to get any benefit from one."

"I wish you would show me the fountain of youth you drink from!"

"Little flatterer! You do not need to play the courtier with me. But I must play the mentor to you, Marie. You will excuse an old lady if she is blunt."

"I have offended?"

"Not me, dear. But . . . What queer cards! How did you come by them?"

"Oh, I—" La Blossette could not think fast enough. She said with gentle deprecation: "Master François lent them to me."

"Exactly." Villon imagined the sage nod of the old lady's head, the pursing of her lips. "My dear Marie, I know you too well to believe that you would do anything you would be ashamed to tell your confessor. But one cannot be careful enough. It is so easy to fall into sin when you think you are only playing."

Marie Blossette spoke as though she were smiling.

"Your ladyship is talking in riddles."

"Come, come, Marie. You understand me. And I understand

246

you, dear child. I was young once. I know what temptation is."

"Your ladyship does not imagine—"

"I imagine nothing. I see what I see. I hear what I hear. And," Simonette Gazille sighed, "I remember." She paused briefly. "This Master François—"

"But he is—" Villon stretched his pointed ears in vain to hear what Master François was: Marie Blossette must have ended with a silent shrug.

"Very ugly," the old lady-in-waiting finished for her. "And very attractive. Those black eyes. And that wicked tongue!"

Behind the curtain, Villon grinned. And pricked his ears again to catch la Blossette's reply. Whatever she said was smothered in a short sharp bark.

"What is it, my little one?"

Villon shrank back. The old lady-in-waiting must have come in with her lapdog on her arm. He heard unmistakably the sound of the little animal sliding to the floor, Marie Blossette's anxious coaxing voice as she called it, the patter of its feet as it trotted across the room.

"Come here, Griffon!"

But Griffon was not diverted. He went nosing on his voyage of exploration.

"Never mind him," said the old lady-in-waiting. "Only give me your promise, my dear, that you will be careful! I am sure—"

"Oh, he will tear the curtain!"

Griffon was sniffing suspiciously at the folds that hid Villon's feet. Marie Blossette ran across the floor to snatch him up in her arms. The little dog barked again crossly.

"My dear Marie, one would almost think—"

Simonette Gazille rose slowly and slowly crossed the room. She was standing directly in front of the hangings, stroking

247

the little dog as Marie held it. Villon wanted to poke out his nose and make a face at her. The old lady-in-waiting put a hand on the curtain, adjusting it. Villon would have drawn further back, but there was no space. It was difficult to breathe. He was afraid any moment a sneeze might betray him.

"Griffon must think I have Master François hidden there!" laughed Marie Blossette. Ah, the shrewd girl! Villon loved her for that bold stroke.

"Naughty dog!" murmured his old mistress tenderly, taking him from her young friend. "Now, my dear, I must be going. Don't be angry with me. There was a proverb when I was a girl: the students are the worst. Of course, Master François is not a child, he is a master of arts, I think, and a poet, they tell me, though not to be compared with Meschinot and Chastellain, of course. But do think of what I have said. God bless you, and give you good night."

"Thank you, your ladyship."

She was going at last. Villon breathed more deeply. At the door she turned.

"I know you mean no harm. But that is just the danger. And, believe me, my dear Marie, once you have made a misstep, you can perhaps do penance and get absolution. But what God in His infinite mercy may forgive, the world never forgets!"

"Yes, your ladyship. I am grateful. Sleep well, Griffon! Good night, your ladyship."

The door closed.

Villon waited a moment to make sure that the coast was clear. Then he stepped out of his hiding place with a great sigh and a wink.

"Phew! That was a near thing. Well, you have been warned now."

La Blossette shook her pretty head.

"I did not need the warning, Master François."

He came closer.

"Would you have cared as much without it?" he asked pointedly.

She dimpled. Villon would have looked into her eyes, but she let him see only the long white lids and the lashes' dark fringe.

"Would you?" he pressed her in a whisper.

She opened her eyes. They were dark and bright and merry. She opened her soft mouth to answer him.

"Marie!"

They had been too deeply absorbed to hear the returning footsteps. The Lady Simonette, her little dog on her arm, confronted them with no further word.

"Oh! Your ladyship . . . Master François just came . . . to ask for his cards . . ."

"It was a presumption, my lady," said Villon quickly. "But it suddenly occurred to me that someone coming in to the Lady Marie's room might find them there and reproach her for having borrowed them from her very humble servant."

"It did not occur to you that someone coming into the room might find you there?" retorted Simonette Gazille sharply.

"And I must confess," pursued Villon, "I wanted to teach her a conjuring trick privately. I can make any card vanish in the twinkling of an eye. Observe: here is the knave of hearts. Now you see him. Now you don't!"

Was Villon the knave of hearts? The card had vanished, with the deck, and himself.

In the great hall below the gentlemen were gathered. They greeted him so cordially that his self-esteem revived at once. He could not worry about what was happening in Marie

Blossette's chamber, now that he had taken himself off. But he was not long in perceiving that it was not the entrance of Master François that unexpectedly delighted these courtiers.

Good news. Disturbing news. They did not know how soon they might receive a call to her Grace's apartments. Master Jean Cailleau had but just been summoned. If his calculations were not amiss, she would be in labor before matins.

Villon twitched his eyebrows. They might be women themselves, a-flutter as they were. Because there was to be another infant in the world. Beginning its journey toward its inevitable end the very hour that it was born. But it was not any infant. It was a duke's son. Or daughter. Not like one of Fat Margot's casual imps, who could be fathered on a dozen men. Even on Master François Villon. He must have children somewhere, he supposed. He wondered about them, but only for a moment. He was thinking that he would not be one of those invited to witness her Grace's safe delivery. He would be expected to write a poem on the occasion. With the proper allusions. No blasphemous breath of reality.

Villon moved away from the buzzing circle of courtiers. Old Guyot Pot, who had returned to the service of the house of Orléans with the Duke's politic marriage to Marie de Clèves, stood in the doorway. He brushed past Villon with scarcely an apology, hurrying toward the gentlemen grouped in front of the great fireplace, and announced huskily:

"My lords, it's begun!"

No one had a thought for Master François now. He laid the blame on the baby. Even if the Lady Simonette had wanted to gossip, no one would have heeded her in the excitement attendant on the birth of the Duke's daughter. Villon looked in vain for Marie Blossette.

250

He looked in vain for his stipend. Belatedly it occurred to him that he might do something to earn it.

Jam nova progenies caelo demittitur alto. Now a new progeny from heaven's height is descended. Had Virgil indeed envisioned the Messiah in his famous tribute to the infant son of the Consul? At any rate, here was inspiration for a poem about the infant Marie, daughter of the Duke of Orléans.

Villon smiled crookedly, thinking that the Roman poet must have felt much as he did about this expenditure of lyrical energy on a scrap of red flesh that squalled and puked like any brothel brat for all its illustrious parentage. The little princess had known no better, when Lorraine d'Anjou had had the honor of holding her for the first time on his satin arm, than to wet his sleeve, discomfiting the poor young man so that he tripped over the impearled draperies of the State bed, where the mother lay smiling at her quondam lover.

The city of Orléans had presented the baby with a handsome silver casket that must have cost the burghers a good deal more than they liked. A penniless poet could at least do goldsmith's work in flattery. And might win his reward.

Villon set to work. If he could not imitate the Roman, he could at least use a Virgilan epigraph, embellish his verses with the gilt of classical learning. The infant was to have the name of her mother, Marie de Clèves, the name of the Queen of Heaven. Stick to the Virgin, my lad, Villon bade himself, if you want to get your stipend. Marie, the most gracious name in the world, the fount of pity, the source of grace, the joy, the solace of our eyes, Who contrived and established our peace. The peace, that is to say, of the rich (he would get that in, though he must add: the sustainer of the poor). He piled one heavy compliment on another, trying to equal in his verses the gorgeous gifts the infant had received from nobler hands.

When he had finished he shoved back his stool and grunted. He had never composed a worse piece in all his life. It made him sick at his stomach. Was the wintry day to blame? But he had written his best things in weather that only a wolf could like.

He made a fair copy painstakingly. At least it might earn him his stipend. He still owed the tailor. He dared not go down to the village for fear of meeting Perdrier. If he did not pay him something soon, the moneylender would be coming up to the castle to dun him.

Previously Villon had received his money at the hands of one of the Duke's secretaries. There had been small ceremony about it. He had simply presented himself at the proper hour in the company of other pensioners, and after, gone down to the village, avoiding the street where old Perdrier's son carried on his father's business, to spend it on drinks at the Silver Swan and to pick up franker gossip than could be gathered in the great house. But on Monday morning he had come to the usual room at the usual time, and found it occupied by three elderly courtiers who broke off talk about "that upstart Sforza" to stare coldly at this intruder upon serious affairs. He met a couple of long-faced fellows whose names he had not troubled to learn but whom he knew to belong to the Duke's hangers-on, wandering about the corridors being laughed at by the Duke's servitors. He encountered Nicolas Astesano, with a manuscript under his arm, going in search of fresh quills. The young man courteously directed him to a tower chamber. But when Villon reached it, he found only Martin the Moor meekly taking abuse from the dwarf. He hurried from one part of the palace to another, greeted by pleasant words, helpless shrugs, chilling ignorance. His stipend mattered to no one but himself. He mattered to no one but himself.

It was understandable that his Grace was not thinking of the necessities of Master François. Not since the triumphal return from England with his young Burgundian bride had there been such excitement at Blois. The ceremonies, the celebrations, feasts in the afternoon, fireworks at night, the special services in the chapel—it was many a long year since the Duke of Orléans had had so many demands on his time and strength.

Yet only yesterday a friendly word from his Grace about Franc Gontier had raised Villon's hopes. The Duke was surprised and pleased by work so unlike his own. And then the Lady Simonette had appeared, and his Grace had lost all interest in poetry, wanting to know how the infant was taking nourishment: there had been some difficulty about getting her to nurse properly. Villon had made a joke about the baby dying of thirst beside the fountain. His Grace had not heard it, which was lucky, to judge by the draught of cold air that seemed to blow through the room at this piece of bad taste. Glancing round for applause, Villon had caught Tignonville's twinkle, but Chastellain had coughed in polite deprecation, Meschinot had looked startled and gravely stroked his beard, there had been plain scorn in the Prince of Sicily's dark face, and Gilles des Ormes had fallen to studying Villon's manuscript as though he liked it better than its author. Perhaps the Lady Simonette had blabbed, and her entrance had recalled the company to the scandalous conduct of Master François. Villon was annoyed by his uncertainty as to whether the Duke himself had ordered his stipend stopped or had merely let drop a word that an officious underling had misinterpreted. The long and the short of it was that he had no money.

It was better business for a man to be in the service of the Great Khan, Villon thought wryly, as he pushed his papers aside and went down the stairs in search of better company than himself, than to be forced to bow and smirk and flatter himself into a comfortable place at Court, where you were well received indeed, and rebuffed by everyone. When all was said, he thought, sticking his head into a doorway and finding only a circle of idle squires dicing before the fire, the underworld was but the rough side of the fabric of which the great world was made. With the Khan, you knew where to go for your pay; you got something worth risking your neck for. So René had argued. Like Colin, he had had traffic with the Khan. And wore a rope round his neck in the end.

"I die of thirst," Villon muttered, "close by the fountain's edge." What did his Grace know of such paradoxes? Because he'd been in exile a quarter of a century, smelling the sweet wind that blew from France and drinking the bitter beer of the English? Because he'd married a pretty creature of fifteen when he was nearer fifty—a grand consummation that left his father's murder unavenged, that must make Louis' ghost howl in Hell to know of it? Because he was cousin to the King, yet at best merely a great vassal in times when the King was swallowing his vassals' privileges like oysters? Oh, he had plenty to complain of, the deaf old rhymester, whose verses made it so plain that in all his long tiresome life he had never really felt anything—not exile, not injury, not insults, not real poverty or honest passion. And since when do you care for honesty, Master François? Villon asked himself as he put his nose into another room and withdrew it hastily, recognizing Henri Perdrier, who undoubtedly had not come to call on his Grace.

Villon moved on. Whether he was on the road or in a palace, he must always be moving on.

As he passed the music room he observed Pierre de Brezé chatting with the harper.

"Ah, Master François." The Grand Seneschal acknowledged him with his usual dry smile.

"I was hoping to find your lordship," said Villon hurriedly. "If I might have the privilege of showing you a trifle I composed in honor of the little Princess? Your lordship could tell me whether it is worthy of being offered to his Grace."

"Do you need an ambassador then?"

"I am not close enough to his Grace to be heard, your lordship. His unfortunate deafness . . ." Villon's smile was rueful but malicious.

"So. Well, let us see it."

"A thousand thanks, my lord." Villon whipped out his manuscript.

His luck was turning at last. He winked joyfully at the harper.

As de Brezé ran his eye over the first sheet, Chastellain, accompanied by two pages costumed like cupids, came hurrying toward them.

"Ah, there you are! We are ready to rehearse now. Will you come?"

"I have just been arranging for the music. You will excuse me, Master François? Another time." De Brezé handed his manuscript back to Villon and went out, arm in arm with the Court poet. They did not invite Villon to go with them.

Villon winked at the harper again, on a different note, as it were, and turned away.

His experience in arranging farces for the lawyers' corporation would have stood them in good stead. More than once at carnival time he had given shrewd hints to the Prince of Fools. He may have bragged of it too loudly. Or else the Court feared the rough humor that suited the Paris mob. Once more his hands were as empty as his purse.

255

If he were writing, he would feel himself his own man again. The ballade in honor of the little Princess was trash. His heart had not been in it. Nothing put him in the vein except the eternal verities of death and love and poverty. And at Court not death nor love nor poverty was frankly faced.

Villon mounted the circular staircase to his room with lagging feet. He halted at the turn. Marie Blossette was coming down.

"My lady!"

"Good day to you, Master François." He could not tell by her voice if she were angry or not. She neither frowned nor smiled.

"It has not been a good day or a good night this long while," he murmured.

"Why, we were never so merry at Blois," she said lightly. "I have not even had time for a game of cards."

"Then you have not tried my tricks?"

"Ah, your tricks." He studied her face in vain, but her gentle gaiety gave him hope.

"You have not forgotten them?"

"I have forgotten nothing." She blushed. Her dimples made long creases in her cheeks. She would have passed on down, but he blocked the way.

" 'What God in His infinite mercy may forgive,' " he quoted slyly, " 'the world never forgets.' Do you prefer to belong to the cruel world, or are you, as a poor clerk dreamed once, of the company of God's angels?"

"I am not an angel, Master François."

"Does your ladyship think I am a devil?"

"I think you are nobody but Master François," she said merrily.

"You think I am nobody."

She shook her head at him:

"You are a poet, are you not?" And then: "Oh, there is Tignonville! Good day, Master François."

She ran lightly down the stairs, and he was left staring after her like any dolt.

He mounted the steps to his room slowly, walking as though all the while he were standing still, staring, not at the image of the flying lady, but like a miserable Narcissus bent over his own reflection. Narcissus leaning over the pool. Over a well, perhaps, like those the carpenter had mended in the spring of the year.

I die of thirst beside the fountain's brink. He could write a better poem on that score than any of your silk-and-velvet lords, sure of their pension, their place, their appointments, their fun, their women, and their deaths in honorable encounter or in a comfortable bed. Here he was in his own country (all France was his country), an exile from the Paris that was the synonym for home. Dressed like a president of parliament, thanks to his Grace's tailor, yet naked as a worm; these were not his clothes; he was no more at home in them than at home in Blois. He was enjoying life—where would you find richer entertainment than a princess's nativity and the Christmas feasts at Court afforded together?—and taking no pleasure in these fat luxuries. He was in despair, and hugging hope. He was at the height of his powers. What! A man of twenty-six, a master of arts from the University of Paris; a poet who could compete with the Duke of Orléans and throw him; a man with the eyes of a lynx, the nose of a hound, the ears of a hunted fox, the tongue of an epicure, the fingers of a pickpocket, the legs of a tennis champion, the wit of the Prince of Fools, the brains of a bishop. A man who knew everyone from those in the palace to those in the stews; a man who had had his trip to

Heaven and had slunk through Hell with the damned; a man
who had all the tunes ever sung in his head, and words more
living than the Logos on his lips. A man young, audacious,
clever enough to compel the world—and strengthless, waiting
on the good will of those in power, dining on morsels fallen
from the tables of the great, knocked about, beaten (damn you,
Jolis!), comforted by a silly servant girl, loved by a fat whore
who was any man's property, a piece of death's meat; a man
received with smiles and shoulder-clappings everywhere, and
rebuffed by everyone. Katherine. Marie Blossette. Gilles des
Ormes. His Grace, the Duke.

Villon stood before the lectern, nibbling gloomily at his
quill. He was miserable enough to make a poem, whether it
would be one to please his Grace or no. He drew a sheet of
paper toward him and dipped into the ink.

> *Beside the fountain's brink I die of thirst,*
> *As hot as fire, with rattling teeth, I quake;*
> *In my own land a foreigner accurst;*
> *Beside the brazier, shivering, I bake;*
> *A naked worm, in clothes of richest make,*
> *I laugh in tears, and hope on, minus hope—*
> *Find solace in despair the while I mope;*
> *Make merry joylessly, nowhere find fun;*
> *I'm strong, but powerless and without scope,*
> *Welcomed with warmth, rebuffed by everyone.*

It was as though he were overhearing the words spoken by
another, by the voice of his private devil. His wretchedness
dictated the lines. The itch for fame, the thirst for love, the
ache of cheated pride, a self-inquisition whose tortures ended
in mounting self-disgust, mixed with a child's desire to howl.
But Villon grinned. "I laugh in tears."

258

He finished it comforted, as no warm wine, no woman's tenderness could comfort him, by his own true speech. He reread it, delighting in his study of himself, in his lovely rhymes, only four of them to thirty-five lines, in the gay lilt of the verse, in the neat envoy addressed to his "clement Prince": whom may it please to know that I understand everything, small though I am in learning; that I have my preferences, subject though I am to every law. What more do I want? Why, only to receive my wage once more, "Welcomed by all, rebuffed by everyone."

Villon frowned and took a restless turn round the room. He imagined his Grace listening to the ballade as he sat at ease after dinner beside the great hearth, one long hand playing with the jeweled charm that hung on his breast, the other cupping his ear, his lips pursed in a smile of condescension and appreciation. His Grace had ever a good word for Villon's verse. He would summon the Blois circle to applaud it and request Astesano to make a fair copy of it in the manuscript book to companion the other lyrics on the same theme. The best of them would look faded by comparison, thought Villon. The hell with it, thought Villon, if it will not bring me my stipend.

He was sick of the castle's finical ways, elaborate rituals, and careful conversation. He was sick of men of letters with their proud learning and their jealous vanity, more poisonous than any brew concocted by an Italian politician. He wanted to push off. To some city in which he could choose his own companions and live in vagabond freedom with the need to please no man but Villon. If only he could get his money he would slip out with the players from Orléans when they returned to the city. If he could get his money!

With a grimace he took up again his fresh sheet. He would

present it to his Grace. Perhaps it would earn the precious necessity.

His Grace was occupied. His Grace's secretaries were working. The librarian was in his closet. The doctor, a friendly old soul whom the Duke loved, though he had no literary taste, and who might be of service in presenting the Duke with bad verses, was in attendance on the Duchess. The small circle of court poets was dispersed. The players were nowhere to be seen—busy, Villon supposed, with the Mystery of the Nativity that they were to perform for the feast of Epiphany. There was no one about but the servants. At every door, at each of the larger windows, stood guards in lustrous grey with violet silk stockings. Their faces smooth as their livery. Not to be bribed or cajoled. With what would he bribe them? He was ready to crumple up his poem and fling it into the fire, but it was a pity for the paper. It was the Duke's paper, the finest Florentine make.

You could buy good paper not too dearly now. Villon's lip curved as he recalled the procession of scholars from the University marching in pairs to buy the annual supply of parchment at the Lendit Fair, the head of the procession reaching the plain of St. Denis before the tail of it was well out of the rue St. Jacques. He supposed they did it still. Nothing was changed. Only François. Was he changed? He twitched a shoulder and turned into another great tapestried empty firelit room.

The grey day had turned to snow. It would be hard to step off in such weather. It had been bad enough when he had been forced to flee Paris in February after doing in the priest. Then at least he met spring on the southern road. The voices of the choristers singing the Christmas hymns came to him through the small leaded panes. And suddenly he was back in his mother's house, alone in the freezing dark, with the plague raging in Paris, the menace of the wolves, and himself sick with cold, hunger, and dread, piping thinly: "News of Noel, now Noel let us sing, New folk, cry God forgive us everything . . ." God had had little enough to forgive him then. He had been happy then, the miserable little wretch.

He became conscious of someone moving behind him. It was Pierre, the Duke's fool, juggling three apples and humming to himself a song about Noel. He eyed Villon's manuscript with a wink.

"Another poem, Master François? I hope it is better than the last one."

"What do you know about the last one?"

"Nothing. But I hope this is better."

Villon frowned, shrugged, and stared out of the leaded windows. The great flakes had ceased falling, and there was only a mild greyness in the air that was the very tone of Blois. But he was surprised by a stir in the courtyard below. Cloaked men bustling about donkeys with heavy panniers—he looked more sharply. The players! Were they leaving?

"Yes," said the Fool in answer to his quick query. "They go back to Orléans."

"I thought they were to play the Nativity before his Grace."

"You thought wrong." The Fool took out his apples again. He had small interest in the disgraced pensioner.

Villon considered swiftly. It might be his last chance before spring. No other company would be leaving Blois except those who accompanied the Duke's ambassador to Hungary. It was to no such outlandish place that Villon desired to go, even if opportunity afforded. To stay on at Blois another three months, another three weeks, would stifle him! He had his fine clothes, thanks to the Duke's tailor. He was well stuffed with meat and cakes, thanks to the Duke's cooks. On the road with the players there were ever ways, straight or crooked, to come by a handful of ducats.

"Pierre," said Villon abruptly, "if you present this manuscript to his Grace, in my name, I warrant he will reward you properly." He thrust his poem hastily into the Fool's hands. "Tell him that as I love and honor him I could not do otherwise."

Sulkily the Fool accepted it. Villon made for the door. As he passed through, he winked to the servant standing there.

"May God bless you," he muttered.

"God bless and save you, sir," stammered the menial with a stupid stare, not understanding that Villon longed superstitiously for some word of grace, if only from this tall dolt in livery, before he shook the snows of Blois from his heels.

He bounced up the stairs, lighter than a juggler's ball, to fetch his cloak, a clean shirt, and a short sword that hung by his bed. In a moment he was down again, having no more baggage. It was only when he was in the courtyard, making himself delightful to the chief of the players before announcing that he would step off with them, that he regretted not having snatched up one of the Duke's bibelots on his way out and stuffed it into his wallet. He comforted himself with the reflection that there was no knowing when he might be passing through Blois again in want of shelter, glad as he was to fly from it now.

"You Orléans men can teach Paris a thing or two," he cried glibly. "How soon do we get there?"

Chapter Seventeen

The Orléans players were glad to avail themselves of Master François' talents. But they requited him in no proper fashion. They got wind of it that he had fallen out of favor with their master. And they proved almost as jealous of their reputation as the poets at Blois.

As soon as the weather softened, Villon deserted them and made his way south with the vague notion of seeking refuge at the Court of the Duke of Bourbon. He was a much younger man than Charles of Orléans, indeed, scarcely older than Villon himself, of a literary turn, and disposed to entertain on a scale only less magnificent than that of his great neighbor.

But even to win patronage one needed money. The suit

Villon had had made at Blois was shabby and stained by now. It would take a neat sum for him to make himself presentable to his Grace. He had unluckily failed to ask the Duke of Orléans for a letter of recommendation to his great neighbor. And, after Blois, he was not too eager for what the Court promised.

Just before turning off to the Bourbonnais he fell in with a couple of odd fellows—muscular men with the jovial passions, the shifty eyes, the knowledgeable command of the jargon that marked them as servants of the Khan. The one, a slow-spoken, thick-set man with three fingers missing, called himself Guillaume Aubin. The other, skinny, sharp-featured, with a wide garrulous mouth, was a certain Perrinet.

Over the tavern table the pair were able to give Villon news of home. Colin was somewhere safe in Normandy. But Tabary was in prison.

Gradually the story came out. About half a year after the robbery, the fat fool had fallen in with a priest, a stranger from Paray, who had pretended an innocent interest in the exploits of the Brethren of the Cockleshell. Tabary had puffed himself up as a devil of a fellow. He had even tried to introduce the nosy prior of Paray to some of the Companions. When he was rebuffed, they being reasonably suspicious of the good Father, Tabary had tried to swell his own reputation by boasting in a drunken lisp about his hand in the robbery of the College of Navarre. The priest had listened eagerly and taken the tale straight to the Provost, who was delighted to be able to turn over the prior's neat notes to the Faculty of Theology.

"My God!" muttered Villon. "Are you sure?"

"Sure as Doomsday," said Perrinet. "I had it from Petit Jehan himself. He got away in time. It was months before they even nabbed Tabary. But he's fixed now."

264

"Did they torture him?" asked Villon eagerly. He didn't give a damn how Tabary had to suffer. But if, with his limbs racked, his bowels bursting, he let slip the name of François Villon, there would be the devil to pay. After all his wanderings, Villon had arrived at an illusion of safety. Perrinet's story was the more terrifying.

"Dunno," murmured Aubin, rubbing the knobby knuckles where his fingers had once been. "You'd best keep away from Paris if you value your hide."

"My God!" Villon repeated angrily.

"What's the matter?" asked Perrinet, wiping his mouth with a dirty sleeve. "You can't make out in a place like Paris anyway. They know too much about you. It ain't safe."

"Damned if I know where to go," said Villon, more to himself than to his companions. It was certain that he could not go with them. Perrinet, to the disgust of the close-mouthed Aubin, had hinted that they had a little job to perform for the Great Khan and needed no help with it, even from so trustworthy a man as Villon.

"Why'n't you try Bourges?" asked Perrinet. "They's swell pickin's there now."

Villon lifted his eyebrows. He was waiting for a word from Aubin. He was the readier to credit the fingerless man because he spoke so little. Aubin nodded agreement.

Perhaps, thought Villon hopefully, he could make a connection in the Cathedral town with some of the shrewder Companions. After what he had just heard, he had no taste for being alone.

"Who's in Bourges?"

"The plague," said Perrinet with an ugly grin.

Villon hunched his shoulders. He had met the plague once

in his starved childhood. He had no craving to meet it again, a hungry hunted man.

"What are y'afraid of?" Perrinet grunted. "It's a decenter death than hanging. Anyway, the town's wide open. Everybody's gone to the country to get away. The servants can be bought with next to nothing. The Watch is sick or dead or don't care. Nobody goes to church: they think they'll catch it there. You can swipe a chalice or a candlestick as easy as if it was a sausage."

Villon had never yet committed sacrilege. But it was not stealing from God—only from that overweening rich bride of God: the Church. He had nothing against such a theft. He was ready for anything that would put gold in his purse and food in his flat wailing stomach. But the plague. He could not get round the dread of that.

"What is it, the sickness?"

"St. Francis's disease."

It was a pest that commonly attacked the poor, who, in addition to their poverty and the taxes that turned feast days into fasts, must suffer the misery of such ills as fatten upon ill-nourished folk. But when a man is prepared to risk his neck in order to fill his belly, he cannot look too narrowly at dangers that scare more comfortable gentry. And Perrinet assured him that by this time the worst was over.

"You try the churches," he advised Villon. "You might even work the Cathedral. And listen: there's a goldsmith, no ordinary fence, who'll take whatever you bring him and give you good value. Name's Marot, Denis Marot."

"Yes?"

"Yes," said Perrinet firmly. "He's new at the job. He won't double-cross you. He don't try to dispose of the stuff: just melts it down. Take my tip."

266

Villon nodded, with a side glance at Aubin.

"Marot's all right," admitted the fingerless man.

That was how Master François Villon, ward of the canon of St. Benoit, one-time guest of the Duke of Orléans, found himself one fine May morning standing in an otherwise empty street in the cathedral town of Bourges, watching a funeral procession on its way to church. He crossed himself mechanically and thought that it must be a rich corpse that could command even so meagre a following in time of plague. Why the devil had he journeyed so far to land in so foul a place? Cheer up, my lad, he bade himself grimly, as he turned away, the plague can't touch you: it would never do to cheat the ropemakers' guild.

The clergy, he reflected, as he limped in the opposite direction, earned their bread in queer ways. Serving the dead as a help to getting their living. They would go home to a good dinner afterwards. He doubted, though, that they dined as well as the regulars. A hungry man could find no better comfort than in the kitchen of the Jacobins' great house on the rue St. Jacques. The Order had given its name to the first dish he would command when he could afford such eating. Oh, the noble soup! Villon's mouth watered: generous slices of toasted bread heaped with the finest cheese in France and soaking in rich beef broth, with small delicately roasted plovers to top it. His nostrils twitched. He spat again glumly.

God's body, if he would eat he had better find the wherewithal. He stepped from the street, bright with spring sunshine, into the candle-lit gloaming of another church, just in time for mass. The tapers shot wavering gleams upon gold and silver vessels. The chalice lifted in the priest's strong white hands was worth a pretty penny. Money, money for soup au Jacobin, money for wine, money for a soft bed and a gay girl to share

267

it. Fat months again, oho! He would get him a finer fiddle than the one he had left behind in Fat Margot's shop. He would be in spirits and make verses again. He had been dumb too long. There was nothing to sing about on the road but the sheep. And he was a sheep who would sing of them.

If only they did not lock the sacristy! He was thin enough to be mistaken for a shadow. He could creep through a crack in the wall. His heart beat faster as he imagined himself actually laying hands on the precious cup, saw himself fleeing with it through the plague-stricken streets. And, as always in moments of excitement, he remembered death.

It was not the funeral procession he had just witnessed, none of the horrible reminders of death that filled the town. It was his own blood running in his veins, crying out in him that as truly as he now lived and breathed so must he one day cease to draw his breath in fear or joy, lie at last with every sense darkened, all motion stilled. The thought swept over him like a black wave. He could not bear to remain, could not support the weight of Judgment, the worse terror of an eternal blank. He turned, half staggering, and fled the place.

Once outside in the sun, with the homely cobbles under his feet, he damned himself for a fool, cursed the hunger that had brought on this weakness. But it was not his empty belly that had betrayed him. It was the same when he was full, when he had a wine cup in his hand and a girl on his bony knees. He could never be free of the terror except when he was absorbed in a song, though the song itself were of death. Or when he was drugged by some dull job like clerking for the shrewd Perdrier. What had brought up before him so sharply the banker's narrow long-nosed face? What but his one-time cronies, Perdrier's elder sons, Jean and François, in the flesh, marching along the other side of the street, too deep in talk to notice a scarecrow like himself. What in the devil's name would they be doing here in Bourges?

He was about to hail them, but, remembering the sum he owed their little brother Henri, he strolled shakily in the opposite direction.

They might have helped him to a meal. They would have relished reviving the gay old days, if only in talk. Or would they? Jean Perdrier had always thought too well of himself, and less of Villon ever since the night he had dared take Katherine to Montfaucon. François Perdrier was become a man of substance, connected with the salt trade, as usurious a business as moneylending, caring more for getting cheap water power in the salt pits than for getting good wine down his gullet, less happy in raising the devil than in the erection of a new distillery in the marshes of Brittany. If the pair had been visiting their brother at Blois, Villon, as a guest of the Duke, might have reminded them of his existence. But here in Bourges, worn in body, clothes, and spirit, he could not face those who had known him when he had been the merriest jokesmith in Paris.

Without fairly noticing where his legs were carrying him, he had come to that quarter of town where the Companions had told him he would find the shop of Denis Marot. Here was the street. That was his sign, with a golden cup, hanging from the penthouse just ahead. Villon cleared the phlegm from his throat, cocked his hat over one eye, and knocked. The boards were old and in need of paint. A poor outlook for the luxury trade.

The door was slow to open and closed after him sharply. The breath of air that entered with him was fresh and warm with spring. But the shop had a close smell, and the shopkeeper shook as though with cold. Villon eyed him—a youngish man but with the prematurely aged look of a dwarf and the eyes of a wild dog that has been injured. It made a man feel taller and stronger to be in his neighborhood. Villon glanced rapidly at the stock in trade. It seemed to consist of no more than a few candlesticks, a row of cups in need of polish, a large copper bowl, a collection of rosaries, and some gold and silver buckles of indifferent workmanship.

Denis hovered, patting his fingers together—delicate hands he had, but the nails were long and dirty. His voice creaked:

"How can I serve you, sir?"

"I am in need of silver." Villon winked and tapped his belt.

"A buckle, perhaps? Or a set of silver buttons?"

"Thanks for the compliment. I doubt they would suit this suit." Villon glanced down at himself with a disparaging grin.

"For another suit, then."

"Use your eyes, my good Denis—your name is Denis, isn't it? Do I look as though I had another suit?"

The goldsmith shook his great puzzled head.

"You must not mistake me for the archbishop," said Villon and waited, in vain, for Denis to laugh at the joke. Perhaps he did not see it. Decidedly, his eyes were bad.

"Do you serve Jean Coeur?"

Denis Marot laughed then mirthlessly.

"What do you take me for?"

"For a good fellow like myself, out of luck like myself, ready to go into partnership with myself."

"You are a goldsmith?" Denis's large-featured face, too big for his meagre body, squinted in surprise.

"In words." Villon thrust his thumbs into his belt and strode magnificently across the dingy room and back again. He stopped in front of the jeweler and tapped him lightly on the chest with one finger. "That does not matter to you, Denis.

270

But we have tastes in common. We both like to hear one coin rhyme with another: it is the sweetest chink in the world. We would give all the bells in Bourges for that music, eh?"

"Business has been bad," Marot admitted tonelessly.

"And the plague, which may God speedily send to the devil, can have done it no good."

The goldsmith crossed himself, mumbling something that Villon could not catch.

"Has it hit you then?"

Denis looked at Villon out of anxious red-rimmed eyes and looked away again.

Villon raised his brows inquiringly.

"My son. The two little girls. I have buried them all."

"You are a young man," Villon ventured, "you will be getting another child."

"I am a widower."

Villon shrugged, lifted a rosary, and put it down again.

"It used to fret me," said Denis in his rusty voice, "how to feed them and care for them—a man all alone."

Villon, looking at him, noticed the Adam's apple moving up and down in his scraggy throat. Marot looked at Villon as though he did not see him. The words that had been slow in coming began to tumble from his cracked lips.

"They are lucky, those, whose children die before they are grown at all.

"My little Denise, she would have been four years old come Michaelmas . . . The three of them, they were a worry and a burden to me." He stopped again. "You are a father?"

Villon shrugged again with a queer look. Perhaps.

"Then you do not know," said the goldsmith dully.

Villon's thought flew to Katherine. She had sometimes seemed to him like his child, young, foolish, in need of cherishing, but dearer than any daughter. You could know, though you had never seen a creature of your own begetting, or cared to see it.

"My son Jacques," said the goldsmith as though he were repeating a lesson that was hard to learn. "Seven years old. I used to whip him. When he lay there, shivering with fever, and his two sisters both dead, I wished I had not behaved to him like a peasant."

Marot was silent.

"It is bad to watch a child die. They do not understand. When they struggle so terribly, and you would die to help them, but God will not let you . . . If they only understood."

"And you," said Villon harshly, "do you understand?"

There was no answer. At last:

"Excuse me, sir. I am forgetting. It is all . . . Well . . . You wanted a silver buckle, was it?"

Villon looked at him sardonically. He was about to reply with a bitter jest when he was stopped by a knocking at the door. Thunderous. The noise knocked the pity and the anger out of him. It reminded him shortly that he was in the company of a receiver of stolen goods. Instinctively he stepped into the darkest corner of the shop.

"Open!" The voice was rough. "Do you want us to bash the door in?"

Villon noticed a coffer under a nail where a long cloak was hanging. He opened it, thinking to leap into it, but it was too full. As Denis moved to obey the summons, Villon quickly stretched out on the lid, hard and knobby it was, digging into his back, and pulled the cloak down over him for cover.

He strained to hear through the musty folds. Heavy steps: two men, not one. The clank of metal. The same rough voice:

"Denis Marot, goldsmith?"

272

"At your service."

"Come along."

The goldsmith stammered something that Villon could not hear.

"That's your story. Come on now."

"Christ have mercy!"

"You don't know anything about the two chalices stolen from St. Jean de Bourges, eh? You'll be walking like your own Saint Denis with your head in your hands for that. Go tell it to the archbishop!"

Villon heard a scuffle and a groan as the sergeant's fist struck poor Denis on his lying mouth. It wasn't a fair fight. But when was the law fair? He prayed silently that they would make their exit without inquiring further into Denis's business. But they were turning the shop upside down, making the most of their visit. Would they notice the coffer? Pluck up the cloak? Villon's heart thumped. His chest felt strained. He couldn't help himself. He let out a horrible treasonous cough.

They've nothing against me, he kept telling himself, as he trudged through the streets of Bourges with the shrinking goldsmith and the great hulks of sergeants toward the arch-bishop's prison. They can't keep me here without evidence, he assured himself, as he sat with Denis in the jail, which was no more dismal than Denis's shop, waiting for trial, listening and not hearing while the goldsmith explained to him again the affair of the chalices.

He had not known where they came from, he had not troubled to ask, the devil had robbed him of his senses when he melted them down; how should a man keep his head who had buried two of his children and must watch his only son go the same way? He had not enough to hold body and soul together, what could he do else? He had seen the worst that life could show a man, but he prayed that they would not torture him, not cut his tongue out, not strike off the hand with which he earned his bread. Christ, Who had given His blood to redeem all sinners, knew that he had meant no evil. Should he have taken his own life for want of food? That was a monstrous sin. He would have been damned from everlasting to everlasting. Villon nodded sagely, thinking: they know nothing about me but my cough—and coughed again and spat.

But what a fool he had been! Rushing to hide at a knock as though he were in league with the goldsmith and feared to be caught. Like that June night when he had been tricked into a murderous quarrel and taken hasty flight from Paris: he could have proved, first as well as last, that it was all in self-defense. He was forever running away. But from himself he could never escape. A damned fool.

He was relieved when they came to take Denis off, big-eyed and moaning, and he was free of the monotonous voice reciting the tale of cureless miseries. The goldsmith could say nothing against him. Did not know his name. It would need more than Tabary's genius for stupidity to implicate him in this case. And there was no malice in that poor man.

But how explain his hiding away on Denis's coffer under Denis's cloak? Villon gnawed his finger. If he had only hailed the Perdriers on the street, he might be free this minute, with a full belly too. There was no getting hold of them now. He had none to curse but François Villon, and him he damned again tersely, saving God the trouble, Who would doubtless damn him more thoroughly in the end.

There was food for hope in the fact that he had been taken to the episcopal prison. Whether because of the magnitude of Denis's offense in trafficking in sacred objects or because the

274

plague had taken lesser judges off the bench, the pair would come for trial before the Archbishop himself.

Villon knew something of his Grace. The great Jacques Coeur had bought the office for his son when the young man was three years under the age of the youngest in the episcopal chair. Villon had heard talk at Blois of the splendors of Jean Coeur's inauguration as Archbishop and Metropolitan, Patriarch (at twenty-seven) and Primate of Aquitaine. At the feast that had followed, the Duke of Orléans had made the young man's father a knight of the Hedgehog, the order established by his own father at his birth, and the worthies present had included nobles from the duchy of Berry, together with the bishops of Agde, Nevers, and Carcassonne. Now that the old fox was dead and dishonored, perhaps Jean Coeur would not be unaware how small a step lay between greatness and nothingness, how easily a man may be accused of sins he had not committed, condemned for crimes he had never planned. He had seen the father who begot him rise from a common mercer to be treasurer to the King of France and sink to an exile's grave. Strange thoughts, strange memories he must have sometimes. He could not be too hard on poor François.

Thank God, this was not the city of Orléans. It would not be like coming up for trial before Thibaut d'Aussigny, a man stern as iron, proud as a king, merciless as a wolf. Or had Jean Coeur's base origin and his father's curious fortunes killed all kindness in him?

There was actual comfort for Villon in being taken from the prison to the court room. The suspense was keener, but now it would be short. He was among men again, though they were but officers of the law, and one, standing there motionless, like a wooden image of despair, was a convicted criminal.

275

The Archbishop was nothing terrible. A slight man, whose face looked small under his mitre and whose body disappeared in the voluminous folds of his cope. His father's disgrace must have cost him plenty, but he was a great lord still. You do not let power slip through your fingers easily, once it is in your grasp. Those fine white fingers with the magnificent rings had not let go of much. His Grace had known how to furnish his palace with the most splendid products, not of France only, but of Florence and Venice—and the golden Indies. Accustomed to luxury, gracious, as befitted his station, hospitable to the poor Greek refugees whom the Turkish conquest had sent scurrying westward, a patron of the arts. Would he know the name of François Villon?

Conscious of others scattered in the great hall, sergeants, underlings, a few observers daring to seek diversion from the sad business that occupied all Bourges, Villon had eyes for none but Jean Coeur. He tried to put himself in the Archbishop's place, to get at the thoughts behind those shrewd blue eyes, at the feelings in the breast that rose and fell almost invisibly beneath the episcopal robes. Were his thoughts fixed on the law, on the poor men before him, or, more likely, on his dinner? Were his feelings mere physical weariness, as he sat there in his heavy clothes, his posture strictly erect? He must shiver and sweat and itch and cough sometimes (Villon cleared his throat) like another. If things had been ordered differently, their positions might well have been reversed, and Master François, impersonal, a little bored, would be dealing out justice to the shabby wretch, Jean Coeur. It was something like that that his mother had dreamed of for him, when she first took him to the Red Door. Did she imagine him in a fix like this? Very possibly. She knew her son. She might be on her knees this minute, praying for him, at the Celestines. Pray, my mother, it may do you good and can do me no harm, he thought.

Perhaps it would pay to be honest. Not unlikely the Archbishop had heard of the poet, François Villon.

He answered with his right name.

No light of recognition kindled in the Archbishop's eyes. There was a slight stir in the courtroom. Villon turned toward the spectators. God's body, there stood François Perdrier and his brother Jean beside him!

"There is one that knows me!" he cried joyfully.

Perdrier smiled strangely. He could scarcely have expected to meet his old companion here. But he was a shrewd one. He would trump up something.

"Who is this man with whom the prisoner claims acquaintance?" asked the Archbishop, clasping his hands deliberately before him. Villon remarked again the beauty of the great square amethyst in the episcopal ring. He felt easier.

"François Perdrier, your Grace, merchant," came the prompt answer, "son of Guillaume Perdrier, banker, of Paris, Number Seventeen on the Grand Pont. He was not unknown to your Grace's late father, God rest his soul. Myself, I have had the honour to provision your Grace's kitchens with salt, and, what gives me deeper satisfaction, I am arranging with the officials at St. Etienne's to supply the salt for the holy water, may it please your Grace."

Villon coughed. Another "your Grace" and he would think himself at the episcopal palace. Was this the Perdrier with whom he had played tennis so merrily half a dozen years ago? Who had been with him the night he took Katherine to Montfaucon? Still, all this obsequious respectability might serve his

277

cause. He grinned, hastily composed his face to gravity again, stroking his scarred lip, and looked from Perdrier to the Archbishop.

"Very good." The young churchman spoke quietly, distinctly, and with no sign of interest. "And what does François Perdrier know of this—eh, Master François Villon, clerk"—there was a scarcely perceptible pause—"found, most regrettably, in hiding in the shop of the goldsmith, Denis Marot, under trial"—the archbishop's voice deepened—"for sacrilege?"

Villon's eyes slewed round and fastened on Perdrier. God's body, help me now, they cried. Remember the good old days. Remember the scrapes I got us out of with a quick tongue. Go to it, Perdrier!

"Master François Villon was employed by my father, your Grace, as a clerk—he is a graduate of the University of Paris."

Villon smiled contentedly.

"He was dismissed, after repeated warnings, for unbecoming conduct. My brother Jean here will bear me out. He is known all over Paris, your Grace, as a ne'er-do-well, a buffoon, a gambler, to be looked for in taverns and whorehouses . . ."

Villon swallowed an oath.

"Will your Grace," he stammered, "be so gracious as to hear me?"

The Archbishop turned an impassive face toward him.

"It is true, your Grace, that I was employed by Guillaume Perdrier. I left his service by mutual consent." Villon cleared his throat and went on rapidly. "He is no great banker such as your late father, of blessed memory, but a small moneylender with a heart as little as his business. His sons have inherited it. It is true that I have come down in the world. Your Grace knows how God humbles those He loves. (That was a neat

278

touch, Villon told himself, warming to the work of self-defense.) Your Grace prays by his Psalter, but I pray your Grace will not listen to the salter Perdrier. Forgive me: puns are my worst sin. But my jests have been commended by no less a nobleman than the Duke of Orléans, who entertained me at Blois last Christmas, and I might be there still, had I not hesitated to trespass on the hospitality of the King's kinsman. There is a poem by François Villon in his Grace's manuscript-book. It sings better than Perdrier's psaltery. But I will not harp on that. Another set of puns! May your Grace be merciful to a poor sinner."

Villon had spoken in a kind of fever, his eyes fixed on the Archbishop's face, which showed a faint smile as he came to a conclusion, and then turned, without a word, toward Perdrier.

The salt merchant was flushed and frowning.

"There is just enough truth in that lying rascal's account to make the devil wonder and the angels weep. He was at Blois, your Grace. I have my brother's word for it. My younger brother, Henri, who is attached to the Duke's service. A banker, like your father, your Grace, and mine. We visited him only recently. He told us that Villon had been at Blois and gone before Twelfthnight. He went off with the Orléans players, that's the kind of rag-tag-and-bobtail he is. He borrowed money from my brother under false pretenses and never troubled to pay it back. Wormed himself into the Duke's favor with his verses. Your Grace sees how he tries to talk folk out of a right conceit of him. We shall see whether he can fool the Archbishop of Bourges!"

"Your Grace!" Villon pleaded.

Jean Coeur's shrewd eyes hardened. He unclasped his fingers and held up his right hand for silence.

"Enough."

There was a short pause. Then he spoke again, with his customary deliberation, odd in so young a man though fitting to his office.

"In these difficult times, when the whole city of Bourges is in mourning, it is not well to pass judgment hastily. We shall duly consider the case of Denis Marot, goldsmith, charged with sacrilege, a monstrous sin"—the Archbishop paused again for emphasis—"and Master François Villon, clerk, of ill reputation, found hidden in the goldsmith's shop. For the present the two prisoners are remanded to await the pleasure of the Archbishop in this matter. The court is dismissed."

Villon watched Jean Coeur as he rose and gravely made his exit followed by his entourage. He saw Denis, who had been waiting with the stupid patience of an animal before the slaughterer, being led out by the sergeants. A heavy hand seized his own shoulder. He must follow the goldsmith back to the Archbishop's prison.

He cast a glance of vehement hatred at the two Perdriers. They stood there, content with the morning's work, Jean crinkling his close-set eyes, François self-righteously smoothing the trimming on his cloak.

He continued to see them through a red haze of rage as he dragged himself up and down the damp twilit hole into which they had been thrust. Denis crouched in the corner on a heap of straw, shivering and saying nothing. There was nothing to be said. What would the Archbishop do? This might be the end of Denis Marot, though God knew a starving man in a plague-stricken city might be forgiven if he did a rogue's work to pay for children's coffins and funeral masses wholesale.

But what did the Archbishop think of Master François Villon? Had it been a mistake to be witty at the salter's expense?

Damn his venomous tongue. Venomous tongue . . . the phrase carried an echo, what was it now? Envious tongue, yes: the ballade made by old Deschamps damning envious tongues, suggesting that they be served up with a sauce of saltpetre and vitriol.

Villon stood still, grinning. He would go the old poet one better. It was but grudging envy of a cleverer man than himself, envy of a free-living vagrant not tied to a counting-house desk or sunk to his eyes in a salt mine, envy of one received as an equal by the Duke of Orléans, that had set the Perdrier tongue on fire. Villon grunted with mixed fury and satisfaction. He'd write a recipe for cooking the Perdrier tongues— not after the fashion of Taillevant, famous chef to the mad King Charles, but such as you might expect from that Macquaire who roasted a devil skin and all to get the full flavor of him. Villon's eyes narrowed, he could feel his nostrils pinch themselves as though he were snuffing up his own hot malice. He turned his back on Denis, the better to concentrate, folded his bony arms, bit his scarred lip.

> *In realgar, in native arsenic,*
> *In quicklime, nitre, and in orpiment,*
> *In boiling lead, so they'll be shredded quick . . .*

Villon paused, hugging himself, as his fury found words. But he must improve on old Deschamps, who had mentioned realgar and arsenic too, along with vitriol and alum and hellebore. He wanted no catalogue of apothecaries' wares. He must choose more horrible ingredients. He had not found his fun in the haunts of the Paris fishwives to no purpose. Some day he must make a poem to them. There were no curses like theirs in all the world. He began swaying back and forth to the beat of the verse, repeating the initial lines before he could proceed:

In realgar, in native arsenic,
In quicklime, nitre, and in orpiment,
In boiling lead, so they'll be shredded quick,
In pitch and tallow, soaked in lye that's blent
With a Jew's urine and hard excrement,
In water that has washed a leper's pox,
In scurf from dirty feet and ancient socks,
In blood of asp and drugs that scarify,
In gall of angry badger, wolf, and fox,
May these invidious tongues be set to fry!

Gaily he went on, piling one nastiness upon another: in the brains of a black cat, such as the sinner hates, so old that it has not a tooth in its gums; in the spittle of a raging cur; in the lather of a broken-winded mule; in water where rats and lizards and such crapulous beasts plunge their snouts, may these invidious tongues be set to fry! In sublimate, dangerous to touch; in the navel of a live adder; in the blood one sees in the barber's basin at full moon, black or greener than chives; in chancre and flux, and in the tubs where nurses soak their sheets; in the little baths of prostitutes (whoever fails to understand me has never visited a brothel), may these invidious tongues be set to fry! Oh, the beautiful stink! thought Villon. And now the envoy. Coprology, never hadst thou so learned a scholar!

Prince, if your sieve or sifter be not fine,
Then you may strain these savouries of mine
Through filthy breech-bottoms, but first, say I,
In ordure of a constipated swine
May these invidious tongues be set to fry!

Eh, ho! What a work. Relieved, as though by casting his

venom into a set of nasty verses he had cleansed himself of physical dirt, feeling miraculously free of malice by virtue of the vile song he had made, Villon swung round upon the goldsmith.

Denis still crouched on the straw, staring at nothing out of his red-rimmed eyes.

"Cheer up, my hearty!" cried Villon. "There's a grain of pity in his grace, or my name's not François Villon. He'll not let you come to harm for trying to save your skin at a time like this. As for your children, they're better off than you are this minute. Think, man, you'll have three little angels praying for your salvation to the Mother of God! You'll be all right. If the archbishop cuts out anyone's tongue it will be mine for making such foul verses. Only he'll never hear them until I'm well out of this place."

He babbled on, pleased with himself, and so able to be generous toward Denis, but, getting no response save a groan, fell silent again. He could hear his stomach rumble emptily. He was suddenly overcome with self-pity.

When would he be able to read his ballade to the Parisiennes on the Petit Pont, who alone could appreciate the rich dirt of it? A string of curses like that would earn him something better than a salt herring from such an audience. His cough caught him again, and he stood with one hand against the damp wall for support.

The coughing fit left him weak and shaken. He walked lamely to Denis's corner and dropped into the straw beside him with a clank of irons. He was crying with hunger, but, whether it was more for a platter of fish or for a word of praise, he could not have said. Christ, they might never hear his ballade at all!

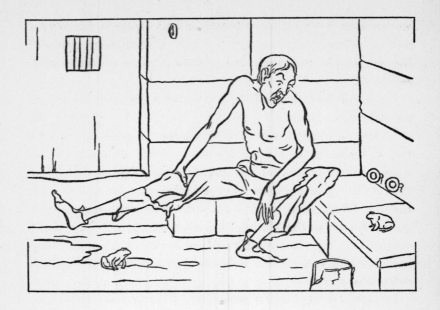

Chapter Eighteen

"Back again, eh?"

Villon, aching in every bone, shivering in spite of the June heat, stared at the jailer out of glazed eyes. He did not trouble to answer. His mouth felt like a mule's, sore from pulling at the bit. He was still choking from the torture of the water they had poured into him. He crawled into a corner and relieved himself, then lay silent in a black misery that would never lift.

"God damn me if I thought I'd ever be seein' you again," the jailer said, eyeing him with a greedy interest in this gallows bird.

He was a very woman for gossip, a fat man with a face like a full moon in August, fringed with white stubble. Villon had once been puzzled as to how he had come by a job that gave him so little chance for wagging his thick tongue. Now he did not care. The words rattled past him as meaninglessly as rolling pebbles.

"You know I didn't half believe you the last time, the stories you filled me with. They tell me I like to talk, and so I do, there's no sin in that. But I was never a patch on you, the tales you told woulda burned the devil's ears off."

The jailer paused, remembering.

"Sure, it was easy to believe you'd been in jail in Bourges, and even that they'd let you go when they remitted that fellow—a goldsmith, was it?—you was working with. But when you told me you went from the Archbishop's prison to the palace of the Duke of Bourbon, borrowed money from the Duke of Bourbon—well, that was a bit hard to swallow, that was." He jingled his keys, grunting.

"And then you land in the prison at Orléans and lie there in charge of me, waitin' for them to finish you. And all the while tellin' me you're hand in glove with the Duke of Bourbon and the Duke of Orléans, too, hobnobbin' with the lords of the land, you a big man of Paris, a scholar and all, wonderin' when I'd be turnin' you over to the strangler. May God burn me if you could get me to believe all that." The jailer scratched his white poll with the biggest key of the lot.

Villon opened one eye and muttered something unintelligible through his swollen lips.

"Eh? Well. It wasn't all a pack of lies, not all of it. I'll not forget when the little Princess Marie made her joyful entrance into Orléans. By Christ, you got your freedom, and they told me the next night you was kickin' your heels at the Duchess's ball. . . . Lord knows, I says to meself, the time of miracles ain't past yet."

The jailer regarded Villon with a mixture of wonder and a kind of bland malice.

"And all the while you was makin' ready to pay us another visit. The Bishop musta been heart-glad to see you again. Thibaut d'Aussigny don't like to see a sinner slip through his fingers so easy. Not he. You'll be stayin' longer this trip, I'm thinkin'. Damn my soul if you'll wriggle out of it this time." He paused reflectively.

"He gave you a taste of the water, eh? What was it for? A chalice did you make off with, or was it a votive lamp, they said? The Bishop don't fancy that. He's a man of God, Thibaut d'Aussigny, he don't let God's property fall into sinners' hands."

Villon groaned. With difficulty, his throat aching, his lips stiff, he cursed the Bishop of Orléans, the heavy-jawed cold-eyed Thibaut d'Aussigny, cursed his Meun dungeon, cursed the garrulous fellow who a year ago in the Orléans prison had listened big-eared to the tales of Paris and Bourges and Blois and Bourbon with which Villon had filled him. How small the world was! The jailer had been transferred to Meun just in time to greet his old prisoner again and sicken him again with his endless chatter. Villon prayed to be shut of him.

The man swung his lantern round the pit, letting the beams fall across the prisoner's twisted face, and with an ugly laugh at this last turn of Fortune went out, leaving Villon to count his pains in the dark. Then there was nothing to listen to but the rats, nothing to think about but the rope.

It was just a year since he had known the same misery in the prison of Orléans, cursing his folly in having so lightly deserted the fatness and gaiety of the castle of Bourbon, whither he had found his way after he had been pardoned and set free by Jean Coeur. He cursed himself for having imagined that he could turn a trick in a town under the thumb of the iron-fisted Bishop of Orléans. Just a year since he had been swinging, as a hanged man swings in the wind, between savage rebellion and black lassitude, wondering how soon they would come for him to put an end to everything. And then—he had not believed it when they told him, as he had not believed in the horror of his sentence—like a veritable miracle, the little Princess Marie, the wrinkled brat become an exquisite child of three years, had made her entry into the city of Orléans, with the old Duke, her father, riding before her on his great white horse and the Duchess, her mother, carried in a gilt and painted litter from which she leaned, bowing and smiling to the huzzas of the crowd, at her side. And all the wretches languishing in prison there, even those who lay waiting for the hangman, had been released in celebration of the grand event. François Villon with the rest. François Villon leaner than a rake, coughing and spitting with a cold he could not cure, but alive, dear Christ, escaped by the skin of his teeth—that ached—saved by a hair—and his hairs were few now—escaped into the sunshine of mid-July. Free! Crazy with joy, he had written a rhymed epistle to the little Princess, chanting her praises, linking her name with the grandest names in history, a paean of ecstasy.

It was all to suffer again: the eternal twilight, the damp, the ache in his chest and his back, his throat and his belly, the verminous itch from the crawling straw, the weight of the irons, the breakfast of moldy bread and water, the dinner of moldy bread and water, the supper of moldy bread and water, the endless hours cracking lice, the rages when he battered his fists on the unyielding wall, the sodden sleep at last, the cool furry feet of the vermin running across his face in the dark, the frightful waking, the night that was like the night of the grave.

This time there would be no escape. This time he would hang. Would it be worse than when they had put him to the Question, gagging him with the wooden choke-pear he had been used to joke about, placing the funnel over his mouth, pouring the water down his throat so that he could not swallow, could not breathe, and must swallow, must breathe, in agony, choking, his mouth stretched, his eyes bulging, his lungs bursting, his blank mind shrieking, When will it be over it will never be over when? Would it be worse than that? Yes. But it would be over. And then? Then nothing. Nothing at all. Hell? That was Hell. There was no punishment could surpass that. And the short years, the little crowded time behind, with so much more to see, to hear, to smell and taste, to touch and handle . . . Gone forever. He turned on the straw. It tickled his face. Not to feel even that. No sight. No sound. The memories blotted out. The hopes: Paris—Katherine. Never to see either again. God, Christ. What other Hell? He put his fist between his teeth and bit on it hard, as though it were the choke-pear, while the flood of bitterness poured through him.

So the hours passed. The day. The evening. The night. Morning came with a far-off ringing of bells, muffled by the walls. Terrible thirst. The tramp of feet outside. The jangling of metal. The heavy door was unlocked. The jailer with a jug of water. Bread, too. But Villon could not swallow that.

The water tasted brackish. But it wetted his sore throat. The jailer's voice, rough as the bray of a mule. Alone then. In the soundless twilight. Only the rustle of the straw under him, the noise of the irons. The sound of his own sighs, his short laugh of self-mockery. At long intervals, the bells. Another day passing. Another night to endure. Thirsty. He had drunk all the water in the jug. Coughing. Praying for the brief mercy of sleep. Fending off sleep for fear of the rats.

So the days passed. The nights. Without change. Without relief. Hours when Villon shuddered as with fever in dread of the end. Hours when he lay sunk in a stupor, wishing for death to put finis to his misery; when his heart lay like lead in his breast, his pulses failed, every breath meant the heaving of an unbearable weight. If he could have had but a sup of wine to warm his veins instead of these mugs of flat water. The Bishop must have the soul of a louse to keep a man drinking what was fit for toads. No wonder Villon had their company.

The dungeon was ancient, and water from the moat seeped in and collected in the corners, giving off miasmal odors. Sometimes it seemed to Villon as though the stench of all the horrors these old walls had sheltered was in his nostrils. As though the souls of the wretches who had lain here before him had taken on the shape of the crawling things that companioned his wretchedness. Who had been here before him? Thieves like himself. Counterfeiters. Rich simoniacs fallen from their high estate. Murderers. Gamblers who had trusted the Lady Fortune once too often. They may have taken Colin here when he was caught at Montpipeau last September, caught and hanged by the neck until he was dead. First René. Then Colin. Would poor François be the luckless third?

The name of one prisoner who had lain here Villon knew— not from the gossiping jailer, it was long before his time— but from the hag who had been the man's mistress in his good days: Nicholas d'Orgemont, canon of Notre Dame. He had not languished in the Meun dungeon for long. He couldn't endure it, an old man by then and used to the soft living in the cloisters.

But the woman had suffered a fate as evil. Villon remembered her, crouching in the street, peering out of dim eyes, mumbling, toothless, with lips that shook and a hand held out like a claw. The beautiful armouress. A fine piece in her young days—now a bag of bones in a wrinkled spotty skin. De Lorris had described her when he pictured Old Age in the *Romance of the Rose*. But he hadn't done her justice. No one had until François Villon wrote the ballade that would make the old bitch live long after her carcass rotted away.

He had told the jailer the story of Nicholas d'Orgemont with the mad notion of reciting to him his ballade of the beautiful armouress. But the jailer, chuckling grimly over the story, had rubbed his white bristles with his fat fingers and spat. You didn't make songs about old whores—they were just a joke.

How could Villon explain to this ox? But that was why a man wrote: to set down what he saw, with terrible clarity; to tell what he knew, with all the force of black truth.

He felt sick with the vile diet, the foulness of this hole in the midsummer heat, the fear of the Bishop's torturer, the Bishop's hangman. But he felt a strange strength in himself too.

The jailer left him alone. The old armouress stayed. He had painted her—ah, how he had painted her!—with merciless power. He saw her again, her mumbling lips and her bony jaw, heard her shrieking hoarsely at the young whores who strolled about looking for custom. They would come to what she was if they lasted that long. She could tell them. An old drab is worth nothing to any man: no more than bastard currency.

Villon saw them as the old hag would have seen them, with the envious eye of cast-off beauty. He saw them tossing their heads and smiling over the wine; he saw them shrunken and withered, crouching beside a foul-smelling fire of refuse:

Girls, if you ask why this despair,
These groans and tears, just look at me:
They will not have me anywhere,
No more than bastard currency.

You could be as young and gay as a May morning: you would be cast off to die alone at last. Little had the beautiful armouress dreamed, as she sat on her lame lover's knee, that he would end in this hole at Meun and leave her to beg from any Christian fool who asked no recompense but a stale whore's blessing. Little had François Villon thought, when he plied the old woman with wine, that he would find himself lying in the very dungeon where the man who once kept her had perished.

He spat a great gobbet of phlegm. Perhaps François Villon would perish here too before they had a chance to take him out and string him up. God send the soul of Thibaut d'Aussigny to burn in Hell! "When he shall be judged, let him be condemned; and let his prayer become sin. Let his days be few: and let another take his office." The Psalmist had spoken well, but St. Paul was better: "Let his habitation be desolate and let no man dwell therein; and his bishopric let another take." He would not like that, the Bishop of Orléans, with his long stern face and his thin lips. He knew how to hold on to his lands, Thibaut d'Aussigny: like that Tacque Thibaut, the breeches maker, who had been a favorite of the old Duke of Berry and whose nasty habits and mean tricks lived on in men's memory still.

God, thought Villon, why should I remember that name now? What a ruck of names I do remember. Names and faces.

Hundreds of faces, seen in the taverns, over the cards, or when the wine and the song went round together. Seen in the streets, in the cloisters, before the parvis of Notre Dame, seen about the University or haunting the Holy Innocents, seen in Perdrier's shop or when I was working for Ferrebouc. Whores' faces and sergeants', thieves, priests, lawyers, money-changers, clerks, students, the Provost's lovely lady, Ambroise de Loré, the red-nosed drunkard, Jean Cotart, the deaf Duke of Orléans, the mean-eyed Noel Jolis, the long-fingered René de Montigny, dead now, the sharp-faced Colin Cayeux, dead too.

How they crowded upon you when you were alone, all the faces you had seen, anxious, angry, eager, sullen, soft with tenderness or sly with greed. The lives behind them that you had only glimpsed, maybe, but that were part of your own life wherever they had touched it.

Colin taking me back of his father's locksmith's shop to show me how to use a crowbar. Old Etienne de Montigny wanting me to meet René, thinking poor clever François would stir the sleeping virtue in his fine wastrel of a nephew. The way Ysabeau said, "Reely!" when I told her I was a better man than Philippe Sermoise. The first time I saw Katherine.

Villon clutched his head. Don't think of it. It is death to think of it. Katherine. And the wasted years. And nothing ahead but the chance of the gallows. The Bishop of Orléans believed that everything must be paid for. A stolen chalice with a life. No matter that Master François Villon was a clerk: so much the worse. He had blackened his calling. Let him swing for it. Or perhaps Master François was stifling here below because the Bishop had forgotten his existence.

And who would know of it, ever? They sang his songs in the streets and the wineshops of Paris, and points south, too.

There was a poem of his in the manuscript-book of the Duke of Orléans. That would outlast him. But his life, all he had done and suffered, François Villon's Book of Hours, illuminated as no colored parchment could ever be with the living colors of nearly thirty years, stained and torn, too, like his soul —who would see it? Who would know what he had known? The pangs and the excitements, the stream of faces that had danced before him a moment since, the drinking and the dancing, these pieces of Hell in the dungeon of Meun. If he could set that down in words fierce as fire, strong as stone. If he could have that immortality. Or must he go like the rest, and all the anguish, like the little joy, be nothing, be vain?

He sank onto the straw, overcome by such a weight of wretchedness that he could not stir. In the whole foul cell, in the whole round world, there was nothing but his misery.

This anguish was not new. It was his familiar, a companion that stuck closer than any mate he had known. In how many odd corners of the realm of France he had suffered it: at night over the gaming table in some hole of a town; waking in the morning beside some cheap whore; tramping the roads in the driving rain or the scorching sun, between one wayside cross and another; listening to the soft deaf voice of the Duke of Orléans discussing dead men's verses; lying in prison with nothing to eat but chaff, nothing to drink but stale well water, nothing to hope for but the next appearance of the jailer, that was a source of infinite dread.

He took a gulp of water. There was nothing else to swallow but his own salt sweat. Christ, the heat! In winter, you prayed for fire. In summer, in prison, you would sell yourself for a mouthful of pure snow. But where are the snows of a bygone year?

Next year, when the snow falls, where will you be, Villon?
Forget it.

He could forget. In hours of physical misery so great that
his mind could fix only on the craving for drink, for air fit to
take into his choked lungs. The joy it would be to strip off his
dirty rags and plunge into a bath. He could forget when he
made his poems.

Never had he composed so much or so freely as he had since
he lay in this hell-hole. Suspended between life and death, tormented by memories and fears, without occupation, without
books, without companions, what could he do but make
poems? Or go mad.

There were nights when a fit of despair would end in something near madness. Sleep was blessed if it was without dreams.
The one escape was song. When a new one refused to come,
he would recite the old ones to himself for comfort. The sad-
dest of them brought him a strange joy. He grinned to himself over the verses in which, with angry malice, he had recalled the injury done him by Katherine de Vauselles.

For hours he had been lying, with a devil on either side
to prod him, with a fire in his breast and in his brains. The
agony of dying was before him, so that it seemed to him he was
strangling as he had strangled in the hands of the Bishop's
torturers. The horror of oblivion dragged him down, lying
heavier upon him than the irons with which they had chained
him to the staples. He had dug his bony elbows into the straw,
gnawing his knuckles, blind with pain. He had cursed himself,
cursed the star under which he had had his unlucky birth,
cursed Ysabeau for tricking him into the murder of Sermoise,
cursed Katherine for every evil hap that had befallen him
since. She was at the root of it all. It was Katherine who had
got him his thrashing from Noel Jolis. It was Katherine who

had sent him to Fat Margot. It was because of Katherine that he had been an accomplice in the robbery of the College of Navarre. It was Katherine's fault that he had been forced on the road, falling from one sin to a worse, until he had sunk to the black misery of the dungeon of Meun. Slowly, out of his torment, out of his rage, had come the bitter gay ballade:

> Make love as often as you will,
> To every festive gathering go—
> The end's the same and always ill:
> A broken head is your least woe,
> For wantons make men beasts: you know
> The tale of smitten Solomon,
> And Samson lost his peepers so.
> Lucky the man who deals with none.

He had gone on, reciting the names of the cheated lovers of history and legend as he had paraded alike the great lords and ladies dead and the prostitutes of his native streets, winding up with mock carelessness:

> Of my poor self a tale I'll spill:
> Stark naked I was beaten, so
> They paddle wash beside a rill.
> That sour cheer, I'd have you know,
> To Katherine de Vauselles I owe.
> Noel was party to the fun;
> Such whacks at weddings lay you low.
> Lucky the man who deals with none.

Katherine: he could not, he would not if he could, shut her out of his memory.

> But does that gay young bachelor will
> To pass those damsels by? Oh, no!

295

Burn him alive, as you would kill
Foul wizards riding broomsticks. Oh,
Not civet is so sweet, he'll crow.
Yet put your trust in them—you're gone;
Brunette or blonde, all's one; and so
Lucky the man who deals with none.

He had played variations on that theme. There was his ballade of good counsel to those mad fellows who hacked and
stole their way to the gallows. There were the savage warnings he had couched in the jargon, to be sung, if they could
issue through these thick walls, to a refrain of guffaws and
oaths in the lowest dives in France. There was his other ballade of advice to those of evil life.

The cheater cheated himself, the thief robbed himself, the
thug battered himself, the slyest fox got caught in the end. No
matter how many smart tricks they turned, or how readily the
money came, it slipped through the fingers faster still. The
wineshops and the wenches wrecked the lot of them; the hangman waited for them, as he was waiting for poor François.
What did they get out of it, the peddlers of faked indulgences
who had never been near Rome, trading on the credulity of
pious fools? The coiners who risked dying in a bath of boiling
oil? The dice-coggers, the petty sneak thieves, the billiard-room
loafers, the card sharpers, wandering from town to town with
strolling players, ragged jongleurs, and loud-mouthed quacks:
where did their winnings go? All to the wineshops and the
girls. Better to earn your bread honestly, better to turn your
shoulder to the heavy plow, groom horses, beat hemp even, if
you weren't lettered enough to do a clerk's job, than end up
with a broken head, an empty wallet, a sick heart.

But—no treasure counts save living at your ease. He had said that too, and meant it. Did he know what he meant?

He knew a good deal. He knew a man by his habit, a tree by its fruit, the monk by his gown, the nun by her veil, the rogue by his jargon, the wine by the tun. He knew lords in velvet and dirty varlets. Horses and mules, and what you paid for them. Prices, how to draw up accounts. Money, and how hard it was to come by. The power of Rome, and the sin of Huss's heretics who were fighting that power. He knew hard labor, and loafing. He knew fools feeding on cream; he knew women. Yes, and what it was to dream. And to sleep, and be nothing. Sleep, and death that devours all. He knew everything, he knew everyone but himself.

A man should know himself. But how? Who was to teach you? Time was when men of active life went into a monastery at the close of it to study their souls and prepare for the end. But the monasteries were no refuge from the world in these days: they were well-endowed schools of rich living where you drank good Beaune and ate soup au Jacobin, and pursued the Church's business. They were no place to find yourself. It was better to go to prison. In the dungeon of Meun he had leisure to examine that unknown: Master François Villon.

He could not get to the bottom of him. Heartsick in the midst of his mirth. Laughing with his eyes full of tears. Mad for life and cursing the bitter meanness of it. Longing for the peace of the grave, shaken by the terror of death. Hating those who squeezed the poor so that they turned into the wolves and rats he chummed with, and filled with a passion of envy for those who lived in comfort, secure, at ease, without fear of the sergeants, the judge, the rope. Loving the poor old canon for a mercy seldom tempered with justice and wounding him at every step. Hating Katherine de Vauselles but ready to damn his soul to be with her once; spending himself on Fat Margot. Mocking the learned and starved for fame; eager for the young men to admire and praise him, for the old men to praise and study him. Wanting to see every sight the world could show, to feel everything a man could feel, to experience luxury and hunger, lust and tenderness, ecstasy and despair, black shame even, and despising the ways that led him to such terrible knowledge. Riddled with doubts of God, casting himself on Christ.

He could fill volumes with what he knew. What were his verses for but to give some poor fragment of it all? Himself he did not know.

He was startled out of his bitter meditations by the noise of the great key, the clank of heavy bolts being shifted. But he was too wretched to greet his unwelcome visitor with so much as a curse.

The jailer stood for a moment looking at him, then set down his rations with a grunt.

If he hasn't come to tell me I'm to hang, why doesn't he get out? thought Villon, not stirring. But the man continued to stand there, looking at the prisoner through half-shut eyes and rubbing his chin with his fat hand. At last, in a disappointed tone:

"Don't you want to hear the news this day, Master François?"

Villon glanced up at the red face in its fringe of white bristle. A shudder of premonition shot through him, rousing him. What was it?

"Christ," he whispered hoarsely.

So soon. Had it come so soon? He was chilled to the marrow. The sweat stood out on his forehead.

298

The jailer's coarse face brightened with a sneer of amusement.

"No, they ain't wanting you yet. Thibaut d'Aussigny's got more important business than the likes o' you."

Villon dragged himself over to the jug and drank thirstily. His knees were weak. His heart was throbbing painfully.

After that deadly fear, respite was almost like a full pardon. He sank into the straw again, trembling, and wiped his face with his sleeve.

"Well. You don't give a damn?"

The jailer could not hold it any longer.

"The King's dead!"

Villon looked up then.

"The King?"

The Great Khan, did he mean? To whom would the Companions pay tribute then? It would have meant something to Colin, this news, and to René. It would mean something to Perrinet and Aubin. It might have meant something to poor François not long ago.

"Charles himself," said the jailer, relishing the fat morsel of news.

Villon let out a guffaw that made his chest ache. It was like him to have thought first of the king of the underworld.

"What's the joke in that? He's dead, save his soul."

"It's no joke." Yet the news of death always made Villon grin. It was the richest, most horrible jest in the world.

"Well." The jailer looked dubious. But he must gossip. "Couple a weeks ago it was. July the twenty-third, they say. We just heard." He paused impressively. "And what of?"

"What of?" Villon repeated stupidly. He had not grasped it. Charles dead. That meant the Dauphin would have the throne.

299

God, they must be in a fever in Paris. All France stirred up. Would the quarrel with Burgundy break out again?

"They say it was a dirty business. Like with Agnes Sorel. Poison, they say."

"Agnes Sorel wasn't poisoned: that was a canard set going by the men who wanted to ruin Jacques Coeur. Who says it?"

"I dunno. But there's talk. Louis was always fightin' his pa. He won't stand no nonsense. Ain't anybody goin' to take anything away from Louis; he's tight-fisted as a peasant. Things'll be different, I'm thinkin'."

What things? The great lords would suffer. Louis was ambitious. But the merchants, the bankers? Villon recalled vaguely the talk he had heard at Blois. He had hardly listened. The power of the King was of small importance to Master François and his friends, the Companions of the Cockleshell: they paid tribute to the Great Khan. Now Villon wished he had attended more closely. It would be something to silence the jailer with. He had made a poem out of it at any rate: Virtue nor vigor are deserved of him who wishes ill toward the realm of France! He grinned feebly, remembering.

And then he remembered the old King's entry into Paris: the processions, the feasts, the bonfires. Would Louis XI make such an entry?

François Villon would not be there to see it. Where would he be then? A prisoner wearing out his life in the Bishop's dungeon? A shred-fleshed scarecrow jigging on the wind? A moment since, terror had chilled his bones at the thought of the news the jailer might be giving him. A vain terror.

Dazed with relief, his thoughts skipping from the dead King to his son and back again, Villon let the harsh voice gossip on unheeded. Suddenly he leaped up from the straw.

"Man! Man! When'll he be crowned?"

"Who? Louis? What's it to you? Next month, I s'pose."

"But then he'll make a tour of France. He'll visit the feuda-tories. Orléans, too. If it's made worth his while. He's close, but he's shrewd as the devil. God, man, there's a chance! If I hold out that long . . . If the Bishop . . ." Villon was stopped by a fit of coughing.

The jailer sniggered.

"Think you'll have the same luck twice? Aagh!"

The man was revenging himself because the prisoner had not made more of his news. Left alone again, Villon chewed on his despair. By the time Louis was crowned, François Vil-lon might be a dead man.

Charles must be entombed by this time. As remote as Char-lemagne himself. And where is the gallant Charlemagne? Where were they all, the buried kings and emperors, the saints and apostles whose graves lay in holy ground? Where were the countless poor knights and small merchants whose bones crowded the charnels, the nameless peddlers, rogues, and thieves, flung into the ditches to rot? Where are they now? The wind has carried them all away.

And poor François? He must not go that way yet. Not yet, O God. He had a chance now, a slim one but a chance! If only he could bribe the jailer. Because Louis might enter Meun, even as the little Princess Marie had entered Orléans, and free the poor devils in its prisons. Once he was at liberty, Master François might even say a good word for the Bishop's jailer. A mouse can help a lion. And he had powerful friends. The Duke of Orléans. The Duke of Bourbon. The canon would turn heaven and earth to save him and to reward those who had done him a service. But the canon was leagues away. And the Bishop might write finis to his page before ever Louis become king. Villon cursed his fate. But the jailer knew he had escaped as narrow a squeeze as this once before. And that, if the Bishop of Orléans was his enemy, the Duke was not so deaf as to fail to hear and admire his verses. Villon felt new power flow into him as his hopes rose. Louis must come this way. François Villon was not dead yet. Nor his poetry either.

Jumping up from the straw, dragging himself back and forth across the strip of earth, coughing, running his fingers through his scant hair, across his unshaven cheek, touching the old scar on his cleft lip, his thoughts still hung on death, but not now on poor François.

He was thinking of Charles, the hapless king whom a girl had crowned, at last equal with the superb Charlemagne, and Charlemagne leveled with him in mortality. He thought of the Maid of Orléans, whose kinsfolk lived on under the protection of another Charles, the melancholy Duke, while her charred bones were washed by the river under the walls of Paris.

Where was she now, the good girl Jeanne? He would like to have known her. And those others, whom Villon should have known: the great courtesans, the stately queens, the ladies so wonderful that the least of men, the sapless masters of the Schools, must speak of them. Where was Flora, the lovely Roman? Where was Thais, the fair Athenian who had followed Alexander into Egypt? And that Burgundian queen who used to look down from her tower and draw her lovers with her eyes and after she had used them had them silenced in the waters of the Seine. All except Jean Buridan, the handsome rector of the University, who fell onto a barge carrying a load of straw and was dragged to safety by his students. Buridan had been famous for his knowledge of mechanics. He had developed a theory of falling bodies, celestial and sublunar. Was it before or after he was thrown from the tower? Villon grim-

aced. But where was Héloïse, whose room in the cloisters of
Notre Dame was still pointed out, where Abélard took her?
The greatest man in Europe her lover, and he made a eunuch
because of her. Villon's thoughts played strangely among the
ladies, remembered in song and story, whom no man would see
again.

They had been living women once, had slept with their
heads on their lovers' arms, had waked, stretching and yawning. Where were they now? The quick eyes, the smooth faces,
the sweetness of the flesh, the majesty of presence, the laughter, the enchantment of long looks and joined lips. Ask, where
is last year's snow.

Villon hummed softly to himself. The music of his own
verses caressed him. He was carried out of himself into a
golden air. But not for long. The dead beauties, the dead kings
reminded him of those dead whom he had spoken with in life,
of Colin, of René, and inevitably of that shaken creature starving in the prison of the Bishop of Meun, sweating to know
when he must die.

So the summer passed, the dreadful nights, the humid burning days, relieved only by the visits of the jailer, that Villon
feared as much as he welcomed. Had the Bishop forgotten
him? August passed without change. Mid-September brought
news that Louis had been crowned. He was on a tour of the
feudatories. Would he be entertained at Blois as Villon had
been before him? Would he hear, from his cousin the Duke,
of the first poet in France?

It was the beginning of October. At the familiar sound of
rasping metal at the door, Villon looked up with a premonitory
shudder.

The jailer stood there silently surveying the prisoner and
scratched his chin with the big key.

Villon's heart was hammering. Excitement fought in his breast with deadly fear. God, why didn't the man speak?

"Damn me," said the jailer slowly, "if you ain't got the devil's own luck."

Villon was dumb with horror.

"The King was in Orléans yesterday. Tomorrow, by sext, he'll be in Meun."

But that meant—that meant—he'd be free. Unless the Bishop chose to hang him out of hand.

In the ecstasy of his relief, Villon swayed on his feet and fell, with a jangling of irons, in a blind heap on the floor of the dungeon.

Chapter Nineteen

It was impossible. It was true. The miracle of the previous year had repeated itself. Then it had been the little Princess Marie whose triumphal entry into her own city of Orléans had freed Villon and his broken comrades from the miseries of the Orléans prison. Now the eleventh Louis, as shrewdly masterful as his saintly forebear had been gentle and humble, now the King of France himself, by passing through Meun, had let Villon out of the Bishop's clutches. The wonder of it would have made him sing for joy, but his voice was cracked.

Hunched over the table in the tavern where he had taken his first dram of wine, his first mouthful of meat in all these lean months, Villon reflected that it was not his voice only that was cracked. He looked at the hand grasping his mug and asked himself if this was the veritable hand of Master François. Could those crooked sticks of fingers, swollen at the joints, that had just been able to grasp the broom in the stableyard, be made to hold a pen? Could this dizzy head, almost hairless now, be made to work well enough to frame so much as a rondel? Would François ever truly be himself again?

The girls wouldn't know him when he got back to Paris.

And the canon. Would the canon recognize the lad he had fathered in this half-bald wretch, his ribs sticking out of his sides as easy to count as the teeth of a rake, his wild jokes stopped by the cough that tore at his chest and left him sweating and trembling like a beaten cur? Villon wanted to see the old man again, however he dreaded the meeting. If anyone could save him from belated Paris justice, it would be the canon.

And his mother? Living or dead, she was better off than her brilliant son.

Villon took another gulp of wine. It warmed your guts. It lightened your heavy humor. Damn the Bishop! Treating him to nothing but water inside and out. There was the very root of poor François' sickness.

But he was alive! By God, he wasn't finished yet. He'd go back to Paris with something to show for all he had seen and suffered.

To show whom? Not Colin. Not René. He would not show off before them ever again, unless it were in Hell. Before Fat Margot perhaps. Who'd give him a job entertaining her customers. It would mean food, at least, drink, and shelter, and love of a sort.

Katherine. He wouldn't be apt to come upon her. Or if he did it would be like the last meeting of Troilus and Cressida,

306

when the knight had seen no more in his erstwhile mistress than a blear-eyed beggar at the gates. But Villon would be the beggar this time.

He took another swallow. Katherine would not know him. Who cared? He'd make Paris know him again, though. By Christ, he would! He'd be safe in going back now. Back to the rue St. Jacques, the Mule, the Pine Cone, St. Benoit, Notre Dame, the fishwives on the Bridge, the rotisseries with their fat juicy capons turning on the spit till your mouth watered, back to the boats on the river, the noises at the armourers', the bustle in the furriers' quarter, back to the University, the Library of the Sorbonne, the College of Navarre . . . And the sergeants, the lawyers, the courts, the prisons, the charnels. Eh, ho! Villon coughed, clutching his chest. Coughed, coughed, and wiped his mouth with a ragged sleeve. But he was alive. No thanks to Thibaut d'Aussigny. Whom may God damn.

Drinking and coughing, sweeping out the stables, grooming the horses to pay for more drinks, Villon spent the next few weeks in an effort to put the prison stench and the prison thirst and the prison solitude behind him. But he could not. Spitting and cursing, with a fire in his guts, he nursed the resolve to get back to Paris, to get near enough to let the canon know he must beg, borrow, or steal the letter of full remission that his release from Meun had not won for him.

Only to get back. For the time was short. Thibaut d'Aussigny had shortened it for him with his damp toad-infested hell, his diet of dry bread and water. The time was short. And he must not go empty-handed. Villon saw to it that in addition to his keep he earned enough to buy himself paper and ink and quills.

Before he left the tavern, to trudge lamely to his next unlovely resting place on the road home, he had written down the first stanzas of his final testament. Written it out of the bitterness of his heart, the sickness of his body, the unquenchable bright malice of his spirit.

> *Set down in this, my thirtieth year,*
> *When all my sins I've swallowed neat—*
> *Not quite a fool, not wise, that's clear,*
> *Despite my many pains: a treat*
> *From him whose fingers bless the street,*
> *Hard-fisted Thibaut d'Aussigny.*
> *Though he sit in a bishop's seat,*
> *He cannot lord it over me!*

All very well, but would the Bishop of Paris have any heartier welcome for poor François? Villon coughed and went on scribbling.

He had escaped so much, the miseries of the road, the envy of the Duke's courtiers, the plague at Bourges, the cruelties of the Bishop's dungeon, the hangman's noose. Was he to die like a sick dog in a ditch? He, the greatest poet France had produced since Jean de Meun, he who outshone Rutebeuf and Deschamps and Alain Chartier? He whom Louis XI had seen fit to pardon because, while the realm held some greater rascals, it held no verse-man who came to his shoulder even?

The canon would guard and cherish him surely. He would give him a decent bed and good food, and the warming wine that was the best medicine in the best city in the world. He would not let him cough himself to death before he had truly lived. Then Master François would turn over a new leaf.

It was possible. Anything was possible to a man in health with money in his purse.

Crazy day dreams of a sick fancy. He would never be well again, never be rich, never be brave or honest or wise. Thibaut

308

d'Aussigny's dungeon had damped the little flame of virtue that was in him. There was nothing left but the fever to live, to make his name shine—the canon's name—with a fame that would outlast his feeble carcass. But to live he must be in Paris.

And so he came there at long last, his tongue hanging out of his mouth like a thirsty dog's, his stained clothes patched with the rags of a friendly country wench, his lean body racked by pains and his eternal cough, and a sheaf in his wallet that made him prouder than all the dukes in the realm.

It would be no surprise to old Guillaume Villon to see him. From his last refuge, the hideout on the outskirts where even so mean a creditor as Robin Turgis could not find him out, he had smuggled messages to his guardian that had at last brought him the coveted letter of remission. It took care of everything.

Everything save the matter of the robbery of the College of Navarre.

And that was no joke. Villon had learned from a chance encounter with one of the Companions that Tabary had been released only on condition that he pay back to the outraged authorities more money than he had ever seen. The beadle of the College, old Laurens Poutrel, who had lost a goodly sum of his own when the treasure was stolen, was still sleuthing with vicious earnestness for the other accomplices. And Tabary, under torture, or more probably out of vainglorious stupidity, had not hesitated to name Master François Villon. No matter.

Nothing mattered now but that Villon was home again. After five years of variegated misery. Sick, sorry, but with the poem that had been kicking at the walls of his mind like a nine-months' child finally delivered. A live thing if ever there was one, and if it seemed to wear horns and to smell slightly of brimstone, what of the hell that had begotten it on the poet's imagination?

The first few days were the strangest Villon had ever known. Stranger than the luxury of Blois, more wonderful than the charmed life at the castle of the Duke of Bourbon, quieter than the vermin-ridden solitude of the Meun dungeon.

He lay in his old attic bed, under clean covers, with the smell of ripening grapes drifting in from the close below, and no noise save the morning cockcrow and the regular chiming and booming of the bells of Paris. Nothing to disturb his vague reveries but the hushed steps of the canon, coming to bring him a bowl of broth, or a broiled bird and a cup of wine, or to see that he had swallowed a decoction of not unpleasant herb tea that was supposed to get the better of the cough. Villon sometimes staggered from his bed to pour it out of the window. But for the most part he lay there between sleep and dreams, grateful even when the dreams were nightmares because he could wake to a miraculous lack of hunger and thirst and dread. The canon served him, nursed him, asked him no questions. The prayers that the old man said over the returned prodigal were as private as his tears. He did not open his lips to the sick man except to medicine him with a mild jest. Everything was as it had been when Villon had first come to the Red Door, a boy sharp for life and learning. Everything was changed, toned down to a minor key, wrapped in a kind of comfortable mist. There was but one new object in the attic room, new to the room, in itself very old: the Florentine image of the Virgin that had always presided over the canon's hearth. Villon's eyes would open upon it when he waked, it would be the last thing he saw before his tired eyes shut again.

Lady of Heaven, Queen of the earth, Empress over the marshes of Hell . . . The holy image wavered before his gaze, confused for him in this twilight mood with one of his earliest memories: the rich greens and blues and reds in the stained-glass windows at the Celestines.

Villon's eyes were closed. All the more clearly he saw the Mother of God, in Her blue mantle, lovelier than any master in Florence or Paris could paint her, gentler than any woman Villon had ever known, and mightier in Her gentleness.

Lady, my Mistress, even my sins cannot exhaust Thy loving-kindness; without it, no soul would merit Heaven or ever win to that place. Nothing short of superhuman kindness, divine womanliness, unstained by desire, utterly merciful, utterly bountiful, could save poor François now. He must not glance into the gulf of unbelief. He stretched out his crooked fingers as though to clutch at the hem of the blue mantle sweeping in soft folds about the Virgin's feet. His fingers closed on air. His hands dropped. He sighed heavily. The image faded. He dared not open his eyes to the painted sculpture on the shelf. Not yet. For She was here, unseen, but very present, very near. Holy Mother of God. I do not lie. He coughed. I do not lie: in this faith I would live and die.

He smiled feebly. He was rhyming again. He must be getting well.

If he was to be saved at all, the Mother of God would turn the trick. She had saved the rascal on the gallows in the nursery tale. His own mother had told it to him often enough.

She must be alive, thought Villon. The canon would have dropped a hint if he were never to see her again. He must go to her. By Heaven, he would take her a present, too. A prayer that was a ballade, a ballade that was a prayer.

He turned on his bed and coughed again. It would be good to stand on his legs. He'd get into his clothes somehow. There was fresh linen and a decent suit hanging over the bed-rail in readiness. Perhaps by tomorrow, Master François, you'll be strong enough to take a stroll down the rue St. Jacques. You might drop in at the Mule. Do you think you can hold a billiard cue?

The new clothes hung loosely on his aching body. The canon could not know how many pounds had been sweated away in the Meun dungeon. But the suit would be stuffed out yet with plenty of meat and drink. And the praises he'd win with his verses would puff out any man's chest. Villon laughed hoarsely to himself, winding up with a cough.

The canon had heard. He was standing at the foot of the stairs, peering up with anxious eager eyes. Villon waved a hand to him, stumbling weakly down the familiar steps.

"Are you all right, my son?"

It was cosy before the canon's fire, though Villon was a little dizzy with the effort of dressing and moving about. He felt reduced to childhood again as he sat there in the old room, beside the old man, holding fast to the secret of sins that the canon would not imagine, secure in the canon's ignorance, leaning on an affection that confession might strain but could not break. It was queer, the old man's love, passing the love of women.

The canon got up to pour him a cup of wine, and coming back with it, hesitated a moment beside the chessboard. It was not a game that François had ever shown a fancy for. Not risky enough. But convalescence, that had turned him to a child, made him something of an oldster too. Perhaps he would suggest a tourney.

Villon coughed and hid his face with his hand, ignoring the tentative gesture as he had always ignored his guardian's wishes. But he was ready for the wine. The canon repressed a sigh and sipped with him.

"Well, my son."

Bald, palsied, half his teeth out of his head, more time's wreck than that beetle-browed, gentle-faced man with the white-fringed tonsure would ever be, Villon was still "son" to the canon. Father, Son, and Holy Ghost. I am the unholy ghost, Villon grinned privately, come back to haunt the poor man. But all he said was:

"There is nothing like a cup of Beaune."

"Except another cup of Beaune," smiled the canon.

"No: the second is never as good as the first. Wine is like a woman. You enjoy her so much that you cannot wait to repeat it. But the edge has been taken off. Desire is blunted. It is never the same."

Had he forgotten to whom he spoke? No, he must show the old man that the devil was in him still.

"I do not know about women," said the canon, who had been sucking his cheek in the funny familiar way he had. "But that is true of every pleasure of the flesh. I am glad you have learned it, François."

"I have learned it with my mind," Villon admitted. "But my body is a damnable dunce."

"Another cup then." The canon rose to fill it for him.

"The pleasures of the spirit are different," said Villon wryly. "Forgiveness remains enjoyable, though it be required seventy times seven times, eh, my father?"

The canon growled softly in the way Villon remembered.

"I cannot forgive myself," he said.

Villon raised his eyebrows.

"Notre Dame always held you to be a sinner," he murmured.

"This has nothing to do with Notre Dame, my dear. Nor with St. Benoit either. I have all but damned your soul, François, and my own along with it."

313

"You!"

"I."

They were silent, the canon sunk in meditation, sucking his cheek, Villon lost in a wonder that quenched his malice.

"I have wronged you, François," muttered the canon at last. "God grant it is not yet too late to undo a little of it all."

"You?" Villon repeated and fell to coughing.

The canon looked at him anxiously. The cough gave over.

"Confess your sins, my father," said Villon then with a reassuring wink. This would be forgiveness with a vengeance. He to pardon the canon. For what, in God's name?

"Do you remember when your mother first brought you to the Red Door? A little street gamin you were. From the looks of you one could have believed that that good Christian woman had stolen you from the gypsies." The canon smiled at the memory. "In all the years I had been teaching, I had never seen a lad like you. Your aunts had bragged to me about you, shaking their heads. They knew you, François, but they had such hopes. . . . And your mother, I think she saw you a bishop as soon as I agreed to take you on. I am not sure I did not think something of the sort myself."

"I never encouraged you in it," said Villon.

"Never," the canon admitted.

"And was that how you wronged me: trying to make a bishop out of a young pickpocket? I have seen pickpockets made out of bishops."

"No, my dear." The canon paused for a moment before he spoke again. "I told you just now that I knew nothing of the love of women. When God made me He seems to have left something out that is given to most men. Assuredly He did not make me quite in His image. But He gave me much to be grateful for." The canon sighed and went on in a lower voice.

314

"I have loved, François. I loved my pupils: the worst of them the most. None more than you."

Set down in this, my thirtieth year, when all my shames I've swallowed neat, thought Villon bitterly. But he gagged on them now. The wave of shame that swept over him was like nausea. He flung himself on his knees before the old man.

Guillaume de Villon frowned.

"Do not kneel to me, boy. Or is it before the good God that you are kneeling?"

But Villon did not rise. He wanted to sob, and could not. He wanted to ask forgiveness, not of his heavenly Father, but of his earthly one, and could not. He was ashamed, and ashamed of his shame. His spirit was as sick as his body. He felt the old man's hand, soft and dry as some fine tissue, laid gently on his head. It was removed, and he rose, turning awkwardly to look into the fire so as not to look at the canon. It was the canon who spoke first.

"I did not beget you in the flesh, my son, though I think you may sometimes have imagined that."

Villon's imagination had indeed once laid that sin to his mother's door and to the canon's. He had been mistaken. The old man had probably never known a woman; the poor parishioner of the Celestines was an honest soul.

The old voice, strained with the hard task of confession, continued:

"But I have been your spiritual father. And like all fathers I wanted you to be everything I had not been. I wanted you to know all that I had not known, to relish what I had not enjoyed, God forgive me, even to suffer what I had not suffered. But that last was only because I thought it would bring you nearer to Christ. You believe me?"

Villon nodded.

"Yes, you may well wonder at me, François." The canon's face showed a strange smile. "You did not see it then for all your wit. You do not understand it yet. But I had been one of those young men who feel no particular urge to sin. What is commonly called virtue came so easily to me that there was no virtue in it. I wanted, as I grew older and knew myself for what I was, I wanted to be one of those who overcome temptation, who are masters of their souls because they have wrestled for them with the devil himself.

"And then you came, as full of life as an egg is of meat. As full of mischief as the sea is full of terror. You were terrible, my dear. And I looked upon your weak childish soul as a surrogate for mine. You were to be what I had not been, to do all that I had not done. You with your zest for the fleshpots, your love of gaiety and splendor, your immense cleverness, your hunger for fame. I was to be famous through you, François, not through your verses, but through your triumph over the old Adam in you. I, your teacher and spiritual father, was to be known throughout Paris and beyond for your humbleness of spirit, for your sainthood! Good God! What a fool I was. What an arrogant fool!"

For a moment there was no sound in the room but the canon's heavy breathing. Villon did not stir.

"You used to wonder at my forgiveness of your peccadillos and then of your greater sins. You thought me an easy mark, I dare say." The canon snorted with anger at himself. "But I remembered the sins of St. Augustine and of St. Francis, your saint, and how they came to repent and to be true sons of God. I always thought: this is the last time."

The canon stopped short. His voice had been dry enough. But his eyes, when at last Villon dared to look at him, were wide with the difficult tears of the aged.

316

"You will be famous, my father," he croaked with indomitable pride. "Don't forget that I bear the name of Villon. It is attached to some of the greatest poetry ever written in the realm of France."

"I do not doubt they will remember you, my dear. There have always been plenty who have recited your verses. Even I heard them occasionally. They will go on singing your songs even after we are both dead, perhaps.

"But where will you be then, François?" the old man cried in an ecstasy of anguish. "What of your soul, my son? And the soul of old Guillaume de Villon?"

Villon grimaced, his restless eyes shining in a face like a dirty rag.

"They say there is excellent company in Hell," he jested hoarsely.

There was a moment of stupefied silence.

"May God—" the old man cried out savagely, and stopped. "May God," he ended on a low harsh note, "have mercy upon me, a sinner."

Villon's eyes slithered away from the canon. He began to cough. He could not stop. The cough tore at his lungs, wrestled in his throat, his chest heaved, his lean body shook. He would promise anything, perform anything, if he could only stop coughing. The canon watched him, the anger gone out of his face, only the pain sharp in his anxious eyes.

At last it was over. Villon lay back in the chair, his heart thudding, and wiped his mouth with an unsteady hand.

"Go back to bed," said the canon in a low voice. "You will be better off there," he added more gently.

Villon shook his head weakly.

He did not want to go back to bed. To lie there and think

and ache. A curse on his cough. A curse on Thibaut d'Aussigny and his Meun dungeon.

He wanted more wine. And the soft arms of a girl. He wanted music and someone begging him for a stave of his own making. He wanted to feel strong and gay, proud and forgetful.

"Help me across the street," Villon muttered in a hoarse whisper. "To the Sign of the Mule. I will come back before curfew. I swear."

"But why?" asked the canon. "For God's sake, my son, why do you want to go there?" He groaned. "Must everything I do be the wrong thing?"

Villon shook his head again.

"You will not repent this time. I will come back early. I cannot lie up there alone now."

"You need not be alone. I will stay with you," said the canon painfully.

"No, no!" Villon would have shouted, but he had no strength.

"If you want me to love God," he croaked, "you will have to let me find life worth loving. There is—not much—time—left," he gasped, trying not to cough. He swallowed the wine that the canon held out to him. "For Christ's sake, my father. Help me over to the Mule!"

It was an old gag. But it worked. The canon took his arm. Even after what had happened he could not so easily give up his faith: there was scarcely a saint in the calendar who had not once been a sinful man.

So they moved, lamely, the old priest supporting the broken young man, across the room and down the stairs, out of the Red Door and the cloisters of St. Benoit, to the Sign of the Mule swinging provocatively in the October wind.

318

Chapter Twenty

The whole place was different. Brighter and gayer than Villon remembered it. He liked it no better for that. The decorations set up when Paris had been celebrating King Louis' ascension to the throne still hung against the walls and from the roof beams, crumpled, fly-specked, but lending the tavern a novel aspect. The faces were none of them those he used to see there. But to sit at a table at the Mule and remember the old days was almost as painful as to lie in the Meun dungeon and know they would never come again.

What girl, seeing that bald head bent over his cup, would think of asking him to stand her a drink? What man, noting that haunted, toothless face, would nudge his companion and whisper eagerly: "D'you see that fellow in the corner, alone? That's Villon, the poet!"

Suppose he were to leap onto the table and recite his ballade on the women of Paris? Suppose he were to sing out one of his gay bitter songs on whoredom? Or his rhymed advice to men of evil life? They'd never guess who it was that was entertaining them. How should they? It was not his looks only or his long absence. His missing teeth would make him lisp like that fool Tabary. His voice, that had been rich as the best play-actor's from Angers, was cracked and broken. They'd cry him down, like as not, for his caterwauling. Boot him out of doors as an impostor. He wept into his mug.

He was an old man. He was thirty. His youth was gone, and nothing to show for it. His life was finished, and nothing to look forward to but the last humiliation of dying.

He'd left them a legacy, though, that would make them think twice of him. They'd grit their teeth over it when he was past grinning back. They'd curse him, when he was beyond their hurt, for the way he'd painted them: the hard-handed pontiff who had starved him through that hellish summer; the old usurers who held the city in their grip (poor little orphans, he'd called them in derision); the overweening canons of Notre Dame, to whom he'd left the rent of that house off the rue St. Jacques long years of litigation had not produced; all the most famous, all the most infamous men and women of Paris were remembered in his Testament, the whores and cheats in patches jostling the big thieves in purple and ermine; all viciously characterized, mocked with gifts as empty as their heads, as foul as their sins, as cruel as their lives. Poor François had nothing to bequeathe, eh? His soul to the blessed Trinity, his body to our great mother, the earth—the worms would get little good of such a skinny carcass—his library and his epic of the

320

Pet-au-Diable to his mother's surrogate, old Guillaume de Villon; a prayer to the poor woman herself; to everyone else alike, great and small, wise and simple, good and evil, comrades and enemies: gibes, japes, wounding wit, savage irony, the quick stabs of a malice that pierced to the bone. The same to Fat Margot. The same to Katherine de Vauselles.

He would like to see Katherine's face when she received his bequest to her: the Ballade to his Dear, with the double acrostic: François, Marthe, to shame her, and the end-rhymes on "r" which carried a naughty suggestion she might guess, having been tutored in such innuendos by himself. He had started the thing six years ago at Fat Margot's. He had finished it in prison. Now it was part of his final Testament. Set down in malice. It would last. No chance of seeing her read it. No chance of seeing her at all. He had not wanted her in the Meun dungeon when he was starving. Why should he want her now when his heart was full of cramps as his belly had been then? He would see Fat Margot first. By God, he would.

His legs were too wobbly, or he would go tonight. But the next night, if he had to get the canon to help him there, sinning his way to sainthood, he'd go.

It was not the next night, for his cough grew worse again. But the canon did help him, by dint of nursing him anxiously back to some semblance of strength, to leave the Red Door for the streets of Paris within less than a week. Villon avoided the Mule, which had afforded him so little joy on his first excursions, and the Pine Cone, where he feared to run into Noel Jolis, and where, moreover, the hostess managed things more strictly since her brother-in-law had died in a bath of boiling oil for his sins.

As he limped down the familiar street he wondered if there would be many changes. He could not imagine that Fat Margot had altered much. She probably had three chins now instead of two. Doubtless she was jolly again, for trade had picked up since Louis had come to the throne. What would she say when she saw him? Which of the Companions would he find there?

The place was fuller than his imagination had pictured it. Eagerly he sniffed the familiar air, with its mixed smells of wine, heavy perfumes, and tallow; pricked his ears to define the welcome hubbub of voices, twanging strings, stamping feet, the slap of cards or of bare hands on bare bodies, and the small clatter of dice on a table. He sat down in a corner, wanting to orient himself before he should ask for Margot, and winked gleefully at the pimpled potboy who took his order. The lad little thought that this queer-looking customer had performed the same service in this place once. Most of the girls were new, but he could have laughed out when he heard a shrill metallic voice behind him cry, "Reely!" The men were strangers, but their hard-bitten swarthy faces, some gashed, some lop-eared, no less than the oaths in the jargon from one wide mouth and the cockles on certain greasy caps, marked them as Companions. He did not see Fat Margot until he was drinking his second cup of wine, and then a creak on the stairs announced her, the roly-poly body supported unbelievably by her tiny feet, and surmounting her full white breasts the ruddy face dimpling professionally. She caught sight of him almost at the same moment and pointed a fat forefinger at him, amused by the bald skeletal figure.

"If he'd give me some of his lean and I'd give him some of my fat, we'd make two proper folks, eh, lads?" she cried gaily.

Some few looked at him and laughed. The fat girl came on heavily down the narrow stairs, blowing a kiss to Villon. Plainly she did not know him.

"Hey, Margot!" he summoned her.

322

"Dear child," she mocked him, "how is it your tutor lets you out so late? D'you want Margot to see you safe home?"

"Maybe," he grinned. "Sit down here, Fatty. How's tricks?"

His clothes were good enough to warrant a full purse. But they could not hide his bony body, his death's-head features. He was good for some drinks, and maybe he would do someone the kindness to lose at cards, but that was all there was to be got out of that one. She crinkled her eyes, vainly trying to place him.

Villon continued to grin, exposing the gaps in his mouth, and then, to cover them, passed a hand over his scarred lip. At the gesture, Fat Margot let out a cry. He nodded.

"It's me, old girl. Come and sit down. We'll drink to the good old days."

She obeyed him, her small blue eyes still stretched with amazement. Her look made him laugh, and he ended up with a coughing fit.

"By God, what did they do to you?"

"Plenty."

She shook her head.

"That's a bad cough you've got, my poor one."

But she soon saw that tenderness was wasted on him. What he wanted was news. He questioned her slyly, about herself, about the new provost, about the other girls, and the Companions who were hanging around them. By God, she repeated at intervals, it was like seeing a ghost.

She thought he'd gone the way of René, of Colin. He stopped her. Had she seen Tabary lately? Ah, no one saw Tabary now. He was still paying his debt to the authorities. The College of Navarre had not taken its loss lightly. And all the expense of replacing the broken locks, too! The beadle wanted his own treasure back. He'd been snooping everywhere. Villon had best

323

watch his step. Maybe he was done with all that? In his grand outfit. She surveyed it appraisingly. He looked like a respectable citizen—from the rear. But no one could mistake the meaning of that slit lip, those eyes moving uneasily in the dark worn face.

Fat Margot tossed her head in the direction of a student who was strumming a lute and singing in an uncertain voice. "Listen to him! Thinks he can play. Why don't you show him, Villon?"

He shrugged.

But Margot had not been his doxy six years ago for nothing. She knew how to coax him. As she talked, his grin widened. His eyes glittered.

He began to improvise a song in the jargon, tumbling out rich rhymes on the cut-throat band, the hangman's hand, the jerk of the noose, the high-hanging goose. The Companions suspended their play to listen. Soon half the room was roaring a chorus the sense of which some had to guess from his playacting, though even the ignorant relished his mysterious slang. Villon did not go back to the Red Door that night, nor the next.

There would have been no need to return at all, had it not been for want of money. He had soon spent more than he could afford on the red wine for which Margot, with her increased affluence, had become famous and on the dishes he commanded from the nearest rotisseries and bakeshops. He could not eat and drink well and often enough to make up for what he had suffered at Thibaut d'Aussigny's niggard hands. Plump oysters, juicy roasts, crisp patties, custards, cakes, the delicious cream tarts that he had rhymed on repeatedly with a watering mouth, always accompanied by jugs of glowing Beaune or fragrant Arbois, were not to be had for a song, even

324

of Villon's singing. Fat Margot might call him "Gogo" again and caress him with careless familiarity, but though she admired his wit she could not be made to feel that this lantern-faced shiny-pated figure of death was the fierce François whom she had once walked the streets to serve. She must turn her charms to account quickly if she did not want to follow his beautiful old armouress into the gutter. She would support Villon no longer. And though he shook the dice ever so shrewdly, there was always a cleverer sharper than he to empty the purses of such young fools as looked for entertainment in that house. He began to wonder where his meals were to come from.

If he were to go back to the Red Door? The canon would take care of him. He would pray for him. He would get up from his knees and sit in his chair by the fire, sucking his cheek and closing one eye, and consider what to do next. He would not rest till he had found the proper work for Master François Villon, late of the Meun dungeon and Fat Margot's stew, protegé of the canon of St. Benoit.

Villon had promised himself, a few short weeks ago, lying sick and shaken in the hideout where he had composed the greater part of his Testament, that he would reform. The game was not worth the candle. He had written more than one bitter sermon in rhyme on the fate of those who gambled and thieved and hacked their way to the gallows. He had sworn he would not risk his neck again. The canon had dreamed of making a saint out of him. He to be another Francis, like the gay bachelor of Assisi who had learned to kiss lepers. He to imitate Augustine, who had turned from his wantoning and chambering to become a Father of the Church. They had never gone his road. They'd not put their fingers in other men's pockets, nor their knives in other men's bodies, nor traded on a whore's passion. But they'd had their youth. Had their wine and their wenches. And were now among the holy ones of Christendom. It happened, then. Men could change. Had he not changed? Christ, look at him, listen to him, peeled bare as a turnip, coughing like a beggar in a ditch.

He could return to the Red Door. There would be no room for luxury and less for lust, but neither would there be the fear that sometimes waked him in the middle darkness with the nightmare on his chest. It was too late now for picnics at Montfaucon, even if it were spring, which it was not. The old thrill would leave him shuddering, the teeth left him would knock against each other. It was too late for everything but the canon's kindness and the mercy of Christ Jesus. He would go back to the Red Door.

Hungry, for Margot had stinted his food, tired, for he had lost the trick of sleeping, chilly because he was tired, and coughing a little now and then, Villon shambled down the narrow street under the signs that rocked in the autumnal wind, wondering what act he should put on for the canon, imagining how the good old man would look when he saw him back again.

Scarcely minding where he went, he found himself approaching the grand mass of Notre Dame, and halted, in spite of the cold, near the parvis, struck by a bleak memory. Here the young Villon had stood, hoping for a glimpse of Katherine, here he had paced, back and forth and back again, waiting to meet Katherine. Here she had come out of the Door of the Virgin, here she had walked with him a little, sat with him in the sunshine, laughed at his jokes, frowned at his caresses, listened to his passion.

Out of a perverse curiosity, wanting to know if he could indeed be made to feel something again, he walked round toward the Door of the Virgin. It was getting on toward vespers, and the usual bustle about the cathedral had thinned out. He shrugged and turned away.

As he walked off he glanced sullenly at the few passers-by. He did not know them. Why should he? They did not know him. François Villon meant nothing to any of them. That lady in the furred mantle would think no more of him than of the blind beggar outside the church door. She would never know who it was had turned aside to give her room. What did she read beside her psalter? Villon reminded himself that he had pleased the Duke of Orléans, that Jean of Bourbon had been his patron. His audience was the Court, and the slingers of the jargon at Fat Margot's. Suddenly he was seized with the absurd desire to make himself noticed by this elegant bourgeoise, this befurred nobody. She would remember him though she would never know his fame.

Within a few feet of her he lifted his cracked voice in an ancient drinking song. The lady walked on, disregarding the broken mountebank. Her servant laughed and pointed. Villon flashed a smile at her in reply, his black eyes livelier and fiercer than his voice. The servant pulled her mistress by the sleeve. Villon was almost upon them. A cough caught him by the throat and stopped his song. He passed them, still coughing, and turned round to grin once more at the servant. Through the hushed twilit air the lady's voice floated back to him in sharp reproval of her companion:

"What is it, Marthe?"

Only then Villon recognized the cowlike stare, the broad foolish face. But then . . . Why then . . .

Like one bewitched, Marthe stood there looking after him. Villon swept off his cap to her in a mocking bow, just as Katherine de Vauselles turned to summon the girl. Villon

327

could think only that she saw his baldness. He clapped his cap back on his head. Marthe said something he did not catch. Now Katherine was looking too. He was pulled toward her on invisible cords. She faced about as though she did not see. But he was beside her. She could not pretend now.

She looped her train higher over her arm in silence. He turned to Marthe.

"How are you, girl?" he asked. "Do you think you could still find the baker's where they have the fresh almond tarts?"

Marthe stared at him with moist open mouth. He looked at Katherine.

Not a word? Was it anger, or fear, or disgust? He eyed her curiously. The small head set on the long neck, the pale skin, the short upper lip, the green eyes under the straight black brows. They were the same. Not quite the same. What had happened to her in the years he had lost? She had not married Jehan de la Garde. She had not married at all.

With a quick step he was in front of her, blocking the way.

"I didn't seek this meeting," he croaked.

"Nor did I," she said, her voice trembling.

"No. But it should be a pleasure. Look, see what you have escaped."

"Please."

When she dismissed him, he had not looked like this. He had not ever been handsome, but he had not been what he was now, a ragged figure of fun. He saw himself as she must see him, with the terrifying face of the prematurely aged: death's varlet.

"A moment," he said hoarsely. "Just a small moment. As small as your charity. By the way, how is Noel?"

Years ago he had been tongue-tied in his lady's presence, having so much to say. He had imagined, if he should ever chance

328

to encounter her again, he would hold his peace, having nothing to say. Now the words tumbled out of him half against his will. Why?

"That was a masterful beating you got me, sweetheart."

Katherine looked away. It was Marthe who burst out in a low shamed voice:

"Oh, Master François! It was not her fault!"

He raised his hairless brows.

"It was . . ."

"Hush, Marthe!"

"Hush, Marthe," repeated Villon, laying a finger against his scarred lip. "Not a word. Not a syllable." His eyes devoured Katherine. "But you are still beautiful!" he muttered. He turned to the servant. "Go inside, Marthe, if you will not go to the bakeshop. Go in to the priest and say confession. You will not have time to name all your sins before I have had two words with your mistress."

Marthe gaped at him sorrowfully, her pale blue eyes wide with wonder and dismay. It was like the old days. He was filled with angry impatience of her. To his astonishment, as long ago to his relief, Katherine yielded.

"Go, Marthe. But do not be long."

Marthe stared and with an awkward gesture of farewell left the strange pair to themselves before the great door.

"Thank you, my lady," Villon grinned. "You are very good. Now perhaps you will be kind enough to tell me: Who put Noel up to it if it wasn't you?"

She answered his question with another:

"What did they do to you?"

That was what Fat Margot had said: "By God, Villon, what did they do to you?" "Plenty," he had told her. To Katherine he said:

329

"What did *you* do?"

As though she were responsible for the horrors of that fierce summer, for the dismal years that led up to it. If it had not been for Katherine, he would never have gone to Fat Margot's in the winter of '56, nor thence to rob the College of Navarre that Christmas Eve, nor afterward on his dreary pilgrimage up and down the roads of France, in and out of its Courts and its prisons. . . .

"I am sorry," she said. "But you were wrong to blame me. I—"

"Yes, I know," he interrupted. "It's cold here." He shivered. "I must be going." He nodded toward the Cathedral with a crooked smile. "Pray for me in there."

He walked off, but then, thinking, or perhaps only wanting to think, that she had called him, he turned back.

"Eh?"

"No, nothing."

After five years, looking at the thing he had become, what could she say? You behaved as any girl would, my dear, he said to her silently, though she be the daughter of a duchess or a brat in a brothel. Some have dowries. Some have beauty. They're all hungry for love. But a long purse does as well. Better.

He glanced at the rich purse she held. And then at her. She seemed subtly changed. Perhaps she had fallen in love with a better man than François Villon. She must have learned something, whether or no. He remembered when he had wanted to tear her heart open and look inside. Praying he would find his own image there. Wondering if her veins ran ice instead of blood. That memory was clearer than the brief time when he had had her love. Now, freezing in good earnest himself in the cold October dusk, he did not care. Yet she had sent Marthe away. Why? What had she to confess to him?

Katherine, this was Katherine, whom he had longed for as a parched man for drink, as a starved man for food, as a lost child for his mother, as a damned soul for God. This was Katherine, who had turned his gayest jests to bitterness, his hopes to ashes, his triumphs to dust. Katherine, whose remembered eyes had wrenched him with pain in the lap of the sweetest comfort, whose remembered touch had soothed him in all but his worst agonies. Here she was, breathing beside him, her green eyes looking down on him, for she was taller than he.

He groaned.

"You must have known: the marriage—it did not take place."

Yes, he had heard that. But there must be so much he had not heard. At the sound of her voice, humble, strained, the old misery awoke. He was filled with rage against whomever she had loved, with joy in her pity, in her evident pain.

"And the beating you got Noel to give me did not take place either," he muttered. "And these five years, these five damnable years. They did not take place. Nor the kisses you gave me. I shall be gone in a moment. And then you will forget that this meeting ever took place."

"Ah, you are cruel. You were always cruel."

She leaned toward him. He could smell her furs and the faint odor of her skin. She glanced hurriedly about the deserted paths, and leaned closer with a little shudder. She did not need to speak, to say: you may kiss me again, once, for remembrance.

Villon's eyes blazed in his twisted face.

"No," he cried harshly. "I will not. But I will have this to remember you by." With a sharp movement he snatched the purse from between her fingers and took to his heels.

Automatically she cried out.

He heard her as he ran, and ducked into a dark doorway. He had never done so stupid a piece of work before. They were certain to catch him. And then it would not be the Red Door again but prison again. The empty paths were suddenly full of people running, shouting: "Stop, thief!" The cold was in his bones. His heart was made of lead. And he was coughing. A hard hand gripped his thin arm.

"Thought you could get away with it? Not this time. Come along, damn you."

Chapter Twenty-One

After the Meun dungeon, the Chatelet was no very terrible place to be confined. Villon was not seriously disturbed by his situation. Katherine, after setting the sergeant after him with her involuntary cry, had disappeared. The jailer ventured that before the first week in November was out Villon would be a free man.

Before the first week in November was out, Villon was standing in the courtroom where Tabary, lisping in anguished gasps, had stood four years earlier, confronting Master Laurens Poutrel, Grand Beadle of the Faculty of Theology of the College of Navarre. Villon had heard that Tabary's mother was making slow restitution of five times Tabary's share in the treasure stolen on that famous Christmas Eve. Colin was beyond the reach of the Faculty, a shredded thing on the gallows or maybe rotting in a pit below them. The Grand Beadle, to whom sixty crowns of the stolen money belonged, had done a deal of traveling trying to find out the other culprits. But the expert Petit Jehan and Dom Nicolas had vanished utterly. Villon must face the music alone.

He eyed Master Poutrel, the narrow lawyer's face, with the eyes set close together, peering down at the papers: Tabary's deposition, which had cost the court something too; the bills for repairing the locks and keys, that would have been a nice job for Colin's late lamented father; the account of the expenses to which he and his colleagues had been put, traveling hither and yon in fruitless efforts to trace the gold, long since scattered in a dozen taverns and whorehouses in and out of Paris. A devil of a lot of money. But here was no Thibaut d'Aussigny, demanding vengeance, savage for punishment. The Grand Beadle would be content to close the case, let the prisoner go, if he could but lay his hands on his savings again.

Master Poutrel put the papers aside, rubbed his chin, cleared his throat. Villon watched the court almost indifferently. What would he be telling them that was not already set forth in Tabary's confession? What did he stand to lose? He knew the law, he knew Master Poutrel, he knew the canon. So did Master Poutrel. Doubtless he had stayed Villon's exit from the Chatelet in the hope of squeezing something out of the canon. Very shrewd of Master Poutrel. After all his vain searchings, how jolly to have one of the culprits fall into his hands like an overripe fig. Villon glanced from the dais to the clerk of the court standing below, fiddling with his quills. Was it the same who had written down what Tabary had spilled out under torture? They need not torture poor François. He was only waiting to speak. At the first question from the bench he flopped down on his knees rehearsing the part of the repentant sinner that he would play yet again on his return to the Red Door.

"If it please the court," he croaked, "I am that François Villon, the unworthy ward of Master Guillaume de Villon, canon of St. Benoit, living at the Sign of the Red Door in the cloisters. I am the man accused in the deposition of the d—"—he caught himself—"of Guy Tabary. I am guilty as charged and would make full confession, and may the good God help me to a better life hereafter."

He shot a glance from under his hairless brows at Master Poutrel. The old dog looked eager, hot on the scent of his money again. That mention of the canon had been the part of wisdom. They would shove him back into the grey cell at the Chatelet to lie on straw and eat the lean prison fare for maybe another week. But the Grand Beadle had not heard the name of his colleague of St. Benoit for nothing. He would go to the Red Door. The canon's heart would be wrung again, his purse would be bled again. It would all come right in the end.

Within a week Villon's shaky hand was setting his signature to a paper containing a promise to repay one hundred and twenty gold crowns to those he had helped to defraud of so great a treasure five years earlier. The canon had lived up to his expectations. Master Poutrel was duly satisfied. The Faculty of Theology of the College of Navarre was silenced. François Villon was a free man.

But it was none too jolly at the Red Door. The canon spent all the time he was not attending to chapter duties in figuring. One hundred and twenty gold crowns. It was a small fortune. He must sell another bit of property. At home they must retrench. They must eat less meat, drink cheaper wines, make the shabby old cloak do another year; the old man must forget forever the beautifully illuminated Book of Hours that was to have been so choice an addition to his library, worst of all, must cut down on certain gifts to the poor parishioners of St. Benoit that had been one of his pleasantest luxuries.

Villon was out of the house oftener than in it. But, with winter drawing in and his cough worrying him, late hours in the taverns were no longer so attractive. His room at the Red Door was tolerable if he could drag his boon companions back there with him.

So it was that, having been treated to supper at the Sign of the Chariot by that good fellow, Robin Dogis, together with the light-fingered Roger Pichart and Hutin Moustier, who had never tried to live on his pay as a sergeant, Villon persuaded the three of them to return with him and make a night of it cosily in his attic. They had already had a glorious lot to drink, and were on the lookout for some fun before they should reach the cloisters.

They had not gone far along the rue St. Jacques when they came to the Sign of the Mule, and next to it the lighted window of the pontifical notary, Master François Ferrebouc, where his clerks were burning tallow even at this late hour over their master's thick parchments.

"Hoo!" shouted Robin thickly with a scornful gesture at the toiling scriveners, "don't they ever quit?"

"Sending some poor devil to the halter, most likely," mumbled Roger Pichart. "Who're they workin' for?"

"Ferrebouc." Villon knew. Had he not worked for him in the old days when he'd been laboring to undo the evidence against the girl Jeanne. A dirty business, though she was innocent, and requiring all the lawyer Ferrebouc's shrewdness. The notary had been active, too, when Tabary was tried in the affair of the College of Navarre. Villon imagined him examining the prisoner, the sharp eyes peering out of the equine face with its deep lines and its ugly wen, the deliberate voice putting the questions that set Tabary, in a sweat, stammering out the whole story, even to the name of François Villon. Damn him.

"Sure. It's a halter they're making. The sun don't shine long enough for that job: they must work by candlelight."

The four companions had halted before Ferrebouc's window and were whistling derision at the young men working there. It was a mild night for November, and the window was open. Roger Pichart staggered forward, stared drunkenly at the clerks bent over their papers, leaned over, and accurately spat.

The scrivener whose page had been so wantonly soiled sprang up with a shout, his fellows with him. They ran out into the street, grabbed the innocent sergeant, and hauled him indoors, roaring "murder" at the top of his lungs. Master Ferrebouc, rushing from his own desk at the clamor, knocked Robin Dogis to the ground. Robin stumbled up, dagger in fist, lunged at the notary, stabbing him in the arm, and ran after Roger Pichart, who had escaped into a dark corner of the cloisters. Villon, running too, remembered as he fled another such fracas, another stabbing, another flight.

Panting up the path to the Red Door, he told himself that they could not seize him for this. It had not been his spittle that had marred the paper nor his knife that had entered Ferrebouc's arm. But as he flung into his attic room, he kept seeing the tortured twist of Ferrebouc's face at the slash of Robin's dagger. Had there not been a glimmer of recognition in his eyes as they fell on his old schoolmate?

Why, in God's name, Villon asked himself, hadn't he stopped Pichart before the row began? They'd go after Pichart. And Robin, who deserved punishment on more scores than stabbing the notary. They had Hutin at the Chatelet by this time, no doubt: now he'd learn what it felt like on the other side of the gate. It was a mean way to spend an evening that had begun so well. Glumly he pulled off his clothes, threw them anyways over the bed-rail, and climbed into bed. He pulled the covers over his aching head and addressed himself to sleep.

But he could not. He had always hated going to bed. It was like practice for dying. All sorts of scarecrow visions came between him and sleep. He could not forget Ferrebouc's face, the long jaw, the ugly wen, the cold angry eyes. When at last he drifted off he still saw it, more like a horse's head than a man's, a horse that kept gnashing its teeth at him, a horse that he had to saddle, but the halter belonged somewhere else—a lout from the rope maker's guild was bent on taking it away from him: it was due at the executioner's house before noon; it was not a horse's halter at all, it was a hangman's rope. And all the while the horse eyeing him madly, looking as though he would like the chance to trample him.

Villon woke in a sweat with the canon's hand shaking his shoulder, the canon's strained voice in his ear:

"François! Come. The sergeants are below. You are wanted at the Chatelet."

So there he was, back in the dim hole again, with Pichart, who couldn't hold his spittle, with Dogis, who couldn't hold his knife, with Hutin, the sergeant, under lock and key. And he had done nothing. Just stood there while Pichart mocked the clerks, stood there like a fool when Ferrebouc knocked Dogis down and Dogis drew his knife. And then run for his life to the noise of Hutin shouting "murder!" He had done nothing. But if Ferrebouc could turn a witch into a saint, he could make an innocent bystander look like a murderer. François Villon was not in the notary's good graces. What had possessed him to take those rowdies to the Red Door? Why did they have to stop to jeer at Ferrebouc's window? But he had done nothing.

Villon's thoughts went round and round like a mule on a treadmill. He was thirty: it was the age of a mule. He was no longer a child. And what had he come to? What, after all he had lived through, did he know? A fly in milk, as the proverb went, black from white, like an idiot. If he were an idiot, there might be some excuse for him. But he must have a head as hard as stone, or find more pleasure in shame than in honor, to be content. He fell to coughing. Devil take it, he didn't care. When he was dead, it wouldn't matter. God, what comfort! What wisdom and eloquence! But it was not his fault. He had been born under a leaden star. The children of Saturn were known to be janglers who came to no good end. There were those who said a wise man has power over the planets and can put their influence to naught. He didn't believe it. He was as God unhappily made him. But he wanted to live. He must leave this folly. He must go back to his books. Christ helping him, he would turn over a new leaf. Once he got out of this place.

How would he get out?

He could not look to the Provost: Robert d'Estouteville was no longer in office. Villon might be a clerk, but he had no more to hope for from the Bishop of Paris than had Colin or René at the end. The Criminal Lieutenant, Pierre de la Dehors, had been sorry enough to discharge his prisoner the last time. He was Master of the Butchers' Guild; he had been on the road to that proud place when Villon was at the University, during the row over the Pet-au-Diable, when the students had stolen the butchers' hooks.

Villon kept pushing these thoughts out of his head. But one morning the archers came for him and marched him into a

339

room in the Chatelet which he had not yet seen. With a shiver he observed the instruments that had been used upon him so effectively at Meun and upon Tabary in this very chamber.

His yelp of dismay was muffled by the funnel clamped over his mouth. Before he could draw a proper breath, the water began pouring down his throat. He gagged, he swallowed, he struggled, he tried to shout and could not. Iron hands gripped him. Endlessly, relentlessly, the water flowed into his mouth, down his throat, choking him, his chest was in a vise so that he could not breathe, his ears rang as though he were deaf, his eyes stretched wide, he snorted, he clamored, the water kept coming till he thought he must burst with it. When at last they let him go, removed the funnel from his sore lips, and he stood shaking between the archers, he was ready to confess anything if they would leave him alone.

But he was innocent. Rage and impotence mixed with the horrors of the torture.

Lying on the straw in his cold cell, aching and shivering, relieved to be done with the torture, remembering with terror what he had mumbled after it was over, wondering if he must go through it another time, he reviewed his case.

They might half kill him, but they had nothing against him. God, they had everything against him. The robbery of the College of Navarre, the theft of the chalice that had landed him in the Meun dungeon, if he had died then he would be out of it all now, the murder of Sermoise, the unforgotten college riots. The Master of the Butchers' Guild lost no love on clerks. The Provost would be glad to prove that he knew how to handle rough customers. Colin had not been saved, clever as he was. René had not escaped, though some of the biggest financiers in Paris had stood ready to help him. To whom could poor François look for aid? To the Perdrier clan perhaps. He would have laughed, but there was no laughter left in that tormented body of his. He was innocent.

He could almost have protested his innocence to the archers who came for him two days later and half pushed, half dragged him up the stairs again to the Provost. To be put to the Question once more? He would plead guilty first, of all the sins in the calendar. But he was innocent. Thank God, they were taking him past the torture chamber into the court hall.

Mournfully Villon observed the Provost, with Master Ferrebouc seated on the dais beside him, eyed the Criminal Lieutenant, who was smoothing his beard with a fist made for hacking an ox, glanced at the clerk of the court, buried in a mountain of crackling parchment, and straightened up feebly as the clerk, having put his papers in order for the third time, began reading from the top of the pile.

All that about poor François? They must have his whole record there. The voice droned on, mechanically repeating the name François Villon at intervals, like a refrain, but there was no rhythm to these lines, they flowed like water from a jug, the throttling water of the Question, as steady, almost as meaningless to Villon's weary ears.

The voice ceased. The clerk looked up from his papers toward the dais. Villon's eyes followed his. The Provost's grim face did not change. Ferrebouc was leaning back, scratching one ear. The Criminal Lieutenant looked at the Provost. Villon's eyes were drawn to the befurred figure set above him, looming taller and broader than a man should be.

"In consideration of all that we have just heard," Villon wished that he had listened more carefully to the clerk's monotonous stream of words, "and since Holy Church has no wish to reclaim this relapsed sinner"—Villon blinked—"it behooves this court to declare that the said François Villon, once Montcorbier, rioter, thief, procurer, and killer"—the Provost cleared his throat, adding, as though it were part of the indictment—"clerk, and eh-h, poet, be removed from further danger to the fair city of Paris."

Villon noted the set of the Provost's jaw, the firm jeweled fingers clasping the carved head on the arm of his chair, Ferrebouc's face beside him with its ugly wen, the brown softness of the fur on the Criminal Lieutenant's gown, the light glancing on a halberd below the dais. He saw these things with a clarity that made him think he must remember them always.

Ferrebouc stirred in his chair. The Criminal Lieutenant looked coldly at the prisoner, but Villon's eyes were fastened on the Provost. Who pronounced sentence with the deliberation of one savoring a small pleasure.

"Let him be taken and hanged by the neck until he is dead."

Villon's body tingled emptily. His mouth was dry as paper. There was a weight like iron in his chest. Then he felt the archers' hands gripping his thin arms. They were in a hurry to hustle the condemned out of the room. He heard his own cry as though it came from the throat of a stranger, as they dragged him away.

François Villon was sick. He lay in a huddle on the straw, no limb moving, but his whole body trembling violently. There was a darkness before his eyes that blotted out even the dim light of his cell. He was alone there now: the others had been removed, he did not know where, or care. He wanted to throw up, but his stomach was empty and denied him that relief. He put a cold hand to his throat. They would have to pull the rope tight round that scrawny neck to choke him properly. He licked his lips. His tongue would stick out, he knew how. He looked down at his legs. They would be kicking madly in spite of him: he could not move them now. A wilder jig than he had danced in any tavern, on any stage. Despair flooded him so that he could not even rage at the Provost, at the Master Butcher.

He did not know how many hours it was before he pulled himself up, crouching on his haunches. Poor François.

> *I'm François, I'm sorry to say,*
> *Born in Paris, near Pontoise city.*
> *At a rope's end, more's the pity,*
> *My neck will learn what my buttocks weigh.*

It was a good joke. He would tell it to the jailer. It was a rotten joke. He would tell it, maybe, to the hangman.

No, he would not! He would not be carted off, with a halter round his neck like butcher's meat, to make a dinner for the crows. His eyes, these two eyes that had seen—God, what had they not seen?—to be pecked out as one gulps oysters. His carcass to twist and turn in the wind, for the sun to blacken and the rain to harry. He fell back on the straw, biting his fists in agony. He would not! He would not!

He must get word to the canon. The canon would go to the Master Butcher. He would go to the Provost on his knees. He would plead with Ferrebouc, his colleague at St. Benoit.

The heavy key was turning in the lock. The jailer was coming with a crust and a jug of water. Villon wanted none of these. But paper. Paper and ink. If only he had money to bribe the man.

"I hear you're not going to be with us much longer."

They would be removing him to the Conciergerie. The condemned cells. Villon threw himself forward on the ground, clutching the jailer by the ankles.

"They won't. They mustn't. I didn't do it, I tell you. When they put you to the torture like that you say anything. God.

343

For a little less hell on earth you damn yourself forever. Listen!"

The jailer tried to kick Villon's hands away, in vain.

"Listen! You've got to help me get out of here. I'm innocent, I tell you. You're a good fellow," Villon stammered the outworn flatteries. "One of the best. I have friends outside. With money. Golden louis. You'll get yours. Bring me some paper and a quill. I'll write it in my blood if I can't get ink. My guardian's a lawyer. Master Guillaume de Villon of St. Benoit. He'll pay you, he'll pay you well. I'll tell him in my letter to reward you properly. For Christ's sake!"

The jailer looked down doubtfully at the man writhing at his feet. Money. Golden louis. A reward. He didn't look like anything a canon of St. Benoit would pay well to see again. Tavern trash. But with a wonderful tongue in his head sometimes. Made you laugh like the Prince of Fools. And he must have seen the inside of a palace once to judge by some of his stories.

"It can't get you in bad to give me ink and some paper. You'll be glad of it in the end, I swear!"

The jailer shrugged.

"I'll see."

He set down the food. Villon burst into a paean of gratitude, urging haste, mumbling wild promises. As the door clanged behind the broad back he turned greedily to the jug. His throat was like the floor of a bake-oven.

Villon spent the night composing the letter he would write to the canon. The old man wouldn't want him to swing by the neck. It was no death for a saint. Frightful visions of Montfaucon mingled with his imagination of the canon's horrified face at the news. Colin and René, neither one as he had looked living, dangled before his eyes, mocking him. He would never

344

mock the things on Montfaucon again. He might be one of them. God forgive him. The terror, the shame mounted and sank and mounted in bitter waves. If he could find words, if there were fit music for this misery, he might bear it.

Slowly, toward morning, it began to subside, to change, to shape itself to a song.

> *You, men and brothers, who after we die*
> *Live on: steel not your hearts against us, pray.*
> *For if you pity us, poor things, hung high,*
> *God will have mercy upon you one day.*
> *Here five or six of us are strung to stay;*
> *As for the flesh we nourished heartily,*
> *It's long since rotten rags, as you may see.*

Villon looked back upon the rich pasties, the cream cakes, the wine, but with no watering at the mouth now: he saw the shredded flesh of the hanged nearer.

> *And we, the bones, to dust and ashes fall.*

He had laughed at them, once, sticking so queerly out of the torn carcasses.

> *Let none who see us vexed so, grin with glee,*
> *But pray to God that He forgive us all.*

Facing the terror, phrasing it in verse, eased his over-burdened heart. But he dared not go on lest he forget the fine things in his letter to the canon. If he could but hear the bells striking prime. If only the jailer would keep his word.

O blessed human compassion! The man was at the door. There was the noise of the key in the lock, the moving of the iron hinges. Paper, paper and ink, and a quill. O God, if it would reach the canon safely! If he could work it! Before the jailer could speak, Villon had snatched sheets and inkhorn and was scribbling literally for dear life.

The letter was written, signed, folded, given into the jailer's horny hand. The door closed behind him. Villon was alone.

It was hard to wait for him to return with news. Meanwhile —meanwhile, there was paper enough for another stanza. He had left the inkhorn and quill behind him.

> *We clamor to you, brothers, clamor and cry:*
> *Do not disdain us. Though we died, you'll say,*
> *By order of the law, and justly, why,*
> *You know how sometimes justice goes astray.*

Whatever sins he had committed, in this case he was free of guilt. But his sins were many and black. That dossier the court clerk had had before him . . .

> *Plead for our pardon, now we're fled away,*
> *To Virgin Mary's blessèd Son, that He*
> *Let not His grace be quenched toward such as we,*
> *And let us not be damned beyond recall.*
> *We are dead: let none harry us endlessly,*
> *But pray to God that He forgive us all.*

Villon dipped the quill into the ink again.

> *Washed by the rain, hung in the sun to dry,*
> *We're shrunk and blackened well this many a day;*
> *Magpies and crows have picked out every eye,*
> *And torn our eyebrows and our beards away.*
> *We'll never more sit down, up here we stay;*
> *At the wind's pleasure we swing merrily*
> *Hither and yon; dinted like thimbles, we*
> *Know the birds' beaks as though each were an awl.*

346

He could not forget those pocked eyeless faces. And his to be one of them?

> *Take warning: never join our company,*
> *But pray to God that He forgive us all.*

There was only the envoy left to compose. To what great lord could he address a ballade like this? No lord on earth would understand the pain and the dread, the hungry shame of it. No prince on earth . . .

> *Prince Jesus, Who hath perfect sovereignty,*
> *Let not Hell have us in its mastery,*
> *Into that pit, O Christ, let us not fall.*
> *Men, here there is no glint of mockery,*
> *But pray to God that He forgive us all.*

Villon drew a broad black line under the last words, his face twisted; he was torn by a harsh dry sob.

His letter was gone. His poem was finished. He had time to think again. Too much time. Was the jailer never coming back? He fingered the sheets nervously. Now. Now he heard something surely. Had the canon been at home or in chapter meeting? Or visiting one of his parishioners? What news? Christ, what word?

He had been mistaken. No one was coming. And perhaps, when the jailer did appear, it would be to say that he had not seen the canon at all.

No. Yes. There was someone at the door. Oh, agony of suspense while the key turned. Villon saw first the coarse face of the jailer which told him nothing. There was another man behind him. The canon himself, so soon?

They entered the cell. It was a priest but not the canon. It was the prison chaplain, come on his ghostly office, to prepare François Villon for his end.

Chapter Twenty-Two

The first week in January, 1463, was a cold time. A season to put a man in mind of his childhood when the wolves, sick of living on wind, had braved the streets of Paris looking for food. Villon was fasting again, not because of the wars and the famine. He was lying in the condemned cell of the Conciergerie, where even the Christmas feast was omitted.

The canon was doing what he could, but that was little at the eleventh hour. An appeal from his sentence had been sent to Parliament. They couldn't butcher an innocent man. Ah, but they could do what they liked, the Master Butcher and the Provost, with Ferrebouc's help. Hanged and strangled.

The past was black. The future—what future for a hairless,

toothless skeleton with a cough? But Villon did not want to die. Not yet, O God. Not so soon. Just past thirty. The age at which Jesus Christ was hung up on the cross. The theologians said that at the resurrection all men would have attained the perfect age of thirty-two. Villon tried to imagine Heaven filled with men of thirty-two, all young, all blessed—and failed. He could not imagine Heaven. It was easier to picture the damned. He looked, at thirty, like one of them. Hanged and strangled. He had imagined dying often enough.

> *So dies Paris, and Helen, too;*
> *Who dies must die with grief and smart:*
> *Breath fails, nothing a man can do,*
> *His gall bursts over his heart!*
> *He sweats then: God, what sweat-drops start!*
> *And there is none, whoever it be,*
> *Child, sister, brother, to take his part,*
> *Endure for him his agony.*

He had set down every hideous detail.

> *Death makes him tremble and turn white,*
> *Makes the flesh flabby, the neck swell,*
> *Makes the nose beaked, strings the veins tight,*
> *Stretches the nerves and joints as well.*
> *Oh, body of woman, so tender, tell:*
> *Must you, smooth, soft, and precious, even*
> *You, suffer a fate so fell?*
> *Yes, or ascend alive to Heaven.*

No man knew anything of death save the dying, for all the priests might say. Question the silence of Lazarus, the man who died twice. Ask René, ask Colin wherever they are. Villon bit his bony fingers.

349

What could he hope for if they spared him? Not again to run and leap in a game of tennis that left a man drenched with good sweat and glad of his weariness. Not to hold Katherine in his arms again. Not even to keep Fat Margot, to whom he had become a laughingstock. Not to match verses with Orléans in the great hall at Blois. Maybe to return to the books that he should have read when he was young and could have learned wisdom. To take refuge in a monastery like another broken Abélard? That was three hundred years since, and Villon had never seen himself a monk. But there were still his five clamoring senses, eyes, ears, and tongue, his sharp nose, his itching fingers. What was starvation, what were the pains in his chest, if he could just go on, seize the poor fragment of life left him to squeeze out of it what no man else could, to set down what he had suffered? He thought he had drunk down all his shames when he wrote his Testament. He had tasted a bitterer drink since. If only the young knew, but they were fools and would not listen. God, he could tell them, if he had time.

The clangor of the bells ringing tierce seemed to echo his miserable thought. The bells penetrated even to the dungeon where those about to die were shuttered. They confused the only other noise that could make a difference to the prisoner: the noise of a key in the lock and the jailer tramping in with his meagre fare.

Villon was startled to see the door open. The priest again? But then his time was up.

They couldn't be coming for him yet.

The jailer was alone and grinning. Villon jumped up and clattered toward him, dragging his chains, the gaunt face fixed with horror.

"Well, man, you've won."

"Won? You don't mean—Parliament has granted my ap-

350

peal? You wouldn't fool me, would you?" Villon stammered.

"I'm telling you: this place'll see no more of you, nor Paris either."

Villon flung himself upon the jailer in a frenzy of mindless joy, burst into a crack-voiced song, and stopped, overcome with tears. He was to live, then. He was to live. The jailer stood by, waiting for the sentence to sink in.

"You understand, don't you, you've got to get out?"

"Get out?" Villon sobbed with relief. "Thank God for that! Or maybe you think I'll be homesick for this place?" he grinned through his tears.

"You've got to get out of Paris."

Leave Paris? It was better than leaving the world.

Villon stood up. He was free. His heart hammered with joy. He wanted to dance, to sing, to summon his friends and drain a keg of wine in celebration. He was to live.

It meant the road again, traipsing from one mean hamlet to another, always on the lookout for the wolfish dogs, hoping for refuge in some great house, being kicked out, finding a night's lodging in an empty bake-oven, tramping on, falling in with a set of purse-proud pilgrims or, if he was lucky, with a group of friendly play-actors, meeting the Companions, who would put him on to a good thing—no, no, not that. Not again!

He must see the canon, get letters of recommendation. They couldn't send him away naked. He must have time to get together some provision for the journey, to take leave of his friends.

His legs shook so that he could hardly walk to the door. As he was about to pass out of it he turned and blew a kiss of mockery to the cell he was quitting. They might have taken him out of here to be hanged and strangled. He could have

351

hugged every member of Parliament for joy. He squeezed the jailer's stout arm. Christ!

When the formalities were concluded and Villon stumbled out into the street, blinking at the harsh January light, he was one loud song of praise and thanksgiving. All the way home to the Red Door he busied himself composing a letter to Parliament, the Sovereign Court, Mother of the Good, Sister of the Blessed Angels, bidding all his five senses cry out his rejoicing, his teeth to chew no food but rather clatter thanks more loudly than bell, organ, or trump, his liver and lungs and spleen, his vile body, fouler than the swine that rolls in filth, to praise the Court, the triumphant Court, Mother of the Good, Sister of the Blessed Angels. By Heaven, he would send them his prayer in rhyme, begging for three days' grace in which to prepare for his ten years' exile.

Late that evening the canon returned to the Red Door, looking older and wearier than Villon had yet seen him, with the news that the three days' grace was granted. Villon had spent the afternoon penning a riotous ballade addressed to Garnier, the clerk who kept the register of the prisoners at the Chatelet, demanding what he thought of his appeal. He had half a mind to show it to the canon, failing a better audience, but when he looked at the old man the gaiety died in his breast. It might have been better for Guillaume de Villon if his ward had ended on the gallows. He could have said masses for the poor damned soul, hanged to satisfy the Master Butcher's vengeance; he would not have had to spend his last years in dreadful ignorance of the exile's fate, fretting over the possible sins into which he yet might fall.

They were sitting in the canon's study with the firelight playing on the canon's worn face, almost as white as the fringe of soft hair that haloed it, on the backs of his books, on the chessmen standing unused in the corner. The old man, finding no appetite for his tardy supper, was letting it cool while he tried with difficulty to talk as though all were as it should be.

"You should rest, my son. You have had a hard time, and it is not an easy road you have ahead of you."

Villon nodded and coughed. It would not be a bad thing to lie down in his old attic bed, under the warm covers, after shivering with cold and fear in the straw at the Conciergerie. It would be the last night but one that he could be sure where he would sleep maybe for the rest of his life.

"And tomorrow," murmured the canon, moving his wine cup but not lifting it to drink, "you can go and say your farewells to your good mother."

Villon grunted assent. He would look in at the Mule, maybe at the Pine Cone, pay a last visit to Fat Margot. And Katherine? He might go and apologize for having stolen her purse. Villon stroked his scarred lip. And why not? He did not know whether she was still living in the old house near the cloisters, but it should not be impossible to find her again if he wanted to try.

He would sleep on it. He was worn out with the miseries of prison and the excitement of his release, eager for bed, glad to escape the canon's helpless kindness, the shames and disappointments that rose between them, stifling speech. He got up.

"Good night, Father."

The canon stirred in his chair, looked at Villon with a smile sadder than tears, and raised his hand to bless him.

"Good night, my son."

Villon hurried out of the room, up the stairs to bed. But tired as he was he could not sleep. The familiar shapes of the furniture bulked large in the little low-ceiled room; the unfamiliar comfort of his bed, the terrors past, the uncertainties

353

ahead would not let him rest. He imagined unhappily the coming visit to his mother. He played with the notion of seeking out Katherine. He wondered what plans the canon had for him: he could not frame any for himself.

Suppose the old man recommended his entering an abbey. It would do one necessary thing for him: it would keep him out of the clutches of the law. Villon a monk. Poverty. Obedience. Chastity. About poverty they could teach him nothing. He had never obeyed any rule save those that govern the making of a ballade. Chastity. He was almost ripe for it now, the broken-down spavined donkey that he had become. Should he try to see Katherine?

Feverish, troubled, in spite of the freedom from the halter that sent his fingers straying tenderly to his lean throat, Villon heard the bells ring matins before he drifted into slumber. He did not wake till the sun was high in the sky, and then with a struggle remembered the events of the day behind him, the glorious gift of life, the dark cruel future, the urgency of preparation to face it.

He stopped in the midst of pulling on his leggings, hopped over to the chest against the wall, and drew out the manuscript of his Testament. He fingered it with a wry face. Should he turn it over to a copyist? It would be like leaving his life behind him. He stuffed it into the breast of his jerkin. If he went to Katherine's, he might show it to her. He shrugged. He must get the visit to his mother over with. He did not look forward to that.

The walk to the neighborhood of the Celestines was a slow progress. It would have been worse bumping along in the hangman's cart on the way to the gallows. But he would scarcely have looked with greedier eyes at the city that had

354

banished him. Already he was used to the fact that his life was
not forfeit. He was not used to the idea of exile.

He had seen his mother only once since his return to Paris.
The meeting had shocked both of them: she had stared with
incredulous pale eyes at the scar-lipped coughing skeleton that
was her son, and he had observed with cruel intentness the
bent shrunken body, the sagging cheeks, marked with brown
stains like old parchment, the munching movements of her
gums, the way she kept wiping her wet lips with the back of
her hand. She reminded him of the old armouress, except that
she had never been beautiful. But she must have been gay once,
when she was a girl, in spite of the wars and the hardships.
And she had had her moments of joy and pride: when she
first took him to the Red Door, for instance, dreaming of how
he was to become learned, become great . . .

He had never found it easy to talk to her, grand talker that
he was. As he walked toward her poor room he reflected that
it would be the very devil to talk to her now. He would give
her his ballade to the Virgin, that would do for conversation.

He had not spent many minutes in the cold bare room when
he made a show of what he had brought her—conscious, as
he drew it forth, that more generally he brought her nothing
but heartache. He made her sit quietly like a good child, and he
the master. He bade her listen.

She sat near him, a hunched figure, her swollen fingers
spread before her mouth, looking at him hard as though she
could hear better with her eyes. He had to force his voice a little,
pretend to himself that he was reading to a stranger (and was
she not a stranger?). But after the first few lines he was in the
swing of it, chanting the words with his unquenchable delight
in poetry, in his own poetry, feeling his old power, justifying

355

himself before her and before that sick rogue, so shortly out of prison, so soon to be out of Paris, poor François.

When he stopped he threw her a glance of triumph with a question at the tail of it. What son had ever left such a legacy to his ancient mother? What did she think of it? Was it not fine?

She thought it fine, truly. She could not help liking what brought vividly before her all the precious hours of her comfortless life: the rich colors in the windows at the Celestines, the glory of the lighted tapers, the silver and gold on the altar and on the priests' vestments on holy days, the grand roll of the organ music and the paradisal voices of the young choir, the blessed words of the service, warmth and wealth and joy, the promise of eternal bliss. "And in this faith I wish to live and die."

She was vaguely troubled about his addressing the Virgin as "high goddess," and he had to explain that this was a literary term common enough in speaking of Christian saints. For the rest, she found the thing plain and satisfying. She marveled at her son, surprised at his having understood her so thoroughly, humbly grateful for this show of religious feeling. Her pale eyes were full of tears, her withered lips shook. She made the sign of the cross over him, and he felt her fingers tremble as she clutched his sleeve and pulled him to his knees beside her while she muttered her thanksgiving.

"Oh, my legs!" she groaned as she rose to her feet. "That's when you're old, François." And at once she stopped complaining to lament that she had nothing to offer so rare a visitor.

"If I had known you were coming, I would have baked some little tarts. But I never know when to expect you. I do not expect you," she explained with a touch of grimness in her hoarse plaintive voice. "Only when you do come, I would like . . ."

356

"If we had oysters, we could have some oysters and wine, if we had some wine," he joked.

She shook her head, smiling at him with tears in her eyes, veritably his mother. It was a treat to see him again, thin, yes, almost bald, and with that cough, but in good spirits, not in any bad trouble now surely, and with those beautiful verses on the true faith.

"It's wine and oysters now," she mumbled. "Do you remember when it used to be turnip tops?"

"I remember."

"You were a clever child, even then, François. You could sing more songs than I could teach you. Ah, yes." She sighed. "And when I took you to the Red Door. You didn't want to go. You fought me. You didn't understand what a fine thing it would be for you. Yes." She wiped her mouth with her swollen fingers.

"I remember," Villon nodded. "You thought he would make a bishop of me."

"The good Lord knows best." Her pale eyes gleamed. "Perhaps you would have made a bad bishop."

"Like Thibaut d'Aussigny?" he asked with sudden savagery. "No, my mother. Whatever sins your François has to lay to his conscience they are not those of the Bishop of Meun."

"Eh," she said, "never mind that. What are you doing now?"

He shrugged. He remembered how she had cursed and wept over him that first time he had left the city, when he had come running to her with a patch on his mouth after the affair with Sermoise. It had been different five years ago when he had escaped the authorities of the College of Navarre. Then he had had his pockets full of gold, and he had made her a little present before he set out on the Orléans road. He had not dreamed of telling her of his plans then. It was evident that she had not heard how nearly he had just escaped the gallows.

He saw no need to enlighten her on that point. Though it might sweeten their farewells for her to know he had at least twisted his neck out of the noose. He wanted her prayers. But he hated the thought of her tears. He would hold his tongue.

"I am going on a journey, my mother," he said lightly.

"Again?" She looked at him with troubled suspicion. "I thought you'd had enough of legging it over the countryside, and you with that cough. You had better stay at the Red Door and take care of it. Or maybe you would stay here?" She glanced anxiously round the mean room. "Have you quarreled with the canon?"

"Whatever about?" Villon asked in a tone of astonishment to put her at ease on that score.

"Well. You never put yourself out to please him, François. But where do you go? What do you do?"

He evaded her questions by coughing.

"May the good saints have you in their keeping. Let me get you a drink."

He accepted the cup she handed him, though he knew the wine would merit the curses he had once put in a song on taverners who trifle with their casks. But he had no sooner drunk it than she began plaguing him again about his journey.

Was he going on the canon's business? Would he by any chance be getting as far as Angers, where his uncle was? She had not seen him since she had been a girl at home, but she knew he had not forgotten her. God grant he was still living. François might even bring back some word from him.

Bring back? In ten years' time? He shot a humorous glance at her. No. He would not be able to do that. Besides, he was taking another direction.

Was he invited again to the Duke of Orléans? Ah, that would be something for his mother to tell her gossip, who went

358

with her to clean at the Celestines and who would let the dirty water in the bucket dry up while she rattled on about her son, the little priest. As though that were something wonderful. François could have been better than a priest if he had had a mind to it.

"You're on your way back to my bishopric," Villon jested.

His mother said nothing, only put out a lame hand to smooth the paper on which was written her son's ballade that she could not read.

He would not speak about the future. Slyly he drew her back into the past.

"It is not your fault, my mother, if I am not a great man. Did you never imagine, when you looked into my cradle, that you saw a changeling lying there?"

"God forbid!" she cried hoarsely, crossing herself.

"Perhaps I am not quite human: perhaps I am a fairy's child."

"What are you saying!"

It was his old way of terrifying and enchanting Katherine. He did not know what possessed him to recall it now to frighten the poor old woman.

"Indeed," he said soothingly, "I am your son. It was you who made a poet of me. Nobody else. Do you remember the stories you used to tell me when I was little, when it was so cold and we were too hungry to sleep?"

"You could always wag your tongue, François. You began to talk before you were two years old."

He blinked at her. What an assortment of memories she must have, of the squalling brat that never could get enough milk, of the sharp-eyed imp who would never be polite to his aunts, the greedy boy roaming the cold streets to snatch what he could, and bringing home nothing but bruises and the threats of the neighbors, a worry out of the house, a plague in it. He had not been much of a joy to her. She had promised him an ugly death more than once. She was wrong about that. The hangman would not have him now. But she did not know that this hour was a kind of dying. He was fumbling for the bleak fragments of his childhood to tell them good-by. He smiled at her coaxingly.

"Do you remember it, my mother, that story you used to tell me about the robber and the Holy Virgin?"

She shook her head at his foolishness. She half remembered it. She did not understand that he wanted to hear it again from her now, to creep back into the imaginary comfort of the old days when they had been poor and wretched together, but she had had hope in her simple heart and his own had been swollen with a huge ambition. She did not know that she was not to set eyes on him for ten years. She would not be alive in ten years.

"It is a beautiful song, François," she said, touching the paper again with an illiterate old woman's reverence for the written word. "I will pray to the Holy Virgin for you while you are gone, and do you pray, too. There is no other help."

Villon nodded, not looking at her. When Jesus was dying on the cross, He gave His mother into the care of the beloved disciple. He had no fears for Her, nor She for Him. Yet She had to watch Him die, She who had sheltered the Godhead in Her virgin womb, had to behold the last agonies of the Son of Man, hanging on the cross, suffering the death of a criminal. She was all-pitiful, the Mother of Sorrows. Pure and immaculate. Knowing no evil. The courtesan whose body had been bought, the clerk who had signed away his soul to the devil in hell could rest on Her intercession and be saved. She waited, in patience, with perfect tenderness, even for so stained a sinner as François Villon to throw himself upon Her grace. And this poor woman whose pale eyes he could feel restlessly searching his face, averted from her, whose crooked swollen fingers kept touching his paper on the table there, this poor mother could do nothing for her son but seek to bring him to the feet of that Other.

He could not tell her what was facing him. Let her learn it from the canon. Or perhaps from her crony, washing up at the Celestines, boasting about her little priest of a son. Or more likely at some crossroads, come upon one of the Provost's criers shouting that François de Montcorbier, called Villon, was sentenced to ten years' banishment from the Town, Provosty, and Viscounty of Paris; and whoso should receive, comfort, or aid in any way the said François de Montcorbier, called Villon, did so on pain of forfeiting body and goods to his lord the King; and whoso should come upon the said François de Montcorbier, called Villon, in any place within the Town, Provosty, or Viscounty of Paris, a holy place excepted, was in duty bound by summoning the people, by crying hallo, by ringing of bells, and in all ways possible, to apprehend him, that the said François de Montcorbier, called Villon, be brought before justice to receive his punishment.

"You are cold? Let me give you another cup of wine."

"No. No, it is time for me to go."

"So soon?"

It was always too soon. Whenever you died, it was too soon. But he was not dead yet.

He got to his feet.

"Thank you for the prayer, François. It is beautiful. The blessed Virgin will not forget that you made it for me. And I won't forget either. But you must come to read it over for me again. As soon as you get back, eh?" She looked at him anxiously. "You are not likely to get into trouble, are you?"

"I!" he said with firm scorn. And then, turning suddenly and taking up the sheet with his ballade, "Do you mind if I take this? It is yours, of course, my mother. But I should like to make a clean copy of it. You would like that, eh?"

The old woman looked disappointed. She would have preferred to keep the paper, even though she could not read it. She could have gotten the priest to read it to her, and then she could have boasted to him about her son, who could make such wonderful prayers to the Virgin and who was indeed a great poet, received by the Duke of Orléans himself. She would have cherished the smudged illegible sheet.

"Well, if you must, François."

"That's a sweet mother! I'll see that you get it back again, handsomer than ever."

"Take care of your cough. And come back soon."

"As soon as I can, you may be sure of that."

He thrust the paper into the breast of his jerkin. He would leave the whole Testament at the copyist's and tell the canon to call for it in good time. He wished he had not put off this business of copying so long. But there had been places here and there to correct and polish, or sharpen. A man didn't write his Testament every day. Not such a one.

"You have a great son, my mother, believe me. He may not be much to look at. But I swear he'll be remembered. By David the Psalmist, I swear it, and he was a grander man than David the King."

"What are you saying, François?" lisped the old woman, looking at him as though he had gone crazy, as for a minute he had. Crazy with the memory of the power that was in him, crazy with the thought of the misery that lay ahead of him, wanting to put his shame out of mind and make his fame ring through all Paris once more.

He snatched her in his arms, trying to dance her down the

room, but she limped and tottered so that he had to set her down on a stool, panting.

"Whatever . . ." she gasped.

"Nothing. Nothing at all. It is a great city, this Paris. It is a great time, this fifteenth century of our Lord. It is a great fellow, I'm telling you, this François Villon. Remember that when you are not saying your prayers. And then say them all over again. With a special intercession to the Virgin for him. 'And in this faith I will to live and die.' Good-by, my mother."

He laughed. He hugged her. He kissed the top of her poor dizzy old head.

Before she knew it, he was gone and with him his precious gift to her. She was never to see either one again.

His pride restored, his manuscript folded against his rapidly beating heart, Villon swung down the street, relieved that the dreaded hour had passed so easily.

He began to think that he could have done the copying job himself if only he had had time. God, what was the stuff made of that it vanished so fast?

It was a long walk to the rue de la Parcheminerie, and he had enough leisure to think where he should carry his script. It would be no small matter, copying above two thousand lines. And he would not be there to receive it when it was done. They might botch it, and he would not know.

He stared greedily at the shops that crowded the narrow street. This was the best place. But the fee would be enormous. When he came back in ten years' time . . . if he came back.

He could turn the manuscript over to the canon. With the bequest of his library and of his tale of the Pet-au-Diable engrossed by that staunch lad, Guy Tabary. More than the canon would expect of him.

He stood for a moment, reflecting, before the window of a scrivener's shop. Hurried passers-by jostled him. Clerks. Merchants. Students. Maybe some of these slim hopefuls were authors, ignorant that they were rubbing shoulders with François Villon: his face was not familiar to the young. Ten years hence they might be great men, and he forgotten. He wanted to dig a sharp elbow into them to make them think of him. He shrugged and shambled on.

He could not loiter here. He had to go to the draper's to fetch a cloak, to the armourers' quarters to pick up a good blade cheap; he wanted to step in at a dozen places: Fat Margot's, the Pine Cone, the Mule, to see whom he could see. He wished he were a lord with a stout horse, or a rich invalid (he felt like a poor one) with a chair and bearers, so that he might move faster and farther, stop at every tavern, halt on every bridge, visit every house where he had danced and joked or recited verses to an admiring circle. The house of Katherine de Vauselles? He was not wanted there. Yes, and why not the gallows of Montfaucon where he was not wanted either?

He returned to the Red Door late and weary, his errands half done, his farewells only half said. The canon had spread a small feast for him of his favorite dishes, from fat soup au Jacobin to the nut cakes he relished most. There was the best Beaune on the table.

It was a queer meal, the canon telling one story after another and Villon punctuating them with short coughing spells, each parrying pauses and thrusting at silences like skilful duellists.

"No more almonds," pleaded the canon at last, pushing the dish away from Villon. "They will make your cough worse. Take some raisins."

"Yes, Father."

364

"That pastry was a trifle on the hot side, I thought," said the canon.

"A good cook uses ginger as God uses hell-fire, for the virtue that comes of it."

The canon smiled and cleared his throat.

"What was it," he grumbled gently, "I wanted to ask you?"

Villon shifted uneasily in his chair. Now it was coming. But the canon wished only to inquire if the draper had done properly by him and if he wanted help with his packing. And, yes, he had written a letter or two addressed to friends at Rheims, at Chartres, and a few lesser towns that might prove useful whensoever François might find himself in their neighborhood. He got up and fussed over his writing table, searching helplessly for a sheaf of papers that lay under his nose. Villon got up too and stood beside him, frowning.

"No. Yes, I have them all right here."

"And I," said Villon abruptly, "have papers to leave with you. A document, a—legal document," he grinned.

The canon raised an eyebrow, and held out his hand, which shook slightly.

"Time enough tomorrow before I leave. But I'd like you to have it copied out in a fair hand."

Villon rose and took a turn about the room, stroking his scarred lip.

"I should have had the benefit of your legal knowledge before—but you'll find it quite in order."

"May I know what it is?"

"Of course. It's—a—set of papers—a— In short, my Testament."

"Testament?"

"No less. No more. You didn't know I had anything to bequeathe, eh?"

The canon shook his head. He looked troubled.

"Don't be anxious, Father. I've not got into a scrape this time. Whatever I've left to my friends was rightfully come by. You'll see. But if you'll only promise to have it copied faithfully. It's all I value." His soul to the blessed Trinity, his body to our great mother, the earth. . .

"Of course, of course." The canon rose too and moved over to the chessboard where he stood, lifting the pieces idly and setting them down again, wondering perhaps what this stripped thief had to leave.

Villon looked at the old man, the tonsured head with its fringe of soft white hair, the thick eyebrows over the sad kind eyes, the strong lines of the profile he knew so well. A handsome old man. A miserable old man. Loving laughter. Loving life. What had he got out of it? Nothing but pains, anxieties, an assortment of heartaches and disappointments. A keen old man, or he would not have come so far. A heart without guile, or he would have gone much farther. If he had not been pulled back repeatedly by the necessity of looking out for his wretched foster son.

And poor François? What might he have done if he had been born under a luckier star?

Villon bent over the fire, holding out his bony hands to the blaze.

"Set down in this, my thirtieth year, when all my shames I've swallowed neat," he quoted to himself silently. And surdenly, harshly, aloud: "Tell me, Father. What is it—the sin against the Holy Ghost?"

The canon turned about the pawn he was holding, set it down on the chessboard, and moved across to the fire. He stood there a moment before he spoke, the firelight brightening the half-smile on the white old face.

"I always like to answer that one," he said, as though it were a game of riddles they were playing. "It is to count too heavily on God's mercy because it is tempered with justice." He frowned into the fire.

There was a sound of a door opening and shutting below. The canon shook his head grumpily.

"That must be Jean, come for his game of chess. I thought I told him—"

Villon whirled about.

"That's all right, Father. You can have your game in peace. And I," he grinned, "shall have mine."

"François—"

"I'll just have a last look-in at the Mule. I'll be back before you've won the second time."

The canon went to the head of the stairs, moving quickly, like a young man. His clear voice struck Villon as having an odd note of gaiety in it as he called down.

"Ask Master Flastrier to be so good as to wait. I have a little business to settle before I see him. He will wait," said the canon contentedly, as he came back into the room. "But your question will not wait. You will be thinking of it again when I am not there. You see, there are two answers, my dear. The first I have told you. It is good, but it is not all."

Villon blinked. He did not want to meet his guardian's nephew, the barber-surgeon. He did not want a sermon on the sin that had so strangely risen up to vex him. He wanted to get to the tavern. But something in the canon's face arrested him in spite of his impatience. It was devilishly true that he would think of the question again, on the road, in nasty little hamlets, strange cities, among the miseries promised by a ten years' exile. He began to cough. The canon waited, his eyes fixed on the hairless haggard scar-lipped face whose black eyes shone so feverishly.

"What were we saying?" he asked.

"We were talking about the sin against the Holy Ghost."

"Yes, yes." The canon looked at Villon with a humorous light in the brown eyes that suddenly jerked Villon back, reminding him of the master's look when he had greeted the sharp-faced, wicked-hearted urchin twenty-odd years ago. For all the sorrows that had passed over him since, nothing had changed that look.

"The sin against the Holy Ghost," he repeated. His voice was deep, earnest, gentle. "You should know that. It is to despair of God's pity."

There was a moment in which the words echoed in the quiet room. Then the canon shoved Villon's shoulder.

"Now go, go to your friends. Jean must not be kept waiting any longer. You will remember, François?"

Villon, at the door, did not reply. The black eyes burned as he turned to the canon a face older than his own, the mouth twisted in a scar-lipped smile. The next moment he was clattering down the stairs, without apology to Flastrier coming deliberately up for his game of chess, and out of the Red Door to the warmth and gaiety of the Mule.

Chapter Twenty-Three

Charles, Duke of Orléans, was feeling more than ordinarily tired. He looked at the little girl before him, a child of seven, her slight body quiet in its velvet sheath, though the anxiety in her eyes, pensive as her father's, showed her eager to be released. She was every inch a princess. And all her life ahead of her. He would not know what she made of it. He prayed he might live to see her safely married. Marriage was a serious affair for a woman, profoundly serious for a great lady. He thought, not of her mother, but of his second wife, the gentle Bonne d'Armignac, from whom he had been parted by exile and death, and of his first unhappy bride, widow of the English king. He thought of his own mother's tragedy. He shook his head and sighed heavily. He had particularly remembered his little daughter in his devotions this morning. He stretched out a long thin hand toward her and smiled.

"You must be off to your dancing lesson, is that it?"

"Yes, my father." She hung between desire to please the old man and desire to run to her companions in the great room where the harpist and the dancing master were waiting.

"Well, go then, do not keep them. You must be first in courtesy, my dear, and tardiness is a kind of ill manners."

He waved his hand, dismissing her.

"Go then with God's blessing."

"Thank you, my father." She curtsied and ran off.

The Duke turned to his companion.

"A treasure, eh, Cailleau? Do you remember when she came into the world?"

Cailleau nodded, pursing his lips. It had been a difficult business.

"Six years is it now, or seven?" he asked. "It seems only yesterday we were struggling to get her to nurse properly." He smiled ruefully. "But what a festival it was! I doubt your Grace exceeded it when your son was born."

"The King was here for the boy's christening."

"Yes, the King," said Cailleau in a dubious voice.

Each man knew the other's opinion of Louis, but it would not do for the Duke of Orléans to speak too freely of his king and cousin before the little doctor from Blois, though he feared the one and cherished the other.

"We were not so grand at Marie's christening," murmured Charles.

"You had one queer fellow here then. A poet from Paris," said the doctor. "He was a short, thin man with a scar on his upper lip. What was his name now?"

370

The Duke's sad old eyes crinkled in amusement.

" 'Welcomed by all, rebuffed by everyone,' " he said. "My good Cailleau doesn't even remember his name! Alas, poor Villon!"

"Villon?" the physician repeated. "I thought, now you mention it, it was de Montcorbier."

"His father came from that region, I understand, but he took the name of his guardian, a canon of St. Benoit, and made him better known than if he had been Bishop of Paris." The Duke smiled faintly. "He left here like a thief in the night, with the players, for no better reason, as far as I know, than that la Blossette refused him her favors. As though she would look at the rake! But he had a neat wit. I heard sad stories of him from the money-lender Perdrier soon afterwards. And charming ones from the Duke of Bourbon, whom he seems to have elected as his patron after leaving us."

"I have not forgotten the face. It looked to me like a hanging face," said the physician. "I'll wager he was born under Saturn."

"You have an eye, Cailleau. But the wheel of Fortune turned in the fellow's favor as often as not. Do you know that when our little Princess made her triumphal entry into Orléans he was one of the poor devils released from prison in honor of the occasion? Would you believe it, my dear doctor, a man whom I had entertained at my own table! And Bourbon too! A man we had both matched verses with!"

"Your Grace is too kind to these poets," said the doctor, leaning forward to poke the fire. "The most of them are no better than play-actors, when you come down to it. There is no honorable guild of poets. There is no manner of science about it."

The Duke smiled.

"You cannot forgive me because I make even you write verses. You do not fancy my prescriptions any more than I do

371

yours. But you will cure me of insomnia, my dear friend, sooner than you will cure me of poetry."

"It is all one. Those infernal double ballades are enough to keep a strong man awake until cockcrow."

"A strong man would be awake until cockcrow for prettier reasons," said Charles of Orléans. "But it is neither the one nor the other that keeps me awake."

"That potion I prepared for you last night did not turn the trick, then?"

Charles shook his head.

"You have seen what it was like this morning, Cailleau: the quarrel to settle between those two priests of my chapel, the pair of them fierce as two dogs—or as the Pope in Rome and the Pope in Avignon; that poor fellow from the village wanting money for a pilgrimage to celebrate his son's recovery, I had to satisfy him; and the steward coming in with bills as long as my face; my dear wife in tears over the death of her favorite falcon. Trifles, of course, but the news of the risings in Brittany was no trifle. It looks as though a hundred years of war were not enough for the poor people of France. Those are the things that keep me awake, my dear doctor, and not all your potions nor all my prayers give me rest."

"It is no easy thing to be Duke of Orléans," the doctor agreed. "But I thought I had prescribed that you at least retire from politics."

Charles cupped his ear with one long hand. His deafness was increasing with age, and now, absorbed in his anxieties, he did not hear his companion at all.

"Eh?" he said softly, and, without letting Cailleau answer, he continued: "Perhaps I unlearned the habit of sleeping in England. And even here, at home, among friends, I am not free. I am a prisoner to bad memories, Cailleau. Bad dreams. I spend whole nights in the rain at Agincourt, my horse in yellow mud up to his ankles, unable to move, and the English archers, like pagan savages, barefoot, in helmets of hide or wicker, armed with hatchets, rushing at us, men and horses stricken, trodden in the mud, and our men shrieking, 'I surrender,' but the English fools not understanding, and then everything confused, shouts and groans and prayers, the living stripped like the dead, lying hacked and naked in a marsh of mud and blood. Christ, God, it is horrible. And I stand there, dripping, unable to stir or cry out, like a soldier of stone. When I wake, I am as wet as though I had been rained on in earnest, sweating with horror. Will there never be an end to it? We are free of the English. But right now in France . . . I cannot bear it, Cailleau. Will there never be peace on earth?"

The doctor rose and poured the Duke a glass of wine.

"Drink this. To the future! You must not live so much in the past."

Charles took the glass from him and turned it between his fingers before he drank.

"I am too old to live in the future, Cailleau. And the past is not all grief and fighting. Even in the years of exile there were times it is a happy thing to remember. Ah, my friend, if we could live somewhere else than in memory or in hope! It is only when we are free of both that we really live. But an old man has nothing but memories. And as a young man I had nothing but my hopes. Perhaps, if God had called me to a humble station, it would have been otherwise." Charles was silent for a little, staring sadly into the fire.

"I recall that young François Villon composed some verses, not bad, either, answering my cousin Anjou on the ease of a countryman's life. It is all very well for such fellows to talk of princely pleasures. They do not need to fret over what is to

373

become of their estates. Take Villon, now, the rascal cannot govern himself. Does he suppose it is easier and pleasanter and more rewarding to govern a dukedom?"

Charles drank off his wine and set the glass down on the heavily carved table beside him before he spoke again.

"He was an impudent fellow, no more to be trusted than—than England," Charles smiled whimsically. "But there was something I fancied about him. I had his belated ballade on the fountain copied with those made at the tourney. He wrote as I would never write, harsh violent verses, but scarcely a line that was not a protest against the evil that he floundered in up to his neck. I wonder he has managed to save that neck!" Charles paused, tapping the physician lightly on the arm, and spoke as though half surprised at his own fancy. "Do you know, my dear doctor, I would give"—he lifted one of the heavy gold chains that hung about his neck—"I would give this to listen to him again."

"That should not be so difficult," said Cailleau, pleased that the old Duke should show à flicker of interest in something. "Where shall we look for him?"

This was the moment when Villon, stumbling down the Orléans road, tripped over a stone and fell, cursing. He had broken his ankle and could not rise.

Back in Paris a fat woman with nothing on but her shirt was sitting on a bed cutting her toe nails. Every now and then she would pause in her task to cast a glance from her small blue eyes at her companion: a young girl who was arranging her hair in front of a mirror of highly polished steel.

"It don't look too bad, dearie," she volunteered in a fat voice, "but it takes more than a smart hair-do and round titties to

374

make a living nowadays. You must wear all the gauds you have if you're to compete with the burghers' daughters, with their fine clothes and good jewelry. And they know the new dances, too," she added, shifting her position heavily, "and they can talk as prettily as you or me, and don't forget the big dowry that goes with 'em to the proper young man. Christ Jesus, I've cut myself!" she shrieked. "Here, give me that rag!"

The girl obliged her in silence and went back to her hair-dressing.

"There, that's better," murmured the fat woman, pursing her lips. "See here, Jehanne, what did you get out of that student last night? He didn't look like much."

The girl at the mirror mumbled sulkily, the comb between her lips.

"I'm only trying to help you, you fool."

"Well"—Jehanne turned from the shining steel oval to the fat figure squatting on the bed—"I've given you yours. And he spent plenty on wine. I saw to that. What can you expect from a student? He promised me a girdle, though, when he gets his money from home."

"D'you think his father figures on buying you girdles? We'll be lucky if the boy comes back for a drink. There isn't anything to get them here now but those casks of Beaune that I bought last autumn. The stuff's too good for them, but I make 'em pay for it."

"What would they come for but us?" asked Jehanne coldly and turned her attention to polishing her fingernails.

The fat woman put her scissors aside. Sitting there cross-legged tailor-fashion, with her arms folded across her great breasts, she looked more like an Oriental image than a Parisian harlot.

"You're not any different or any better than the girls they

can pick up at the Holy Innocents or in one of the other houses on the street. You've got to offer 'em something more than the others if the place isn't to go to the dogs. Ah, you'd know if you'd been here a few years ago when I had my Gogo."

"Who's Gogo?"

"François Villon to you. The biggest poet in Paris."

"Was he rich? Never heard of him."

Fat Margot laughed.

"Christ, what do you know!"

"Well, why should I? Who is he, anyway?" said Jehanne contemptuously. "Poets ain't made of money either."

"Maybe not. But he brought more custom with his songs and his play-acting than you and Ysabeau and Marion with all your tricks put together."

"Why don't you get him back then?" Jehanne was not interested.

"I wish to God I could. But he's not the man he once was. Poor Gogo! They did for him, right enough."

Jehanne looked sharply at the fat woman.

"You mean they let him swing?"

"Mighty near it. He has such a tongue in his head, though, he'd talk the devil out of snatching the soul given in a contract written with his own blood. God knows he talked me out of my bit of savings and all I earned for more months than I like to think about, and that's no joke, Jehanne, believe me."

"I believe you." Jehanne snorted. "I shouldn't think you'd want him about."

"Not the way he looks now, poor devil, with the skin hanging on his bones like the picture of a dried herring. Bald as a fish too. But you'll travel to the gates of Paris and beyond, my lady, before you'll find the match of him. And the poor fool knew the way of it as no man else."

376

"You don't mean he was in love with you?" asked Jehanne incredulously.

"With me! Him! No. He was in love with a young miss lived in the neighborhood of St. Benoit. A fine piece she was, with a nose that turned up at him the way yours does at the stink in the alley. That was what burned him. He'd be thinking of her when he was with me until I made him forget her, and maybe you think I don't know how, and me thinking of none but him every breath I drew, the mean devil he was, the dear little cabbage!"

"I'll bet you're crazy about him still."

"I'd be crazy if I were. He's banished the city for ten years, and he was half dead when he left it."

"What for?"

Fat Margot shrugged.

"Had sticky fingers when he handled other men's money. And there was a new provost: he'd been hand in glove with the old one. We all thought he'd end with his toes turned up at Montfaucon."

Jehanne sat down on a stool near the window and examined her fingers carefully.

"He don't sound like anything to make you hot and cold all over. The man who did for me wasn't one of your gallows' birds. He's a rich merchant now. Worth a hundred of your Gogos. His father was a furrier. Real ermine he gave me." She looked at Fat Margot. "I'll bet your poet never gave you anything but his silly songs."

"You're wrong there," said Fat Margot with an ugly laugh. "Many's a black eye he gave me, all for nothing."

"And you call me a fool," muttered Jehanne. She got up, yawning and stretching.

"Listen, dearie." Margot stuck out a fat forefinger and

pointed it at her for emphasis. "You can have your little rat catcher of a furrier. Not that he stuck to you, or you wouldn't be here this minute. Before you're as old as I am you'll be sick and tired of it, many's the time, wishing yourself back home or maybe in the river, and never once remembering a pair of hot black eyes and a face sharp as a knife, with a slit lip in it that gave salt to a kiss." Fat Margot stopped to scratch her back. "I tell you, you'll be saving up what you get, penny by penny, counting your golden louis like masses to get you into Heaven, just to have your old age in peace without a creature in britches anywhere about to make God's image hateful to you. You'll be sending your bit of ermine to the rag market for what it'll bring so you can have a house, not like this house, a bit of a cottage in the country with a garden to it and chickens and a pig, and the priest coming in the way he did when you were home with your father to have the breast of the roast goose at the feast of Epiphany." She nodded sagely.

"Yes, my girl, all that. And you'll go to bed at night to sleep, and glad of it, by your lone."

"What's got into you?" Jehanne asked scornfully. "Do you mean you really want that sort of thing?"

"By God, Jehanne, and I'm going to have it too. Before I'm too old to enjoy it. I've seen enough of the other thing."

"Where'll you get the money? And how will you ever stand it? Oh, forget it: even if you try it, you'll be back here in a week."

"Maybe," sighed Fat Margot. "But I've been thinking of it a long while now. Ever since Gogo beat me up the first time. A bit of a cottage outside the city, with a pig and chickens."

"And a cock," added Jehanne with a laugh, strolling up to the mirror and surveying herself again.

378

"Of course a cock," said Fat Margot. "And I'll call him Gogo."

"Your poet should hear you!"

"I wish to God he would. Jesus, I wonder wherever he is this minute."

Villon had dragged himself and his broken ankle to the edge of the road. A cold drop of rain from the cloud he had been watching doubtfully since morning fell on him, and he flinched.

Rain was falling in Paris, too, darkening the room at the Red Door where the canon, limping a little with rheumatism, was pacing back and forth, from the table with his famous chessmen to the flaming hearth and back, under the serene gaze of the Virgin, to the chess table again. The fire was newly made, and there were fresh rushes on the floor, but all else was worn and old. The few pieces of furniture had a shabby look, the man tramping from one end of the room to the other was white and weary with years, the thoughts that moved behind the frowning brow were old.

He paused for a moment beside the table, studying the pieces with absent eyes, and sighed. He seemed to be waiting for something.

There was a muffled stir below, and hurried feet on the stairs that brought him to a halt facing the door. Before his visitor could knock, he cried: "Come in!"

Jean Flastrier came in, without speaking but with a rapid head-shake that made the canon lift his hands and let them drop in a gesture of resignation.

"She's gone, uncle," said the barber-surgeon, letting the canon help him off with his dripping cloak and going to dry himself

379

before the fire. "God rest her soul. There was nothing for me to do."

"God receive her soul," said the canon softly. He knit the shaggy white brows. "I should have gone with you," he fretted.

"Her parish priest was with her. She died peacefully. I'm glad you didn't travel all that way in this wretched weather. We might have you sick, too. There'd be no manner of good in that."

"I should have gone," repeated the canon. "I didn't know the end was so near. We must have masses said for her soul. Poor François!"

The barber-surgeon shrugged one shoulder and accepted the cup of wine that the canon held out to him.

"How did you like that new gambit?" he asked to divert the old man. "Did you work out another move for the king's bishop?"

"Eh? Oh, yes." The canon sat down opposite his nephew. "An excellent gambit, my dear, I must try it on Etienne. But I wonder if I shall make a success even with that opening." He paused, rubbing his chin. "Chess is something like life, Jean, if you will forgive an old priest's maxims: the gambit is more than half the battle, but one cannot win the game without Grace."

Flastrier smiled briefly, then looked out at the evil weather that made the November afternoon wear the look of dusk.

"What a rain!"

"Yes," murmured the canon and sighed. "Poor woman. Poor François."

Flastrier crossed his legs, hugging one knee.

"She is well out of her misery, uncle. As for your precious François, you were more of a mother to him than the woman who bore him."

"So he said once," the canon smiled sadly. "But how did I mother him: letting him perish like that!"

"What! Is he dead?"

The canon shook his head, frowning.

"I do not know where he is or what he is doing. When I said 'perish' I was not thinking of his mortal body but of his immortal soul."

"Immortal fiddlesticks," said Flastrier impatiently. "If he has a soul he signed it away to the devil long ago. I'm sorry, uncle! But when I stood at that poor creature's deathbed this morning and thought what her life had been and what she might have had if her son had taken advantage of the opportunities you gave him, my gorge rose at it. Why, he might have been a bishop!"

The canon smiled. "He said that, too. Yes, the gambit was good enough. But he lacked what was needful to let him win the game. You know a good deal about the body, my dear, though I don't doubt you could get to know more. But about the soul—" the canon hesitated. "You surgeons . . ." he said then, and did not finish.

Flastrier hunched his shoulders, squinting into the fire.

"It's no mean thing to do good surgery," he said. "Did I ever tell you about the Sicilian who performed that miraculous nose operation? A countryman of his had his nose half torn away by a splinter of shell. This Branca, Antony is his Christian name, he's the son of a surgeon, cut a bit of skin from the man's arm and pieced out the mutilated nose with it. He inserted what remained of the nose and bound the whole so tightly that the patient could not move his head for more than a fortnight. After about twenty days Branca gradually cut open the bit of flesh that adhered to the nose and reshaped it into nostrils! He did it so skilfully that the deformity was entirely removed. Can you match that?" he cried triumphantly.

"That's wonderful," admitted the canon. "Truly wonderful! Yes, but the cure of souls," he added, smiling, "is another matter. You cannot so easily cut a piece from one part and insert it in another to mend a mutilation." He was silent a moment, sucking his cheek reflectively. Then he got up and moved over to the shelf of books. He passed his hand with a hesitating tenderness over the backs, drew out a thin manuscript bound in parchment, and, coming back, laid it on the barber-surgeon's knee. "Have I ever shown you this, Jean?"

Flastrier turned it over, leafing it casually.

"What is it? Verse? Not Villon's by the look of it." He glanced at the title page: *"The Light for Laymen,"* he read aloud.

"It's a good deal older than François, or you, or even I," said the canon. "It was composed a hundred years ago, no, more: back in the thirteenth century. We have not learned very much since that is better worth thinking of." He took the book from his nephew's hands and paged it with the affectionate touch of long familiarity. "Here, you see," he said at last. "This passage on the Holy Trinity.

" 'The sun is the image of the Trinity: the substance of it represents God; the light that comes from it symbolizes Christ, but they are one, for while there is sun there is light; and the warmth it gives reminds us of the Holy Ghost.

" 'The creative power of Divinity rests with the Father. That which maintains creation belongs to the Son; as in human life, the father is the begetter, and the child is the continuance of life. The Holy Ghost: the warmth of love, ornaments and vivifies creation. Or again, the Father is memory, the Son is understanding, the Holy Ghost is the will, which derives from both.' "

382

Flastrier unclasped his fingers and clasped them round his knee again. He was bored by the canon's exposition of thirteenth-century theology.

"I am not as far away from a point as you think, Jean," the old priest twinkled at his nephew. "We were speaking just now of poor François," he said more slowly, "and of the cure of souls. This little book, it is truly a wonderful little work, speaks of that, too.

"Man was made, we are told, in the image of God. How? This kind of animal, with its beastly impulses, lusting, drinking, feeding on carrion, to become itself carrion, this flesh you surgeons cut and piece like tailor's cloth—is this God's image? No. It is the soul of man that is the image of God. The soul: that is memory and reason and will. This is man's immortal part."

Flastrier nodded.

"Yes, uncle. But what I say is—" but he stopped and would not say.

"You say that François is a damned soul. I know. And it is true, how often I have seen it and wrung my hands over it and fallen into the sin of despair because of that one thing wanting in him. It is his will that is weak. How often he has said it himself, in tears, on his knees, in this very room, and I beside him, listening to the child, helpless to give him comfort because when he was young and innocent I did not strengthen his will, as a good doctor with exercise strengthens a lame member.

" 'For what I would, that I do not; but what I hate, that do I.' The terrible words of St. Paul in his Epistle to the Romans. 'For the good that I would, I do not: but the evil that I would not, that I do. . . O wretched man that I am! Who shall deliver me from the body of this death?' "

383

"No!" said Flastrier harshly, getting up and striding to the window, where the chess table stood.

The canon looked after him, puzzled.

"What are you denying? That he is weak? That he repents his weakness in anguish of spirit?"

"I am denying that you are to blame. He always got the better of you, repenting, yes, crawling back and whining to you whenever he was in trouble. Playing the devil with your money and your patience. Pretending that he was going to reform and keep to the straight and narrow. And no sooner out of your sight than he was back in the muck again up to his neck. How he escaped without a rope round it, God only knows. Or maybe you know, wearing your life out over a worthless rascal. What did he ever give you but endless worry and pain, and he's bound to turn up again, damn him, like a bad penny, and go back like a dog to his vomit. Have masses said for his poor mother's soul. You will have done your last duty by her then. And pray that you'll not set eyes on her son again."

"It is no kindness to me," said the canon sternly, "to be harsh with him."

"I'm sorry," said Flastrier for the second time.

Then he burst out again.

"He couldn't have so much as signed his name if it hadn't been for your teaching."

"Oh, my teaching!" The canon had a sad smile for that. "I didn't teach him to compose verses."

"No," said Flastrier scornfully. "And what virtue is there in verses? Have you forgotten your favorite maxim: the love of money is the root of all evil? What did your precious Villon do but nourish that root in the richest dirt in Paris?" Flastrier shook his head. "You are well rid of him."

"I shall never be rid of him," said the canon gently. "You

384

think he will come back. I hope he will. It is one of my reasons for wanting to go on living, tired as I am sometimes." He sucked at his cheek again before he continued: "But you are wrong: it wasn't money he was after. Did you ever read his Testament? It cries out against usury as no money-grubber could cry out. If he wants wealth, it is because he loves life and he thinks that money can buy it. And so it can, but not the best life. And then there is that girl, Katherine de Vauselles. She was in his blood like a disease. How could I have saved him from that?"

"You couldn't save him. That's what I'm trying to tell you," said Flastrier in a kinder voice. "Never mind him. He's gone, banished, and sick enough, I imagine, to repent truly. He can't expect to play the gay dog now, the shape he was in when he left. He may yet cough himself into holy orders."

The canon knitted his shaggy eyebrows.

"Do you think so?" he asked eagerly.

"You want to see him again. You think he'll save his soul or you will save it for him?" Flastrier said.

The canon answered his nephew's question with a steady look, earnest and tender. The glimmer that shone in his brown eyes made the worn face indomitably young.

"'We are saved by hope,'" he quoted softly, "'but hope that is seen is not hope: for what a man seeth, what does he yet hope for?'" He passed his hand slowly over his face. Then he said self-reproachfully: "But I am keeping you, without even the excuse of a new gambit. And I must go to chapter meeting soon: in a moment the bells will be ringing nones."

At that hour Villon, crouched under a leafless tree at the edge of the road, straining his ears for the sound of cartwheels or the distant yelp of a dog, shuddered under the pelting rain

385

and stopped rubbing his ankle to clutch at his chest: he had
begun to cough.

In a tall narrow house not far from the cloisters, a woman
was kneeling before an open chest, tumbling its contents about
with impatient hands.

"I can*not* find it, Marthe," she complained.

The servant standing beside her stared unhappily at the
boxes, ribbands, and trinkets lying in loose heaps on the floor.
Without answering her mistress, she tugged hard at the bottom
drawer and pulled it out with a jerk: it was crammed with an
assortment of colored stuffs, hoods and laces.

"Heavens!" The lady leaned over to take between her fingers
a bit of green stuff that stuck out from the rest. Drawing it
slowly forth, she held at arm's length a curious garment that
looked like nothing so much as a pair of hose such as a young
man might wear.

"What is it?" asked Marthe.

"Hose, you great goose."

"But however did they get in there?"

The demoiselle Katherine shrugged her shoulders and, standing up, held the leggings against her body.

"Phoo!" she grimaced. "How fat I've grown. I couldn't get
into them now."

Marthe laughed, surprised, excited.

"Did you wear them, truly? Was it a masquerade? Whose
are they?"

"Yes. No." Katherine answered the questions shortly, in
order. "Villon's."

"Oh!" Marthe stretched out her hand and touched the gar-
ments as though that would convince her of their ownership.

"They're spotted," she said. "Look!"

386

"Do you know where I wore them?" There was a glint in the green eyes. Katherine leaned close to Marthe, pressed her plump arm, and whispered: "Montfaucon!"

"No!"

"But yes." Katherine flung the hose onto the heap of oddments that lay beside the chest and dropped to a hassock. She sat there, her hands clasped tightly about her knees, looking into the brazier standing near her on its little tripod.

"Look, Marthe!" she pointed. "D'you see that crooked piece of charcoal? That's the way the gibbets look when the bonfires light them from below."

Marthe, who had been smoothing the leggings and laying them straight, gave a little shiver.

"How could you?" she breathed, trying to imagine the demoiselle Katherine in that region of the damned, and failing. "But you're joking," she said then. "I would have known."

"You were away, visiting your sister who was sick. It wasn't so hard to slip off. I jumped down from that window." Katherine nodded in the direction of the balcony. "Villon was waiting for me. He had lent me his suit. It was a bit tight, I remember: he's shorter than I, and he was always thin." She paused.

"Did you ever see a gibbet, Marthe, with—with something on it?"

"Who hasn't? I saw a hanging once. But I wouldn't want to again."

"This was different."

"What was it like?" breathed Marthe.

Katherine could not tell her. She was seeing it all again, the tall black timbers under the pale cloudy spring sky, the corpses dangling dreadfully, the flame of the bonfire like a piece of hell, and beside her a sharp eager young face, the black eyes smiling into her own.

Marthe sighed.

"Poor Villon."

"Why do you pity him?" asked Katherine. "He is nothing but a thief. He belongs at Montfaucon. Do you remember that afternoon in front of Notre Dame when he stole my purse?"

"He was hungry," Marthe excused him.

"He was angry," Katherine corrected her. "He never forgave me the beating he got from Noel Jolis. It was after that he sent me those verses with your name and his in an acrostic."

"My name—Marthe—and his?"

Katherine nodded, her lips set.

"You—don't have it?"

"No. Why? Did you want me to read it to you?" Katherine shook her head. "There's not a scrap of him left in this house except those old hose."

"Don't you think," Marthe spoke hesitatingly, not looking at the demoiselle Katherine, "we ought to give them back to him? Take them to the Red Door?"

"So you can ask him for a copy of his verses?" asked Katherine shrewdly but not unkindly. "No. You shan't try to find him. We're going to forget him, Marthe."

The sound of the church bells came faintly into the room, a cold sweet clanging that softened the wintriness of the rain beating on the window. The fire in the brazier flickered as though to greet the music of the bells, but could not change the sadness of the servant staring down at a pair of stained green hose or the bitter mood of her mistress, looking away from the lost past to the lost years ahead.

"He's been terribly punished," said Marthe, "for all the wrong things he did. The way he looked that day, it was cruel."

She halted, unable to say what was in her thought. She felt

388

dimly that Villon was not as other men, that judgment of him should be left to the God Who had made him what he was. She was jealous of Katherine because Villon had loved her, and proud that she herself had known and loved this strange clerk, whatever else he may have been besides. She was angry too because the demoiselle Katherine had not shown her the verses in which he had linked her name with his own, even if it was only done in wounding jest. She feared to meet him again, so horribly changed he had looked at that last encounter, and she ached with pity for him. She did not know herself what she felt, conscious only of miserable confusion and meaningless heartache.

"Cruel?" repeated Katherine, unclasping her hands and turning them about, looking at them as if they belonged to another woman. Even her hands, she thought, looked old. Villon was a poet. He could have made her beauty live forever like the beauty of Héloïse that Abélard sang, so it had not faded in three hundred years. Villon had told her of the letters of Héloïse and of how she had said she would rather be Abélard's harlot than queen and empress of the world. That was magnificent. But Villon had made Katherine de Vauselles a true harlot in the mouths of men, a girl who gives herself for a long purse, who weighs the world against her soul and takes the world though her soul is damned for it. Oh, Villon had made her remembered in Paris. So that she burned to think of it. And what happier thing had she to think of?

It was not as though she could have married him. But he would not let her marry anyone else. No man would have her who had heard what he had said of her. Ah, but he would have made a mock of her marriage though she never saw him again. And now he would not leave her. He was here, peering at her from her balcony, jumping out of her chest. When she would dress for a feast he dragged her back to picnic with the hanged at Montfaucon. When she would take her lute and sing, he killed the song on her lips and whispered to her of old age and poverty, of shame and death.

Katherine took up the small ivory-backed mirror that hung at her girdle and looked into it with sad appraisal. He had left her with nothing but bitter memories. Oh, and grinding remorse.

She let the mirror fall, and burst into a passion of tears.

"Have pity on yourself," murmured Marthe, leaning over her, trying to draw her against her breast as once, how differently, how long ago, she had drawn Villon himself.

But Katherine de Vauselles would not yield. She thrust Marthe away and flung herself down, sobbing, sick with a despair that she knew would be more terrible when she could no longer cry.

She sat up at last and dried her eyes. Her heart was lead in her breast. It was hard to breathe.

"Look," she whispered hoarsely, trying to smile at her own joke, too poor for Villon's making: "the rain is over."

She got slowly to her feet and went to the little window. "The clouds are gone now. The wind has carried them all away." It was what Villon had said about kings and beggars, but this she did not know.

The wind had carried away the clouds from the Orléans road too and was ruffling peacock colors in the puddles. But where Villon's head rested there was a little pool that was dark and stiff.

He was no longer alone. Two men had come out of the

near-by wood when the rain ceased and were bending over him with sullen faces. They spoke the jargon of the Companions, but they did not recognize him, nor could he know them.

"You don't want to be nabbed here," said the one, "they'll think we did it."

"Button your mouth," retorted the other, his fingers busy with a rain-soaked wallet. "Let me see what's here."

The first man bent closer, not to be cheated. The wallet was open now, and the quick rough hands of the second were turning over a wad of papers, damp with rain.

"What is it?"

"Am I a clerk that I should know? Some sort of scrawl."

"What else is there?"

"Not a damn penny," the second cursed and spat.

"Maybe the writing's worth something. It might be a letter of remission. We could use that."

"The rain's spoiled it, you fool, nobody could make it out. And he don't look like the sort that gets the King's pardon." The thief glanced rapidly up and down the road. "Come on now."

The other shook his head, reluctant to go.

"Maybe you think it's his testament and he left you a legacy," the second rascal laughed hoarsely. "What's he got to leave? His carcass to his mother, the earth, the worms won't fatten on that."

"And his soul to the blessed Trinity," muttered the other, crossing himself.

The second man shoved the shrunken body with the toe of his boot and turned aside.

"The wallet's worth something when it's dry," said the first greedily.

The other thrust his fingers searchingly into the wet pouch and flung it to his companion with a grunt. Then the pair, shrugging to keep out the cold, trudged off down the muddy road. They did not look back.

The rain-blurred pages lay on the ground. A gust of wind caught them and carried them away.

As François Villon said himself: "It's a great city, this Paris. It is a great time, this fifteenth century of our Lord. It is a great fellow, I'm telling you, this François Villon." Of these three — France's greatest century, her greatest city, and the father of her poets (the first of modern poets) — *Rogue's Legacy* has been written: a novel based upon what Villon has told us of himself and what his own world thought of him, with the gaps filled in by the intuition and imagination of one of America's best-known poets and critics.

It was in 1456 that François Villon, the wildest wit in Paris, first fled the city, after killing a priest in a quarrel. He saw the countryside of France that year, its taverns, its highwaymen, its jails. And, the more he saw, the more he longed for Paris. But when, at last, he dared return, through the influence of his long-suffering guardian, Guillaume de Villon, canon of the church of St. Benoit, he hurried back to his old haunts, the taverns, his old comrades, the roistering thieves led by that slim aristocrat René de Mon-